*Praise for delightful novels of*

## Donna Kauffman

### Dear Prince Charming

"*Dear Prince Charming* kept me up all night and left me satisfied in the morning. For pure fun served piping hot, get yourself a book by Donna Kauffman!"

—Vicki Lewis Thompson,
*New York Times* bestselling author of *Nerd in Shining Armor*

"Sports reporter spars with ditzy publicist. Kauffman has a wonderful knack for turning nothing into sparkling fun."

—*Kirkus Reviews*

"Sexy, funny, entertaining . . . *Dear Prince Charming* may not solve real-life romantic dilemmas, but it will certainly bring a smile to your face."

—America Online's Romance Fiction Forum

"Laughter, passion, and friendship combine in *Dear Prince Charming* to create an enjoyable, fast, and highly entertaining read. *Prince Charming* will entertain and enchant the reader with its cast of captivating characters, humorous dialogue, and heartfelt romance. For a story that's guaranteed to find a place on your keeper shelf, grab *Dear Prince Charming!*"

—*Romance Reviews Today*

"*Dear Prince Charming* is campy, ridiculous fun. Kauffman plays happily with gender stereotypes and sexual chemistry, offering manly men for boys and girls alike. Her zippy prose and direct sensibility are a breeze to read, perfectly suited to romantic comedy. There'a bit of substance to complement the fluff, making for the perfect afternoon read."

—*Contra Costa Times*

"Ms. Kauffman writes a savvy, no-nonsense story with a strong heroine and a sexy hero. Fast-paced and witty, this story is a must-read."

—*BestReviews.com*

"Kauffman does it again. [*Dear Prince Charming*] is light and fun, filled with zingers and humorous scenes."

—*The Facts, Texas*

"*Dear Prince Charming* is a fun-filled story with characters that will touch your heart and lift your spirits. Filled with a lot of humor, romance, and sensitive situations, the book is a fast read and a perfect solution to a lonely day."

—*Inglewood News*

## The Cinderella Rules

"Fun banter and sizzling sex."

—*Entertainment Weekly*

"Kauffman writes with warmth, wit and swashbuckling energy."

—*Publishers Weekly*

"*The Cinderella Rules* is a captivating, modern day fairytale that will delight readers from beginning to end. Well written with humor, passion and a dash of mystery, *The Cinderella Rules* delivers."

—*Romance Reviews Today*

"A sexy, spicy romp."

—*Booklist*

"Kauffman has written an action-packed, sexy, humorous, intricate story with zany characters who will touch your heart, tickle your funny bone and leave you wanting more. Smart, with sizzling romance and a captivating plot. It will make every woman want to follow *The Cinderella Rules*."

—*Old Book Barn Gazette*

## The Big Bad Wolf Tells All

"Women everywhere will be taking *Big Bad Wolf* to bed with them. Donna Kauffman writes smart and sexy, with sizzle to spare . . . and no batteries required!"

—Janet Evanovich

"Deftly spun . . . with a zippy style."

—*Kirkus Reviews*

"Entertaining . . . sure to find an audience with the beach-reading crowd."

—*Booklist*

"Humor and suspense . . . fans of Laura Zigman will enjoy this book."

—*Library Journal*

"This is one sheepish tale that stands out from the flock of chick-lit patter with a unique zest and fire all its own."

—*Bookpage*

## The Charm Stone

"Give me more!"

—Linda Howard

## The Royal Hunter

"Kauffman . . . anchors her readers with sensuality, humor and compassion."

—*Publishers Weekly*

"Action packed adventure, steamy sensuality, and a bewitching plot all come together in a surprising and dramatic ending."

—*Rendezvous*

## Your Wish is My Command

"Whimsical and sexy!"

—Jennifer Crusie

## Legend of the Sorcerer

"Kauffman has written a spellbinding romance that is so hot it near sizzles when the pages are turned . . . a superb book to curl up with and get lost in."

—*New Age Bookshelf*

"Kauffman knows how to set our hearts afire with passion and romance."

—*Rendezvous*

"Ms. Kauffman is an amazing talent."

—*Affaire du Coeur*

## The Legend MacKinnon

"Intricately woven together . . . a terrific read."

—*Rendezvous*

"A uniquely exciting, captivating and sensational read."

—*Romantic Times*

Also by Donna Kauffman

Dear Prince Charming

The Cinderella Rules

The Big Bad Wolf Tells All

The Charm Stone

The Royal Hunter

Your Wish Is My Command

Legend of the Sorcerer

The Legend MacKinnon

Yours 2 Keep

*with Kay Hooper, Marilyn Pappano,*
*Jill Shalvis, and Michelle Martin*

# Sleeping with Beauty

Donna Kauffman

Bantam Books

SLEEPING WITH BEAUTY
A Bantam Book / July 2005

Published by
Bantam Dell
A Division of Random House, Inc.
New York, New York

This is a work of fiction. Names, characters, places, and incidents either are the product of the author's imagination or are used fictitiously. Any resemblance to actual persons, living or dead, events, or locales is entirely coincidental.


Cover design by Lynn Andreozzi



Library of Congress Cataloging-in-Publication Data

Kauffman, Donna.
Sleeping with Beauty / Donna Kauffman.
p. cm.
ISBN 0-553-38306-X
1. Single women—Fiction. 2. Women teachers—Fiction. 3. Class reunions—Fiction.
4. Self-realization—Fiction. 5. Elementary school teachers—Fiction. I. Title.
PS3561.A816 S55 2005
813'.6 22 2005041117

Printed in the United States of America
Published simultaneously in Canada

www.bantamdell.com

BVG 10 9 8 7 6 5 4 3 2 1

*This book is dedicated to friendship.*
*I certainly couldn't have finished this one if not for the power of that very special bond.*
*Thank you Mom, Jill, Kathy, Diane, Micahlyn, Karen, Anne Marie, Mary, Mary Kay, Pat & Nora.*
*I don't know what I'd have done without you all.*

# Prologue

*Once upon a time, long, long ago, in a kingdom known as Potomac Middle School, there lived a young girl named Lucy Harper. Brave of heart (if not quite fleet of foot), our plucky yet coordination-challenged heroine struggled valiantly to confront her own shortcomings—and they were many—so that she could once again set forth and navigate her way through the dangerous and often uncharted waters of the preteen social strata (also known as the sixth-grade lunchroom) . . .*

*Oh, God. Why me? Why?* Lucy struggled to keep her tray steady. She'd been so focused on making her way through the jostling crowds and trying to avoid ending up with food globbed to the front of her sweater or worse, like yesterday, accidentally allowing the ends of her ponytails to drag through her gravy, that she'd failed to chart a course to a predetermined safe harbor.

As usual, there was no answer to her silent plea. The only seats left in the whole lunchroom were at Buddy Aversom's table. She sighed. Even God couldn't save her now.

"We could always go sit outside." Jana Fraser, best friend and fellow pariah geek, stood just behind Lucy's left elbow, her own tray in balance.

Lucy didn't dare glance Jana's way. She was already doing two things at once, and that seemed to be her limit before causing catastrophic damage. "It's freezing out there," she reminded her. October had started off cold and nasty.

Jana jostled her own tray as she moved to one side to avoid getting plowed into by the students flowing around them. They were, as they had always been, invisible to their peers. "Well, we'll just deal with it." She sighed now, too. "Like always."

Lucy made a face. "He's doing that thing with the french fries up his nose again." Buddy was the proverbial class clown for the entire sixth grade. Lucy, along with most of the girls on the planet, didn't really appreciate his brand of humor. But most of the girls on the planet weren't his favorite target. Lucy was. Of course, the rest of the sixth-grade girls had their own tables, their own cliques, so they didn't care. Jana was the only one who understood what it was like, sticking out in all the ways a twelve-year-old girl didn't want to. Too tall, too dorky, too klutzy, too smart. Which was why Jana usually brown-bagged it and spent more time in the library than the lunchroom.

Lucy, on the other hand, was just stubborn enough to stick it out, regardless of the torture, if for no other reason than to make it no easier on them than they made it on her. At the moment, however, she was seriously questioning that strategy. Buddy's lunchroom specialty was doing this thing where he hiccuped and forced milk through his nose, resulting in the dislodgement of whatever food item he'd shoved into his nostrils. Last time she'd been forced to sit near him, he'd snorted Tater Tots into her reconstituted mashed potatoes. Much to the delight of all who knew him.

She and Jana shuffled their way over to the table and took their seats without making any more eye contact with the enemy than absolutely necessary. She was all about not backing down, but she didn't see any reason to encourage them, either.

"Hey, if it isn't Pippi and Bozo," Buddy chimed, causing a ripple of laughter down the length of the table. "You know, if you'd put those wires in your pigtails like a real Longstocking, your hair wouldn't drag in your gravy."

Lucy immediately yanked her head back, looking down, expecting to discover the worst. There was nothing in her hair or on her sweater. But when she'd jerked back, she'd dragged the edge of her sleeve across her applesauce. She endured the laughter that followed the gag, telling herself she was just thankful her hair was still clean. She'd just wash her sleeve off in the washroom later. She was used to that anyway.

"Very amusing, Buddy," Jana said bravely. "About as attractive as the Tater-Tot bits you have stuck in your nose hairs."

Buddy didn't fall for the poke, probably because he didn't really care much if there were Tater bits in his nose. But Lucy felt a rush of affection for her best friend anyway. Fate might have set them up as targets since they'd first stepped onto the playground together in preschool, but fate had also given them each other to endure it with. Lucy thought it was a pretty decent trade.

While Lucy dealt with her Pippi Longstocking pigtails and giraffelike arms and legs and all the coordination issues accompanying it, Jana had been dealt a head of frizzy red hair, an overabundance of freckles, and the heart and soul of a jock who had absolutely zero athletic ability whatsoever. Alone, they both were strong in their identities, smug in the knowledge that they were too smart for these immature idiots, beyond their years in what was really important in life: true friendship and goals for the future.

But though she'd never say it to Jana, privately Lucy would give almost anything to make it through just one lunch break as a welcome guest at a table. Any table.

"So, Stilts," Buddy said, taunting Lucy with yet another one of the many oh-so-original nicknames her peer group had labeled her with. "Why don't you give it a try?"

Lucy could all but feel Jana's sideways stare, silently commanding her to just ignore the stupid jerk. Of course she couldn't. Not that Buddy Aversom held any kind of secret allure, even to someone as attention deprived as Lucy. She likened it more to responding to a challenge. At least, that was what she told herself. A far more palatable truth than the real one, which was that she was desperate to feel like she fit in somewhere. Even with Buddy and his moron friends. She lasted about five seconds before looking across the table. "Try what?"

It might have been her imagination, but it felt like the noise level of the room dimmed, that heads were turning their way. Buddy, who for some fathomless reason was still quite popular despite his disgusting and frequent display of proboscis prowess, smiled at her as he handed over two french fries and the rest of his milk. Even with Jana drilling holes into the side of Lucy's head with her fierce gaze, Lucy was forced to admit that, for a teeny tiny moment, anyway, she debated taking him up on the dare. If she couldn't be one of the popular girls, or one of any other kind of girl, really, except the dorky spaz kind, maybe she could milk-snort her way into the cool-kids culture by being "one of the guys."

Everyone in the whole cafeteria seemed to hold their collective breath, as the moments ticked away and her mashed potatoes and gravy grew more congealed. In the end, all she heard was Jana's disgusted sigh when she finally cracked under the pressure and began to reach for the fries.

"Wait just a minute. You don't have to do that."

Lucy jerked her head up, wincing as she heard the distinctive *slurp* of her ponytail hitting gravy. Closing in on the table was a tall boy with the unruliest mop of hair she'd ever seen. The new kid, Grady Matthews. She'd seen him in the halls. Being one of the only boys in her grade as lanky and geeky as she was, he was hard to miss. Her hands stilled in midreach, unable to pull her gaze away from those lost-puppy-dog brown eyes of his. Puppy-dog eyes that were currently blazing mad at something. What, she had no idea. She managed to look around, then realized he was heading their way. Surely he wasn't coming over to this table. He couldn't be—

"Don't let him work you like that," Grady said, making it clear he was talking to her, and pretty angrily, to boot.

Now he was mad at her? What the heck had she done to him?

"Leave her alone," Buddy said. "Let her shoot the fries."

"Yeah," one of Buddy's moron friends said, "let her shoot the fries." Then he began to beat a tattoo on the tabletop, which was quickly picked up by the rest of the people lining their table, then grew like wildfire through the rest of the room, until the noise was almost deafening. Everyone was shouting, "Shoot the fries, Pippi, shoot the fries!"

Her hands wavered, her gaze darting from Grady, to Buddy, to Jana, then around the room in a quickly growing panic. How had she gotten herself into another mess like this? All she wanted to do was eat her lunch in relative peace and quiet.

"Put them down, Lucy," Grady ordered.

He knew her name? How did he know her name? Sure, they had one class together, but it wasn't like they even sat near each other, much less talked to each other.

"Make her," Buddy said, shoving his milk at Lucy so it sloshed out of the spout and onto her sleeve. The clean one, of course.

Lucy jerked her hand back, slipping in her seat as she did, just as Grady came even with the table. What happened next panned out like a grotesque sort of slow-motion disaster film-strip. Grady tripped over her big foot, which had inadvertently slid out into the aisle, and which sent him sprawling across the table. Causing—of course, because Loopy Lucy was involved—Grady to dump his entire tray of ketchup-laden Tater Tots directly into Buddy's lap. Her potentially life-altering moment of indecision was lost in the ensuing tussle, which, given that Buddy had an entire posse of lugheads leap to his immediate defense, ended swiftly and quite unfortunately for Grady.

Before the lunchroom monitor could reach their table, Grady was already heading to the exit, scrubbing angrily at the ketchup stains on his shirt and flicking the Tater Tots from his hair and ears. Amid the sound of raucous laughter and much jeering, a horrified Lucy followed him out the double doors, with Jana right on her heels.

Grady didn't stop until he was outside in the barren courtyard. Lucy sucked in a breath as the cold air snatched at her throat. Folding her arms around the waist of her button-down sweater, she followed her young knight-errant. "Why did you do that?" she demanded, not sounding as much the grateful princess as she'd meant to. But then, no one had ever mistaken Lucy Harper for any kind of princess. "You just made everything worse."

Grady spun around. "You shouldn't let them get to you like that. Bullies like Aversom aren't worth your time."

"What do you know about Buddy Aversom? You just transferred here."

Grady scraped the rest of the goop off his shirt. "I've met enough of Buddy Aversom's type to know one when I see one. You shouldn't let him get to you like that."

Lucy folded her arms. "I didn't exactly have anywhere else to sit. And he'd just have kept at me until I did something stupid. So

I figured it was best to get it over with up front, before my food got cold." As bravado went, this was one of her better performances. It would probably have gone over even better if her teeth weren't chattering. And gravy wasn't dripping from her ponytails.

"He's right, you know," Jana said. "You really should have ignored him. I tell you that all the time. But do you listen?" She sniffed for dramatic effect.

Lucy gaped at her turncoat best friend. "What?"

"You should listen to your friend," Grady said. "Strength in numbers works."

Lucy rolled her eyes. "We're two against . . . well, all of them."

Grady smiled. "Now you're three." He stepped forward and reached out his hand, then thought better of it, and wiped it on his pants first. "Sorry."

Lucy was still standing there openmouthed.

Jana moved in and stuck her own hand out. "Don't be. You're right. We should stand up for ourselves more often. Hi, I'm Jana Fraser."

"Grady Matthews." He shook Jana's hand, then turned to Lucy and stuck his hand out to her.

"Why did you do that for me?" she asked, ignoring his hand for the moment. "I didn't need saving. I can take care of myself." Which was patently untrue. She was a walking land mine on most days. But that didn't mean she didn't try hard not to be.

"We all need saving sometime. And bullies shouldn't get away with that kind of crap, but they do all the time. Most of them are just insecure scaredy-cats who pick on others to draw attention away from their own shortcomings. It's a sad attempt at self-affirmation through domination. Pathetic, really."

Lucy just gaped. "'Insecure scaredy-cats'? 'Self-affirmation through domination'?"

Jana grinned. "I'm liking you more and more by the minute, Grady Matthews."

He smiled, and those sad-puppy eyes were suddenly lit with a devilish, almost impish light that was impossible not to respond to. "So, what do you say? Can the new kid join your exclusive little clique?"

Lucy and Jana looked at each other. "We're not a clique."

"I know. That's what's so great about you."

Lucy glanced at him, at that smile, and felt her cheeks heat up while Jana nudged her in the back.

"Tomorrow, why don't you come sit in the back with me and some of my new friends."

"'In the back'?" Lucy tried to picture what table Grady was talking about. "You mean—"

Grady nodded. "The exchange-student table."

Lucy had been about to say "the foreigner table." Not that she had anything against them at all. Potomac Middle School had a special program they ran for a number of foreign-exchange students, almost all of them from India and Asia. Most of them didn't speak English well, if at all, but managed to be some kind of freaky geniuses anyway. She was more awed by them than anything. "You understand them?" she asked.

Grady shrugged. "A little. Science is science, you know?"

Lucy had no idea, really, but she wasn't about to admit that.

He smiled again. "One thing I do know is that they'll never make you do anything untoward with a french fry."

Jana snorted a laugh. "'Untoward.' " She nudged Lucy. "He's funny."

"What do you say?" Grady asked.

Jana looked to Lucy. "Come tomorrow, we're going to need a safe port."

"I was thinking I'd stay home sick," Lucy said, only half kidding. "For a week, maybe."

"Come on," she begged.

"Listen to your friend," Grady advised again.

"What about Buddy and his stupid friends?" Lucy asked, wanting what Grady was offering almost too much. There had to be some kind of catch. There always was with anything good that happened to her. "What if they try something else? I don't want you to bring trouble to your table."

"They'll be fine. They'll slide-rule Buddy and his friends to death or something. Besides, I think most of the students here are half afraid of their brains anyway. Collectively, you'll be well protected by the force of their knowledge."

Even Lucy laughed now. "You make it sound like something out of *Star Wars*. 'May the force be with you.' "

"Whatever works, right?"

"Right," Jana chimed in, beaming even as she shivered.

Lucy looked between her oldest friend . . . and her newest one. "Okay," she said, finally reaching out her hand.

When Grady took it in his own, Jana impulsively stuck hers on top of it. "Okay."

Grady grinned and capped their hands with his other one. "Okay."

*And just like that, it was settled between them. Like the knights of old, every day they met around the lunch table, for that year, and every year after until graduation, sharing stories of battles won and battles lost, shielding themselves from the slings and arrows of their brethren (along with the occasional french-fry launch from a nearby table) using nothing more than wry observation and a well-placed barb as their weapon of choice. Little did they know that the bond formed that blustery afternoon would someday be tested, and by the very peasants who brought them together in the first place. Which is where our story really begins . . .*

# Chapter 1

Looking back, she could blame the whole thing on an impulse purchase. Well, that and the invitation to her tenth high school reunion, which landed in her mailbox the very same day. Divine providence? Cruel cosmic joke? Hard to decide. Experience pointed to it being the latter. Then again, Fate had never done her any favors, either.

Before buying that issue of *Glass Slipper* magazine, Lucy Harper had pretty much accepted the fact that she was forever destined to play the Sandra Bullock role in *Miss Congeniality*. Only there was no Michael Caine. She was never going to make it to the transformation scene.

There were two truths in Lucy's life. One she'd learned very early on. The other had crystallized the night of her senior prom.

First: She would never be one of the popular girls. That had been made painfully clear, oh, pretty much the first time she'd been stuck in a preschool playgroup with Andrea Steiner and Miriam Thompson.

Andrea, she of the perfect, glossy ringlets and shiny patent-leather shoes that never scuffed, not even on the playground. And Andrea's best friend, Miriam, of the perfectly freckled nose and adorable matching dimples, complete with endearing lisp that Lucy pretended to hate but secretly coveted.

These two Benetton princesses took one look at Lucy, with her hazel eyes, magnified by bookworm-thick glasses, her mousy brown hair, lumpy rather than wavy, no matter how often she brushed it, topped with the fresh chicken-pox scar on her right cheek, and immediately decided she was not fit to climb the same monkey bars they were. The preschool version of the Corporate Model for Advancement.

Lucy Harper, already a corporate failure at age four.

Things didn't change much in elementary school. Quiet, but more out of insecurity than shyness, she'd at least learned to tame her unruly hair by then. The Pippi Longstocking nickname had arrived shortly thereafter. Privately, she'd always thought Pippi rocked. But then, Pippi didn't have to contend with both the whack braids *and* being the class beanstalk.

Taller than anyone her age from second grade on, she still had gangly awkward long legs, complete with matching big feet that refused to steer clear of even the most insignificant obstacle. Her arms were freakishly strong, yet still scrawny-looking, and her nose wasn't quite straight due to an unfortunate flip-turn incident in the pool the summer of fifth grade, when she'd worked up the nerve to join the local swim team. The great thing about swimming, she'd discovered, was that it favored long legs and freakish arm strength, but didn't require perfect eye-hand coordination, like basketball or softball. And, as long as she remained in the pool, she didn't have to worry about tripping over her own feet. She'd prayed nightly that she was merely a late bloomer.

At twenty-eight, she was still praying.

Which brought her to truth number two: Popular boys never, ever fell for the geeky, beanpole, wallflower girl. Any doubts she might have harbored regarding this law of nature were completely and resolutely put to rest that long-ago June night.

Emboldened by a new pair of contacts that still kind of made her eyes water, skin imperfections only partly disguised by strict adherence to the tips outlined in the "Make Him Notice You, Not Your Pimples!" article in *Teen* magazine, and a black formal she'd begged her mother to let her wear—one that finally hugged her meager curves rather than hanging from her shoulders like the Shrouds of Dances Past—she'd worked up the nerve to approach the surprisingly stag Jason Prescott.

Jason was the magnificent, blue-eyed, broad-shouldered point guard of Grant High School's varsity basketball team. And the best part wasn't his blinding white smile, quick wit, or even his participation on the student council—long a haven for her fellow nerds and geeks. No, Jason's number one attraction was the fact that, at six feet five, he towered over Lucy's five-eleven frame. Whenever she could position herself in his orbit, which was as often as humanly possible—without ever actually being noticed, of course—she enjoyed the fleeting sensation of feeling almost girlishly feminine. And, dare she say it, petite.

Grady and Jana had both warned her, of course. But she'd known it was her last chance before they were all cut loose into the big bad world of unpredictable futures. Well, in her case, as much of the big bad world as was encompassed by the Georgetown University campus. Her future wasn't all that unpredictable either, really, seeing as her father was a tenured professor in the English department, and her mother held a similar position at nearby American U. But Jason was heading off, scholarship already in hand, to play for Duke.

So Lucy knew she had to make her move now . . . or never.

Just one dance in Jason's arms. That was all it would take. One dance, with everyone watching them, their bodies so perfectly aligned. Lucy, surefooted for the first time, as would surely be the case with his oh-so-natural grace guiding her, her arms lightly around his neck as he smiled down—down!—at her. The crowd would part, all other dancing would cease, as every eye was drawn to their absolute perfection. And when it was over, and the final strains of Seal's "Kiss From a Rose" were but a mere echo in their minds, she'd accept his kiss upon her cheek, maybe even a brushing of the lips, then she'd smile knowingly up into his perfect blue eyes . . . and turn and walk away without so much as a backward glance. Mysterious Lucy Harper, so poised, so controlled. *How did we misjudge her all these years?* they'd all wonder. Yes! Twelve hellish years in the public school system eradicated in that one, perfect exit.

It was *her* dream, after all.

Her best friends had used a less flattering term, but in their defense they were only trying to look out for her. They didn't want her hurt. Again. But that hardly made the plan delusional. Yes, Grady Matthews and Jana Fraser had seen that look of determination before, and okay, so it had rarely resulted in a positive outcome. But her pathetic little sigh of infatuation, bolstered by a plastic tumbler's worth of spiked punch, and they both knew all the reasoning in the world wasn't going to stop her.

She'd had a crush on Jason Prescott since freshman summer, when he'd been a lifeguard at her community pool. Her carefully orchestrated dives off the high board—the only mostly graceful thing she could do—had never seemed to get his attention. And her one attempt at drowning in order to secure a romantic rescue, complete with at least two minutes of glorious mouth-to-mouth resuscitation, had gone embarrassingly awry. It turns out it's hard to get anyone to believe you're drowning while wearing your local swim-team Speedo, rubber skullcap, and goggles. Planning ahead was never her forte when her hormones got the better of her.

But on that glorious June night, she'd planned everything down to the last detail, including bribing the DJ to play Their Song. Or what would be Their Song, just as soon as their one perfect dance was over. For years to come, every time Jason heard that song, he'd think about that night. That dance. And the mysterious Lucy Harper.

Fate had given her a sign by sending Jason Prescott stag to his own senior prom. Looking back, she supposed she should have realized that Fate had been trying to tell her to give up after that pool incident. For someone with a 4.5 GPA, she had serious learning disabilities when it came to matters of the heart.

Not only had Jason not fallen for her starry-eyed, sequin-splattered, come-hither charms—much less the opening chords of "Kiss From a Rose"—he'd thought she was joking when she'd asked him to dance. *Joking!*

*Yeah, such a kidder, that Lucy Harper.*

Lucy thought she'd done an admirable job of covering up the additional humiliation of having him not only laugh in her face, but pat her on the head before turning away. Like she was his bratty kid sister or something.

Then, because Fate wanted to make sure she got it this time, without so much as a backward glance at the conspicuously partnerless, hollow shell of a girl he'd left behind, Jason walked right into the arms of the blonde, blue-eyed perfection that was head cheerleader, Debbie Markham. She of the no-visible-panty-lines and questionable virginal status.

Unlike her heart, already shattered into so many irreparable pieces, Lucy's smile had barely wobbled. She was pretty sure she'd made a halfhearted attempt at joking her way out of the situation—an automatic fallback position she'd mastered long before. Except no one was paying attention to her at that point. She supposed that should have made her feel a little better, being invisible and all. She knew from personal experience that it could have gone much worse for her. But Boyz II Men were crooning "On Bended Knee" now, and everyone around them had moved on without her. She stood there alone, completely ignored by the swaying couples surrounding her, which felt worse somehow. She wasn't quite sure how to make that exit now, knowing it would feel a lot more like running away.

In the end, Grady had emerged through the crowd and quickly dragged her outside. He'd told her he was merely protecting himself from the stalkeresque wiles of Marching Band Girl, Paige Fernlow. But Lucy had known the real reason. (Although after spying the two of them leaving together, Paige *had* left rather disturbing tuba solos on the Harper family answering machine for three nights running. To this day Lucy could not sit through halftime at a football game without feeling a prickle of paranoia.)

No, Grady had been protecting her, as always. She'd been insisting she didn't need rescuing since the day they met over the infamous Tater Tot incident in sixth grade, but her protestations were still met with the same response: *"Everybody needs rescuing sometimes. It's what friends do."* Then he'd trump her with the old "You'd do the same thing for me" routine. Which she would have. Gladly. Except it never had seemed to work out that way. One more thing Fate tossed her way that she couldn't seem to alter.

Since the day Grady had firmly wedged himself into her and Jana's life, he'd been routinely saving them both. So, okay, more often her than Jana. Could she help it if Jana didn't seem to get into as many scrapes? He was still the quiet observer around others, but never with her or Jana. He was wicked smart, possessing a bordering-on-nerdlike fixation with all things mathematical and technological. Okay, so it wasn't "bordering." But it was his wry commentary on how the human condition afflicted the majority of their peer group that had kept Lucy and Jana sitting at his lunchroom table all the way through high school. They still enjoyed a rather loose interpretation of those erudite lunchroom discussions, only instead of being accompanied by the less-than-savory chili mac surprise and warm milk, they now took place over pizza and beer.

Jana had been in her life since the days of the Benetton princesses. (Jana flunked Playground Politics 101, too. She and Lucy were immediate best friends.) At that time, the Frasers and Harpers lived in the same apartment building in Arlington, Virginia. Their mothers wouldn't be considered close friends, or even casual friends by the loosest of standards. Lucy's mom was every English professor cliché rolled into one, from the serviceable clothes and bobby-pinned bun, to the wire-rimmed glasses perched on the end of her long, slender nose, a nose that was generally immersed in a book. Mary Harper was far more at home dealing with fictional characters than she was with real people. Not because she didn't like real people, mind you. Real people were just fine. It took real people to write books, after all. It's just that she was usually so distracted with writing her next lecture that observing even the basic tenets of friendship building were beyond her.

Jana's mom, on the other hand, made friends very easily. Too easily, some might have said. Of course, that might have been envy talking. Or jealousy. Because most, okay all, of Angie Fraser's "friends" were men. And because it was no secret that not all of them were single.

But Mary and Angie did have one thing in common—they shared car-pool duty, ferrying their daughters to and from Tiny Tots Preschool.

Jana had her mother's bright red hair, but the similarity

ended there. Angie Fraser was very Tina Louise as Ginger. Jana was more Lucille Ball as, well, Lucille Ball. Except with huge splotchy freckles, and big white teeth that were just a bit crooked, and still were, despite three years of braces, complete with the ever-so-attractive head appliance.

Of course, to mousy, unfreckled, and uninterestingly toothed Lucy, Jana was some kind of exotic creature, and the source of immediate fascination. Unlike the television-commercial cuteness of Miriam and the preppy perfection of Andrea, Jana was an absolute original. Lucy remembered thinking that her new friend must be something really special if God made her stand out like that.

Lucy had since learned that God merely had a peculiar sense of humor.

But her belief in the unique force that was Jana Fraser had never wavered. Unfortunately, that unique force, even when combined with Grady's global-rescue theory, couldn't protect Lucy from her own self-destructive crush tendencies. The Senior Prom Fiasco had only been a temporary setback to her apparently indestructible—and obviously deluded—libido. Jason Prescott had merely been the first in a string of unattainable men Lucy fell hopelessly for.

Through four years of college, not once did she find herself remotely attracted to any of her horn-rimmed-glasses-wearing, but ever-so-nice-and-dependable, lab partners. The same went for the unfocused yet earnest struggling poet in her English composition class, and the naïve but sweetly endearing member of her study group. She lost her virginity, but never her heart. She'd lost track of the number of end-of-date kisses where she'd close her eyes and pray that this time she would feel something. Anything. Nada.

But she knew she wasn't holding out for the impossible. There was that Halloween keg party in her sophomore year, after all. Proof positive she could feel something. A whole lot of something, actually. As a joke, she and Jana had dressed up like cheerleaders. With their wigs, orange-hued fake Coppertone tans, and bust-enhancing Victoria's Secret bras, even Debbie Markham would have believed they'd earned their pom-poms. Okay, only if the lighting was sort of bad. And a lot of beer had been ingested. Which was exactly the case when Lucy ran into the current target of her unrequited—hell, totally unnoticed—affections: junior-varsity quarterback Steve Van Kelting.

He'd mistaken her for the real thing, and the next thing Lucy knew, she was on her back in one of the frat-house bedrooms. A small, insignificant part of her knew she should tell him she really wasn't Wanda—which is what he'd called her as he'd pulled off her letter sweater—but then his hands were on her, and his mouth found hers, and well . . . what Wanda didn't know wouldn't hurt her.

The earth definitely moved that night. Okay, so maybe there was someone else beneath the pile of coats she and Steve were making out on. The fact remained, she'd finally felt *something.*

After that—and despite the fact that Steve not only didn't call her, but didn't so much as notice she was still in bed next to him the following morning (she blamed it on all the coats)—the idea of settling for less than *something* was pretty much impossible.

Now getting ready to begin her fifth year teaching perpetually rowdy third-graders at Meadow Lane Elementary (no, not exactly the tenured position her parents had hoped for, but the apple hadn't fallen so far from the tree after all), she was still searching for *something.*

The thing that Lucy envied most about her parents wasn't their professional accomplishments, but that they had each found someone who appreciated their unique attributes. From the very first time her mother and father had laid eyes on each other, like had recognized like, and *bam!*, that had been that.

Thirty-two years later, they still made a solid team, with common interests. It was clear, despite the rather cerebral nature of their relationship, how much love, support, and respect there was between them.

So why couldn't she find herself madly in love, or even respectfully smitten, with some nice, average guy who'd appreciate her for her sharp mind and cutting wit? She had absolutely nothing against average guys. In fact, she'd hoped and prayed with each successive average-guy date that she'd get that like-recognizes-like thing and the *bam!* would happen. But there was never any *bam!* with them.

Now, put her in the path of the Jasons and Steves of the world? *Bam! bam! bam!* Problem was, there was never a reciprocal *bam*ming. Back to that like-recognizing-like thing, she supposed. Except her "like" was still incognito. At twenty-eight, she was still a Pippi. On the outside. But on the inside, she felt like a Ginger. No one got that about her, though.

Why was she cursed with swooning only for the unattainable? Why was she so attached to the need to swoon in the first place? With thirty looming on the horizon, maybe it was time for her to let go of the need to swoon.

Jana, now a sports editor for the *Washington Post,* had found her *bam!*. She'd married him two years after graduating with a degree in journalism. Of course, Jana's "like" had come out of hiding by then. She'd bloomed in their second year as college roommates. Although not exactly a swan, Jana had learned to make the most of her unique attributes. Attributes her husband, Dave, worshiped ad nauseam. Apparently the man had a thing for playing connect-a-dot with his wife's freckles. Lucy, though privately fascinated, didn't ask for intimate details for fear Jana would actually tell her.

Quebec-born Dave Pelletier, second-string goalie for the Washington Capitals hockey team, had been Jana's first interview after getting the job with the sports editor at the *Washington Post.* Dave had fallen head over hockey sticks for the cagey redhead. (Lucy wanted a flashy moniker like that—"cagey redhead." Brunette elementary-school teacher just didn't have the same flair.) Jana had flair now, and she also had freckle-worshiping Dave. They'd married eight months later.

Not only did Dave think her splotchy freckles were endearing, he loved her frizzy, corkscrew red hair, calling it unbelievably sexy. Dave had a scar across his forehead from a hairline skull fracture he'd received his first year in the majors, and a nose that had been broken more times than a heavyweight boxer's, which might explain his questionable judgment regarding beauty. But Jana adored his French-Canadian accent, his oddball sense of humor . . . and of course there was that quirky discovery that having a husband with removable front teeth made for some very interesting sexual side benefits. Lucy supposed there were other reasons, but she'd always gotten a little hung up on that one. Anyway, it was obviously yet another match made in heaven.

And this was all fine with Lucy. She was happy for her friend. Dave traveled a good part of the year, and other than being forced to bear occasional witness to their somewhat gooey attachment to each other, Lucy and Jana still had plenty of free time to continue their friendship relatively unencumbered by the change in Jana's marital status. The only real downside was that in her three-plus years of wedded bliss, Jana had joined the ranks of the Come in, the Water's Fine Club.

Just when Lucy had finally adopted her Single Pride mantra with a believable note of sincerity.

Not that it had been all *that* challenging, really. Jana's occupation regularly put her in the direct path of hockey goalies, point guards, and shortstops. Lucy's options within her immediate office dating pool were somewhat more limited. As in extreme to the point of laughable. Most of the elementary-school staff were female—though choral teacher, Bonnie Colvin, had given Lucy a few looks that could only be described as "suggestive." Which left her to choose between Jared, the still-closeted art teacher; Ramon, the janitor, who, in addition to using gold dental plating as his main fashion accessory, was also married with three small children; or the former Navy bomber-cum-PE teacher, Ed Foley, who, though widowed and available, was old enough to be her father. Possibly her grandfather. There would be no *bam!* with him. Not ever. Even she was not that desperate.

Jana had taken it upon herself to fix her best friend up with the occasional athlete, newspaper reporter, or franchise executive. This was not a bad thing, in theory. Jana knew the kind of guy Lucy went for and came through like a champ. The problem? The only ones who called her back were the recent Russian athletic imports, who spoke next-to-no English but were very willing to let her do their laundry and fix them breakfast in the morning. Or the vertically challenged Washington power execs who thought that having an almost-six-foot woman on their arm—even a mousy, fashion-challenged klutz such as herself (she was the anti–Heidi Klum)—somehow compensated for their, uh, shortcomings.

It wasn't like she was looking for wedded bliss. Or even a seriously committed relationship. But it would be nice on the nights that Dave was in town to have someone else to rely on as a movie-and-coffee date. Sex was optional, though preferred. Of course, there was Grady, providing he wasn't working. Except he always was.

He'd become a think-tank genius for some government setup, in charge of creating God-only-knew-what kind of technological wonders. Lucy had asked him for details once, but with his typical deadpan humor, he'd spouted the very tired "I could tell you, but then I'd have to kill you" line. With anyone else, she'd have rolled her eyes. Only, where Grady was concerned, well, she still wasn't entirely certain he hadn't been telling her the truth. Of course, macho as all that sounded, the bottom line was, whatever he did for their government, he was doing it in a lab. Hardly James Bond. More like Q.

Not that he didn't socialize in between designing fountain pens that were actually poison darts or nametags that secretly harbored powerful zoom lenses. He jogged and played racquetball—two activities he'd invited her to participate in a total of once. Her insurance through the school system just wasn't that broad-ranging, and his first-aid skills were negligible. Apparently his mad-inventor genius didn't extend to devising a racquet that magnetically attracted the ball to it, thereby rendering skill and coordination a noncompetitive factor.

Grady dated, but he didn't talk about the women in his life much. Still, she and Jana knew they existed. You could always tell when Grady had gotten laid. He sprang for the pizza *and* the beer at their quasiregular get-togethers. But he still didn't talk about them. Probably because he'd so wittily eviscerated every guy Lucy had ever dated, that he didn't dare. But she and Jana suspected that if he ever got serious, they'd know, because he'd bring her to one of their get-togethers. That's how they'd met Dave. It was like introducing your intended to family. They each had their own families, of course—in a manner of speaking, anyway—but the opinions that truly mattered would always be one another's.

Lucy considered it a blessing that, despite his critiques, Grady never offered to fix her up. She'd met several of his coworkers over the years. *Bam!* candidates they were not.

But Grady came through for her in far more important ways. He'd long since stopped having to rescue her, of course. Well, not counting that time two Thanksgivings ago when she'd been craning her neck to get a look at the new frozen-food guy and ended up plowing her grocery cart into the carefully arranged display of pumpkin-pie filling, condensed milk, and canned cranberries. Grady had managed to calm the store manager down *and* get the hunky frozen-food guy to put a bag of frozen limas on the lump that had sprouted so becomingly on her forehead. Truly her hero, that Grady, even if the frozen-food guy had turned out to be more interested in getting Grady's phone number than hers. But really, most of the time she hardly ever needed rescuing. Physically, anyway.

In the words of the great Mick Jagger, Grady was oftentimes her "emotional rescue." The best thing about him was that she knew with absolute certainty he would stop whatever he was doing, possibly jeopardizing national security, to be there for her if she really needed him.

Of course, her parents were more than glad to fix her up, and did, with painful frequency. It seemed beyond their academia-saturated comprehension that their nice, well-educated, and respectably employed twenty-eight-year-old daughter wouldn't fall for "a catch" like American alumnus and department head Hugh Wadell. A forty-two-year-old divorced anthropology professor with alternate-weekend visitation rights. She supposed it was her fault for not making a romance match while her parents were still going through the staff roster of single men in their thirties. She loved her parents dearly, but unlike her mother, she didn't feel the urge to order wedding invitations simply because the guy in question could complete the Sunday *Post* crossword in pen. If these were her choices, she'd rather stay solo, *bam!* or no *bam!*

It was just, sometimes it got a little depressing that the guys who called her back weren't the ones that sparked her. And the ones that did spark her didn't even look in her direction, much less ask for a phone number. Not that she hadn't put herself out there. But the result of her attempts? She could write a book on "I'm Hot, and . . . Well, You're Not" letdowns:

*"You're such a nice person, I know the perfect guy is out there for you."*

*"I wish I was the one for you, you have so much to offer the right man."*

*"It's totally me."*

*"You're so together and, well, I guess I still have some growing up to do."*

And her personal favorite:

*"You understand me better than anyone I've ever met. Let's stay friends, okay?"*

She understood, all right.

But was it so wrong of her to want what she wanted? To be honest, and very possibly shallow, she wanted to experience, at least once in her life, a night of wild, out-of-control, down-and-dirty, multiple-condom sex. With a sober partner who called her by the right name. And no coats on the bed. Or other drunken party guests.

What she wanted was a guy who was as turned on by her as she was by him. At this point she'd be happy with missionary position and an orgasm, as long as both parties were still in the same room for Part A and Part B.

Did that make her pathetic? Desperate? She didn't think so. A girl could dream, couldn't she? Fantasize? Hallucinate?

Then the reunion invitation had arrived. The very same day she'd tossed *Glass Slipper* into her shopping cart. Who could have guessed that one innocent little postcard and a makeover magazine would start a chain of events that would turn her entire life upside down. Or at the very least, the last two weeks of her summer break.

Lucy opened the magazine to the "Inner Beauty Boot Camp" article she'd marked with the reunion postcard. They promised miracles.

So what if she decided to go to the reunion after all? Maybe what she needed to get her head on straight was to take this opportunity to go back and revise past history, beginning with getting the attention of a rumored-to-be still-single Jason Prescott. Well then, a miracle was exactly what she needed.

Fate had long since given up sending her signs. So, probably, had God.

It was time she took matters into her own hands.

# Chapter 2

"How is it that Debbie Markham still manages to come across petite and blonde on an e-mail loop?" Lucy straightened from her hunched position behind her friend's shoulder. She didn't want to read any more reunion posts.

"You're just projecting," Jana told her, stuffing the last of her Sun Chips in her mouth. "For all you know, she's turned into a leather-skinned tanning-bed junkie with overprocessed highlights, saggy tits, a flabby ass, and married to a balding, nearsighted CPA who likes it when she wears that leopard-print nightie he bought her at Marshall's for Mother's Day."

Lucy's smile was decidedly unkind as she clasped her hands beneath her chin. "Do you think?" Then her shoulders drooped. "Nah. My karma would never be that good." She sighed and balled up her sandwich wrapper. "But I appreciate the visual, so thanks for that."

"I live to serve."

"I still say you should consider writing fiction. You're a natural."

"Right. Then you'd give it to your mother, who would delight in desecrating it with her beloved red pen."

"My mother loves you."

"Me, yes. My work, not so much. I get enough of that kind of love from my editor, thanks."

Jana was probably right. But then her mother, much like the rest of the Harper clan, really wasn't a sports person. Lucy brushed crumbs off her shirt and slid from her perch on the computer-lab table. Instead of reading about the exaggerated exploits of a group of people she'd once loathed and had long since ceased to care about, she should be using her remaining summer break time to put her classroom in order. "I guess I'm just not a loop person."

"Truer words," Jana agreed, having been the first one to point that out two weeks earlier when Lucy had signed up on a whim after they'd received their invitations from the reunion committee, complete with information on how to join the reunion group on Yahoo! Thankfully she didn't rub it in. But then, the look on her face precluded that necessity. "You've become a first-class lurker, I'll give you that. Most entertaining lunch breaks I've had in years. Of course, anything beats the hell out of listening to that insufferable asshole Frank belch out his latest know-it-all opinions on the Redskins, the Wizards, the Capitals, the effect of the Cold War on American sports, the dawn of the solar system—"

"You're just pissed because his column got picked up for syndication."

"Damn straight I am. His columns are pompous and arrogant, not to mention out of step and uninformed. And I don't care if his father once played for the Senators. It's not like he's an effing sports guru just because his dad had a .341 career batting average and came within one season of tying DiMaggio's record." She lobbed her wadded-up trash at the small wastebasket beside Lucy's desk, missing by a wide margin, despite being less than two feet away. It was a good thing Jana only wrote about sports.

"Yeah," Lucy said, "but can he consistently miss an easy two-pointer with his fanny wedged in a third-grade desk? I think not."

Jana sighed and let the front legs of her chair *thump* back on the tile floor. "True. My wrist action sucks and my release is all wrong. I shoot like a girl."

Lucy lowered her chin and shot Jana a look. "Please don't tell me you bribed Dave into trying to teach you how to play hoops again."

She shouldn't give her friend a hard time. It was sad, really. Jana was a die-hard jock, always had been. Maybe it was the very lack of any kind of continuous male influence in her life, but she'd been hooked on sports as long as Lucy had known her. From the time she could read, she devoured the sports section of the *Post* and every issue of *Sports Illustrated.* ESPN's SportsCenter was her version of CNN.

Jana could tell you the starting lineup for any team, college or pro, in any of the major sports. She could whip out stats, debate the merits of the most complex coaching strategy, and pretty much wipe the floor with you in terms of predicting draft choices and win-loss records well before the season started. Any season. She worshiped sports. All sports.

She was just completely inept at actually playing any of them. But it didn't stop her from trying. Bless her heart.

Lucy, quite happy with her status as an avowed—and therefore injury-free—couch potato, said, "He's a hockey player, Jana. How many times—"

"A hockey player with excellent eye-hand coordination. The man can routinely stop a puck flying at him over eighty miles an hour, while wearing skates *and* more pads than the Michelin Man. You'd think he'd be able to teach me how to sink a simple layup." Jana frowned. "I tried hockey, remember? It's too many things at once. Skating *and* trying to stay upright *and* trying to hit a ball with a stick? I can't do any of that individually yet, much less combined. So I went for something more straightforward." She pointed her Snapple bottle at Lucy. "And, more important, something that can be played in sneakers and shorts. Put the ball in the net. It just shouldn't be that hard."

After a "there, there" pat to Jana's shoulder, Lucy went back to unpacking school supplies. One thing she loved about her best friend was that, while Jana might be quick to boil—a much-hated redhead cliché that she nevertheless owned up to—she simmered down just as fast. "I agree with you, if it makes any difference," Lucy offered. "About the syndication thing. I like your columns. You're not condescending, and you have the kind of style and energy in your writing that can make even fellow uncoordinated losers like me read the sports page. Well, a column of it, anyway." She glanced over her shoulder at Jana, who'd turned back to the computer terminal. "Of course, you're no Christine Brennan, but—"

"I have deadly aim and a whole box of Crayolas within easy reach," Jana reminded Lucy, never looking away from the screen as she casually clicked through posts.

Lucy snorted. "Deadly aim. Right."

"All I have to do is aim for the chalkboard and I could nail you in the back of the head with no problem. Trust me."

Lucy grinned and went back to stocking tempera paint and brushes in the locking overhead cabinet, well away from the ever-questing fingers of her next batch of heathens. She'd given up on the honor system last year after coming back from a quick hallway consultation with the principal to find Billy Cantrell drinking Sunshine Yellow, straight up, no twist. Fellow classmate Doug "The Instigator" Blackwell had convinced him it would make him fly. Doug was her prime candidate for the first student ever busted in Meadow Lane Elementary for selling a controlled substance. Billy would probably be his first customer.

"So, should we unsubscribe?" Jana's finger hovered over the DELETE button..

"No!" Lucy almost dumped a whole carton of Sky Blue in her efforts to get to Jana before she could act.

"Whoa there, hoss," Jana said, laughing. "What's up with that? Did we not just agree that reestablishing any kind of umbilical relationship with these people is detrimental to our psychological health? Not to mention our hard-won self-esteem?"

Lucy vainly attempted to reclaim what was left of her dignity. "That doesn't mean we have to stop anonymously enjoying ourselves at their expense, right? I mean, they did that to us for years, right to our faces. Come on, Grady'll be here soon. You know he'll make you laugh. Besides, it's only for a few more weeks."

"Six," Jana corrected, then her gaze narrowed. "You are *not* still considering actually going to the stupid reunion, are you?"

Lucy waited a beat too long in answering. She hadn't quite gotten around to telling Jana about the appointment she'd already set up at Glass Slipper, Inc. She needed to do that. The last two-week session of their special miracle camp started this weekend. Someone had to water her plants.

Jana swore beneath her breath. "Didn't we take enough abuse at the hands of these people? Are we such gluttons for punishment that, ten years later, we want to give them another shot? Why would you even consider putting yourself in that position?"

"Maybe I'm holding out hope that Debbie Markham really does have flabby tits."

"Ass. Saggy tits."

"Works either way."

"Don't jump off topic here."

"Why are you drilling me about this? What are you writing, an article or something?"

"Hmm, maybe I should," Jana said, tapping a finger to her chin. "How about: 'Gearing Up for Your High School Reunion: A Full-Contact Psychological Sport, Not for the Timid.' "

Lucy squeezed herself into the seat next to Jana. "Maybe the whole point of going back is to prove we've progressed beyond allowing others to define ourselves." That sounded pretty good, she thought. She almost believed it herself.

"There is nothing wrong with mocking our pretentious, overzealous, label-conscious classmates in the sanctity of your empty classroom. Considering it's like a million degrees outside, this is the best lunchtime sport going. But why ruin the fun by giving them a chance to reciprocate?" Jana clicked through the messages posted since their last lunch get-together, skimming for something juicy they could pounce on. "You know, I thought we were on the same team here. Unified in our conviction to let the overbearing assholes inflict themselves on one another while we go out and do something less painful, like getting matching root canals. Why the sudden change of heart?" Then her fingers paused on the keys, before quickly clicking back to the previous message. "What in the *what* what?" Jana pushed her glasses up and leaned closer to the screen. Then turned an accusing glare at Lucy.

Who suddenly pretended a great interest in the last dregs of her Diet Coke. Dammit, why hadn't she just let Jana unsubscribe when she had the chance?

Redheads, as it happened, made the best glarers. They'd known each other for over twenty years now and Lucy still was not immune.

Lucy fidgeted, which was hard to do, wedged as she was in the tiny desk/chair combo. "What?" she finally asked, feigning complete innocence even though she knew she was already busted. She set her empty can on the desk. Where was a good stiff belt of Sunshine Yellow when you needed it?

"Jason Prescott, is what. And you damn well know it. Did you think I wouldn't find out? My God, I'm surprised every other freaking post isn't about the golden boy coming home. Fatted calves are probably being slaughtered as we speak."

"It's been ten years. I'm pretty sure 'the golden boy' statute runs out somewhere by sophomore year of college."

"Maybe for mere mortals."

"My wanting to go has nothing to do with Jason," she said, making a valiant effort. Then failing miserably by adding, "Not specifically, anyway."

"Ah-hah!"

"Don't *ah-hah* me." Lucy fished the rolled-up magazine from her shoulder bag and smoothed it open. "If blame must be placed, focus your derision and scorn here."

Jana adjusted her glasses and picked up the magazine, folding it back to the article Lucy had dog-eared. She read silently. Well, mostly silently. There was the occasional snort, punctuated with an intermittent eye roll or sigh of disgust. Finally she dropped the magazine back on the computer station like a piece of contaminated sewage, then lowered her glasses and looked at Lucy over the skinny black rims. Another thing redheads were good at, it turned out. "So, you're honestly considering going to Beauty Queen Boot Camp? Have you completely lost your mind?"

"See why I didn't tell you?" Lucy snatched the magazine back and stuffed it in her purse. "I knew you'd be judgmental."

Jana just laughed. "Ch-yeah. And with good reason. Ten years of maintaining absolute distance from those jerks, a decade of proving to yourself that you're everything they claimed you'd never be." She ticked them off on her fingers. "Successful. Happy."

"Alone." Lucy hadn't meant to say that out loud, it just popped out.

Jana goggled. "And?" She waved Lucy silent. "First off, you're single. Hardly alone. And hardly a curse, I might add."

"Says the happily married woman who found someone who adores her." Lucy's tone turned dust-dry. "Frizzy hair, obnoxious attitude and all."

"Yeah. A guy who gets hit in the head with flying pieces of rubber for a living. Obviously he's an anomaly of the species." But she had that smile. That smile she always got when the subject of Dave came up. Jana might be all harsh talk and frizzy edges, but mention her husband, and something in her demeanor softened in a way Lucy had never seen before.

Was it so wrong that she envied her best friend that telltale softening moment?

"But being single has nothing to do with this," Lucy said, determined to get control of this conversation. She just wished she'd thought out her defense a little bit better before revealing her decision. "I'm not going for the makeover so I can go to the reunion to meet men."

"Maybe not *men*, plural. But are you telling me that finding out Prescott is single and RSVP'd, didn't seal the deal?" She waved her nail-bitten fingers in Lucy's face. "Hello? I was at the prom, too, remember? And I was also by your side that whole summer, listening to you moon and moan over that jerk until we finally got to Georgetown and got your head out of your ass."

"Thank you for that kind analysis. But he's not—"

Jana flipped her hand up. "Uh-uh. Not another word."

"He's not the reason," Lucy finished stubbornly. "I was already considering going to Glass Slipper and the reunion before I found out for sure that Jason was coming back. It just so happened that I picked up the issue with that article the same day the invitation for the reunion came. I couldn't help wondering—"

"Hallucinating."

Lucy just made a face at her friend. "—what it would be like to get the full makeover, then show up and blow them all away. You can hardly blame me for that little fantasy, can you?"

" 'Fantasy.' Exactly."

Lucy studied her own short, chipped nails. "Okay, okay. Maybe reading that post about Jason did cement the decision." She looked up at Jana, serious now. "Is it really so awful that I want to get back some of what they took from me? Not just Jason. All of them."

Jana sighed now and reached for Lucy's hands, folding them in her grip. "It's been ten years. How can you let them matter to you again?" She squeezed her fingers. "You're a fabulous person. And the very last group you need to prove that to is a bunch of egotistical idiots we haven't seen since high school. And don't get mad at me for saying this, but part of me feels you'd be selling out. Admitting you're not good enough the way you are. And you're just damn fine."

Lucy threw up her hands. "Easy for you to say. You have everything you want!"

"Not everything," she muttered. "But I didn't have to turn myself into someone I'm not to get what I do have." Jana blew out a heavy breath. "I can't even believe we have to have this conversation, but come on. You don't have to change the way you look to prove anything to anyone. And please, you're tall and skinny; do you know how many women would kill to have your metabolism?"

"Yeah. I'm the Janeane Garofalo of supermodels. Please." Before Jana could get wound up again, Lucy tugged her hands free. "I don't want to argue about this, okay? If any two people have hashed and rehashed why appearances aren't everything, it's you and me. And it's not like I'm the walking wounded, ten years later." Her gaze flickered to the computer screen, then back to Jana's raised eyebrows. "Okay, yes, the invite and reading these posts did dredge up a few unpleasant emotions that I thought were long since buried. I'm not proud that I let them get to me." She fingered the corners of the magazine. "But I can't deny that when I saw the cover story about this two-week intensive program, I was a little tempted. Only, I don't see it as giving in, more like beating them at their own game. You know, Julia Roberts rubbing it in the face of those snotty boutique bitches in *Pretty Woman* with her 'big mistake' comment. Everyone cheered her, everyone got that moment of triumph."

"Lucy—"

"No, let me finish. You know, you kind of came into your own in college." She ignored Jana's snort. They both knew it was true. "I never felt like I did. And then you met Dave, and, well, I'm not saying you need him to validate your existence or complete you or anything ridiculous like that, but in terms of self-confidence, there has to be some sort of inner sense of satisfaction that comes with knowing you can fit in with another person like that. Share who you are with someone else on that intimate, connected level."

"I understand," Jana said sincerely. "I do, but—"

"Well, who doesn't want that? I do. But I can't make that happen. It either will, or it won't. So is it really so bad to want at least a moment of satisfaction that I *can* make happen?" Lucy asked. "I know it's a hollow victory, that these people mean nothing to me in my life today. But . . ." She shrugged. "I don't know. Maybe it's not about them. Maybe it's about me, and they're just a convenient measuring stick. All I know is I have something I need to prove to myself."

"Then prove it by going back the way you are right now and being fine in your own skin."

There was no point stalling any longer. "I've already signed up," she admitted, then forced a smile in the face of Jana's sincere concern. "If nothing else, it will make for a great 'How I Spent My Summer Vacation' story, right?"

Jana gave her a halfhearted smile. "I want you to be happy. I guess I just wish you didn't feel you needed this. The makeover or the reunion."

Lucy unwedged herself from her chair and stood. "If I go to Glass Slipper and I don't feel comfortable with how it turns out, I don't have to go to the reunion. But you know, it's not like they're going to cut into my flesh. I'm not going to come out permanently altered or anything. They'll primp and prod, and who knows, maybe I'll finally learn the secret to putting on eyeliner so I don't look like Tammy Faye. But really, what's the worst that could happen?"

The door to the classroom opened just then and Grady walked in carrying a Domino's box and a six-pack. He took in Lucy with her fists on her hips and Jana's set expression and said, "What did I miss?"

Lucy jumped in before Jana could speak. "You can't have alcohol on school premises." She nodded to the six-pack.

"It's root beer," he told her, rattling the brown glass bottles in the cardboard carrier.

"Oh. With pizza? Ew." But the pizza smelled so good she could almost convince herself she was still hungry. Okay, so it didn't take that much convincing. He flipped open the box. Deep dish, loaded. She shot him a wry smile. "So I guess dinner went well last night?"

Grady gave his customary half shrug and changed the subject as he always did. "So tell me what's wrong with you two. Nothing amusing on the reunion loop today?"

"You know," Lucy began, wishing she'd never told Jana anything, "maybe we should head out somewhere. I can finish this stuff later, and a cold beer—a real beer—is actually sounding pretty good right about now."

"She's going to Barbie Boot Camp," Jana informed him.

Grady looked at Lucy, then at Jana, then back to Lucy again. Then he smiled. It really was his best feature. His hair was still a mop of brown curls, albeit a shorter, salon-managed mop, and his eyes just as brown and soulful. Most of the time he looked exactly like what he was: a slightly distracted, somewhat overserious tech engineer who was probably right that minute thinking about something involving quadratic equations and microchips.

But when he smiled, everything changed. It brought this kind of charming yet devilish glint to his eyes. Add in the tousled hair, and he looked somewhat impish, like he might take delight in doing something a bit naughty. Jana and Lucy had long since decided this was the weapon he used to get women into bed. Because, unless they got turned on discussing things like complex atomic particle theory, it was pretty much the only weapon he had.

"'Barbie Boot Camp'?" He sat on top of one of the desks and hooked his feet through the seat. When Lucy said nothing, he took a healthy bite of pizza and motioned Jana to continue.

"I'm not going to talk about it," Lucy blurted, already disgusted with the two of them. "You two can dissect this all you want, but I've already sent in my deposit. It's my two-week vacation; I can use it however I want."

Grady just ignored her and motioned to Jana again.

"It's the reunion," she told him. "Lucy has this unhinged notion that if she turns herself into some kind of Stepford Graduate, the stunned reactions of our former classmates will magically erase the indignities she suffered at their hands." Jana reached over and snatched a slice, carefully flicking off the offending olives first. "And then there's the whole Jason Prescott element," she added, pointedly ignoring Lucy's openmouthed look of protest as she sank her teeth into her pizza.

Grady swung his gaze immediately to Lucy, all traces of his impish smile gone. "What about Prescott?"

"It's nothing," she said stubbornly, glaring at them both.

Jana snorted. "The teen idol of Grant High School is coming to the reunion." She used her pizza to punctuate her statement. "Solo." She looked at Lucy. "Don't *even* try to convince Grady that wasn't part of your plan." She sat back then and enjoyed the rest of her slice, satisfied that Grady would finish things for her.

They both knew that Grady had never forgiven Jason for what he'd done to his best friend. Unfortunately, Grady hadn't the requisite posse of defensive linesmen to help him do anything about it. Three guys from the math debate team weren't quite going to cut it. But during her heartbroken months afterward, he'd made no secret of the fact that Lucy was wasting her tears on a guy like Jason Prescott.

She agreed with him wholeheartedly. Now, anyway. But that didn't lessen her desire for a little payback. If anything, it did the opposite.

"I said it all ten years ago," Grady said, tossing his uneaten crust back in the box. He looked at her as if he was going to add something, then looked away, shaking his head. "I give up. You're going to do what you want to do anyway. Enjoy the rest of the pie." He shoved off the desk and headed toward the door.

Lucy moved after him. "Grady, come on."

"I have to get back to the lab. I'll talk to you later." The door swung shut behind him.

Lucy spun back to Jana, but one look at her set expression told her she wasn't going to find any regret there. Slumping against the bulletin board, she folded her arms and said, "Well, he didn't have to stalk out of here like that."

"You can hardly blame him. You know how he felt about all that."

"*You* didn't have to bring it up," Lucy said, but Jana didn't have to respond that he'd have found out anyway. Feeling lousy now and not exactly sure it was fair that she was the bad guy in all this, she blew out a sigh and pushed away from the wall. "I'm sorry you guys are so against me trying to improve myself." Okay, so that sounded petulant. But bad guys were allowed to pout, weren't they?

Jana clicked the program closed and shut down the computer. "I've got nothing against self-improvement. It was the motive behind your decision that got me." She cleaned up her trash and closed the pizza box before finally looking over at Lucy. After a brief standoff, she let her shoulders slump in resignation. "I'm not trying to rain on your Barbie Makeover parade, okay? I just . . . you know, I just don't want you to do things for the wrong reasons and get yourself hurt all over again. It's not worth it. Not for this."

Lucy walked over and helped her clean up. "I know. And I'm sorry I ruined our last lunch before school starts up again."

"It wasn't all you," she admitted. "I helped. Don't worry, I'll talk to Grady. He'll get over it. He—"

"—always does," Lucy finished with her, and they both smiled briefly. "I know. And I know you guys are only saying what you think I need to hear." She paused then, knowing it was probably best to just leave it at that. She didn't need her best friends' permission to go to Glass Slipper, Inc. Or their blessing. But she couldn't deny she'd feel a lot better about the whole thing if they at least saw her side of it.

Looking for the right words, she finally paced to the front of the room and started shelving supplies again. "You know, it's about more than the reunion. I've felt . . . I don't know . . . unfinished for some time now. Like my outside doesn't match my inside. Only I don't know how to go about reconciling the two."

Lucy darted a glance at Jana, and relaxed a little when she saw her friend was paying attention and not chomping at the bit, waiting for the chance to leap to the defense of her opposing point of view. That was the downside of having a reporter for a best friend. They loved playing the role of devil's advocate. Always made for the best stories, if not the most soothing or complacent friend. "I think getting the invite to the reunion and seeing that article at the same time was like some kind of—"

Now Jana raised her palm. "If you use the words 'fate,' 'sign,' or 'destiny,' I'm going to be forced to hurt you."

Lucy smiled. Okay, so Jana was never going to be soothing or complacent. Honestly, she wouldn't have it any other way. "Well, whatever you want to call it, it *was* what gave me enough of a nudge to take an active role in doing something about this . . . I don't know, ennui."

"God, now you sound like the daughter of two English professors or something."

Lucy smiled again. "Imagine that."

Jana sighed and shoved off her desk, then slung her arms around Lucy's shoulders for a quick, tight hug. "I want you to be happy with yourself," she said. "I just wish you didn't feel you had to try so hard."

Lucy stepped back. "It's just a new hairstyle and some makeup tips, okay? If we hate it, you and Grady can both mock me for an entire Sunday afternoon after I get back. I'll even provide the brownies."

"I'm going to hold you to that," Jana said, waving a finger.

"I'm sure you will," Lucy responded, relieved they were okay again. It wasn't the acceptance she'd hoped for, but she'd take grudging support. And she knew Jana would get Grady to see her side, though he'd probably never admit it.

"And if we unanimously agree you don't look like you, then you won't go to the reunion?"

Lucy sighed. Close. "I'm not making any promises there." She held up her hand to stall Jana's argument. "One step at a time. The reunion isn't till the end of September. You and Grady will have plenty of time to devise all kinds of mental torture for after I get back."

Jana chewed her nail. "True. We could be so much better organized about it, too."

"Oh, great. Now I know what you two will be doing for *your* summer vacation."

Jana grinned. "Yeah. And our vacation won't involve waxing or plucking or ripping anything out by its roots."

Lucy winced inwardly. She hadn't thought about that part. "Yeah, well, I'll be pampered and waited on hand and foot. And I bet my scenery will be better, too. Possibly buff, half naked, and tanned."

"So I'll get Dave some spray-on stuff and hide his favorite shirt."

They both looked at each other for a second, then burst out laughing.

"Okay, okay," Jana said, hugging her one last time. "You win. I'll reserve judgment until you get back."

"Thank you. That's all I wanted."

Jana paused at the classroom door. "Can we at least mock you behind your back while you're gone?"

"Sure. Get it all out of your system." She pointed a bottle of tempera at her. "Because you're going to eat every one of your words, Ms. Reporter." She grinned then. "And them's a whole lot of words, so wear something baggy."

Jana's laughter floated down the hall as the classroom door drifted shut behind her.

Finally alone, Lucy wasn't surprised to find herself fighting the encroaching fear that maybe, just maybe, Jana and Grady were right. (Waxing and plucking and ripping . . . oh, my!) But no. Now was not the time to buckle and cave. She was big on buckling and caving. Which was exactly what had led her to this point, right? She'd made the decision to do something about her growing self-discontent, and frivolous or not, the first step was going to Barbie Boot Camp.

She had to start somewhere, after all.

Lucy went back to stocking paint. She had to get the rest of this room in shape before the weekend. Because as of Saturday noon, she became the exclusive property of Glass Slipper, Inc. And for the next two weeks she would have her own personal fairy godmothers.

She shoved the last bottle in the cupboard, closed it, and clicked the lock in place. "I hope you have your magic wands charged and at the ready, ladies," she muttered. "I have a feeling I'm going to need every trick you've got."

# Chapter 3

"I think you turn here," Lucy told Grady, looking at the map to Glass Slipper that had been included with her boot-camp packet. "Almost there." She shot him a fast smile.

Grady saw right past the smile to the nerves beneath, but then he'd always been able to read Lucy Harper like a book. His fingers tightened slightly on the wheel as he turned down the majestic, oak-lined drive. He knew from doing a little online research that the private road wound its way back to a stately Potomac manse that had once been home to a state senator, the late Way Favreaux. His widow, the genteel southern magnolia, Aurora, had joined with two of her oldest and dearest friends—Mercedes Browning, former New England girls school headmistress, and Vivian dePalma, former Hollywood fashion maven and dresser to the stars—to open Glass Slipper, Incorporated, their self-termed "life makeover" business, several years before.

Grady still thought the whole thing was ridiculous.

"I appreciate you driving me." Lucy folded and refolded the map, plucking at the corners with her stubby nails, as they slowly progressed down the winding private lane.

"They provided you with a gilded pumpkin carriage—excuse me, I mean, a limo," he reminded her.

Her lips flickered briefly in a smile. "I know." She reached over and laid her hand on his arm. "And I know you and Jana still don't really approve of this. I wanted a last-ditch chance to explain. For all the good it did me."

He heard the dry tone, shot her a brief smile. It was hard not to. What you saw with Lucy Harper was what you got. He wished more people were like that. "Shoot me," he said, honest with her as always, "but I'm not sorry that I think you're fine the way you are."

"Thank you." Then she made a gun with her fingers and clicked the mock trigger. "You're being such a guy about this."

"At least I get that much credit," he muttered as the car emerged from the tree-lined drive into a huge circular driveway. The mansion, the outbuildings—or "private guest cottages" as they were called on-line—along with the surrounding manicured and landscaped grounds were even more impressive in person. A sprawling ode to Victorian elegance, the entire place dripped with southern charm. Probably just like its current owners, he thought, imagining the "godmothers" (as they'd been dubbed by former clients in their gushing and endless tributes) as a trio of aging pageant directors whose vision of an ideal world included a tiara for every highlighted and hairsprayed head. That world was so not the Lucy Harper he knew.

"All you guys have to do is shower, shave, and rub a towel over your hair and you consider yourselves presentable to the world," she explained. "It's a little more complicated for the opposite gender."

Not seeing a parking lot or additional signs indicating a visitors entrance, he simply parked in front of the fieldstone path leading to the big house itself. Then he shifted in his seat and looked directly at Lucy for the first time since picking her up at her Alexandria apartment forty-five minutes earlier. "And sometimes the opposite gender has a tendency to overcomplicate things."

"Oh, sure, like you don't enjoy the mascara-enhanced batted lashes, the perfectly painted lips, hair that looks like a weekend of wild sex—"

"Guys aren't all that hung up on war paint and hairspray."

"Please. You might not care to know the particulars of how that war paint goes on, but you like the results. Men are visual creatures. Well, maybe not you. You seem to appreciate personality over cup size, but trust me, you're the diamond in the rough there. And I mean 'rough.' A wilderness full of rough."

There was no point in asking her why she didn't just go for the so-called diamonds. He knew the answer to that. And it had a lot to do with the proverbial pot calling the kettle black. She didn't want to hear about that.

"Most guys can't get past what they see to find out if there's anything else worth investigating," she told him. "Much less take out to dinner, or home afterward for dessert."

*No, but neither do you,* he thought, wishing for the umpteenth time he'd locked himself in his lab all night. It was all Jason Prescott's fault. Again. "So, by transforming yourself into Hooter Barbie, you think the Neanderthals will take you out to dinner and be mesmerized by your scintillating wit and sharp mind?"

"'Hooter Barbie'?" She laughed. "Okay, since when do you hang out at the boobie bar?"

"I'll have you know that I can be just as turned on by a pair of big knockers as the next Neanderthal."

She looked at him for a long moment, then shook her head, clearly thinking he was kidding. In her mind, he was apparently above such an earthy male response. He didn't bother to correct her. What was the use? One of the things he most appreciated about their friendship was that she was so easy to talk to. Always had been. Where Jana was quick with an opinion and never shied away from defending it, popular or not, Lucy was the opposite. She was open and guileless, never meaning to offend. She was the first to laugh at her mistakes and quick to smooth over those of others. She didn't let him off the hook when he didn't deserve it, but always came up with a tension-deflating, smart-ass comeback when he did.

And because he valued her friendship above all else, this was the one topic he'd never broached with her. He didn't plan to start now.

"Well, I'm not here to get big knockers." She glanced down. "Even the fairy godmothers aren't that good." Grinning, she said, "Anyway, this isn't *Extreme Makeover.* I'm just going to learn how to, you know, enhance the positive." Then she rolled her eyes and slumped back in her seat. "God. Who am I kidding, right?"

And that was the paradox of Lucy Harper. Such a confident smart-ass one minute, then that flicker of sincere vulnerability the next. Never failed to draw him in. *Yeah,* he thought, *like a fly to the web.* Christ, what a pair they were.

He blew out a deep sigh and reached for her hand, tugging it between his even when she tugged back. "I can't believe you're wheedling this out of me, but you know I just want you to be happy. With yourself, or whatever it is you think needs improving. Both Jana and I want that. We just don't want you setting yourself up for disappointment, that's all."

Lucy stared at him with those frank hazel eyes of hers. "I'm not a teenager anymore. This isn't a whim. Okay, so coming here might have been. But I've wanted to fix this . . . I don't know, this feeling that I don't match up, for a long time. I just had no idea how to go about doing it. I tried convincing myself that I should settle for what I've got. But after a while, that began to feel an awful lot like copping out." She shifted her hands so she now held his. "If you want to improve your mind, you take another class, right? Well, I like my mind just fine. I want to improve whatever it is that keeps people from seeing the real me. Only it's not as simple as signing up for another college course."

He just sighed. She'd never get it.

"Worst case is I find out this is all there is. That this is the real me people are seeing. And then I guess I accept it and go from there. But I have to know I tried. Can you at least trust me that this is something I have to do?"

Grady rubbed his thumbs along the outside of her hands. "Yeah. I just wish you didn't feel so incomplete." Because it made him feel like he'd failed her somehow.

"I know you think this is a shallow endeavor, but—"

He shook his head. "Like you said, it's what you have to do."

She smiled. "A ringing endorsement." She pulled him forward and gave him a resounding kiss on the cheek. "But I'll take it."

On impulse he hugged her. Not that he didn't ever hug her. He did all the time. Just not when he was feeling . . . well, like he was feeling at the moment. "Just come back the same Lucy Harper I know and love, okay?" he murmured against her hair. Then sat her back and quickly shifted the tone. "Or Jana and I will be forced to confiscate your secret decoder ring to the Up with Homely People Club. Not to mention the 'Don't Hate Me Because I'm Beautiful, Hate Me Because I Can Program My VCR' T-shirt."

Lucy laughed. "Don't you mean, 'not beautiful'?"

Grady's smile shifted to one of pure affection. "No," he said, shaking his head. "I got it right."

"Aw, Grady," she said, her bottom lip wavering just a little. Then she reached out and punched him on the arm. "Don't pull that 'special moment on *Friends*' thing on me right now. I don't want to meet the godmothers with tears leaking down my cheeks."

He rolled his eyes in mock exasperation. "Make up your mind, will ya? Hey, dry your eyes fast." He motioned behind her with his chin. "The pageant directors triumvirate is approaching."

"'Pageant directors'?" She turned to look out her window, and gasped. "It's them." Glancing back at Grady, she made a *tsk*-ing sound. "'Pageant directors,' honestly. You'd better behave."

"Boy, remind me to not answer the phone next time you call for a favor." He got a better look at the trio of older women as they closed in on his car. "Wow, I take it back about the pageant thing. What the hell is that one on the right wearing, anyway? No wonder their pictures aren't up on the website."

Lucy's attention darted from the godmothers to him. "'Website'? What were you doing on the Glass Slipper website?"

"Making sure you weren't being sold into white slavery."

*"What?"*

*Or worse, that they'll make you into something you're not. The world has enough Debbie Markhams. It only has one Lucy Harper.* "Smile, they're here."

The tall, severe-looking one reached for the door handle. Grady guessed that one was Mercedes. She reminded him of the sort who'd left ruler marks on more than a few sets of knuckles.

"Welcome to Glass Slipper. Ms. Harper, I presume?"

Lucy nodded, smiled nervously, went to step out of the car . . . and began choking.

Grady reached over and undid her seat belt for her.

Smiling sheepishly, she looked back at him. "Thanks. For everything."

He nodded.

"I mean it. I'll be fine, you know."

"I know," he lied.

And then she was stepping out of the car and into the waiting arms of her Barbie Boot Camp drill sergeants. They'd been through the stress of puberty, peer pressure, the drama of high school, the freedom of college, and somehow becoming responsible adults anyway, all with their tight bond still intact.

So it was silly to worry about a two-week beauty camp. And yet he couldn't shake the feeling that she'd finally crossed a boundary that would change things between them forever.

He watched her walk down the stone path, praying he was wrong. Halfway down, she tripped and went sprawling into the grass. *Ah, Luce.* Grinning and shaking his head, his hand was already on the door. He'd been her rescuer for so long, he was out of the car without another thought. But before he could take another step, he watched Lucy scramble to a stand. She shoved her hair from her face, and he could tell by her goofy smile that she was making fun of herself, deflecting the embarrassment he knew she was really feeling.

He sank back against the car as the godmothers helped Lucy brush off her pants before continuing down the path and up the stairs. And he realized that his resistance to this idea wasn't about her getting hurt. It was about him getting hurt.

If she gained enough confidence, she might abandon the security their friendship provided. And that might mean she no longer needed him.

Welcome to Glass Slipper," Aurora said, gesturing to the sprawling Victorian with the deep, shaded porch that wrapped around the house. "We're so glad you're here."

Still recovering from her less-than-graceful entrance, Lucy forced a smile and nodded, but furtively she was scoping out the grounds. Other than a few people bustling along the shaded walkways that led from the house to the cottages tucked back beneath the oak trees and azaleas, she didn't see a single soul. The bustlers were all wearing matching linen blazers, discreet headsets, and carrying clipboards, so she assumed they were employees. What she didn't see were any other guests. They prided themselves on maintaining the privacy of their guests, but this was ridiculous. Surely she wasn't the only one who'd spent her entire savings on summer makeover camp.

"Let's go inside and I'll introduce you to Audrey. She'll be your personal director during your stay," Aurora was saying. "She'll explain the program to you, schedule your first round of appointments, then see that you're settled into your room."

"Thank you, Ms. Favreaux," Lucy said. "I'm excited to be here." In truth, she felt like she was going to throw up. What in the hell had she gotten herself into? She glanced over her shoulder, but Grady had already driven off. *Why hadn't she listened to him?*

"Aurora, please," the older woman once again assured her.

" 'Aurora,' " she repeated with a brief smile. "Your place here is beautiful." She'd received a glossy pamphlet full of background material and instructions on what she was supposed to bring with her. "The photos don't do it justice."

"Why, thank you, dear," Aurora said, a pleased smile creasing her perfectly preserved face.

Aurora seemed the softest of the three. Her makeup appeared as airbrushed in person as it did in her brochure photo, disguising the wrinkles without appearing troweled on; from her perfectly penciled auburn eyebrows, to her carefully lined and painted, deep rose lips. Her hair was an amazingly natural-looking strawberry blonde, all swept up in a loose bun on top of her head, with curled tendrils at her forehead and trailing along her neck. She wore a flowing caftanlike dress of gauzy silk, with a swirling pattern of russet and gold. That, along with the benevolent smile and southern accent, gave the impression she sort of floated along on the cloud of White Shoulders she'd doused herself with. Somehow, on her, it wasn't overpowering.

No, that description belonged to the shortest of the three, Vivian dePalma. Lucy knew from what she'd read that Vivian was the former Hollywood fashionista and dresser to the stars. She just wasn't sure what stars Vivian had dressed. Cher seemed an obvious choice. Or Elvis. Her hair was a theatrical red, cut in an equally flamboyant asymmetric style, above-the-ears short on one side, the front dipping over her brow in a dramatic sweep toward a chin-length bob on the other. Her lips matched her hair in tone. So did her eyebrows, in terms of flamboyance. Her snug black suede suit was ruthlessly cut to fit her short, fireplug frame and showed a scary amount of cleavage for a woman over sixty, but the heavy mantle of gold and onyx around her neck and dripping from her ears somehow made it work.

Then there was Mercedes, tall and lean, and the only one whose hair remained its natural color. The vivid steel-gray-and-white upswept do was actually flattering to her pale skin tone and subdued makeup, but her natural expression seemed permanently severe, even when she was smiling. Might be the patrician features. But it was probably more about the dark Beatrice Arthur eyebrows. One look from her made Lucy want to hide her knuckles. And she'd never even been taught by nuns.

"Audrey will have someone show you around the house and grounds later on this evening, but first we'd like you to come in and enjoy a light tea with the three of us."

Lucy glanced from Aurora to Vivian, who were both smiling approvingly, to Mercedes, who was merely smiling. "That sounds wonderful," she lied, surprised by the offer and nervous about what a "light tea" with this trio would entail. She hadn't expected such personal treatment.

She knew they catered to a pretty exclusive clientele, had even hoped to glimpse a Capitol Hill wife or two, but she was an elementary-school teacher. Aka Nobody. The camp was pricey, but she had the distinct impression from the magazine article that their purpose in hosting it was to allow the Everyday Woman to avail herself of their otherwise too-expensive services. She was Charity Barbie.

So, rather than flatter her, their attention made her feel wary and a little nervous. Lucy Harper didn't rate red-carpet treatments. Didn't they have an empire to run? Surely they didn't do this with every client. Could it be she really was the only pathetic idiot to sign up for this?

There was no polite way to ask (and she wasn't really sure she wanted the answer, anyway), so she was left trailing Aurora as they climbed the wide steps to the veranda and entered the house through a matched set of gorgeous oak doors, each inlaid with oval-shaped stained-glass windows.

"Right this way," Aurora said, sweeping her arm in an elegant arc, motioning Lucy forward with her heavily ringed fingers. "We serve tea out back on the veranda."

Lucy followed Aurora, so overly conscious of the two women behind her—Were they sizing her up? Staring at the way she walked? Making mental notes on her hideous hair and fashion sense?—that she could hardly do more than take in her surroundings. The open, two-story foyer had a tile floor set in a swirling circular pattern, with a beautifully restored round walnut table placed at its center. The table bore a towering arrangement of perfectly blooming flowers beneath a stunning crystal chandelier. The hallway leading from the foyer was a polished, dark inlaid wood; the walls were painted a deep leaf green below walnut wainscoting that matched the floors, and papered with a light cream magnolia linen pattern above.

Paneled walnut doors, also with inlaid stained-glass ovals,

lined one side of the hallway, but because of the wavy, colored glass, she couldn't see what went on behind any of them. They passed two sherbet-colored-blazer-clad Glass Slipper employees in the hall before entering a short service hall leading to yet another set of doors—this pair was French in design, with louvered white jalousies covering the glass panes—before leaving the house once again.

The veranda was expansive and shaded beneath a massive white canvas tent. A slowly swirling ceiling fan dropped down from the central peak and provided a steady breeze. The furniture was white wicker padded with thick, flower-patterned cushions. The table was smoked glass, set with an enormous sterling-silver tea set and two three-tiered trays filled with tiny fruit tarts, scones, and assorted pastries and finger sandwiches.

The whole thing was a masterpiece of *Southern Living* perfection.

Adjusting her glasses, Lucy looked down at her sensible shoes and grass-stained knees and realized she'd never felt gawkier or more out of place.

Where was a patented Grady Rescue when she needed it?

"Have a seat, dear," instructed Mercedes.

They each took their seats spaced evenly around the glass table, but she was still left feeling as if she'd been seated in front of a panel of pageant judges. A feeling that quickly proved to be prescient.

Their business was immensely successful. With the added success of their newly launched magazine, and the opening of another Glass Slipper in Europe, it was truly a global empire. So, despite the fact that, on its face, it looked like Glass Slipper was being run by three women more suited to heading a Broadway revue (*The Headmistress, the Southern Belle, and the Showgirl*), the truth was, Lucy was completely intimidated.

Linen napkins were spread on laps, scones and pastries were

selected and arranged on china plates, tea was poured. Lucy cautiously waited for the other three to drink first, slightly relieved when none of them extended their pinky fingers or balanced the delicate china teacups and saucers on their knees. Lucy was just praying to get through the next thirty minutes without dropping a blob of fruit onto her blouse or knocking her knee into the table leg and shattering something valuable.

"So," Vivian said abruptly, dabbing the corners of her vividly painted lips as she spoke, "tell us why you chose to come to Glass Slipper."

Surprised by the sudden direct question, Lucy bobbled her teacup, but managed to save it from teetering to the floor at the last possible second. She sent a sheepish smile to the three women and said, "Well, if I can leave here more graceful than I arrived, that would be a nice start."

Aurora reached over to pat the back of her hand. "There dear, you're doing marvelously." Her faded eyes twinkled when she smiled and Lucy found herself wanting to trust in the genuine affection they seemed to be telegraphing.

She took what strength she found there and faced the other two again. There was no way she could explain the complex reasons that had driven her to do this, when she didn't entirely understand them herself. And she was beginning to think Grady and Jana had a point when they said she was setting herself up for disappointment. A two-week makeover was not going to cure what ailed her.

So she gave them the easy answer. "I picked up a copy of your magazine the same day I received the invitation to my ten-year high school reunion." She flashed what she hoped looked like an easy smile. "I wasn't what anyone could term 'popular' in those days. So I suppose I'd hoped you could help turn the duckling into a swan, even if it's only for a night." Her smile grew. "Don't worry. I'm not expecting miracles."

They didn't immediately smile at her self-deprecating attempt at humor. She twisted the corners of her napkin in her lap.

Vivian spoke first. "You don't need a miracle. You're a lovely young woman."

"I appreciate you saying that," Lucy said, not believing a word of it. She was paying them to be nice, after all. "But I would feel more confident with a few tricks up my sleeves. I'm afraid I'm severely makeup impaired. And as you can see," she added, motioning to her shoulder-length hair, pulled back with a wide barrette, "I've never exactly gotten the hang of styling my own hair."

"So, you've come for beauty tips?" Mercedes said, the comment sounding more like an accusation.

Lucy faltered. Had she offended them? "I'm sorry, I didn't mean—"

"Mercy," Aurora gently chided. "Don't rattle the poor child." She turned her beneficent smile on Lucy. "Of course, we can give you confidence in the surface things," she said, "but there is a great deal more we do here than teach makeup application."

"Of—of course there is," Lucy began. This was all going horribly wrong. Barbie Camp was supposed to be fun. She'd imagined perky counselors spouting sunny affirmations while they waved their mascara wands and twirled their round brushes. Not these overly serious, dour old women. Well, not exactly dour, but still.

Vivian chose that moment to lay her napkin next to her plate and shift her chair back. "If you'll please excuse me."

Aurora's gaze went from Lucy's stricken expression to her partner. "Vivi, must you rush off? We've just started."

*Just started?* Lucy fought against the almost desperate urge to bolt. She'd followed the strict directions to leave the demands of the real world behind, which precluded bringing things like cell phones. But surely she could flag down a passing car. Then she would call Grady or Jana and prostrate herself on the Altar of Eternal I-Told-You-Sos if it meant getting herself the hell out of here.

"Don't get your fancy lace knickers in a twist," Vivian calmly told Aurora. "I'm merely going to consult with Audrey." She turned a smile on Lucy that, if it was meant to reassure, wildly missed the mark. "Finish your tea, darling. We'll see you when you're ready."

*Hell will freeze over first,* Lucy thought as she watched Vivian sashay back into the house. She'd pay big money to be able to sashay on four-inch heels, or sashay, period. But she was pretty sure that was an inborn trait.

She looked back to the remaining two godmothers. And it hit her. She had, in fact, paid big money. Big to her meager savings account, anyway. But it was all relative, wasn't it? She might not be the wife of some powerful Capitol Hill bigwig, but she deserved to get what she paid for. And if she had to sit through a grueling tea to get to the good part, well then, she was certainly made of stern-enough stuff, wasn't she?

She hadn't survived the public school system for nothing.

In a personal show of defiance, she placed her hands on the table. *Bring it on,* she thought rebelliously. Parochial schoolkids had nothing on her when it came to brazening her way through a bad situation.

Pasting a brave smile on her face, she looked at both women and just put it out there. What the hell did she have to lose? It wasn't like she'd wowed them thus far. "You're right. I need more than makeup tips. There are a lot of things I want, more than we could possibly cover in two weeks. But most of all, I want to walk into my high school reunion and feel bulletproof. For that, I need help. A lot of it. I came here because you're the best." She lifted her palms. "So I'm putting myself in your hands. I'll do whatever it takes."

Aurora beamed and Lucy thought she even spied a hint of grudging admiration in Mercedes's expression. Or it could be she was just dizzy from trying not to hyperventilate.

Both women stood. "Well, then," Mercedes said, "no point in wasting any more time on pleasantries."

Lucy almost choked. This had been the pleasant part? She took a last fortifying sip of caffeine and stood. It cost her to resist the urge to present them with her wrists and ask them to take her to their leader. This was, after all, about as alien an experience as she was ever likely to have. But she didn't think they had much use for her brand of humor. Or any humor, as far as she could tell.

She followed Mercedes into the house and down another long hallway. They stopped in front of a matching walnut-and-stained-glass door. "Audrey is waiting," she instructed. "You'll work together to develop your regimen here. She'll be here for you anytime of the day or night for the duration of your stay, should you have any questions or concerns. Of course, we'll do our best to make ourselves available to you, as well." She smiled tightly. Or maybe that was the only way she knew how to smile. "Welcome to Glass Slipper, Lucy."

Lucy nodded. "Thank you. And thank you for the tea, the personal meeting. I didn't expect that."

The door opened and Vivian stepped out. "It's our trademark," she said. "We like to make each guest feel as if they are receiving one hundred percent of our attention."

She was certain they meant to make her feel coddled and special, but she was feeling self-conscious enough right then that she'd have gladly accepted, say, fifty percent of their attention. Or less. It wasn't their fault. She just wasn't used to this kind of beneficent scrutiny. *Bugs felt more secure under microscopes than she did at that moment.*

Mercedes and Vivian retreated down the hall, heads together, but Lucy couldn't make out whatever they were whispering about. She had the distinct impression it was about her.

Aurora put her hand on Lucy's arm. "You're going to be magnificent, you know," she said gently. Her smile grew and the fairy-godmother twinkle returned to her eyes. "I always have a feeling for these things."

"Thank—thank you," Lucy said, surprised to realize how badly she wanted to believe the older woman. Where was the cynic inside her when she needed her most?

"Don't worry so much. Trust us," she said, as if she'd read Lucy's thoughts. "You're right. We are the best. Do what we ask of you, and you'll see I'm right." She grinned and it almost looked a bit mischievous. "I usually am. Just don't tell Vivian. She'll want to think this is all her idea."

"'This'?" Lucy asked, beginning to wonder just what kind of "tea" Aurora had been sipping.

"It's exciting, isn't it? You've taken destiny into your own hands, dear."

That proclamation probably wasn't intended to fill her with dread.

She was gently nudged into the office. Aurora remained out in the hallway. The soft *click* of the door shutting behind her echoed in her mind as loudly as the jarring sound of a jail cell clanking shut.

*Don't worry so much.*

"Sure," she muttered under her breath. "Easy for you to say."

With a deep breath, pasting a fake confident smile on her face, she squared her shoulders and prepared herself to take her destiny like a big girl.

# Chapter 4

Lucy rubbed damp palms on the sides of her khaki trousers and pushed up her glasses. Day two at Glass Slipper and she'd yet to have the first eyebrow hair plucked.

She twisted the antique crystal knob and opened yet another walnut-and-stained-glass door. This time, instead of one of the godmothers, or Audrey, her personal cheerleader, there was a shrink waiting for her on the other side. Her purpose today was to delve into the reasons behind Lucy's desire to change her appearance.

Oh, goody. It just kept getting better and better.

Who wanted to spend their morning talking about why they were a perennial wallflower? Wasn't it obvious what kind of help she needed? Did they really have to sit around and discuss it?

"Welcome, Lucy," a familiar voice greeted her cheerfully.

Lucy stopped short just inside the door, surprised. "Aurora, I mean, Ms. Favreaux."

Aurora lifted one perfectly stenciled brow.

"Aurora," Lucy corrected herself again, gave a nervous smile. "I, uh, you surprised me. I thought I was meeting with Dr. Sullivan." She leaned in and looked around to see if maybe this was to be another one of those panel type of discussions. But Aurora was the only one in the beautifully appointed room.

"Phoebe was called away. Family matter." She smiled and that reassuring godmother twinkle emerged once again.

Assuming Phoebe was Dr. Sullivan, Lucy tried not to collapse in immediate relief. But all she could think was, *Oh, thank God, no alien mind probe today!* "What a shame, I'm sor-sorry," she stuttered, the lie not coming easily. "Has the appointment been rescheduled?" She did her best not to look too hopeful.

Aurora motioned for Lucy to sit down, the stack of bracelets on her wrist jangling at the motion. "Why don't you sit down."

Not an encouraging sign. Lucy stepped into the room and closed the door behind her. She'd expected some kind of tasteful office decor geared toward exerting a calming influence on those forced to enter. Instead, it looked more like the sitting room off an elaborate boudoir.

It was small, or perhaps it was the illusion created by the fact that the walls were covered in a wine-colored linen with a raised-velvet fleur-de-lis print. The floor was carpeted with two colorful, densely woven Oriental rugs, topped with a collection of overstuffed, brocade-covered, antique chairs, all grouped to face one another around a beautifully restored teak tea table. Lighting was soft, provided by several standing lamps, each with dark cream-colored antique shades and elaborate pull chains sporting crystal knobs at the end.

The sensual decor exuded a warmth and coziness that went at least a short way toward soothing her nerves. Definitely more so than in the clinical feng shui setup she'd expected to find.

Aurora, dressed in a burgundy-and-gold silk caftan, was

seated in the chair with the highest back, leaving Lucy to choose between two other chairs of slightly less stature. A light tea had been set on the table in a pretty silver service that Lucy did her best not to bump into as she chose the seat most directly across from Aurora.

"I hope you don't mind the last-minute substitution, dear," Aurora began, as she leaned forward and poured two cups of tea with the sort of elegant grace Lucy could only dream of having. "We didn't want to delay the beginning of your program here, so I offered to step in and conduct this initial discussion."

Lucy was unable to hide her surprise. "You're going to conduct the session?"

Aurora's smile was self-deprecating and quite charming. "Not that I have a degree, but I think we can cover the basics well enough. I'm sure Phoebe will fill in all the gaps when you see her next."

" 'Next'?" Lucy blurted before she could stop herself. Did they think she was in such bad shape that she needed a battery of discussions with a shrink? All because she said she wanted to be bulletproof? Maybe it had been a poor choice of words. Did they think she was going to go back and mow down her evil classmates or something?

Aurora handed her a cup and saucer, her serene smile easily in place. "Why don't we just focus on our little talk today, hm?"

Lucy took the cup and saucer, the china pieces clattering harder against each other the more she struggled to keep them steady. With an apologetic smile, she finally placed the set on the table between them. "It's such a nice set. No point in ruining it."

Aurora graciously made no comment as she settled herself back in her chair. When the silence spun out as the older woman sipped her tea, Lucy realized it was up to her to start things off. It felt like a test. She gave tests all the time. It was what teachers did. That didn't mean she enjoyed taking them.

Feeling a little desperate, she nodded at the framed prints on the walls. Each one featured a door. Some open, some shut. Some fancy, some austere. Garden doors, castle doors, random doors. "Interesting photographs," she said, by way of nothing except to delay this talk as long as possible. "Did you take these yourself?"

Aurora shifted her gaze, too, and her smile softened as true affection lit her eyes. "My late husband, Way, took those." She looked to Lucy. "He was in politics, and we traveled often together. These were sort of a hobby of his." She looked back at the prints. "I like them. It always makes me remember that life is an adventure. Doors will close. Others will open." She shot Lucy a fast smile. "And you never know what's behind the next one."

"Good philosophy," Lucy said, feeling her own mouth curve in response. Despite the general intimidation she'd felt since setting foot on the perfectly manicured grounds, she'd been drawn to Aurora from the moment they'd met. Soft and a bit ethereal, with that twinkle thing she had going on, she seemed to embody the fairy-godmother spirit.

"So," Aurora began, her teacup and saucer balanced perfectly on top of her caftan-covered knee. "Why don't we talk a little bit about your reunion."

"Aurora," Lucy began warily, only to be interrupted.

"I know the visit with Dr. Sullivan wasn't something you expected," Aurora broke in, her face wreathed in an understanding smile. "But you need to trust we know what we're doing. In fact, you'd be surprised to know how helpful these little sessions are for us. By asking you some questions and chatting a bit about a few things, we'll be able to build the program that will provide you with the greatest benefit."

"So this is standard? I didn't see it mentioned in the literature."

"No," Aurora admitted, "it's not 'standard.' We don't have

'standard' plans here. Every person is unique, and so are their concerns. We approach each of our guests as individuals and plan their program accordingly."

"Is it really all that complicated?"

Aurora took another measured sip. "Are you saying your reasons for wanting to attend your reunion as something of a knockout are simple?"

Lucy shrugged, feeling another twinge of discomfort. *Chatting a bit, my ass.* Aurora might have the smile of a fairy godmother, but those faded blue eyes told the real story. And they were shrewd. "If we're going to get existential, then no, of course not. On one plane, even the simplest decision is a resolution reached after assessing complex layers of motivation and desire." Aurora didn't appear to be impressed by her academic bullshit. Rats. "But what I want here is pretty basic. Both the motivation and desire are, I would imagine, fairly common. I wasn't one of the swans in high school. Far from it. I've long since accepted that." So much for keeping her school issues out of the conversation, too. "But when I got the reunion notice and your magazine article in the same day, I figured, why not get a little outside help, scrape off a layer or two of ugly duckling, and go back with my head held high? Trust me, I won't hold anyone at Glass Slipper accountable if I don't get the reunion-queen crown. I just want to . . ." *Wow them. Blow their collective snotty minds. Make an entrance, dammit.* "Fit in," she finished lamely.

Aurora's gaze grew more attentive. "When you were talking with us during our initial visit, I believe you used the word 'bulletproof.' What exactly did you mean by that?"

Lucy sank back in her chair, pulled into the conversation despite the little voice in her head urging her to *flee now, flee fast!* Aurora's twinkling gaze was like some kind of tractor beam, compelling her testimony as if she were under some kind of self-improvement oath. "It's not about being a knockout." Lucy adjusted her reliable, if not-so-trendy, wire-rim glasses and gestured to her pleated khakis, pinstriped blouse, and Naturalizer sandals so boring they weren't even on the cutting edge of schoolmarm fashion. "I mean, who are we kidding here?" She sighed. "I just want—hope—to feel confident enough so that when I walk in the door, the whispers and comments won't shake me."

"It's been ten years. Perhaps your classmates have matured."

"With the invitation came an invite to join an e-mail reunion loop. I signed up to see what was going on, who was attending, that sort of thing."

Aurora made one of those *hmm*ing sounds. "And from what you've read, you feel like they would still find such behavior amusing?"

Lucy's lips quirked. "Not all of them. But you know what they say about leopards and spots. Some have used the intervening years to elevate their catty behavior to an art form."

"You don't have any interest in renewing ties with any of them?"

"God, no." Lucy waved her hand. "I know what you're going to say. Why go through all this for a bunch of losers who aren't even relevant to my life?"

Aurora didn't respond to that. Instead, she said, "You said you want to be a knockout. And that you want to fit in. Do you think you need the former to get the latter?"

Lucy shrugged. "It's a start. But I don't want to fit in the way you mean it. It's not about acceptance into their tribe. I don't want to actually *be* one of them."

Aurora's eyes lit up a bit. "Then this is about going back and getting revenge, hm? Do you want to prove to them that you're worthy of their acceptance, only to reject it when it's offered?"

Lucy opened her mouth to deny it, then stopped, reflected for a moment. "Maybe a little of both."

"You're very honest with yourself." Her smile widened. "That's good."

Lucy lifted a shoulder, not quite sure how to respond to that.

"Wanting revenge is human, if not always healthy."

"It's not like I'm fixated on it or anything."

Aurora's smile turned knowing. "I know. It's . . . complicated, isn't it?"

*Hoist by my own petard.*

"Yes. But I don't see how telling you all the sordid details will really impact my two-week stay here. Just teach me how to do my hair, put on my makeup, give me some remedial fashion help, and make sure I don't trip over my own two feet. I'll be more than happy."

"What have you read about Glass Slipper, Inc.?"

"What do you mean? I read your magazine occasionally. I know you do makeovers. That you're considered the best in the business." Lucy shot her a self-deprecating smile. "I figured that's what it was going to take. Your two-week program sounded like it was the kind of all-around intensive program I'd need. A kind of makeover camp."

"Have you heard the phrase 'life makeover'?"

"I know that's what you call what it is you do here. And I know you do a lot more than help make ugly ducklings into swans, but I don't need all that. I don't need help getting a better job or finding a husband. I just want to get through one night looking like someone who has her act together. Unshakable."

"Bulletproof," Aurora said.

"Exactly. And honestly, I am realistic about all this. Short of applying for *Extreme Makeover,* I know my improvement options here are limited."

"What do you think about the phrase 'Beauty comes from the inside'?"

Lucy snorted. "I think that no one cares about Pam Anderson's insides. But I know what you're really asking. And sure, some people might not be conventionally attractive and yet they are still compelling. I think that comes from having a certain level of self-confidence that they have their act together."

"And do you think those people you went to high school with all have their acts together?"

"Of course not. And I realize that rather than finding solace in like recognizing like, they feel compelled to confirm the status of their peer group by denigrating all those who they feel don't measure up."

"So maybe they're the ones who need their head examined. Not you."

Lucy smiled a little. "You said it, I didn't."

Aurora sat forward in her chair and set her cup and saucer back on the table. "I'm happy with the progress we made today." She slid a small spiral-bound notebook out from the folds of her caftan.

Lucy recognized it as the chart Audrey had begun for her earlier.

"I see you have a session first thing in the morning," she said, tapping the schedule with a long fingernail. "So we'll schedule you in at ten." She looked up and smiled. "Phoebe should be back by then."

"Tomorrow? I have another appointment?"

Aurora nodded. "I can't really pursue much further than this. She's more qualified, dear. Trust me, you'll get a greater benefit from continuing with her."

"But—"

Just then there was a chirping noise. Aurora fumbled in the folds of her caftan and produced a slender cell phone. Lucy wondered what the hell else she might be concealing. Probably a tape recorder, she thought with a defeated sigh.

"I'm terribly sorry," Aurora told her, "but I have to take this. I'll have Audrey confirm your appointment for tomorrow."

As if so commanded, the office door cracked open and there was Audrey, beckoning Lucy to follow her. How long had she been out there? Had she been listening to the whole session?

Lucy lifted her hand in response to Aurora's brief wave and smile, then stood and followed Audrey out as if on autopilot. She wasn't in Barbie Boot Camp, she thought as she followed the back of Audrey's perfectly pressed linen blazer. She was in Stepford Wife Hell.

Well. Not for long. She wasn't exactly a prisoner here.

# Chapter 5

I wonder how it's going," Jana mused, peeling the skin off her orange.

"She'll be fine," Grady said shortly. He tore off a piece of hot-dog roll and tossed it out to the pigeons gathering around their bench.

*Yeah, but will* you *be fine?* Jana sent him a sideways glance, worried about her best friend. Both of them. She'd finished up her preseason interview with head coach Joe Gibbs earlier than expected, so she'd left Redskin Park and made a beeline for D.C. with the sole purpose of ambushing Grady.

She'd been wrestling with her conscience over what to do ever since the invitation had shown up and Lucy had gotten it into her head to make herself over. Should she barge in and potentially change things between them forever? Or play it safe and keep her mouth shut? After all, she'd been keeping her mouth shut for what, going on fifteen years now?

She knew Grady jogged every afternoon, alternating his path between laps around The Mall or the Tidal Basin. It was Monday; Lucy had been gone two days now. Jana staked out a bench on The Mall, across from the Museum of Natural History, and waited. He hadn't seemed completely surprised to see her. Wary, but not completely surprised. Of course, he'd been avoiding her calls since he'd dropped Lucy off at Glass Slipper headquarters. He had to know she wasn't going to stand for that very long.

Only now that she was here, with no chance of Lucy popping up or calling, the perfect opportunity she'd so carefully staged staring her right in the face . . . she was chickening out. "Maybe we shouldn't have given her such a hard time about this," she said, inwardly cursing her cowardice. "If she feels she needs to do this for herself, who are we to say she's wrong? Right?" She picked at her orange. "What was the place like?"

"Very Tara Meets Capitol Hill."

A smile tugged at the corners of Jana's mouth. "Pretty much what we'd deduced from the website, then." She hazarded another glance, but he wasn't looking at her, didn't so much as nod. *To pry, or not to pry?* "Did you meet the godmothers?"

"I saw them. Interesting lot. Not surprised they don't include their photos on their home page."

Jana straightened, both intrigued and shamelessly relieved to put off the Very Important Talk a bit longer. "Really? Why?"

"They were quite . . . colorful." He didn't add anything else.

Jana knew he wasn't in the mood to dish. Of course, delivering one-liners while she and Lucy dished on the subject of the moment was more his thing. Another time she'd have dragged every last cynical detail out of him anyway. But not today. "So, was Lucy excited? Nervous?"

"Both."

Christ, it was like pulling teeth. "Did she say anything else to try and convince you how great an idea this really is?"

Jana watched Grady as he threw the rest of his crumbs at the expanding, grateful flock, then leaned his rangy body back on the park bench. There had been times over the years when Jana had found herself looking at his body in more of an opposite-sex way, not a best-friend way. She'd even dared to quiz Lucy a time or two, when she thought she could get away with it, without giving away what she knew. What the whole world would know if it paid the slightest damn bit of attention. Lucy's responses had generally been vague, like those of a sister being asked to rate her brother on a scale of one to hottie. Lucy said she found it hard to be objective about a guy she'd watched go through puberty; zits, developing body hair, and all.

Maybe it was because Jana was married. Or maybe it was because she had the analytical, objective eye of a reporter. Or maybe it was because she'd never been able to look at any member of the opposite sex without mentally ranking or undressing them—yet another reason why her coworker, Frank Winston, made her cringe with loathing—but at the moment, Jana found herself eyeing Grady's mop of damp curls, the contemplative look on his oh-so-serious face, the way his sweat-soaked T-shirt clung to his lean but well-defined torso, the ropy muscles lining his long runner's legs . . . and thought he ranked pretty damn high on the hottie chart. Especially for a self-admitted geek who was mostly clueless about his hottie potential. Which actually gave him added points.

"Yes, she did make a last-ditch effort," he said. "And no, it didn't exactly work."

" 'Exactly'?"

He shot her a sideways glare. "Journalists are worse than lawyers. Don't look for some hidden story in my every word."

Jana smiled and half shrugged. "Can't help it."

"You could have saved the trip and interrogated me via cell phone."

She chucked a piece of orange rind at him. "Which you never pick up when you're in the lab," she pointed out. "Which is where you always are. I figured with Lucy in Barbie Rehab, you might not surface for the whole two weeks."

"Contrary to popular belief, my social calendar is not co-dependent on Lucy's calendar." He crossed his ankles and glared at the pigeons. "Or yours."

It was the perfect opening. And he had to know it. A cry for help? Did he *want* her to out him? "You have no social calendar," she said dryly. "Nailing that movie-geek manager at Blockbuster is hardly a social calendar."

She saw his lips twitch. "You're forgetting I also get first-run releases up to forty-eight hours before the general viewing public."

Jana rolled her eyes. "I was happier thinking you were more interested in her for the sex. Sometimes you worry me."

There was a slight pause, then he said, "Sometimes I worry me, too."

Then there was silence. Followed by more silence. And she wasn't jumping in with the obvious follow-up. It wasn't because she'd suddenly lost her knack for knowing how to pin an interview subject to the wall. It was because she cared very deeply about this particular subject. And once she opened Pandora's box, there would be no going back.

Finally, Grady filled the chasm of awkwardness with a long, whistling sigh. He rolled his head toward her. "Why did you come down here, Jana?"

And there it was. The moment of truth. She looked at him, at those soft, serious, studious dark eyes of his, and her heart jerked a little. *Please forgive me if I'm about to screw up one of the best friendships I've ever had.* "You know why I came down here, right?" she said quietly, earnestly. Chickenshittedly. *Yeah, that's courage, all right. Make him say it first.*

He shifted his gaze back across The Mall. "To talk about Lucy."

Oh, great. Soft lob, followed by an even softer one. Bastard. Who was the journalist here, anyway? "Yeah. Yeah, I did." She took a deep breath. "I've often wondered why I waited this long. I thought about it once before, back during senior year. But we were heading off to college, and it didn't seem right. Since then, I guess, uh, I guess it never felt . . . I don't know. Critical." She stole a glance at him. He was still watching a bunch of college students play football Frisbee. "Like it does now," she added. Meaningfully.

He didn't say anything right away. Just left his arms resting on the back of the bench, keeping his gaze forward. And very much not on her. "What makes you say that?" he asked at long last.

"The reunion. Glass Slipper." She did watch him now, gauging his reaction. "Jason Prescott."

Bingo. The stoic mask slipped. You had to be looking for it. But there it was. She hadn't imagined that flicker of anger, that flinch.

"You don't want her to go through that again," she said, pressing on slowly, gently. Praying he'd jump in anytime now and just freaking relieve her of this horrible burden.

"Of course not. But she's a big girl now. She can make her own mistakes." Then, under his breath, she thought she heard him mutter, "Again and again."

"Grady—"

He sat up abruptly, pressed his hands on his knees, and looked at her before standing. "Neither of us wants to see her get hurt. No shit. We're her friends. I get that. Now, I have to get back to work."

"Yeah, well, friends don't let friends—" She broke off. "Okay, so I've got nothing clever to end that with. But you know what I'm saying here, Grady, right?"

"You're saying I should do something to fix things so she doesn't get her heart skewered like a shish kebab and handed to her on a reunion-size platter." He did stand then. "I've spent a lifetime trying to do that. Maybe I shouldn't have." He looked down at her, his expression all inscrutable. Geeks occasionally had a real advantage that way. "Maybe real friends let friends figure things out on their own."

Jana felt the prick of accusation. Of condemnation. He knew that she knew. And he didn't appreciate or want her blurting it out. It should have been a giant relief. They could just go back to pretending they were all nothing more than good friends. Except it wasn't a relief. If anything, the burden felt all the heavier because it was obvious he wasn't going to shoulder any of it. "Yeah," she said, just as quietly. "Maybe."

"I'll catch up with you later."

She didn't want him to take off. Not yet. Even though they'd basically agreed to disagree on how to handle things where his feelings for Lucy were concerned, she was still afraid she'd done harm to their friendship. "Dave and I are trying to have a baby."

It took a second for her blurted confession to sink in. For both of them. She'd had no intention of telling Grady or Lucy about this very recent, still somewhat shaky decision she and Dave had made. She'd wanted to tell them. Badly. But with everything else going on, the tension between them all, she'd decided it could wait.

"What?" Grady asked, sitting back down next to her. He took her hand between his wide palms and curled his long fingers over hers. "A baby?"

She couldn't help it. She smiled. And maybe she got a little glassy-eyed. What he didn't know was that it was more from sheer terror than a misty-eyed reverie. At the look of awe and wonder in his eyes, her throat got a little tight and she couldn't spit that part out. She managed a nod.

He pulled her into a spontaneous hug, then immediately pushed her back. "Sorry, didn't mean to sweat on you," he said, but he was beaming at her. All thoughts of Lucy and their uncomfortable confrontation of moments ago were apparently forgotten. "That's fantastic news. Does Lucy know?"

For a few seconds, anyway. "We really just started seriously considering it. I haven't . . . I haven't even really come to terms with it myself."

Grady's smile dimmed a little. "You're not sure? Was this Dave's idea, then?"

She shook her head. "No, no. It was mutual. We've been sort of dancing around the subject for a while. You know he's from a huge family, so it's no secret he wants one of his own."

"And only-child you? How do you feel about that?"

She lifted a shoulder, wishing now she hadn't been so quick to use her personal situation as a diversion from the Lucy situation. "I'm not sure."

He smiled encouragingly. "It's normal to be nervous. It's a big step. If it helps, I think you two will make awesome parents."

She couldn't tell him it was more than being a little nervous. She managed a dry smile. "God knows we'll be relying far more heavily on his experiences than on mine."

"Hey, do any first-time parents really know what the hell they're doing?" He rubbed her shoulders. "I mean, except for Lucy, we're poster children for family dysfunction. And look how we turned out."

Jana laughed at that. "Why do you think I'm so terrified?"

"Well, I think it's great. I'm happy for you two."

"Says the guy who thinks commitment is actually writing down a woman's phone number in case you want to use it again. Someday."

His easy smile remained, but something flickered in the depths of his puppy-dog eyes that had her mentally kicking herself. If she was going to offer up her big life decision and plop it on the altar of their friendship, the least she could do was not waste it by taking giant steps backward into awkwardness.

"Give Dave a manly handshake for me" was all Grady said, his smile still a sincere one.

"What, no 'Way to go, dude' beer toast, followed by a macho 'You're-a-procreating-stud' high five?"

"I'll save that for when I see him in person."

"And the womenfolk who would kick your sexist-pig ass aren't around."

He grinned. "That, too."

"Yeah, yeah."

Then there was another slight pause, the beginning of an awkward moment. Grady stood up before it loomed any larger and lobbed his balled-up hot-dog wrapper in the nearby trash can. "Thanks for the nitrates and carcinogens."

She wrinkled her nose and looked at the half-eaten hot dog still nestled in its aluminum-foil wrapper on her lap. "Anytime," she said, knowing he was teasing her. But still. "What are friends for, right?" she added without thinking. *Jeez.* Apparently, she was a walking friendship time bomb.

There was a beat, then he looked down at her, all serious again. "You're the best kind a guy could have. That's why I know you'll make a great mom." And with that he took off at a loping run, down the wide path, heading toward the Washington Monument.

She watched him retreat through blurred vision. Sniffling, with a golf ball–size lump in her throat, she sat on the bench long after he'd disappeared, more confused than ever on what course of action to take next. It was clear Grady wanted her to leave it alone. But since when did Grady know what was best for him? That's what best friends were really for. Right?

# Chapter 6

Still intent on leaving, Lucy was already zipping up her suitcase when a knock came at the door. Squaring her shoulders, she marched over to it, prepared to battle Audrey to the death if necessary—or at least until her blazer wrinkled. Whatever it took.

"My mind is made up," she said as she opened the door. "Oh. Sorry."

Vivian didn't wait for an invitation. She strutted right in.

Lucy glanced down at the four-inch black lacquer, gold-tipped spikes that Vivian was sporting and once again marveled at her ability to stay upright, much less strut. She closed the door and turned to find Vivian sifting through her things. "I beg your pardon?"

"That won't be necessary," Vivian replied, not looking the least bit abashed. "However, you should beg the pardon of whoever sold you this." She lifted a khaki skirt, making a *tsk*ing noise as she observed the front placket pockets. "As a fashion statement, it fairly screams—"

"Elementary-school teacher?" Lucy queried dryly. She couldn't afford to let Vivian intimidate her again.

Vivian laid the skirt on the bed, then picked up a cotton camp shirt in a pink-and-tan plaid, turning it this way and that, as if unsure just what to make of it.

"I work with twenty-two third-graders," Lucy pointed out. "It pays to think stain camouflage wash-and-wear."

"How . . . functional of you, darling." Vivian tossed the shirt back on the bed, then finally turned to face her. "But you're not presently teaching school, are you?"

*Do not let her make you defensive. Do not apologize for what you do.* "Not for a few weeks yet, no."

"Ah" was all she said before returning her attention back to the contents of Lucy's suitcase. She began unceremoniously removing her pleated khaki trousers, skirts, and blouses and placing them on the bed.

"I just finished packing those," Lucy said, though in a somewhat less strident tone than she'd hoped for. She was too busy praying that Vivian would stop before she got to her underwear. So what if she liked cotton over silk? What was wrong with comfort, she wanted to know? Besides, silk always rode up.

"Forgive me," Vivian said, not sounding even remotely repentant. "I'm simply looking for your other clothes."

"What 'other clothes'?"

"Exactly," Vivian said, giving up her search, but not before casting a pitying look on Lucy's comfortable brown flats. "You need us, you know."

"That's why I paid you the big bucks, isn't it?"

Vivian didn't even blink, though her expression did turn a shade more considering. "I understand you're not happy with our services, thus far."

"I was hoping for wardrobe and makeup help. And the only kind of analysis I'd figured on going through had to do with determining my season."

"I realize that our methods might not be exactly as you'd assumed, but it seems a rather snap judgment, if you ask me."

Lucy lifted a shoulder. "I just don't see the point of it." She gestured toward her suitcase. "All you have to do is look in there, and look at me, and you get a fairly good idea of the kind of help I need. So why the need for a bunch of psychobabble?"

"Because anyone can slap a fresh coat of paint on a dated piece of furniture and make it look all shiny and new. Would it be passable? Certainly. Interesting? Rarely. You see, the problem with the quick fix is that it buries the chance of finding the real potential of the piece. And that true potential is buried deeper with every cosmetic coat of paint we slap on." Warming to her analogy, Vivian crossed her arms beneath her gravity-defying bosom. "However, imagine if that same someone had taken the time to chip away a little at the old paint. They just might discover the gorgeous wood beneath. Strip away those layers and you have something real to work with. With time and the right kind of attention, the original piece will glow to life with richness and depth that no one could have expected was possible. Place the pieces side by side, and there will never be any comparison." She looked Lucy right in the eye. "Any day spa can slap on a new coat of paint, darling. We get paid the big bucks because we work on polishing what's underneath."

There wasn't much Lucy could say to that. She sank down on the edge of the bed, quiet in her defeat.

"Come now," Vivian admonished. "Where is the challenger from moments ago?"

"Buried under coats of chipped paint." Lucy kept her gaze on her sensible flats, probably looking as miserable as she felt. But then, she'd just been compared to a major restoration project. Surely she was allowed at least a moment of self-pity.

"Now, now. You obviously have some sense of what lies beneath, or you wouldn't have dumped out your piggy bank to come here and let us help you find it, now, would you?"

She sighed and finally looked at Vivian. "So, okay, I talk to Aurora or your shrink and reveal my most torturous secrets. When do we get to the polishing phase?" She frowned then. "You do always get to the polishing stage, don't you?"

Vivian's perfectly painted lips quirked at the corners. "Of course we do." She came over and sat down next to Lucy, taking her hand between her own and urging Lucy to maintain her gaze. "If I didn't think yours was going to be particularly gratifying, I wouldn't have come in here to talk to you in the first place."

Lucy snorted before she could stop herself.

"You're thinking I say that to everyone."

"I'm thinking this whole intervention is very good for public relations, and a way to safeguard the investment I've already made in your company."

Vivian's smile spread. "I'm no fool, that's for certain. Glass Slipper's sterling reputation means a great deal to me."

The thing about Vivian that had struck Lucy from the moment they'd first met was that she didn't seem to have any problem speaking her mind. And while it wasn't always easy to hear what she had to say, blunt as she was about it, Lucy did appreciate her honesty. In fact, it was a relief of sorts, knowing she could trust at least one person around here to tell her the unvarnished truth.

"But though I am a businesswoman," Vivian added, "and a smart one at that, I also excel in making sure the services I provide here meet with success." She leaned closer. "We've each already made our fortunes, Lucy, but we've never once discussed retirement. Why? Because we honestly enjoy helping people find the best within themselves. It's extremely satisfying, and quite selfish when you think about it."

"'Selfish'?"

"Knowing you can alter someone's life for the better is a major power trip, darling. It gives me a real—what do they call it these days? 'Buzz'?" She grinned and her eyes gleamed. "Quite addictive."

"I imagine it would be," Lucy said, fighting a surprising urge to smile. Vivian was both a power trip and just a plain trip. Lucy found herself almost liking the older woman, despite her initial misgivings.

"Much like it must be for you," Vivian told her, "shaping those young minds. Powerful stuff. Quite empowering, I would imagine."

Lucy had never really thought about it that way. Most days it was about keeping her students in line, praying nothing got destroyed, no one got hurt, and, if she was really lucky, that something of what she'd taught them sank in. But there were other times . . . Like when she got "The Look."

"The Look" occurred when, after struggling with a concept for what seemed like forever, something she said finally made the information click into place with a particular student. That young face would light up, the eyes would glow with triumph as understanding dawned. There was little in life that made her feel better than those moments. "I guess it is kind of empowering."

"What made you decide to teach?" Vivian asked.

"My parents are both college professors," she said, giving the stock answer.

"So it was expected of you?"

"Not really. My parents would have been content with whatever I'd decided to do, as long as I was happy with it."

"So, did you choose it to make them proud of you?"

Lucy laughed. "Hardly. Of course, when I told them I'd

decided to go into teaching, they were pleased, but if I'd wanted to make them proud, I'd have had to shoot a lot higher than teaching at a local public school."

"So why did you choose to teach?"

It occurred to Lucy that she'd left Aurora's boudoir office to avoid being poked and prodded, only to find herself grilled once again. But somehow with Vivian, it seemed more imperative to make her understand. "Teaching just seemed a natural course for me. I was a good student. Learning new things was always easy for me. Intellectually, anyway. When it came to learning anything that required physical coordination, I was a disaster. I grasped the concepts easily enough. I just had trouble with the execution."

"That's why life doles out checks and balances. Keeps one from becoming insufferably perfect."

Lucy snorted. "Oh, I was hardly that. And being smart wasn't always a bonus, either. I was also the tallest kid in class pretty much from kindergarten on. I never did like standing out in a crowd, but I always did. Literally. I hated that. Maybe if I'd have been less of a klutz, things would have gone easier on me and I'd have minded less. But I was both a dork at sports and a spaz in general, always tripping over things. Mostly my own big feet. Now factor back in the whole scholastic-geek thing, and, well, I was hardly a triple threat by anyone's standard of measurement. Quite the opposite."

"And yet you chose to teach. Talk about standing out in a crowd. You must have known it would put you directly in front of one."

"You've heard the saying, 'Those that can't do, teach'?" Lucy responded. "Like I said, I was very good at grasping the concept of just about anything, but I didn't seem to actually excel in *doing* anything other than learning. So, it was either vent my vast storage of knowledge on the unsuspecting youth of today, or become a reference librarian."

"Interesting which choice you made."

"What is that supposed to mean?"

"Just that given the option of hiding yourself in the stacks or standing out in a crowd, you chose the latter."

"I hated the spotlight because I never knew what to do in it. I was afraid I'd do something dorky, mostly because I always did."

"Maybe it was simply a self-fulfilling prophecy. Had you expected a different outcome, perhaps you'd have achieved it."

"Easy for you to say."

"You'd be surprised," Vivian murmured.

"Avoiding situations where the probability factor of me looking like a loser was even remotely high doesn't mean I was shy or introverted. Teaching itself isn't intimidating to me. But I did choose my venue carefully." She smiled. "Why do you think I teach eight-year-olds instead of high school or college students?"

"It's been my experience—not directly, mind you—that young children usually have the best 'loser' radar on the planet."

Lucy laughed. "True, in many respects. It's funny, but rather than worry about looking foolish in front of them, I worry more about not living up to their expectations. I think they sort of automatically put their teacher on a pedestal. So I try and teach them to laugh at themselves when they make mistakes, and lighten up when others do, as well. I tell them none of us are perfect, even their teacher."

"So you teach children as a way to make up, perhaps, for your own school experience."

Lucy shrugged a little self-consciously. "I can't deny that wasn't part of the decision to teach grade school. It's obviously something I'm empathetic toward. But it's not like I'm on a crusade or anything. I'm not even sure if something their third-grade teacher says to them will really matter in the scheme of things. I just know it would have helped me feel less alienated at their age."

"And how does it go over?"

"I think for the most part it's a relief to them. To sort of be given permission that it's okay to be wrong sometimes, to screw up, to look silly in front of others."

Vivian turned her focused, far-too-intuitive gaze directly on Lucy. "So," she asked with a challenging smile, "why aren't you taking your own advice?"

"I—I'm not sure I get what you mean." Although she suspected whatever it was, she didn't want to hear it.

"The way I see it, you're a schoolteacher with an obvious love for what you're doing. You're content with your career choice. You have friends you enjoy. A lifestyle that is comfortable for you. Am I pretty much in the ballpark with that assessment?"

"Yes," Lucy responded, still wary.

"You don't wake up every morning and get ready for work worrying about being judged on what you wear, how you look, what you might say."

"Not really. That doesn't mean—"

But Vivian didn't let her finish. "So you've left high school and college behind and become a successful, stable working woman who has supportive friends and family. You lead a pretty decent life."

"I'm not ungrateful for what I have, if that's what you're saying."

"I said nothing of the kind. I'm merely pointing out that, day-to-day, you're fairly confident in yourself and what's expected of you."

Lucy nodded, still bracing herself for what was to come. Not that she had a clue at this point, but she was pretty certain it wasn't going to be good.

"And then along comes this invitation to your high school reunion. An invitation to revisit memories that were, from what I gather, less than wonderful, with a bunch of people who helped make them that way." She lifted her hand to stop Lucy's rebuttal. "But rather than trot your all-grown-up, confident, successful self off to the event, unconcerned about these people—strangers to you now—and their opinions . . . you immediately revert to the same insecure, hate-the-spotlight, self-described 'spaz' you long ago left behind."

"Except that's where you're wrong," Lucy pointed out. "I didn't leave that self-conscious spaz behind. I'm still the uncoordinated smarty-pants dork who will trip over her own feet given half a chance. Sure, I love what I do. So what? I've gained the respect of a bunch of eight-year-olds. Yes, I have supportive friends. Friends who have been with me since grade school precisely because they're a lot like me and therefore don't pass judgment. But that doesn't mean I'm content with who I am, or that I haven't dreamed of being more than I am."

Vivian's silence encouraged her to continue.

"I'm not secure and self-assured. I still feel like that dorky schoolgirl because I am that dorky schoolgirl. Nothing has changed. Not really. Look at me, for God's sake. I can teach, sure, but I'm still fashion challenged, date challenged, everything challenged. When I got that reunion card in the mail, I didn't make an appointment here because I was worried about looking like a nerd in front of a bunch of people I don't even know anymore. I made the appointment because the fact is, I don't want to feel like that nerd anymore. I don't want to go back and knock them dead to prove a point to them. I want to go back and knock them on their collective asses to prove a point to me!"

She'd gotten so wound up she'd emphasized that last part by thumping her chest with her fist. Feeling self-conscious and not a little like a drama queen, she let her hand drop and looked away.

Vivian snagged her arm and gently turned Lucy around.

When Lucy met her gaze, Vivian gently rapped her knuckle on Lucy's forehead. "Now," she said, eyes gleaming, "now we're getting down to the wood."

# Chapter 7

Darling, can I be frank?"

"You mean, you haven't been?" Lucy blurted.

Vivian barked out a laugh. "You see? That's why this is going to work. Just hold on to that edge. It really works on you."

Lucy couldn't help but smile. "Okay. Work on keeping my edge. Check. Was that it?"

"No. I wanted to talk to you about men. And sex. I take it you're not getting much, am I right?"

If she'd been drinking something, Lucy would have either snorted it through her nose or aspirated it. As it was, she choked on her own spit. "What?" she finally managed, after she got done coughing and Vivian brought her a glass of water from the bathroom.

"I don't mean to pry—well, actually, that's exactly what I mean to do. But trust me, it's only because I'm trying to help."

"And knowing about my sex life is going to help exactly how?"

More of the gleaming-eye thing. "Consider it another layer of paint."

Lucy shifted on the bed, trying not to scowl. "Yeah, well, I'm showing a bit more wood than I'm comfortable exposing at the moment."

Vivian took the glass from her and patted her on the shoulder. "Facing your discomfort will do wonders. Besides, it's just between us girls." She placed the glass on the dresser, then turned and folded her arms, all ears and eager to listen. "So, tell me, when was the last time you had sex?"

Lucy just stared at her, wondering how it was their conversation had taken such a drastic turn. "I, uh, well . . ."

"That long?" Vivian broke in, saving her from actually having to do the math. She made another *tsk*ing sound. "Darling, you really have been hiding your light, haven't you?"

She'd gone from a restoration project to a lighthouse shrouded in thick fog. "I wouldn't say I've been hiding it so much as the beam itself doesn't seem to attract the men I'm interested in."

"Yes, well, men can be such dense creatures."

"They're visual creatures," Lucy said, then gestured to herself. "Even Grady goes to Hooters, for God's sake."

"And Grady would be?"

"One of my two best friends. Very cerebral guy, kind of a dork, like me, but a very endearing one. He's much more at ease in his own skin than I am. Wickedly funny. And actually appreciates intellectual stimulation."

"Sounds like a catch. Is he married?"

"To his job. But for all of his smarts and common sense, I recently discovered even he's not immune to a hard body and firm set of, well, hooters."

"You sound dismayed."

"Not really. He's certainly free to do whatever he wants. He's been nothing but the most loyal friend to me. I'd trust him with my life. In fact, he brought me here even though he was against the whole thing."

" 'Against' it? But you just said his head could be turned by a hot piece."

Lucy's eyebrows lifted a fraction. Vivian was a source of constant amazement. "Which is why it was so frustrating for him not to understand why I'd want to find some tiny, infinitesimal element of that inside myself."

"You said Grady is at ease in his own skin. Is that what you want? To be more at ease in your own skin?"

Lucy laughed a little. "Maybe women are visual creatures, too. I'm not much of a vision. And for me, being at ease in my own skin means liking the shell a bit more than I do at the moment, maybe feeling a bit more coordinated with it, as well. Which was where I'd hoped you'd come in."

"So this is only partly about developing your sense of self, searching for your inner goddess, as it were. You're thinking that an improved shell will help attract the kind of male attention you've been missing?"

Lucy smiled. "Well, let's just say I wouldn't argue if an improved sex life turned out to be a side benefit of my transformation. And I don't know about 'goddess.' I'd be happy with 'passably attractive' and 'moderately graceful.' "

"You're already all those things."

"On the inside," Lucy finished for her.

"That wasn't what I was going to say. I merely meant that you have beauty, and you have charm and grace. You're also smart, with a sharp mind and, I'm betting, a rather wicked sense of humor. It's confidence and belief in yourself that you're sorely lacking."

Lucy didn't have any trouble buying that part of it. "So how do I get that? I mean, it's not like you can wave a magic wand, right?"

"Well, they don't call us 'the godmothers' for nothing."

Lucy smiled. "When I signed up for this, I was hoping that with proper instruction on things like makeup, help on styling my hair and . . . I don't know, someone to help me develop a better sense of fashion, help me find a look. If I had all that, wouldn't the confidence come along naturally?"

"Certainly looking good can do a world of wonders for a person's attitude. But it's still a surface change. You need to learn to trust in yourself. Trust that you're interesting, witty, fun to be around, and an all-around fabulous girl . . . with or without the cosmetic trappings. That's just icing. You need to believe you're fabulous no matter what state the shell is in." Before Lucy could comment on that, Vivian said, "Is it Grady's attention you want from this?"

"God, no," she said on a shocked laugh. "He's like a brother to me, and an oftentimes annoying one at that. I'm the same to him, I'm sure. I'd just hoped he'd be more understanding about my need to at least try and find that easy sense of self he already has."

"Maybe he thinks you have that already. That you're already a hot piece."

"Ch-yeah," Lucy snorted. "Except, not. Of all the people in the world, Grady better than anyone understands just how not hot I am. He's seen me firsthand at my absolute dorkiest."

"Uh-huh," Vivian said. "Maybe he sees nothing wrong with that. Does he date what you'd term 'hot' women?"

"What do you mean?"

"You said he was kind of dorky like you, but that he liked looking at hot women. You also said the men you find attractive don't seem to notice you. So I'm asking if he's been able to get the attention of women who are comparable to these men you referred to." She folded her arms. "Or does he merely stare at them at Hooters to get fodder for nights spent alone with his right hand?"

Lucy gaped, choking on a laugh. "He dates real women. All kinds of women, I guess you'd say. It's that confidence thing, I think. But I can't really tell you much more than that." She paused, then added on a snicker, "Except that he's left-handed."

"Ha!" Vivian hooted and made a little mark in the air with her finger, as if putting a point in the Lucy column. "So why can't you tell me more? Haven't you met his dates? Gone out together as a group, that sort of thing?"

"Not really. Like I said, the only serious relationship he's ever had has been with his work. He's a brainiac engineer who designs hush-hush super-secret spy gizmos. Which would be more fascinating if he was actually allowed to tell us anything about them. But he's completely devoted to his lab. So he doesn't date anyone long enough to introduce them to us. 'Us' being me and Jana, our other close friend. She's already married. We're family to one another, and you don't just bring anyone home to family."

"I see."

Lucy had the feeling Vivian did, in fact, see a great deal. Of course, it helped that she'd somehow gotten Lucy to open up about every damn thing. It was a little unnerving to realize how easily she'd managed it, too.

"What about Jana?" Vivian asked. "Did she support your decision to come here?"

"She wasn't as bad as Grady, but no, not really. I think she thought I was looking for a cosmetic Band-Aid or something. She was more concerned that I'd get my hopes up, only to have them dashed again."

"'Again'?"

Lucy sighed. See? This was exactly the thing. Vivian had her spewing out all kinds of information she'd never intended to reveal. "Back in high school, there was a boy—a guy—that I had a crush on. At our senior prom, I got myself all dolled up, or so I thought, with the idea that I was going to make him notice me or die trying."

"And?"

"I wish I'd died before trying. It would have been less mortifying."

"And this guy, he's going to be at the reunion, I take it? Still single?"

She was like cellophane, apparently. A woman of mystery, Lucy Harper was not. And never would be, it seemed. "As a matter of fact, yes. But I swear, I'm not here because of Jason Prescott. Granted, it would be a nice bonus to make him grovel and beg, but despite my dreams of goddess grandeur, I assure you I'm still grounded in cold, hard, dorky reality."

"But Grady and Jana think this is about Jason. Haven't you told them how unsettled you've been feeling? That you've felt like you weren't reaching your potential?"

In two sentences, Vivian had nailed down exactly how Lucy had been feeling for ages. Hell, most of her entire life. It was amazing how good it felt for someone to finally hear what she'd been saying. For that one moment alone, this whole endeavor was worth every penny.

"No. I—I guess I didn't have the right words. I mean, we bitch about this kind of stuff all the time, and have ever since we realized there was a cool crowd, and then there was us. I've certainly whined about the unfairness of it all. You know, the 'Why me? Why do I have to be such a dork?' kind of thing." She paused, looked down for a moment. "But no, I've never told anyone exactly how I feel. Like I'm . . . unfinished." She looked up at Vivian. "It's like, just when I start to let go, feel good about myself, trust that there is more to me than meets the eye . . . I'll inevitably catch my reflection, totally off guard. And every time there is this moment of shock, like, 'Who is that?' That gawky klutz with the lumpy hair and knobby knees isn't me. That's not how I feel on the inside. On the inside, I'm capable of being fabulous. Fabulous doesn't look like that." She gave a dry laugh. "That probably sounds insane. In fact, it did sound insane. Which is precisely why I've never said it out loud before."

"Maybe you should have. You'd have discovered that we all feel like that, to some degree."

"Maybe," Lucy said, though privately she didn't believe it. "But it goes back to being easy in your own skin. Some people most definitely are. Like Grady. And, for a while now, Jana, too. I'm definitely not there yet. And I'm not sure I'll ever be without a little help. Guidance."

"Your inner goddess," Vivian said.

"What?"

"That's what you were feeling. When you're not self-conscious and worried about how you look or sound or act, you're realizing your inner goddess. The fabulous you that you already are."

Lucy thought about that for a moment, then shook her head. "Maybe, but that doesn't change the fact that on the outside, I'm still all geek. I can't seem to fuse the two together. And the geek side wins out every time."

"There are plenty of women, and men, who aren't what anyone would call classically beautiful. Some of them are, in fact, quite geeky. Maybe even klutzy. And yet they still draw the eye, command attention. Because rather than hide their vulnerability, their lack of utter perfection, or worse, feel shamed by it, they sort of embrace it, accept it, and go on anyway. At ease in their own dorky skin. I think you'd be surprised to know how very endearing that sort of self-acceptance can be. Sexy, even."

"Grady has that," Lucy said, thinking on what Vivian had said. "Although if you tell him I thought he was sexy, I'll go to the grave denying it." She grinned. "He'd never let me live that down. But I envy him that sense of self."

Vivian waved a hand the length of her body. "I'm hardly what anyone would call a beauty, and yet I've never lacked for attention of any sort. It's attitude, darling. And belief in your inner fabulousness."

"So you're saying I should embrace my dorkiness and all will be fine?" It was clear from Lucy's tone what her opinion of that solution was. "That won't keep me from tripping over my own fabulous size-ten feet."

"I think you'd be surprised at the results." Vivian sighed a little and looked Lucy over. Really looked her over. "But, you know, I'm also thinking that maybe what you said earlier has merit. About how feeling good about yourself allows your confidence to take deeper root. Maybe you do need some visual proof of the goddess within, to truly believe it." She tugged Lucy to a stand, then turned her all the way around until she was facing her again. "With the time frame available to us, I think we will tackle both the inside and the out simultaneously." She beamed. "And when the two come together, darling, I can promise you, you won't have a choice but to believe just how fabulous you really are." She clapped her hands, then her face lit with purpose and excitement. "This is going to be vastly rewarding."

*Rewarding.* So why was it Lucy felt like she was going to throw up? She wished she felt the same free and easy sense of anticipation that Vivian did. *That'll teach you to be careful what you wish for.* Lucy looked at the real-life incarnation of her very own fairy godmother, noted the devilish twinkle in her eyes . . . and wondered what in the hell she'd gotten herself into now.

"Come now, darling, we need to start developing your regimen right away."

Yeah, that's what worried her. But one ray of hope shone through the new batch of fears threatening to send her into a panic. "Does this mean no appointment with the shrink?"

"That won't be necessary."

But before Lucy could complete her *whoosh*ing sigh of relief, Vivian added, "From now on, you'll be working directly with me."

# Chapter 8

I heard from Lucy."

Grady froze with the pizza halfway to his mouth. "She called you?" It shouldn't have bothered him. After all, Jana was her best friend. "I thought any contact with the non-Barbie world was verboten."

"She left a message on my cell yesterday." Jana wrapped a piece of dangling cheese around her finger, then popped it into her mouth. "SOS call."

Okay, he was definitely bothered. Jana might be her best friend, the one Lucy turned to for gossip and anything PMS related, but when it came to rescues, that was his job. He bit off the end of his pizza, then grew reflective as he chewed. There was a potential bright side to this. If Lucy was trying to break out after only one day, maybe they could put this whole self-improvement thing behind them and go back to the way things were.

Jana plucked an olive off her pizza and flicked it at him.

"Hey!" He peeled the offensive black ring from his forehead, then tossed it into the almost empty box with a grimace. "Olives, yuck. I can't believe they got our order wrong. We've only been ordering pizza from Brick Oven for how many years now?"

"They didn't get the order wrong," Jana said as she chewed.

Grady glanced at her, eyebrows raised. "Since when do you like olives?"

"I have no idea." She lifted a shoulder in a half shrug. "I just looked at the picture on the coupon and thought it looked good and heard myself order it when the person came on the line."

Grady just looked at her, but finally shrugged. Women. Sometimes even the ones he knew the best stumped him. "So why the flickage?" He rubbed at the little grease spot on his forehead. "What was that about?"

She polished off the last bit of crust and reached for her Coke. "Perfectly good waste of an olive?"

First the flickage, now evasiveness. He definitely should have stayed in the lab. He wasn't up to playing Decipher Her Thoughts tonight. But before he could comment, he watched as she reached for her fourth slice. Grinning, he motioned to the cheese-heavy slice she'd already taken a huge bite out of. "What, didn't they let the girl reporter eat today?"

Jana just sighed in mozzarella bliss as she swallowed. "Reporting is hard work. And the reason for the flickage was that face you made when I mentioned the SOS call."

"What face?"

Jana pulled a hangdog expression. "That face."

"I never make that face."

"No, you're right. You do it much better than me. More practice."

"Great, just great. I come over here for Pizza Night, bring you

Coke"—he mock shuddered and downed a slug of his beer—"and even paid for the damn pie when you couldn't find your wallet—"

"I told you, it's in my car. Must have fallen out of my bag when I got home. I offered to go down and check. I don't know where my brain is these days."

Grady waved his hand in a faux magnanimous gesture. "No, no. I don't mind. And I know exactly where your brain is. All that baby-making with Dave. But now you're going to flick condiments at me and tell me I look funny. Is that any kind of gratitude for babysitting you through Dave's layover in Vancouver?"

Jana spluttered, as he'd known she would. "'Babysitting'? This is Pizza Night. We have them all the time."

"Except we weren't going to this week because of Lucy being gone and you and Dave doing—you know." He covered his eyes. "Visuals of which I really just don't want to think about, if it's all right with you."

"What, did the Blockbuster manager turn you down?"

He peered through his fingers. "She got promoted. Transferred to someplace in Prince Georges."

"Ah," Jana said, not looking remotely sorry for his predicament.

Frankly, he hadn't been that put out, either. He'd hoped to distract himself from the whole Lucy/Barbie makeover thing with an advance screening of something interesting, followed by whatever he could manage afterward. He should have been more disappointed to find out Pam had left the area and not even bothered to let him know. It wasn't like they were exclusive. Hell, it wasn't even like they were dating. One date did not a relationship make. "But like I told you before, my social schedule doesn't hinge on Lucy's whereabouts."

"Which is why I called and invited you over for pizza, dummy." She polished off the last bite. "But let's not debate who is babysitting whom here."

Grady let the jab pass, mostly because he realized he was happier here, anyway, despite the lack of sex in his immediate future. He missed Lucy. And though he'd been a bit concerned that Jana might get all weird on him like she had on The Mall the other day, he'd chalked that up to the whole baby thing. He'd been happy to hear from her, and so far, other than killing half a large pie all by herself, she'd been pretty much normal. Until the olive flick. "So, what happened with the SOS?"

"I got an abort-mission text message about an hour later." Jana slid off the kitchen stool and wiped the grease off her hands with a paper towel. "I don't know, maybe she panicked or something. I never got to talk to her. I'm guessing she got past whatever it was that spooked her into wanting to leave."

Grady let that information settle as he finished his last slice and washed it down with the last of his beer. He didn't like the idea of Lucy being stuck somewhere she didn't want to be. But maybe it was for the best. Some things she had to figure out for herself. He could only hope that realizing this was all a phenomenal waste of time was one of them. "Wonder what happened," he said, after promising himself he wouldn't.

Jana grinned. "I'm guessing she's past the welcome stage and into the plucking stage. And we both know Lucy's not big on pain management."

Grady flinched in automatic sympathy. The idea of having any body hair removed in any manner other than shaving . . .

Jana just laughed. "God, you two are such a pair."

Grady made big business of cleaning up the empty pizza carton and tossing the empty cans in the recycling bin. *Yeah,* he thought, *we're a pair, all right.* He just hoped that status remained quo.

"Ouch! Shit! Christ!" Lucy all but came off the padded table entirely as the swatch of linen was ripped quite rudely, not to mention abruptly, from her skin. Her very tender skin. The kind of tender skin, she was now quite certain, that was never meant to be abused in this fashion. When she finally blinked away the tears that had sprung instantly to her eyes, she glared at the woman seated at the base of the table.

The woman, whom Lucy had already christened Sadistic Susie and her Wonder Wax of Death, smiled blandly in return. "Relax. You must relax. It will go much easier."

"'*Relax*'?" She didn't exactly screech the word, but only because her throat had closed over when Sadistic Sue had lifted another glob. "Are you on crack?" Fighting not to hyperventilate, Lucy immediately craned her head around until she found Vivian, who, true to her pledge, had not left her side since she'd entered this torture chamber. "Is this part really necess— *Holy Mother of God!*" She jerked her thigh away from Susie, who was currently slathering very hot wax on parts of her anatomy that had never been exposed to sunlight, much less a tongue depressor coated in molten lava. "When you said I could have baby-smooth skin, I was thinking more along the lines of softening the skin on my face."

With a knowing, if not entirely soothing smile, Vivian stepped over and gently pushed her back down on the table. "I know this is difficult the first time. But I assure you, you'll thank me later."

*And if I don't?* Lucy grumbled silently. "I find it hard to believe that women actually put themselves through this willingly. *OW!*" She yelped as another strip of wax-coated fabric was stripped from her skin, snatching yet another patch of her privates bald. She covered herself with her hands and glared at Sue yet again, all but daring her to even think about putting hot wax on her skin. "Wait a minute, okay?" She glanced up at Vivian, tears pricking her eyes again. "You know, I don't have a high threshold for this kind of thing. Actually, I don't have any threshold. I'm a total wuss with pain. And I don't really feel the need to overcome that particular fault." Her neck developed a crick and her glasses were sliding down her nose, but one glance at Sue and her Tongue Depressor of Torture, and she kept her hands right where they were. She shot a hopeful look back at Vivian, tried for a winning smile, but missed it when her lips trembled. "I mean, don't they make products that just dissolve the hair now? Couldn't we just do that?"

"It's not the same thing," Vivian informed her kindly. "This does a far better job and lasts much longer. Besides, you're half done. You can't stop now."

Lucy removed her hands and hiked herself up on her elbows. Her glasses slid almost completely off, and when she went to push them back up, she almost rolled off the table, and would have if Vivian and Sue hadn't grabbed an arm and a leg respectively. Blushing sheepishly, she angled herself up, then craned her neck and looked . . . down there. Sue helpfully held up a small hand mirror. Lucy gasped and her eyes went wide. "Wow."

Vivian's smile widened. "Exactly, darling." She stroked Lucy's hair and settled her back down on the padded table. "The first time is always the worst. It will get easier each time you do it."

Lucy hated to break it to Vivian, but baby smooth or not, even with a gun pointed to her head, she was never going to do this again. "I still don't see the benefit. I mean, not when contrasted with the pain," she added, not wanting Vivian to think her ungrateful for the change. "It's not like it even matters. I wear a bathing suit a maximum of, like, five days out of a whole year. And that's just with Jana when we do our girls weekend in Rehoboth. And I'm not even going this year because I came here instead." She heard Jana's I-told-you-sos echo clearly through her mind.

"I'm not concerned with making you presentable for bathing-suit season, darling. Think of it this way: one of the benefits of this is rather like that of making sure your man has a really close shave."

Lucy craned her neck again, hissing in a breath as more hot wax met more fragile virgin skin. Virgin in more ways than one, it seemed. "Huh?"

"Razor burn. Men don't like it any more than we women do."

It was probably the haze of pain she was currently enveloped in, more than the fact that she was out of step with the specifics of giving and receiving sexual pleasure. At least, that's what she told herself. Just because the opportunity hadn't presented itself lately—okay, ever!—didn't mean she was naïve to such things. She read *Cosmo*.

"Can I just go on record as saying that, while I appreciate doing what I can to ensure my partner's pleasure," Lucy paused long enough to send what she hoped was a feral scowl in the direction of Sadistic Sue as she began fingering yet another cloth strip, "I honestly don't think this makes even the top-ten list of things I'm most concerned with at the moment. Or the top twenty, for that matter. Shouldn't we be focusing on the more . . . obvious? SHIT!" Through watery eyes, she propped herself up on her elbows and glared at the tiny blonde woman seated at the other end of the table. "You enjoy this, don't you?"

The Glass Slipper skin-care tech glanced nervously at Vivian, who smiled and merely made a small motion for her to ignore Lucy's outburst.

"Vivian, come on," Lucy pleaded. "Is it really that important? It's not like anyone's even going to know."

"Have faith, darling," she admonished. "Besides, most important in this is the fact that you'll know." A rather wicked smile curved Vivian's perfectly painted lips. "Trust me, I can always tell when a woman has had a Brazilian. She carries herself completely differently."

"Yeah. Bowlegged from permanent scarring."

Vivian laughed. "You'll see what I mean when this is all done."

Lucy grumbled but lay down again. "I just don't see why we couldn't have started on something a little easier and more obvious, like my eyebrows."

"We'll get to that. But we haven't much time here. I thought it best to start right off with something that would alter your very state of being."

"Plucking me bald will do that?"

"Darling, nicely shaped eyebrows are important, but when you're walking down the street, you don't feel them, so you don't really feel the difference. You know they're there, but it's a rather detached appreciation. With this, every single step you take, you will feel differently about yourself, about your body. You'll feel voluptuous, sensual. Ripe."

Considering the pain radiating from every single violated pore, it was more than a little disconcerting to feel a sort of stirring sensation. Down there. Vivian spoke with the kind of conviction that only a woman who's walked the same path could possibly have. Lucy tilted her head back. "'Ripe,' huh?"

Vivian's smile widened further, but her thoughts had seemed to turn inward as she took a deep, appreciative breath that threatened to strain her well-strapped-in bosom. "You'll see."

Lucy was still contemplating Vivian's promised rewards when the sadist patted her on the knee and announced, "It is done. In a few days, when you have sufficient growth, we'll do your legs."

"Oh, goody," Lucy muttered.

"I'm going to step out and take care of some other business," Vivian told her. "Sue, you can handle things from here."

"Wait—" Lucy said, lifting her head, but Vivian had already

left. Lucy looked warily back at Sue, wishing now she'd been a little nicer to her. "Listen, if you'll just let me leave now, I swear I won't say a word. You can get some time off, and I can go have a nice soak in the tub. In my room." Alone. This had all been a shock to her system in more ways than one.

Sue gave her the standard Glass Slipper Stepford smile. "You've made it through the hard part. Now comes the nice part. Close your eyes. Lie back. Relax. No more pain. I promise."

Lucy stared at her for another moment longer, trying to deduce Sue's exact intent. After all, she was lying on a padded table, naked except for the folded sheet draped discreetly across her torso. Up until right now, she'd felt more like an assembly-line part than a woman. But something about the way Sue was smiling at her had her wondering. "What exactly does come next?"

"Close your eyes. I'm going to dim the lights down now."

Lucy complied, but her eyes flew back open on that last part. "Excuse me?"

Sue's smile might have become a tad more pronounced, but she maintained the Glass Slipper status quo and managed not to laugh directly at Lucy's less-than-worldly reaction. "It's okay," she assured her. "I'm just going to make the pain go away. I promise. Now close your eyes."

Still wary, Lucy closed her eyes, but secretly she tensed her muscles, ready to leap off the table like a well-oiled spring if Sue so much as breathed on her in a way that could be even loosely interpreted as sexual. Okay, who was she kidding. "Well-oiled spring" was probably overstating her abilities. She'd likely drag the table over, splattering hot wax all over the walls and floor, before tripping over the neat stack of towels and linens on the low side table, landing in a sticky heap somewhere over by the door.

Besides, when you thought about it, Sue had already performed acts on her that were all kinds of socially unacceptable.

Exhausted by the whole process, both mentally and physically, she just let it go. What the hell. Pleasure was pleasure, right? Considering her love life of late, she could hardly afford to discriminate. Who knows, maybe she'd even learn something new.

The light through her eyelids dimmed. And the soft sounds of running water, like a fountain or a waterfall, filled the room. A moment later she was gasping in absolute pleasure. "God, that feels amazing."

"Just lie still," Sue said softly, perhaps the barest hint of smugness in her tone.

That was totally okay. Lucy didn't mind. The wet, warm, and very soft towel she'd just had draped between her legs felt so good against her freshly abused skin that she didn't care if Sue stripped naked and danced around the room like some kind of a forest sprite. Ripe and sensual, huh? Yeah, baby!

"Now we work on smoothing the rest of your skin."

Lucy managed enough alarm, despite the languor swiftly spreading through her body, to crack one eye open. "Beg pardon?"

Sue moved behind her head. "Full massage. Then facial. Manicure and pedicure come next."

Lucy sighed and let herself completely relax for the first time. "Now *that's* what I'm talking about." *Jana and Grady, eat your heart out.*

---

"Do you feel this is necessary, Vivi?" Aurora slid off her tiny, gold-framed bifocals and let them dangle from the long beaded chain around her neck. One of many. She put down the folder of papers she'd been studying and gave her partner her full attention. "It's not standard protocol."

"Says the woman who sat in for Phoebe's initial interview." Vivian waved off Aurora's defense, causing the lamp lighting to bounce off the multiple gemstones adorning her hands. "Since when do we place store by standard protocol? We didn't get where we are today by not following our instincts. That's all I'm doing." Under Aurora's studied gaze, Vivian examined her nails, noticing that the diamond in her right pinky was situated slightly lower than the one in her left. "Consider it my pet project."

Mercedes signed several documents, then sighed as she closed another file and handed it off to Aurora. "Vivian, we're in the middle of negotiations with a new distributor for the magazine, and we have yet to firm up our somewhat extensive travel plans for our overseas trip. It's one thing for Aurora to step in and help out in a staffing emergency, quite another to take on a client's entire program."

"I don't believe I've dropped the ball anywhere, Mercy," Vivian said, rising to her own defense now. "Are you intimating otherwise?"

If Mercedes was surprised by the edge to Vivian's tone, she didn't comment. Which was just as well, because it wasn't until she'd had to defend her position on this that Vivian truly realized how important working with Lucy had become to her.

"I'm merely saying that this is why we hire the best personnel," Mercedes went on. "Certainly we have the appropriate staff to handle this particular client."

"Yes, of course we do. I simply happen to feel Lucy will benefit more from some direct attention."

"Honestly, Vivian, must you complicate matters by—" Mercedes broke off, massaged the bridge of her nose. "What am I saying, of course you must. It's like a disease with you."

Vivian's smile didn't so much as waver. "Much like micromanaging is an addiction for you, Mercy darling."

Never one to tolerate the least hint of tension, Aurora's hands fluttered as she shushed them both. "Come now, surely we can all discuss business without being snarky."

Vivian raised an eyebrow in Aurora's direction. "Watching *Saturday Night Live* again, are we?"

She merely sniffed. "MTV. One must remain current. And don't tell me you weren't glued to the set watching that nice young man, what was his name? Bad Mo Z? Z Dog? I can't keep them straight."

"Being the rap afficionado that you are and all," Vivian murmured, ignoring Mercedes when she motioned her quiet.

"I happen to like music with a distinctive bass line," Aurora said. "I don't quite understand the fashion statement they're making by allowing their briefs to show above the waistband of their trousers, however." Her brow crinkled. "And perhaps they are a little heavy-handed with the jewelry, but—"

"Bling-bling," Vivian supplied.

She blinked. "I beg your pardon?"

"Nothing. Can we move on to the next order of business?"

Aurora looked nonplussed for a moment, then pointed a heavily ringed finger in her direction. "You've gone and distracted me from the point I was making, don't think I didn't notice."

"Of course not," Vivian deadpanned. "Nothing gets by you."

Aurora huffed a little. Mercedes merely lifted her gaze to the ceiling.

Ever the mediator, Aurora gentled her tone. "You know I adore Lucy, too, Vivi. There is something endearing about her. We're just concerned, Mercy and I, that this distraction will prevent you from focusing your attention on these other, more pressing matters." She slid her glasses on again and opened the next file.

Vivian tapped the gold-tipped end of her slender cigarette holder against the arm of her chair, wishing like mad she hadn't given up smoking. Truth was, it had been harder to give up what she'd always referred to as her "tiny little social habit" than she'd expected. And she'd die before admitting as much to these two. In addition to other things, Lucy Harper had been a welcome distraction from nicotine withdrawal.

Of course, her interest was far more complicated than that. She'd dealt with her share of wallflowers before, but there was something about Lucy that called to her specifically. She didn't have to dig too deep to understand what that was. Vivian hadn't always been the maven of fashion she was today, the former dresser to the stars whose every stylish whim had become an instant trend; adopted, copied, and relentlessly covered in every major magazine during the sixties and seventies. Until the nightmare that was disco erupted, anyway. The thought of all that polyester still made her shudder.

Long before all that, she'd just been chubby little Vivian from Chelsea. Like Lucy, she'd been teased relentlessly by her classmates. Nor was "graceful" the adjective anyone ever associated with her as a child. Vivian had long since packed away the memories of her less-than-lovely youth. Then Lucy had tripped on the walkway, making the kind of embarrassing entrance only the child Vivian had been could truly appreciate, and *bam!*, all those memories had rushed to the surface.

But the connection went further than that. What the girl lacked in style and grace, she more than made up for with grit and determination. Vivian distinctly remembered her own stubborn refusal to cave to the greater force of peer pressure. She'd defiantly worn her beloved rhinestone-studded, bright blue cat's eye glasses to school every single day, even knowing it would earn her nothing more than being ostracized and ridiculed by every table in the lunchroom.

Whereas Lucy had been teased for her gawky, gangly height, Vivian had been a short, stout fireplug of a girl, with an unfortunately pronounced Roman nose and as questionable a taste in fashion as she'd had in eyewear. But though she'd cried buckets of tears in private, in public she'd refused to let the bastards see how much their torment hurt. In the end, with gritted perseverance, a lot of hard work, and a little luck (and the help of a lovely plastic surgeon in Tribeca), she'd shown them all, hadn't she?

Lucy Harper had shown the same defiance, in her own way, but she'd never truly broken out of her shell. Nevertheless, beneath it all, she still harbored the belief that she was more than she appeared. It may have taken her a bit longer to validate that feeling than it should have, but she'd done so. And despite the complete lack of support she'd received for this epiphany, she'd acted on it anyway by coming here. Vivian understood the strength that had taken in a way very few others would realize. And she felt an obligation that was inherently personal to not let Lucy Harper down.

"I'll handle it, darlings," she said quietly, her tone not inviting a response. "Next on the agenda?"

Aurora and Mercedes both glanced up, but after taking note of the finality of her expression, they turned once again back to business. There was a small, but telltale smile hovering around Aurora's mouth, and Vivian realized she had her partner's full approval and all of that had been for Mercy's benefit. Of course, she'd never let Aurora know how much she appreciated it. Nor would Aurora thank her for taking on the task itself.

Inwardly, Vivian smiled and allowed the anticipation inside her to swell. Lucy Harper knew she had potential, but she had no idea the real strength of it. Vivian did. And she couldn't wait to unleash it.

*This,* she thought, tapping a rapid staccato with her cigarette holder as the thoughts and ideas began to tumble about and take shape, *could be the most fun I've had in years.*

Roll your hips, darling. Roll. Don't jerk them about."

"I'm just trying to stay upright!" Lucy clenched her jaw in growing exasperation as she took another tottering step forward. "I don't know how you do this."

"An undying desire to be taller was a great motivator," Vivian told her.

"I'm already a giraffe," Lucy said. "I know what you told me, about claiming my height. But I can claim my height with two-inch heels and still tower over almost everybody."

Vivian crossed the room to stand closer to the mock runway in the Glass Slipper modeling room. "Darling, in this case it's not about how tall you are. There is something very empowering about stalking into a room in come-do-me heels. Two inches doesn't say 'Come do me.' " She smiled. "It says why bother. Four inches, on the other hand, will grab the attention of every man in the room. That was my other motivation. And it was worth every blister."

Lucy tried to fold her arms, but even that motion had her wobbling dangerously. Arms pinwheeling, she bent at the waist and tried desperately to keep from pitching off the raised dais. "No one is going to want to 'come do me' no matter how tall my heels are," she said, breathing easier as the panic receded. If she stood completely and perfectly still, she might survive this. Might. "I already tower over most men. Adding inches is only going to make me more intimidating." *Or provide endless entertainment when I fly headlong into the closest table.*

"How tall is Jason Prescott?"

" 'Jason'?" Lucy was surprised by the question. Surprised Vivian even recalled his name. They hadn't so much as talked about her final exam, aka the reunion, since beginning her swan lessons in earnest two days ago.

"Yes, Jason. I presume he's taller than you, am I correct?"

"Why would you presume—"

"Women's intuition," she cut in. "Now, tell me truthfully, even in four-inch heels, he'll still be taller than you. Am I right?"

Lucy flashed back to her endless fantasizing leading up to the prom, about how amazing it would feel to be in Jason's arms. For all her klutziness, she hadn't been afraid of stepping onto the dance floor with him. She'd been certain that from the moment he first touched her, she'd find her inner balance. Jason was bigger, stronger, with enough confidence to guide both of them. She'd only have to follow his lead, and she'd become the princess of the ball, her inner Sleeping Beauty awakened by her prince.

There was a little clutch in her chest as she recalled how her fantasy scenario had played out. "Yes," she said quietly. "He's taller than me. Even in heels."

"You have to go into this as his equal," Vivian said, her tone quite serious. "There can't be even a whiff of inferiority in your mind. You don't just want him to notice you. You want to *command* his attention. You want him to be unable to do anything else *but* look at you."

Lucy looked up and their gazes caught, held. Vivian understood. It was clear, right there in her eyes, that she was completely aware of what Lucy was up against. Without having to relive every detail, share every humiliation, Vivian still got it. Her fairy godmother, after all. She didn't preach about why this was all a big mistake, like Jana and Grady had, how she was setting herself up for failure. No, Vivian believed Lucy could do this. But more than that, she understood why she had to do it. It wasn't about Jason, or even the reunion.

It was about Lucy.

"Yes," Lucy said, feeling a thread of defiance begin to build inside her. As she continued to stare at Vivian, who so clearly believed in her, the feeling grew. A life-affirming breath filled her lungs and she stood a little straighter. Not too much; she didn't want to lose her big moment by falling flat on her ass. "Yes," she said, stronger this time. "Yes, I do!" When Vivian nodded, pride shining in her eyes, Lucy grinned. "I want to blow his freaking mind!"

"That's my girl," Vivian crowed. "So come on. Let's do this!"

Her victorious moment wavered. Badly. As did she at the thought of actually moving. It was one thing to imagine herself striding—no, sashaying—into the reunion hall, dragging every eye toward her like a magnet. But to get that, she had to take that first step. Quite literally, as it turned out. And while on the inside she was Lucy Harper, femme fatale, in reality, she was still Lucy Harper, hopeless klutz.

"Maybe we should start with short heels and work our way up?" Lucy suggested with a hopeful, upbeat smile. No more whining. She could do this. Would do this. Just, maybe, at a wee bit slower pace. "This might be too big a step for me. No pun intended. It's just, I could hurt someone with these things." Herself, mostly. But still. She could hardly be a femme fatale if she was on crutches, now, could she?

Vivian's smile was steady. "I know we're pushing things here, but you have to trust me. I was right about the Brazilian, was I not?"

Lucy had to admit she'd been somewhat surprised after her foray with Sadistic Susie. She might not feel exactly ripe, but there was something to be said for the feel of silk against smooth, bare skin. It was quite sensuous, in an almost naughty kind of way. And she rather liked it. Not enough to ever do that again, mind you, but she would enjoy it while it lasted.

"With every step, I want you to imagine you're as smooth as that silk you're wearing," Vivian said, as if reading her mind. Of course, Vivian knew firsthand what Lucy was wearing beneath her lone remaining pair of khaki trousers.

After her pampering session, Lucy had arrived back at her room to find several tissue-lined boxes, each layered with some of the most exquisite lingerie she'd ever seen. Far too fantastic for her budget, to be sure. She couldn't even afford Victoria's Secret, much less Dior. Oh, but each piece had felt incredible to the touch. She'd had to indulge herself at least that much. Just the memory of how that silk and satin had felt slipping through her fingers made her shiver a little. And okay, maybe she'd rubbed it on her skin. Just for a moment.

Then Vivian had shown up and explained they were her little gift. No matter how strenuously Lucy objected to accepting anything so lavish, Vivian would have none of it. And secretly Lucy was thrilled she had pushed the issue. Anything that decadent . . . well, she could only imagine how they were going to feel on her body. Her Brazilian-waxed body.

She'd tried them on almost immediately after Vivian had left her for the evening. Deciding to preserve the fantasy that she was centerfold material—because that's how they made her feel, especially the padded bra—she hadn't dared to look in the mirror. But everything had fit. Perfectly.

She'd even been tempted to wear a set to bed. Just because. Never in her life had she felt so . . . feminine. Between the facial, the manicure, pedicure . . . and yes, the wax job, she felt beautiful and pampered. Pretty.

This morning it had felt criminal putting on her regular old pants and blouse. But they were all she had at the moment. Her luggage had mysteriously disappeared. She'd yet to have a talk with Vivian about that, but she planned to. Just as soon as she got down off this runway without killing herself. And if she felt like a fraud in silk, the come-do-me pumps she'd received along with her in-room breakfast this morning made her feel even more the pretender.

"You know what? I have an idea," Vivian said, tapping her glossy red talon of a fingernail against her chin. She turned and motioned to the man sitting behind the bank of electronic equipment. "Mr. DeMay, can you give us a few moments? Thank you, David, darling."

"Not a problem," he said with an easy smile. "Just buzz me when you're ready."

"If only all men were that easy," Vivian told him, smiling shamelessly.

David the Video Tech (and temporary DJ) was apparently used to such banter. He grinned, tipped his chin, then slid obediently from his perch and stepped out of the small auditorium-style room.

Lucy sighed in relief. She'd been given a reprieve from strutting her stuff on the catwalk. The very idea of watching a tape of herself—she shuddered inwardly. There was no music David could have played that would have helped, either. Not only was she high-heel impaired, she had no sense of rhythm whatsoever. This white girl definitely could not dance.

Hopefully she could talk Vivian out of this little idea completely. Besides, she didn't need come-do-me heels to feel more confident. There were plenty of other fixer-upper projects they could do to her. For example, they hadn't even touched her hair or makeup yet.

"Shimmy down here," Vivian instructed.

"I beg your pardon?"

Vivian smiled. "I mean, sit down and slide off the runway."

*Thank God.*

Except, tottering on her tiptoes as she was, she wasn't entirely sure how to go about sitting down without keeling off the runway entirely. She tried leaning forward and bending her knees, thinking she'd kneel first, then sit. But that sent her pitching forward instead. With a little squeal, she swung her arms and stutter-stepped forward again, managing, just barely, to stop before she came to the end of the runway. "Um, how exactly—"

"One step forward, then kneel on the rear leg."

That proved to be too many moving parts. The end result was Lucy stuck in a half split. "Vivian!"

"Bend your knees! Put your hands down to break your fall."

"*'Fall'?*" But it was too late. Over she went. "Aeeiii!"

"Dear Lord!"

Sprawled in a tangle of khaki and death spikes, one leg and one arm dangling off the runway, Lucy had time to appreciate just how fast Vivian could move in her own come-do-me heels. Thoughts of Carrie Bradshaw flashed through her mind. Fashion roadkill, indeed.

"I'm sorry," she told her, as Vivian carefully unhooked Lucy's heel from where it was wedged into the side trim of the runway, then rolled her to her back. "I really am a hopeless case," she said morosely. "You can be honest with me. I won't hold it against you, or Glass Slipper, I swear."

"Now, now," Vivian admonished. "Where is that fire and determination I saw moments ago?"

"It left the building with Mr. DeMay."

"Come on, now." With a little grunt, she helped Lucy to sit up, then edged her off the chest-high platform until her toes touched the carpeted floor.

*Terra firma. Finally.* Lucy wobbled as she put her full weight on her feet, and clung to the edge of the runway for balance. "Would you mind helping me take these off?"

"'Off'?" Vivian chuckled. "Oh no, we're not done here. I simply thought that you'd get the hang of it faster if you could practice a bit while using the edge here for balance."

Lucy's heart sank. "Maybe we should—"

"No more 'maybes,' " Vivian said sternly. "Now, turn sideways. Grip with one hand, and hold your other arm out like so." She moved behind her and pulled—okay, tugged—one hand free, moving it away from Lucy's body. "Loosen up a bit. You're arms are stiff like a robot. Concentrate on relaxing; don't think about your feet, or the heels."

Concentrate. Lucy took a steadying breath, wobbled slightly, then finally centered her weight over her feet. She focused first on relaxing her right arm, the one Vivian had propped out to her side. Next she tried to lessen her white-knuckled grip on the runway trim.

"Okay, as before, I want you to find a focal point in the distance, out in front of you. The EXIT sign, or the door to the hall."

"Okay."

"Now, pretend you are walking on your tippy toes."

"I am walking on my tippy toes," Lucy reminded her. "If these heels were any higher, I'd be en pointe."

Vivian ignored her. "Firm up your thighs." She tapped Lucy on the outer flank of one leg. "Tighten your butt." A little tap to her fanny. "A small arch in your back, shoulders square, chest forward."

It was a lot to think about all at once.

"Now, one step. Just one. Looking at the door."

Breathing in, breathing out. Relaxed arm, tight butt, firm thighs. Chin up, boobs out front. She took a step. Tripped on the carpet.

Vivian's grip on Lucy's free arm tightened immediately. "It's okay. Square up. Try again."

Lucy clamped down on her jaw. It just couldn't be that hard. She was all but using a walker, for God's sake. "One step," she murmured.

"Good girl."

Step. Carpet snag. Trip. Another Vivian save.

"Pick up your foot," Vivian instructed calmly. "Don't drag the heel."

Wobble. Wobble even more. Claw at runway to keep from going down. Feel Vivian's nails in the skin.

"Not like a prancing stallion," Vivian said, sounding a tiny bit winded.

Lucy didn't dare so much as a glance toward Vivian. Her gaze was fixed, glazed almost, on the exit door. Oh, if she could just get that far. Then she could run. Run for the hills. As motivation went, it was better than nothing.

Step. Freeze. No wobble. No wobble!

She swung her gaze to Vivian . . . and promptly went down.

But she was smiling, even as she sat in an undignified sprawl at Vivian's feet. "I didn't wobble," she said proudly. "For a few seconds there, I had it!"

Vivian beamed. "Yes, yes you did. You're on your way."

"I don't know about that."

Vivian plucked out her phone and punched in a number. "Yes, David. We're ready."

Lucy gaped. "It was one step! I'm hardly ready for the runway."

"No runway," Vivian assured her. "But I have another idea. I was going to save this for later, but I think it's time we leave the prescribed path behind us and just wing it."

"'Wing it'?" Lucy said warily, and quite within reason, she thought.

Vivian's eyes twinkled and she buzzed David again. "Send me Arturo."

# Chapter 9

As it turned out, Arturo was a dance instructor.

"Isn't this is a bit premature?" Lucy whispered to Vivian as she watched Arturo confer with David, presumably about the music selection. "I can hardly walk. Don't you think dancing is somewhat beyond me at the moment?" Or ever.

Vivian turned, shielding Lucy from the two men, and took hold of both her elbows, drawing her complete attention. "We've discussed my thoughts on confidence and what it can get a woman, have we not?"

*Yes,* Lucy thought. Apparently, being comfortable in your own skin was only a worthwhile endeavor if you could then share said skin with someone else. Preferably when the skin in question was naked.

Vivian touched her arm just then. "Arturo is wonderful; you'll be in very good hands." She arched one brow and shifted closer, lowering her voice. "Men who move like he does . . . well, you know what they say. We should all be so lucky."

Lucy cast a sideways glance at Vivian, who was once again staring at Arturo, who bore a striking resemblance to a young Antonio Banderas, circa *Mambo Kings.* She couldn't help but wonder if Vivian knew firsthand about getting lucky with Arturo.

Then he lifted his head, as if sensing their attention, and smiled congenially in their direction, lifting his hand to motion that he'd be with them momentarily. Panic set in the moment he broke eye contact.

"You want to feel comfortable in your own skin, darling. We have to change your inner rhythm. Once you find that, the rest will fall into place." Vivian patted her arm. "Here is the expert!" she said brightly, as Arturo came to stand with them. "This is Lucy."

"Who can't dance," Lucy said, by way of introduction.

Arturo's smile widened as he extended his hand to Lucy.

He was roughly the same height as she was in the heels, and while somewhat slim of build, from what she could see via the black pants and white collared shirt, what he did have was all sinew and muscle.

"I have a few details to oversee," Vivian told them. "I'll check back in a little while." She scooted away before Lucy had swallowed her panic. But not before Arturo could pull Vivian aside for a quick, murmured consultation.

"Of course," Vivian agreed. "I should have thought of that myself. I'll take care of it." And with a wave and smile of encouragement in Lucy's direction, she left the small auditorium.

Arturo took Lucy's hand in his, and his palm all but engulfed hers.

"You should know," she told Arturo, "that not only do I not

have any discernible rhythm, I can't walk in these heels. I'm liable to do permanent damage to your feet." When he kept smiling, she added, "I'm not kidding. I've maimed before."

His smile didn't so much as flicker as his broad palms spanned her waist and lifted her, effortlessly, to the side of the runway. She was still gasping in surprise—okay, shock—at being lifted as if she weighed less than . . . well, far less than she actually did, when she then felt those hands caress her ankle. She barely stifled a soft moan.

"These will come off," he informed her, his accent slight but distinct. He smiled up at her as he slid off first one heel, then the other. "For now."

"Thank you," she said, telling herself the tremulous note in her voice was merely the result of her abject appreciation for being freed from foot bondage. Not because the brush of his hands against the sensitive skin of her ankles made her think impure thoughts. Lusty, R-rated thoughts. Thoughts that she hadn't been aware of in a very long time.

Just then the door to the auditorium opened and a Glass Slipper employee in a ubiquitous GS blazer—peach was the sherbet shade for today—hurried in carrying a plastic garment bag.

"Ms. Harper?" she queried, motioning Lucy to follow her.

Arturo and his hands were there without her having to ask. She was whisked—truly, it was whisking—off the runway and set lightly on her feet. "You're stronger than you look," she told Arturo, realizing too late that she'd spoken out loud.

"I danced in the corps de ballet from the time I was twelve. You are but a feather."

She was still blushing when Sherbet Blazer took her gently by the arm and steered her to a small set of stairs behind a curtain to the side of the runway. "You can change behind this."

"'Change'?"

The woman nodded with a ready smile as she handed Lucy

the garment bag. "Just come back out when you're ready and Arturo and David will take it from there."

Lucy was efficiently shuffled behind the curtain and Sherbet Blazer was gone before she could ask any questions. "So," she muttered, eyeing the garment bag, "this is what the whispering was about." She unzipped it and found a body-hugging, long-sleeved black leotard and a wraparound skirt made of even filmier fabric. *Dance clothes. Of course. Except, no.*

She started to flip the curtain aside and explain why she wasn't going to wear that getup, but stopped herself. She looked over the outfit again. On a ballerina, the clingy, stretch fabric would look graceful and elegant, showcasing the flow and curve of the female body in its most beautiful form. On her skinny frame, the female form would more closely resemble a knobby giraffe stuffed in spandex.

"Is okay?" came Arturo's voice, disconcertingly close to the other side of the curtain.

"I—I don't know. It's . . . not my style. Exactly." Of course, that was why she was here, right? Because she had no style.

"In order to learn the rhythm of your body, you have to be able to feel it moving, arching, turning with you. For that, *mi amiga*, you must have something on that moves with you." There was a pause. "Or nothing at all."

She gulped. Was he teasing? Of course. Of course he was. Still . . . hmm . . . *Remember, Lucy, you're paying them to teach you new things, so challenge yourself a little.* She let out a short, shuddering breath. "Okay. I—I'll try it on."

"That is wonderful. I will be here when you are ready."

Checking to make sure the curtain was pulled tightly shut, Lucy quickly shed her blouse, then realized she was going to have to take off everything to put on the leotard.

The space between the curtain and the stairs was small, and her elbow caught in the draping as she bent over to slide her pants off. When she straightened, the curtain adhered to her arm with a crackle of static electricity. She tried to tug it off while hopping out of her pants, which were now down around her ankles, but quickly lost her balance and grabbed the first thing she could for support. Turns out the curtain wasn't her best bet for gaining leverage.

With a muffled shriek, a half-naked Lucy and the twisted curtain crashed to the floor. Arturo really was nimble on his feet, thank God, and managed to leap clear to avoid being taken down himself.

"Ms. Harper? Are you okay?"

*Define "okay,"* she wanted to ask. If "okay" meant once again being betrayed by the uncoordinated phenomenon that was her body, then yeah, she was peachy keen. She pasted on a determined smile. "I'm fine. Really. But, uh, would you and David mind giving me a moment or two of privacy?"

Arturo sent a concerned glance to David, and then another back to Lucy.

Did they think she was going to bolt if they turned their back on her for more than two seconds? She tried her best to look reassuring. "Seriously, I'm okay. I just need a minute or two to untangle and finish dressing."

"If you are certain." He still looked worried.

"I won't say anything to Vivian, if that's what concerns you. I swear."

He looked affronted. "It's not that—"

"Okay, okay. Just saying." She waited a beat, and he didn't move. Her leg was beginning to cramp and her pants were wrapped so tightly around her other ankle that she was pretty sure she'd lost blood flow to at least one of her feet. Or it could be the aftermath of the heels. Either way, she wasn't going to budge an inch until they left.

Mercifully, David motioned for Arturo to step outside the

auditorium door with him. "We will be right in the hall. Just call out."

She nodded and would have given him a jaunty salute to prove how fine she was, except her hands were handcuffed in the leotard at the moment.

As soon as she heard the door shut, she rolled to her back, looking, she was certain, like a hapless insect caught in a web. Only in this case, it was a web of her own making. Wiggling and thrashing, she fought her way out of her pants, managing to work up a light sweat as she finally kicked the twisted fabric off her feet. Damp skin would make pulling on the clingy leotard about as easy as getting into a wet suit that was already wet.

For a split second, staring at the demolition zone around her, then the mangled ball of spandex she now had to unknot and get into without further destruction of property or self . . . she felt the urge to cry. Just for a brief moment. Really hard.

Instead she sucked it up . . . and took it all out on the hapless leotard. By the time she had it untangled and on her body, it was stretched out to the point that it had lost its clinginess. Okay, so maybe the odd puckers and baggy spots had more to do with her bony body—so much for the wet-suit look.

She then dug the skirt out of the twisted heap of curtain and tied that around her waist, intensely grateful there were no mirrors around.

Heaving a disgusted sigh, she stepped away from the mess, only to feel the filmy skirt slide across her thighs for the first time. She stopped and let the mid-thigh-length skirt swish around her legs. Then stepped again.

*Oh. Maybe Arturo has a point.* The leotard might not be body hugging, but she kind of liked how the wrapped skirt felt, all shifty and flowy around her body. She took one step, then another, lengthening her stride each time, just to feel the slippery fabric slide across her skin again. Then again. And again.

And, hell, why not, once more after that, just for grins. A smile rose to Lucy's lips, unbidden, and she suddenly felt like twirling.

"Ms. Harper?" Arturo's voice floated through the door. "Are you ready?"

"I'm dressed," she called out. It was the best she could commit to.

David took his place behind the music and video equipment, and Arturo beckoned her to come join him in the relatively open space between the runway and David's setup.

*Concentrate on the swish,* she told herself as she walked, barefooted, thank God, to Arturo.

He beamed enthusiastically and lifted his hands to her. "Come now. We will learn to move with the salsa beat."

*Salsa? I don't even eat salsa, much less dance to it.* "Don't you need, you know, rhythm for that?"

"You will find your rhythm, *mi amiga,* don't fear. And Latin music is best for this. Now turn so you face away from me."

That she could do. The less she had to actually look at anyone while she humiliated herself, the better.

"Now," he said, so close to her ear it made her jump a little, "I want you to take a deep breath."

She did. And maybe it felt a little good when the leotard pulled against her skin as she did. Just a little.

"Now release."

She did, maybe too heavily.

"Again," he instructed.

He was standing so close—well inside her personal space, and she had to remind herself that Arturo was a professional, an instructor. So what if he'd teased her about dancing naked. She quickly pushed that from her mind. She needed all her wits about her if she was going to even attempt doing this.

"Breathe in," Arturo reminded her.

She did.

"Now, when you breathe out, I want you to do so slowly. I want you to feel your breath and your tension ease from your body as you release." She could feel his body just behind hers and began to grow twitchy at the sensations it roused in her. And maybe a little dizzy. Or perhaps she was hyperventilating from all the heavy breathing.

"Breathe out," he instructed.

*Oh. Right.*

"Slowly."

He drew the word out. His deep voice and that accent made him sound almost hypnotic.

*Just give yourself over to the feeling,* she told herself. *Don't think, just feel.*

"Now," he said, his voice softer, quieter, just behind her ear, "we will have some music."

She shivered, just a little. He was so close. And that voice.

Then a slow, throbbing beat pulsed from the speakers, making her start. His hands immediately closed around her hips, making her gasp and jerk forward.

For a sickening moment, she thought they were both going down. But for a man with a slim build, he really was quite strong. He righted her rather easily, in fact.

*I am a feather.*

The music continued.

"Another breath," he coaxed.

She slid air into her lungs, fighting to let the tension go once again. It was harder than it seemed. His hands were still on her hips. And she was . . . feeling things.

"Okay," he said, after she sighed, barely keeping it from turning into a moan. "Now, let the tension slide from your lower back." To help her, he pressed his thumbs there.

This time she did let out a soft moan as her body eased into his.

"Good, good," he crooned. "Now, I will move you. Let me move you."

*Dear God in heaven.*

"Don't fight it," he told her.

Like she could have.

Then he was moving her hips.

"Shhh," he schooled her, pressing his thumbs again into the base of her spine, until her pelvis rocked forward and her hips relaxed again.

"Left," he told her, shifting her hips left. "Right." He swayed her to the right. "Let me move you."

*Oh, you have no idea.*

"Feel the music."

All she could feel was Arturo's hands. On her.

"Left again," he said, swinging her hips. "Then right."

Thinking of what would happen if he just swung her forward . . . then back, she couldn't help it as the rhythm of the music slid past her defenses and eased into her body, until it felt like the hot, thrumming beat was part of her pulse. Latin music was the music of love, was it not?

God, the way he moved her hips. Swish, swing. She felt warm. Ripe. Remembering Vivian's favorite word made her lips curve.

"Very good," Arturo said, sounding vastly pleased.

Yes, well, if he only knew what she was thinking.

"Wonderful, you have it now," he said, disrupting her fantasy just long enough for her to realize that he was no longer guiding her hips. In fact, she was swinging them from side to side with relative abandon. The key to finding her inner rhythm was, apparently, fantasizing about humping her dance instructor.

Arturo expertly turned her to face him with one easy grip and swing of her hips. She gasped in surprise, but he caught her easily enough, and then they were face-to-face.

Her breath caught as his gaze locked onto hers.

He kept one hand tight on her hip and grasped her hand with the other, pulling it out to the side, and up, so her elbow was bent and they were in classic dance position.

"Now—" She stopped, cleared her throat. "Now what?"

"Close your eyes. Let me guide you."

*If you only knew.*

And then the hand on her hip was urging her to sway again. His grip on her palm was just as sure. He didn't move his feet, or hers, but through subtle pressure with his hand and their interlocked arms, guided her body to match the rhythm of his.

"Feel the music. Let it back in. Left, right. In, out."

*In. Out.* Oh, God. Was he kidding?

His hand slid to her lower back again. Her thighs trembled and Lucy impulsively let her head tilt dramatically back, willing the music to take her once again.

Concentrating on the feel of his hand on her hip, his wide, warm palm mated with hers, his body so close, a mere step would bring them into full alignment—

"Yes, yes," he said, "fantastic."

*Let the music be your pulse. You are a feather.* " 'Yes, yes,' " she responded. " 'Fantastic.' "

"Now, come to me," he said.

*Yes!* She stepped forward quite willingly.

Only he now stepped back. So she stepped again. Again he stepped back.

"Slide your foot back."

So caught up in the moment, she didn't even question the command.

"Good, good."

Then he spun her around and tugged her back, so her left butt cheek was snuggled against his right hip pocket. The edge of her body, aligned perfectly along the edge of his. He still held her hand. She held her breath.

"Lift on your toes," came the command in her ear.

She lifted, swallowing a groan as her spandex-covered body slid along his hard frame.

"Forward," he commanded, pushing his hip into her. "Hips first."

She moved forward, one step, then another. Eyes tightly shut, feeling only his body so perfectly aligned with hers as they moved forward, as if flowing through water. Again, she felt her head tilt backward, her hair brushing his cheek.

"Lift and move. Yes, yes," he said, his breath coming faster, his voice sounding even deeper.

Her heart was pounding, hoping for the moment when he would whip her around and pull her tight against him.

He whipped her around. Her breath caught. Her entire body yearned.

"You've got it!" he said. "You are ready!" Then as her eyes flew open—now she wanted to see him, see the look in his eyes, the desire—only to have him choose that exact moment to put on another display of his freakish strength and lift her easily onto the edge of the runway.

"I will get the shoes," he announced.

"Shoes. Yes, get the shoes." Her lips parted, her body tensed, waiting to see if he'd slide his hands down her hips, then up the length of her thighs to where she most needed him to— *What? What did he just say? What do shoes have to do with this? I don't give a shit about the shoes!*

Her eyes flew open again as his hands left her. She swooned back, catching herself by banging her elbows sharply on the runway behind her, then shoving herself back into a sitting position.

Cheeks flaming, the rest of her body rapidly cooling, she closed her parted lips . . . then after a glance downward, quickly did the same with her parted thighs. *Christ, Luce, if you're a feather, you're a damn slutty one.*

Arturo popped up, instruments of torture in hand. "You were magnificent," he told her. "All you needed was help to feel the rhythm."

"Yeah" was the best she could do. What a complete fool she was. God, had he noticed? One quick glance down at the front of her leotard had her inwardly cringing. She should have kept her bra—complete with camouflage padding—on, and the hell with visible bra straps. There was no way Arturo could miss her twin beacons of lust. She was mortified.

She noticed he kept his gaze carefully averted while he strapped the heels back on her feet. She wanted to die.

*Wait a minute.* "Why the shoes?"

He straightened. "Because you are ready." He said it quite matter-of-factly.

As easily as he'd lifted her to the runway, he vaulted himself up next to her. Moving gracefully into a crouch, he offered his hand. "Come. You will see."

She didn't get to a standing position nearly as gracefully as he had. In fact, it was a miracle they both didn't take a header off the side. But she finally crawled and clawed her way to a wobbly stand. "Arturo, really, I—"

He shushed her. And, still smarting from her embarrassing hormonal overload, she shushed without further comment.

He motioned to David. "Play the music from the start."

The opening of the song pulsed once again and Arturo turned to her, all confident smiles and easy charm. "We will do just as before."

*What, is he trying to kill me?*

But Arturo was already taking her by the shoulders, lifting her arms until her hands rested on his shoulders. "Close your eyes."

"I can't walk in these. If I take one step, we're both likely to crack our skulls open."

"We are not walking, merely finding the rhythm once again. Close your eyes, *mi amiga.*"

*Men with accents. There should be a law.*

Lucy closed her eyes.

"Up on your toes," he instructed, his voice a low rumble, mixing with the heated Latin beat.

She lifted on her toes, then realized she was already on tippy toe. Right. The shoes. But Arturo stepped back and her body instinctively followed.

Right hip. Swish. Step. Left hip.

"Ah, *carina,*" he murmured. He stepped farther back, his fingers sliding along hers, then gone altogether. *"Fantastico!"*

Lucy's eyes blinked open, as if awakening from a trance.

"Come, come," he bade her, curling his fingers, beckoning her forward.

She moved as if on automatic pilot, then her surroundings snapped into place. She was three quarters of the way down the runway! *How is this happening?*

Her eyes went wide as she gaped at Arturo. She lost her rhythm . . . then she lost her balance.

Arms flailing, she lurched forward. Arturo sprang forward and caught her before she could take a header off the ramp. But she was laughing too hard to be embarrassed this time.

"I did it!" she gushed.

Arturo turned her in his arms, his own handsome face split in a wide, beaming grin. "*Sí, sí.* That you did."

Before she could register being in his arms, the wide, toothy grin, or the fact that her body was very naturally leaning in closer to his, all on its own . . . the door to the hall swung open and Vivian stepped back inside.

"Success?" she asked.

Arturo kept a steadying hand on Lucy's arm, but shifted around her so he could see Vivian. "We will watch the tape and see. I think you will be pleased."

" 'Tape'?" Lucy's mouth dropped open. All thoughts of Arturo and doing an altogether different kind of tango faded as that one word sank in.

Oh. My. God. She'd barely survived the faux salsa sex. Now she had to watch it on tape? Could she be any more mortified?

# Chapter 10

"Too short," Lucy said, as Vivian handed her another hanger. It was now day five of Barbie Boot Camp, and after Lucy's successful session with Arturo, Vivian had decided she needed more runway clothes. The season in Milan being over, the next best thing had been a field trip to Georgetown. Lucy's schoolteacher budget was toast.

"It's not too short," Vivian assured her.

"My principal would have a heart attack if I wore this."

Vivian lowered her chin and merely stared at Lucy over the rims of her trendy minispectacles. "Good lord, Lucy, who said anything about wearing this to work?"

"I can't afford an off-work wardrobe. Beyond jeans and shorts, anyway."

"Darling, don't take this the wrong way, but you can be quite exasperating at times."

Lucy swallowed a sigh. "I know, but—"

" 'But' nothing. You're a vibrant young woman with many diverse facets, only one of which is dispensing knowledge to the youth of today. So I'd say you can hardly afford not to do whatever necessary to showcase those other facets." She turned and hung the clothes on the dressing-room rack. "However, we can do our hunting in another place that has a smattering of top designers at bargain prices. Come with me."

Lucy tugged on her khakis and buttoned up her camp shirt.

"That skirt would have been smashing with your legs. Which reminds me, we have to go shoe shopping."

"I don't think spike heels are ever going to be a staple of my off-hours life."

"They don't have to be, darling." She and Lucy stepped outside into the hot August sun and quickly into the waiting Glass Slipper limo. "Lorna's Closet," Vivian told the driver, then turned to Lucy. "Lorna Swinson runs an adorable little boutique in Old Town. She takes Junior League castoffs on commission. We'll find something there, I'm certain of it."

Lucy settled into the soft leather seat and let her gaze drift beyond the smoked-glass passenger window. She wondered what Grady and Jana were doing. Grady was probably hard at work in the lab. Jana was out playing girl reporter. And Lucy was shopping. If they only knew. She could picture them, sitting around, eating lunch, reading the e-mail loop without her . . . and worrying about her immortal soul.

She stifled a little sigh. For all her doubts early on, since Vivian had taken over her transformation, Lucy had to admit she was becoming more hopeful. To look in the mirror, you wouldn't guess anything had changed. Her hair, face, and makeup—or lack thereof—looked just as it had when she'd arrived. But that didn't matter. What mattered was that she felt different. She felt . . . transformed, from the inside out. Okay, so they were just getting to the outside part.

But when she'd caught her reflection in the mirror, she saw past the lumpy brown hair and plain face. She saw anticipation, a banked excitement, and she wondered what other hidden talents she might possess.

Vivian had been right about the Brazilian wax, the silk lingerie, strutting her stuff on the runway in heels that she'd now been forced to admit actually did make her long legs look more lanky than knobby.

But she wasn't confident enough to take a spin in the real world just yet. She had another week yet to practice. During which time she could only pray her outside self caught up with her newly awakened inside self.

"Here we are," Vivian announced.

The limo pulled over on the shaded side of a tree-lined street, filled with small, trendy, and expensive-looking boutiques.

"Are you sure this will fit my budget?" Lucy clutched her purse, pledging she'd keep the escalating balance on her credit card from escalating any higher.

"You forget, I used to do this for a living. And not always with a fabulous studio budget." Vivian slid out of the backseat as the driver held the door for both of them.

Her eyes were alight with such excitement that Lucy had to admit it was becoming a little contagious.

"Let's see what treasures we can find. I know Lorna always keeps some fun things tucked away for her regulars."

Twenty minutes later Lucy was naked once more, standing behind a ruffled floral curtain in a tiny rear dressing room, an assortment of dresses, skirts, and blouses hanging on every available hook.

"The little black number first," Vivian told her. "Every femme fatale needs a little black dress. From Bette Davis to Sharon Stone, a little number like that can make a career." She smiled. "Trust me on that, darling."

Lucy dug around through the tangle of hangers until she found what looked more like a little black slip than a dress. She very carefully slid the dress over her head.

It was a bit clingier than she'd anticipated and didn't drop as far down on her thighs as she'd hoped. The neckline was a loose, drapy affair that dipped daringly low between her breasts. "At least Sharon Stone had cleavage," she muttered.

"Come show me, darling. Remember to slip the heels on."

A pair of black, strappy sling-backs were nudged beneath the curtain.

"I don't even want to show myself," she muttered.

"Do you need a different size?"

"No," she said. *A different body*. Knowing Vivian wasn't going to let this go, she grabbed the clothes hook and leaned against the wall as she carefully slid her feet into the shoes. She kept her death grip on the hook until she got her wobbling under control. These heels weren't as high as the ones she'd practiced with on the runway, but she still wasn't entirely confident she wouldn't fall on her face. She needed to find that inner rhythm again.

Humming a Latin rumba under her breath, she relaxed a little, moved her hips a little, and slowly straightened away from the wall. "You can do this," she whispered. She pushed the curtain aside and took two stuttering steps.

"Now that's what I'm talking about!" Vivian pronounced, punctuating the remark by waving her ebony cigarette holder in the air. No cigarette, just the holder. On her it worked. Bette Davis had nothing on Vivian dePalma when it came to owning her own eccentricities. "Absolutely stunning."

Lucy wished she had that kind of natural élan that made eccentricities seem glamorous.

"Turn around, darling, now let's see the back. Your exit is as important as your entrance. No femme fatale worth her

Christian Dior handbag would turn her back on anyone without making sure she's still turning heads."

Lucy had only the curtain for support. Refusing to make that mistake again, she shot a rather helpless look to Vivian.

"Oh, come now, just pretend you're turning into Arturo's arms."

"Don't I wish," she muttered.

Vivian let out a sly laugh. "I know, darling. All I have to do is look at that man and I crave a cigarette."

Smiling, Lucy closed her eyes and focused on listening to her inner rumba. Then, with a tiny hip swing, she shifted her body around until her back was to Vivian.

"So, what do you think?" Vivian asked.

"What?" Lucy opened her eyes and realized she was staring into a full-length, three-way mirror. "Oh. Wow."

"Exactly, darling."

From the neck up, she was still third-grade teacher Lucy Harper. But from the neck down? Yowza! Who was that sexpot, anyway?

"Sharon Stone *and* Bette Davis, eat your heart out," Vivian crowed triumphantly. "That dress was made for you. Slinky could be your signature look, darling."

Lucy had to admit that the drapy front thing actually made her meager curves look less so. And the heels along with the short length of the dress made her legs look kind of sleek. She looked up and caught Vivian's wide grin of approval, and for the very first time, she allowed herself to believe that she could pull this off.

Impulsively, Lucy struck her best Madonna "Vogue" pose, throwing her head back for good divalike measure. "How you like me now, boys?" she purred.

Vivian let out a delighted hoot of laughter, and Lucy couldn't help but join in.

There was sudden applause from behind them. Still laughing, both Lucy and Vivian turned to find the store owner and several patrons clapping and nodding in an endorsement of her ensemble. Lucy gave them a giddy little curtsy and caught the approving wink from Vivian, who also put her hands together, as well. "Brava, darling, brava!"

# Chapter 11

Lucy finished putting the protective coating of lotion on her nails and palms, as instructed. "God, it's freezing in here," she muttered, adjusting the blue paper shower cap so the elastic band was right on her hairline, protecting her newly highlighted locks. She still wasn't used to herself with lighter hair. "Ve vill make you honey blonde," she said, mimicking her stylist's, Roget's, French accent. There was no time to think about that now.

Shivering and naked again, she resolutely turned toward the huge blue-and-silver, space-age-looking booth. Until twenty minutes ago, she'd never even heard of spray-on tans. It made the sci-fi-movie-extra head of foil she'd sported earlier seem low-tech by comparison. "I cannot believe I'm doing this." But what else was new? She couldn't believe half the things she'd done in the past twelve days.

The new hairstyle was simply the latest in a long list of new experiences. She'd come to love the eclectic wardrobe Vivian had put together for her during their shopping spree the week before. She'd almost completely gotten over her fear of heels; even her bruises had pretty much faded. And she had to admit that after Vivian had all but dragged her back to Sadistic Sue to finish the wax job on her legs, she did feel rather smooth and soft.

Vivian had even helped her pick out her "signature scent." Smell being the most powerful of the senses, Vivian had assured Lucy that years after a woman left her lover, every time he got a whiff of her perfume, he would long for her again. Lucy wasn't sure about that, but there was an undeniable thrill at the idea of even having discarded lovers.

She still didn't feel exactly bulletproof—she was still afraid she might do someone bodily harm with the acrylic nails she now sported—but she did feel like she might actually turn a man's head for reasons other than that she'd just taken out the sunglasses display at the mall by inadvertently tripping over the metal base.

"Ms. Harper?"

Lucy jumped and instinctively covered her breasts. Then she realized the voice was coming from the little intercom. "Y-yes?"

"Are you ready?"

Still clutching her breasts, she looked at the booth. "I guess," she mumbled under her breath.

"Just step inside and close the door. When you're ready, press the blue button. Then you have five seconds to get in your stance. Don't forget to curve your hands like Robin showed you. Make sure you keep your eyes and mouth closed. It's a little noisy, so don't let that startle you. The spray will move up and down for ten seconds, then it will stop. You'll have five seconds to turn around before the second spray. Any questions?"

"No, I think I have it. Thanks." Gingerly she stepped into the booth and clicked the door shut behind her. "Okay," she murmured, "press button, curve hands, close eyes and mouth. Hold breath for ten seconds."

She pressed the button, looked down to align her feet on the helpful footprint-patterned mat, then shut her eyes and got into position. Her mind wandered a little. *Hard to believe that twenty seconds in here will give me a golden glowing tan. Hasn't it been five seconds? Better take a deep breath just in case.*

The instant she opened her mouth, something that sounded like a 747 jet engine rumbled abruptly to life. She jumped, squealed—and opened her eyes in surprise. "A little loud, my as—" The nozzles cut on in that instant, spewing spray from every angle, stinging her eyes, and worse, filling her mouth.

Gagging and spitting, she immediately abandoned her stance and covered her eyes as the nozzles began moving up and down. Panic rose inside her as her heart immediately began pounding as loudly as the thundering motors operating the nozzles. She couldn't get her breathing under control, much less in sync with the up-and-down motion of the spray. Hell, she couldn't get her breath at all. She was hyperventilating. *Shit, shit, shit!*

Apparently she must have said that last part out loud, because in the next instant when the motors cut off, she heard pounding on the door to the small tanning chamber. Okay, so maybe she might have screamed. A little.

"Ms. Harper! Ms. Harper! Are you all right?"

Mortified, she immediately turned and began fumbling for the door handle, with every intention of escaping. So what if her boobs were tan and her ass was still white? Who was going to know? Her eyes stinging from the spray still dripping into them, she couldn't find the damn handle. Heart still pounding, she felt the panic rise again and was going to call out for assistance—it wasn't like she could be less embarrassed at this point—but just then the motors cut back on for the second round of spraying.

Trapped and whimpering, she turned her back and cowered,

abandoning any pretense of her instructed stance. She remained in a huddled position as she got blasted all over again, her heart immediately leaping right back into overdrive. *Please be over, please be over.* She didn't even want to think about what this was going to look like. Talk about your uneven coverage!

And just as suddenly it was over, and the room fell silent.

"Ms. Harper!"

"I—" She stopped, gagged, spat out brown spray. "Fine," she said raggedly. She fumbled around the now slippery booth with her hands until she found the knob and all but fell to the floor of the small room in a grateful heap when she was finally free. "Fine," she managed again, staggering to a stand, right before she stuffed the closest towel into her mouth and began scrubbing her tongue.

"Don't forget, rub yourself dry from the feet up," Robin called out, "or you'll streak."

"Shit," she swore, the word muffled by the towel. She tugged it out, realized it was the only one she had, and immediately began vigorously scrubbing her legs and feet. She was probably the only one who'd ever screwed up a twenty-second fake tanning session.

When she finally got her robe back on and staggered through the door, no less than three Glass Slipper employees were huddled there, concerned looks wreathing their perfectly made-up faces.

"Are you all right, then?" Robin asked, her British accent making her sound even more sweet and sincere.

Lucy managed a nod and tried for a brave smile. "Just took me a bit off guard. How long before the color starts to come out?"

"Two to four hours."

*Super,* Lucy thought, barely managing to keep the fake smile on her face. Only four hours before the zebra-size streaks came to life.

"Vivian is waiting for you down the hall," Robin informed her with an encouraging look. "Maryann here will take you to her." Her smile brightened. "You're to have your makeup done next. Then a hairstyling lesson."

Hair and makeup, the two things Lucy had really wanted most. And now all she could think about was whether there was enough foundation to even out the results of her tanning disaster.

Vivian greeted her with a breezy smile. "So, darling. Ready for your next step?"

Apparently, word of her tanning-booth meltdown hadn't traveled to Vivian. Well, at least there was one thing in her favor. She pulled her robe more tightly around her. "Ready as I'll ever be," she said. *Just as long as there aren't any spray nozzles and jet engines involved.* Her heart still hadn't fully recovered.

Vivian steered her into another room that was all decked out with mirrors and a table filled with more makeup than all the department-store counters in Hecht's combined. Glancing at the various pots, compacts, trays, and bottles, she didn't even know what half the stuff was for.

Something of her anxiety must have shown on her face, because Vivian patted her arm. "Carol here is a magician with nothing more than mascara and a pair of tweezers. You'll see. But first, Margo will show you how to manage your new cut."

Maybe it was because Vivian sounded so excited about everything, or because she'd been so patient and kind. Or maybe it was because Lucy was still traumatized by the tanning booth. Probably a little bit of all three, but suddenly Lucy's eyes filled with unexpected tears.

Vivian *tsk*ed and immediately pulled a tissue from somewhere inside her formfitting red blazer and began dabbing at Lucy's face. "Now, now, darling. The hardest part is over." She gave Lucy an encouraging smile. "This is the fun girly stuff you've been waiting for."

"It's just—" Lucy stopped. She was so very grateful for everything Vivian had done for her. So she had no idea how to put into words the absolute terror that had just struck her as she realized she was about to leave here, and she wasn't remotely ready to attempt doing any of this on her own, without sounding horribly ungrateful.

Some of what she was feeling must have shown on her face, as Vivian's expression softened. "Darling, we're not going to abandon you, you know. In fact, I will be quite hurt if I'm not kept in the loop. I expect a full report on how things turn out." Vivian smiled with her typical confidence and assurance.

In that moment Lucy would have killed for even a shred of that élan to come naturally to her.

"Practice doesn't always make perfect," Vivian told her. "But it will put you at ease. You'll have plenty of time for more practice once you leave." Before she could say anything else, Vivian shooed her off into Margo's capable hands.

Three hours and a few singe marks later, Margo stepped back and smiled. "I think you're finally getting the hang of it."

Lucy smiled weakly and gladly put the flatiron down. "I guess there isn't a wash-and-wear hairstyle that would look this nice, huh?"

Margo just grinned. "The price we pay for beauty."

Lucy looked back in the mirror. The blonde streaks in her hair were so wispy thin they weren't all that noticeable, but the overall effect had turned her hair the warm shade of honey. That, along with her new fake tan—which so far appeared to be amazingly streak-free—made her eyes look brighter. They were still hazel, but at least they didn't look as muddy.

Overall, the new hair color had been a shock, but once they'd started cutting, the color had been the least of her concerns. She now sported a fringe of wispy bangs, while the rest barely brushed her shoulders. She told them that she'd only kept it long because the heavier it was, the less lumpy it tended to look. Plus it was easier for her to put in a bun during class. All that bending over little desks, when her hair swung in her face, was a pain.

Margo had laughed off her protestations and told her she'd teach her how to smooth her hair. Smooth, hell. Flatten it with a smoking iron was what she meant.

But looking in the mirror now at her wispy bangs, tanned face, and poker-straight honey-blonde hair . . . well, hell, if she didn't know the person in the mirror was her, she might actually find her downright attractive. She'd been so caught up in learning how to use the flatiron without taking off a patch of her face, she hadn't really taken any time to look at the overall picture.

Margo had stepped out to see if Carol was ready for her, prompting Lucy to lean forward, closer to the mirror, a smile flirting around her lips.

"So . . ." she said, allowing the smile that suddenly bubbled up inside her to surface as she leaned in to the mirror, "how you doin'?" Her Joey Tribbiani imitation needed some work, but she found herself laughing in almost giddy delight, nonetheless.

Vivian chose that moment to stride in. "Ah! Look at you, darling. As with Catherine Deneuve, another timeless beauty is born."

Lucy turned, smiling a bit sheepishly at being caught mugging at her own reflection.

"Well, darling, what do you think?"

Lucy opened her mouth, shut it again, then shrugged as she grinned helplessly. "Thank you," she finally managed, through a throat suddenly tight with emotion.

"Oh, honey," Vivian responded, immediately striding to her

with arms outstretched. She drew Lucy from her styling chair and pulled her into an embrace, which was only slightly awkward with their foot-plus difference in height.

Both of them sniffling, she then held Lucy at arm's length. "Are you beginning to feel the power of your own magic, darling? Sleeping Beauty has been awakened."

Lucy let out a watery snort. "I don't know if I've fully embraced my inner princess, but I'm trying."

"Let me have a look at you," Vivian said, then turned her this way and that so she could see all sides. When she turned Lucy back to face her, her expression was more serious than Lucy had ever seen it, except perhaps that very first day, which now seemed like a lifetime ago.

"You're lovely. But I want you to tell me one thing. I want to make sure you know you have this power with or without all the trappings and accessorizing."

"I wish I could say I'm as confident of that as you are. I have definitely learned a great deal about myself. And I'm vain enough to admit that sprucing up the exterior has helped me really begin to believe in all the interior restoration work we've done." Her cheeky grin faded a bit. "But I can tell you that you were right about chipping off the layers and getting down to solid wood. It's a whole lot more than just a hairdo and eyebrows with a graceful arch. I wouldn't have pushed myself like this if it hadn't been for you. Hell, if it hadn't been for you, I wouldn't have stayed."

"And what a loss for both of us."

Lucy's eyes stung again. "All that time you spent with me." She took a shaky breath. "I know you don't normally do that, and I know I can never repay you, but—"

Vivian gave her a surprising little shake. "You go to your reunion and prove to yourself that what you've learned here is real. That you're one hot mama and they're lucky you found time in what will soon be your very busy social schedule to squeeze them in."

"Yeah, I'll do that," Lucy said dryly between sniffles.

Vivian's infamous knowing smile curved her red-painted lips. "Darling, you doubt me. But your life will change. Whether you keep up with the highlights or not. Although I think they really do bring out your eyes."

"I was thinking the same thing," she blurted excitedly before she could stop herself.

Vivian's grin widened. "We both know it's what is on the inside that matters." Her grin widened. "But you know, it never hurts to keep the chassis in mint condition." She did a graceful turn, then shot Lucy a wink. "I should know, darling. I'm considered a collectible."

Lucy laughed. "I'm really going to miss you."

"Why? Am I going somewhere?"

"Tomorrow is my last day."

"At Glass Slipper. But don't think you can get rid of me that easily. I've invested a great deal of time in you. You don't think I'm just going to abandon all my hard work and leave an amateur in charge."

It was pure Vivian sass. And Lucy loved it. "Well, though I should be telling you that I've taken up enough of your time, the rookie in me would greatly appreciate the follow-up support."

Vivian surprised her by tipping up even higher on her tippy toes and planting a kiss on Lucy's cheek. Well, jaw. "Just try and stop me," she said, wiping off the lipstick smear with the side of her thumb. "I might just have to get a date to this reunion myself," she teased.

"And make it that much harder to get Jason's attention? I don't think I'm up to that level of competition yet."

Vivian hooted. "I knew I picked a winner." She grinned. "Such a sharp little smart-ass you are."

"Thank you," Lucy said sincerely. "I think that's the nicest thing you've said about me."

Margo popped her head in just then. "Carol is ready for you."

Lucy nodded, then turned back to Vivian, but before she could find the words, Vivian merely squeezed her arms and nudged her toward the door.

Vivian watched Lucy walk out the door, wondering if she even realized how differently she carried herself now. She didn't hunch her shoulders to downplay her height. Her strides were longer now, more assured. There was a swing in her hips. And a more confident smile on her happy face.

"And I'd kill for those damn legs of hers," Vivian murmured under her breath. "Arturo wouldn't stand a chance."

Aurora tapped on the door and stuck her head in. "Vivi? You ready? It's almost time for us to leave. You know how terrible traffic is getting around the Kennedy Center. The curtain goes up in an hour."

Vivian allowed her gaze to linger a moment longer on the empty doorway Lucy had passed through. She remembered the day she'd gotten her first job as an assistant dresser. Her new boss, Dessora Claudette, had taken one look at Vivian's eclectic, pieced-together ensemble of a print velveteen skirt, magenta bustier jacket, with a man's striped satin tie tucked beneath, the ends trailing from the bustier hemline, and had hired her on the spot. "You think you have vision, do you, Vivian?" she'd demanded in her accented, three-packs-a-day voice.

Vivian had nodded, then straightened her shoulders and announced that yes, she thought she did. Always had.

She'd never forgotten Dessora's wicked smile. "Good. Because you're mine now. And together we're going to knock those

Hollywood bitches on their collective fanny-tucked asses. This town won't know what hit it until it's too late."

Vivian smiled, thinking of Lucy and the impact she was about to make on her own life and that of everyone who crossed her path. *Go out there and knock them on their collective asses, Lucy Harper.*

# Chapter 12

"Are you sure you didn't mind my coming along?" Jana looked out at the Glass Slipper mansion as it came into view. "I mean, I wouldn't have, except I got a message saying she wanted us both here and . . . Wow. What a place, huh?"

"Yeah," Grady said on a small sigh. " 'What a place,' indeed." He hadn't minded the company. In fact, he'd been relieved when Jana had called this morning and asked to tag along. He'd been dreading this day since he'd dropped Lucy off two weeks earlier.

It had been two of the longest weeks of his life. The funding for his latest project was stalled while State and the Department of Defense argued about God-only-knew-what this time. He'd been expecting—counting on—being ass-deep in nanotechnology and defense applications for liquid memory. Instead, he'd had more free time on his hands than he'd had since taking this job.

Plenty of free time. To think. About Lucy. About what she was doing to herself. About why she was doing it.

About fucking Jason Prescott.

Sure, intellectually he knew that Jason was peripheral to this venture Lucy had undertaken. He was merely a symbol. But there was no law saying Grady couldn't hate the symbol.

"Check that trio out," Jana was saying as he coasted around the circular drive toward the stone walkway leading to the house.

"Ah," Grady said, as he watched the three diversely coiffed older ladies emerge through the stained-glass doors and pause on the porch at the top of the stairs. "Those would be Lucy's fairy godmothers."

Jana half stifled a snorted giggle. "Honestly? You said they were an interesting bunch, but wow, how different are they from one another? Hard to really picture them as makeover mavens."

"True. But they have a hell of a track record." When Jana shot him a considering look, he haltingly added, "Business section of the *Post*, you should read it sometime."

She continued her considering gaze for a moment longer. "Yeah. Right. Because I don't follow the news enough as it is."

"Whether or not the Capitals have a hope in hell of making the Stanley Cup play-offs this season—or any season, really—is not news."

Jana clutched her heart. "Blasphemer!" Then, when he grinned, she stuck her tongue out at him before turning back to the house. "Well, well, well. Maybe you know something I don't." She pointed. "That one didn't turn out too badly."

A tall woman with straight blonde hair emerged from the house and paused next to the godmothers. Even without the tottering high heels, she towered over two of them, and had an inch or two easy on the third.

Grady watched the young woman because, well, he was male. Her legs went on forever, the fitted pin-striped blazer, short suit skirt, and downright hormone-inciting come-fuck-me spikes merely enhancing nature's gift. But if this was the result, he was all for enhancement.

She hugged the redheaded godmother the longest. Vivian dePalma, Grady recalled. Then, after another bit of chatting, turned toward the stairs.

"Good thing Lucy doesn't have to watch supermodel there," Jana said dryly. "She'd be in rehab before even leaving the joint."

Grady only half listened to Jana. His heart had come to a complete stop and was presently lodged in his throat. It was a battle with the sick knot in his gut as to which might kill him first.

"She . . . ah, damn," was all Grady managed.

"I can't imagine why someone who looks like that thought she had to come here," Jana said. "I mean, I know models can be vain and all, but how bad could she have looked befo—oh, my God."

All Grady could do was nod dumbly. The testosterone side of him wanted to thump his chest and howl. His heart, on the other hand, wanted to splinter into a thousand tiny pieces.

"That can't really be—" Jana broke off yet again, shaking her head wordlessly as the "supermodel" descended the porch stairs, her slender, elegant hand resting lightly on the railing.

"Lucy," Grady groaned. Dear God. What had they done with his Lucy? And yet he couldn't have dragged his gaze away from her under penalty of torture.

He'd have thought himself incapable of any movement, but when Jana started to open the car door, his hand flashed out and locked onto her arm. "Not yet."

Jana shot him a surprised look, but even she couldn't keep

her eyes off the miracle presently walking toward them. "Why? My God! Look at her. I'm—it's—she's . . . I just can't believe it," she ended on a hushed note of awe.

"Yeah" was all he could mumble. "Me, either."

Jana seemed to snap out of it then. Or so the sudden fist thwack she delivered to his chest would seem to indicate.

"Ow! What was that for?"

Jana turned on him. "You better not ruin this for her," she said hurriedly as Lucy drew closer.

"What? What makes you think I'm not happy for her?"

Jana merely rolled her eyes. "Please. I didn't say anything last week down on The Mall because your puppy-dog eyes beseeched me not to."

Grady's chest tightened even further. Oh, for Christ's sake, she wasn't going to do this now of all times, was she? "Jana, please." He heard the begging note in his voice and didn't give a damn how pathetic he sounded.

"Don't worry. I haven't said anything in all the years I've known you two, have I? I love you both, you know that. I know this is probably eating you up inside, just like I know it doesn't have to if you'd just stand up for yourself and—"

"Jana," he said, warning her.

She waved a hand. "God, of all the millions of ways I'd planned to talk to you about this, this was definitely not the place or time I'd have chosen. But it's situation critical, dammit. You're going to have to suck it up and realize that if you're never going to stake a claim, then you sure as hell can't keep her from figuring out how to go out and stake one of her own. She's been unhappily alone long enough. If this is what she needs to believe in herself, well then, you'd damn well better—"

A tentative knock on the window had them both jumping around in their seats. Lucy waved at them, a big smile creasing her new face.

Only Grady noticed the nerves pinching the skin around her eyes. The eyes were still the same. His Lucy was still in there somewhere.

Rather than lower his window, he opened his door to get out. Jana was right, Lucy clearly was worried about introducing them to the new her. And since that was the role he'd cast himself into, it wasn't fair to hold the final destruction of everything he'd held dear against her.

Only, when he swung his door open, it caught her off guard. She took a quick step back, then teetered dangerously on her heels.

Jana had climbed out of the other side, but she couldn't clear the front of the car fast enough. Grady shrugged out of his seat belt and scooted out just in time to grab her arms and yank her forward before she went down.

The momentum shift bucked her forward so hard she plastered him back against his car . . . and herself all over him. From knee to chest they were perfectly aligned.

Lucy laughed self-consciously. "Miss Congeniality in the flesh," she quipped, though there was still a hint of nervousness in her expression. She struggled to get her balance, making Grady clench his teeth . . . and several other parts of his anatomy, in an effort not to react in a way even Lucy couldn't possibly mistake.

"Sandra Bullock's got nothing on you," he said, hoping the raspy edge to his voice was mistaken for having the wind temporarily knocked out of him.

More like his common sense. He should be helping her straighten away from him, and he did have his hands on her elbows, with the intent to do exactly that. But his gaze was momentarily all caught up in hers, and for a second longer, he couldn't do anything but stare.

"What have you done to yourself, Luce?" he murmured.

Her eyes widened a bit, and a tiny telltale blush bloomed on her expertly made-up cheeks. "You hate it, right?"

"I don't know what I think."

Jana was there, then, tugging her away. "I do," she said, shooting Grady a sideways glare. "God, turn around so I can see all of you."

Lucy did a little twist turn, only wobbling for a moment, then held her arms out to the side. "Can you believe it?"

Jana shook her head. "My little Lucy, all grown-up," she said, her accompanying sniff only half teasing. She stepped closer and peered intently at Lucy's face. "Nice makeup job. And your brows. Fantastic arch." She brushed her fingers over them. "Are they stenciled on or what?"

Laughing self-consciously, Lucy batted Jana's hand away. "No, they're all mine, but with a little pencil." She grabbed Jana's arms and leaned in. "The real shocker is I put on my makeup myself today. Brows and all. And I only look partly like Frankenstein's bride."

Jana's teasing smile faded. "Honey, you look amazing." She brushed a hand over Lucy's newly straightened and streaked hair. "My best bud is a hottie. Good thing I'm already taken or I'd be jealous as hell."

Lucy snorted. "Yeah, I'll be lucky if I make it home in this getup. I was out here practicing those front-porch stairs for an hour this morning so I wouldn't humiliate myself in front of you guys."

"Aww," Jana said, hugging her.

Grady stayed back, watching the reunion, saying nothing. It wasn't that he couldn't contribute, or had nothing nice to say. He just couldn't seem to pull his head out of his ass long enough to stifle the stupid sense of betrayal he felt. Stupid because he knew it was totally unfair to Lucy. But there it was.

Beyond the hugging twosome, he spied the godmother trio approaching, along with several Glass Slipper employees toting the suitcase Lucy had arrived with and several garment bags and shoe boxes she definitely hadn't.

Vivian reached them first. "Isn't she marvelous?"

Her smile was wide and sincere, but Grady didn't miss the intent look in her eye, warning them to tread carefully. So, Grady thought, Lucy had managed to find herself another rescuer. He supposed he should be thankful her White Knight was female this time. Even if she did look more the dragon than the knight.

"Yes, she is," Jana gushed, her eyes glassy now, as she stood back and looked at Lucy again.

"I owe it all to Vivian," Lucy explained. "I was ready to walk on day two, but she stopped me."

Now Grady had a real reason to dislike Dragon Lady.

"She kind of took me under her wing."

Dragons had wings.

"And really forced me to dig deeper than I thought I had it in me to dig." She smiled at Vivian, then stepped over, with more grace than she might realize she had, bent down and hugged the much-shorter woman. "I know I've thanked you a zillion times, but—" She broke off, sniffed, then, horrified, dabbed her finger under her eyes. "I'm going to ruin my masterpiece here."

Vivian laughed and whipped out a tissue, dabbing her clear. "Now, now, you know I'm only a phone call away."

"Thank you," she sniffled. She looked over her shoulder and realized her gear had been packed safely in the trunk, then glanced back at Vivian. "Here goes nothing."

"Knock 'em dead," Vivian told her, then looked at Grady and Jana. "And if she chickens out at the last minute, I expect you both will see to it that she follows through, or contact me and I will. She's worked quite hard and she deserves to ace her final exam." She looked to Lucy. "I'll expect a full dishy, gossipy report the morning after." She winked. "Or the afternoon after, as the case may be."

Grady watched the byplay between the two women. Out of the three, he would never have picked Vivian as a role model for Lucy. The soft and maternal-looking Aurora was more the kind of person he'd presumed she'd gravitate toward. But then, what he was witnessing was so far afield of what he'd dared to imagine, why bother second-guessing any of it at this point?

Vivian fussed over Lucy for another couple of minutes. Jana even got pulled into their little hen circle. Traitor. It took considerable willpower on his part to stay put, appearing to lean casually on his car, as if he had all the time in the world, when there was absolutely nothing casual about the way Lucy was making him feel at the moment.

He couldn't even begin to sort out the myriad emotions whirling around inside of him. Only one stood out, and that was the undeniable and quite cavemanlike urge to stuff Lucy in the car and take her far, far away from here. Not because she was so hot now that his libido had gone into overdrive. Well, not that parts of him weren't threatening an all-out mutiny. But the predominant thought was to get her away from Glass Slipper and Wicked Witch Vivian so he could start detoxing her. He wanted his old Lucy back. Gorgeous women were a dime a dozen and usually about as interesting. Once you got past the lacquer and heels, there wasn't much left to stimulate the mind.

Lucy was different. She was vibrant and funny, smart and compassionate, and a complete and total klutz. They could find a way to heatedly debate the stupidest of points for hours on end, or just as easily sit side by side in complete, companionable silence.

He'd found women who turned him on. He'd found women who stimulated his brain. He'd even found women who were sharp and funny and vibrant. He'd just never found one who had it all in one package, who called to his heart like Lucy Harper.

He carefully avoided catching Jana's eye. He kept his expression neutral, but she probably knew this was far from easy for him. He didn't need her to tell him that maybe the reason he'd never fallen in love with anyone else was because he'd never stopped loving Lucy. Truth be told, other than his aborted attempt at leaving her behind when he'd gone off to MIT, he hadn't even tried. It seemed like a wasted effort. Besides, how does a person fall out of love without a concrete reason to make him feel differently?

In the back of his mind, he'd always kind of hoped that someday some woman would just step into his path—maybe crash into it, just to get his attention—and his feelings for Lucy would mutate back into friendship as his feelings for the love of his life grew. It wasn't like he was blocking women from doing just that. Not in any real sense. Because, if Woman X was his soul mate, it wouldn't matter what he did, right? A true soul mate would have to connect, shake his heart loose, demand his full and complete attention.

"Earth to Grady?"

He jerked his head up from where he'd apparently been contemplating his navel to find Lucy standing in front of him, arms folded. The godmothers had retreated. Jana had already gotten back in the car. In the backseat, he noted with a scowl.

"So, can we get this show on the road?" She cocked her head. "You really do hate it, don't you?"

"Hate" was a strong word. He felt pretty strongly. "What do you think about it?" he asked instead. "Is it what you wanted?"

Her response surprised him. Her smile took its time emerging, almost a bit warily. "Honestly? I . . . well, it's still taking some getting used to."

"In a good way or a bad way?"

The smile grew stronger. "Good. I'm pretty sure, anyway," she added, self-deprecating to the end. "You know I'm still the same person on the inside."

Actually, that's what bothered him most. The exterior overhaul was startling enough, but she had changed in less obvious ways, as well. And that's what really terrified him. Earlier wobbling notwithstanding, she carried herself entirely differently, with a bit more grace, and most definitely a new attitude. Soon other people would see that change in her, too. Some of them men. One of them, Jason Prescott. And act accordingly. Then what the hell would he do?

He did not, under any circumstances, look at Jana.

"You have every right to do whatever you want to yourself if it makes you feel better," he told her, striving for polite, fair, decent. Happy with not shouting, growling, or begging.

"I just wanted to be more comfortable in my own skin."

He couldn't help it, his gaze traveled down her body, then back up again. Christ. She looked amazing. "And are you?"

She lifted a shoulder. An elegantly suited, slender shoulder. "Getting there. It takes some getting used to, the superficial stuff. But I'm liking the changes so far. I feel . . . I don't know, more confident, I guess." She grinned suddenly. "Maybe not about the heels. I'm still pretty sure I'm going to do major damage with those. But I do like the idea of them, of how they make me feel. I'll get better with practice."

She didn't say it, but he knew she was looking for confirmation from him. As they often did with each other when embarking on some new venture or path in life.

He forced a hint of a smile and it cost him more than she'd ever know. "I'm sure the first wolf whistle will make it all more bearable."

She waved off his comment, so certain he had to be kidding.

He so wasn't, but perversely it was that momentary peek at the Lucy he knew and loved that brought the first honest smile to his face. "You underestimate the power of the wand," he told her, when what he'd always thought was that men had always underestimated the power of her. He pushed off the car and walked around to the passenger side, opening her door with a flourish. "Your economy-size carriage awaits."

She took a bit longer than usual to catch up, but he privately thought she was far more balanced on those towering sticks than she let on.

"Hey, I'm already starting to see the perks. I guess Vivian was right about the heels."

Grady glanced up, realizing he'd been staring at her legs. "What's that?"

She grinned as she stepped between the open door and the waiting seat. "You've never opened a car door for me in your life."

"Or stared at your legs like a man just emerging from a long prison stint," Jana offered oh-so-helpfully.

"I have to," he said, caught off guard by the ambush. "Open your door, I mean," he added with an uncustomary stammer. Christ.

Grady stood holding the door in silence as Jana and Lucy swapped grins over his tongue-tied state.

Lucy gripped the edge of the car door as she lowered herself in, and without thinking, Grady automatically reached out to block her head from hitting the frame, but, still chattering with Jana, she dipped down and sat, then swung her ever-so-long and shapely-looking legs expertly into the car. She reached for the handle as he straightened, stupified by the natural act of grace and coordination he'd just witnessed. The Lucy Harper he knew could never have pulled that off, not without breaking one heel, ripping her hose, and likely ruining that tight and far-too-short skirt.

He swung the door shut with perhaps a tad more force than necessary, but only earned a quick glance and thank-you smile before she continued to shift around to look at Jana so she could continue her story.

Grady trudged around the back of the car, trying not to snarl. She already didn't need him anymore. When she wasn't self-conscious about her new skills, she didn't so much as wobble on those heels. In fact, he'd bet she was far more practiced with her new wiles than she'd let on. It was probably only because she'd been worried about them seeing her for the first time, not wanting them to give her too hard a time about her dramatic makeover, that she'd done that tripping thing earlier.

"Safe journey," someone called out from behind him as he opened the driver-side door. He turned to find Vivian waving from the base of the porch stairs. He stared at her for a moment, not quite sure why, except she seemed to be staring at him. Hard. Despite the cheery grin. Or maybe "cheeky" was a better word. That woman had to be a handful.

"Take care of our girl," she called out.

He didn't know what to say to that. *Our girl.* If only that were still true. He sketched a light salute, then ducked into the driver's seat next to Lucy.

He'd ridden beside Lucy any one of a million different times in any one of a million different circumstances. Like the time in their sophomore year when they'd taken the debate team road trip down to North Carolina and had been crammed on a school bus bench seat together, along with their overnight bags.

He'd been so excited when they'd won the regional title and advanced on to the East Coast championship. Three days away from home and the stifling and ever-increasing tension had been a godsend to him.

He'd lived with his uncle Frank back then, his mom's older brother and only sibling. He'd taken over as sole caregiver after Grady's mom died when he was ten. Grady had never known his dad. Even though Frank hadn't been completely receptive to fostering his sister's kid—Frank was a dedicated bachelor and cop who had no idea what to do with his egghead nephew, or kids in general, for that matter—he'd tried hard, under what Grady realized as he got older, had to have been difficult and painful circumstances.

They had next to nothing in common, and Frank's clumsy attempts at bonding had left Grady feeling even more like an outcast than he already did. As he'd entered his teen years, the tension between them had mounted. And any excuse to be gone for a few days was cause for major celebration. Spending those three days with Lucy Harper made it even better.

Until he'd been crammed on that bus with her. It had turned into a miserable trip for him. Lucy chattering away, oblivious to the fact that when he'd woken up after a night on the bus to find her sleeping against his shoulder, he'd been awarded with a mortifying hard-on that would not go away . . . and the sickening realization that from that point on, being "just buddies" was going to be a lot more difficult for him. Guys didn't get that excited about being with their best friends. But they definitely got that excited about spending time with a girl they were falling in love with.

It had been three days of agony, with part of him wanting to just grab her and kiss her and let her deal with his feelings for her, and the other wiser-than-his-years part telling him that if he did, he'd likely freak her out completely and ruin their friendship, which, along with knowing Jana, was the best thing that had ever happened to him.

*Funny how as much as things change, they stay the same,* Grady thought, not remotely amused. He didn't glance over at her as he slid on his seat belt and put the car into gear.

Something told him this ride home was going to be even more brutal than that stupid bus trip.

# Chapter 13

"Where's Grady?" Lucy looked behind Jana as she let herself into her own apartment and bumped the door shut with her hip.

Jana waggled the six-pack of Diet Coke at Lucy. "Not coming," she said, juggling the pizza box, her purse, and a bag of Milano cookies.

Lucy took the Coke and nipped the cookies off the top of the pizza box.

"Hey!"

She shot Jana a smug smile. "Don't whine. We only have to split them two ways." She tore open the bag. "And without Grady here to lecture us on appropriate pizza-eating protocol, we can eat the cookies first."

"True," Jana said, then flopped down on Lucy's couch with a deep sigh. "God, I'm beat."

Lucy snagged a chair from her breakfast-nook table and

dragged it close to the couch. Her Alexandria apartment was small by any definition, except perhaps when compared to those in New York City. It consisted of one great room that was living area, breakfast nook, and tiny kitchen (separated by a counter with no room for stools on either side). A single bathroom and her bedroom finished out the place. She also had a standing-room-only balcony overlooking pretty much nothing, but if she leaned to the side of the railing and craned her neck really far, she could get a glimpse of the Potomac River. Well, almost. Were it not for the row of buildings blocking the one shred of river view left. But she knew it was there, right behind them.

Her decorating style was Early Schoolteacher, meaning bookcases large and small took up most of the wall space (bathroom, bedroom, and hallway included), each of them crammed with pretty much everything she'd ever read, dating from The Baby-Sitters Club onward, plus all of the many additional volumes she'd picked up over the years and had every intention of reading someday. She easily bought three titles for every one she read, and even her students could do that math, but that didn't keep her from compulsively snooping through every library and garage sale, usually coming away with a cardboard box full of new treasures. Okay, so it was a geeky addiction, but a harmless one. It wasn't like she collected cats. Yet.

What little room was left over was filled with whatever furniture she'd been able to snag from her parents' place, combined with Marlo clearance items and more garage-sale finds. She viewed her decorating taste as whimsical bordering on eclectic. Other people would probably use a less-flattering description. Rummage Sale Kitsch came to mind.

Fortunately, those "other people" were just Jana and Grady, who had both long since gotten used to her off-center approach to decorating. From her retro metal lunch box collection and the rack of vinyl record albums she was continually adding to, despite the fact that she had no turntable on which to play any of them, to the six-foot-tall stuffed ostrich she'd won on a fluke basketball throw at the Virginia State Fair her sophomore year in college. It was the only thing she'd ever won—and while ostensibly playing a sport, to boot! Naturally, she was very proud.

Crunching on a Milano, she sat and offered the bag to Jana.

"Thanks." Jana slid out a cookie, but didn't snarf it down like they usually did with their Pizza Night contraband.

"So, did Grady give a reason?" Lucy asked, kicking herself as soon as the question was out. This made two Pizza Nights in a row he'd missed, but she already knew what the reason was, and she'd sworn she wasn't going to say anything if he didn't show. Again. She shouldn't force Jana to cover for him by putting her on the spot, but it was like the two of them had some kind of unspoken understanding about his recent no-show status, and she was feeling a bit miffed about being left out.

Even though she knew *she* was the reason.

"Never mind," Lucy said, crunching on another cookie. She'd been looking forward to this all day. Hell, all week. Since returning from Glass Slipper, her life had been hectic, to say the least. She was still adjusting to the new Lucy, and school had begun, as well. She was still trying to get a handle on her new students, and the always stressful Back-to-School night was looming. As was the reunion.

She wanted to obsess over the upcoming dance much as she would about any final exam; meaning ad nauseam, until even she was sick of talking about it. She wanted to examine every minute detail, from what she should wear, to how she should make her entrance, or even if she should make one. She'd thought about striding in like some kind of towering Runway Barbie, getting a collective gasp from the crowd as they realized it was nerdy Lucy Harper all grown-up. But then, she thought, maybe it would be even better to slide in undetected, then spring up, *pow!*, smack in the middle of the dance floor, right in front of Jason.

Even the steady pressure of starting up a new school year and getting to know her students, dealing with the administration, and attending the endless staff meetings hadn't kept her from spending almost every other waking second—and most of her sleeping ones—thinking about the dance.

But she knew better than to go there with Jana. While she hadn't been as obvious in her lack of enthusiasm over the new Lucy as Grady had, they had known each other forever. So her real feelings were hard to mask. Though at least Jana was making an effort.

"Tough day at the office?" Lucy asked, scooting around to snag the Coke. *Absolution in a can,* she thought, still munching her last Milano as if the zero calories in the drink made up for the fat-saturated calories in the cookie. But hey, the equation worked for her. She opened two cans and handed one to Jana, who took a healthy slug, then burped before answering.

"Ah, sweet Coke buzz," Jana said, then let out another deep sigh.

It was then Lucy noticed the fatigue lingering around Jana's eyes, the pinched corners around her mouth. And she immediately felt like the leading candidate for Worst Friend Ever.

She knew she'd spent the past two weeks in All-About-Lucy Land, but given the big changes she'd made, it had been kind of hard not to be. Unleashing her new self on the world had been both exciting—and exhausting. Perversely, that made accepting those changes herself that much more difficult. It was sort of like having your arm in a sling and having everyone question you endlessly about what happened.

Old acquaintances took very satisfying double takes, and a surprising number of new people paid attention to her. Sometimes at night she'd lie in bed and wonder why appearances counted for so much, why having blonde streaks and a perfect arch to her eyebrows made such a difference. Which was silly because she knew damn well they did, having been on the other side all of her life. So all this attention should be making her feel wonderful. And mostly it did. But it could also be surprisingly disconcerting. Sometimes it even kind of pissed her off, which made no sense whatsoever. She'd wanted the self-improvement makeover and was thrilled with the results.

And yet, she was the same Lucy Harper inside, and no one had cared to get to know her before. The same guys who smiled at her now, with her tan legs and shorter skirts, wouldn't have given her the time of day before. She tried to think of it as having come up with an improved marketing plan for meeting people. Sort of like slapping a new cover on an old brand of cereal. She'd just improved her odds of getting picked up off the shelf, that was all.

To quiet her silly, niggling concerns, she'd naturally turned to Jana. Jana might not agree that the makeover had been necessary, but even she had to admit that Lucy 2.0 was the better model. Not that Jana had come out and said so, but, well, *duh*. Just look at her.

Vivian had been right about one thing, though. It was all a matter of finding her inner rhythm. Even Jana had given her that much. But she wasn't confident enough to let go of the surface changes and hope that her newfound rhythm would garner her the same kind of attention straight hair and spike heels did. Then there was Grady, who was no help whatsoever. He wouldn't even give the new her a chance. She had to believe he'd come around in time. He had to. Because otherwise who was going to help her get a handle on it?

"I'm sorry. I know I've been a rotten friend since I've gotten back. No talk about Glass Slipper or any reunion crap tonight. Scout's honor."

Jana snorted. "Neither one of us was ever a Scout."

"Only because Andrea Steiner's mother was troop leader. And I still say we should have joined. God, could you imagine their faces when we bumbled in, in all our divine dorkiness, right into the middle of the Junior League of Brownie Troops?"

Jana just shuddered. "I'd rather not, thanks."

"So, tell me what's up with you. I know Dave was thrilled to get the chance to go to Europe to play those exhibition games, but it had to have been hard having him gone. I still say it sucks that you couldn't go with him. First I abandon you on our annual beach trip, and then that."

"I couldn't get the time off from work then, anyway. I would have lost whatever toehold I had on covering the opening of football season."

"Well, you must be happy to have him home finally."

"Yes, definitely happy." She'd said it easily enough, and sounded as sincere as ever, but then she looked away, then down at her uneaten cookie.

Though Jana was good at putting up the tough-chick front, Lucy knew it was hard on her when Dave was traveling. Jana wasn't used to leaning on anyone, but Lucy had watched her best friend fall hopelessly in love, and as much as it had thrilled and excited Jana, it had also rattled her pretty badly. Jana had grown up with a mother who found true love every Friday night around closing time, leaving her a bit shaky on concepts like intimacy and commitment. And yet with Dave, Jana had finally found something real.

Lucy had envied her as much as she'd been in awe of the personal strength she knew it had taken for her best friend to reach out and grab on to what she wanted. Especially when it was a long-term relationship with the first man she'd ever truly loved. It came easy to Jana when it was about a career move, or telling someone else—namely Lucy—how to run her love life. But this had been the first time she'd been confronted with such a personal emotional challenge, and the concept of trying and failing was terrifying.

And though it wasn't easy for Jana to admit she loved him as much as she did, much less that she'd somehow found herself leaning on him, counting on him, depending on him . . . they'd made it work. And Lucy had never been prouder of her, or happier for her. And, sure, a little envious, as well.

So the idea that there might be trouble in paradise pinged at her heart and her conscience. God, just how far up her ass had she stuck her head, anyway? It's no wonder Grady was in absentia. "Is everything all right between you two?"

Jana's lips curled a little, but since she was still staring down at her lap, Lucy couldn't tell if it was a smile or a grimace. "Everything is fine," she said.

Lucy leaned down to catch her eye. "Really?"

Jana finally glanced at her, and her eyes were shiny with unshed tears. "Really."

Lucy gasped. "Oh, honey, what's wrong?"

Jana, who never cried, not even when they'd skipped school—twice—to see a matinee of *The Last of the Mohicans*, sniffled. "Nothing. Everything." She hiccuped as she tried to stifle the tears. "Dave and I are fine. So take the Worried Mama Look off your face, okay?"

"Okay," Lucy said, knowing she couldn't. "So, if you and Dave are fine, what's with the tears?"

"I seem to be doing that a lot lately. But don't worry, they are tears of joy. Terror-filled joy," she added, more under her breath, "but joy."

"So, you're happy." It was, understandably, a tentative statement. When Jana merely nodded, sniffled, then downed a whole Milano in two bites, Lucy shook her head and said, "You wanna buy me a vowel here or something?"

"Didn't Grady tell you?" she said around the crumbs on her lips.

"Grady and I have spoken a grand total of twice since he dropped me off here two weeks ago. Neither conversation lasted longer than five minutes. Apparently, he's extremely busy." Her tone made it clear what she thought of that excuse. "I know he's probably neck-deep in some top-secret, hush-hush project, but when isn't he? And since when has that prevented him from making time for his two closest friends?" Or one of the two.

And she knew the answer to that one. Since one of those friends turned herself into something he could no longer identify with.

Jana looked shocked. "Really?" she said, the word muffled by the last of the cookie crumbs. "When you said you hadn't talked much, I didn't realize—" She broke off, sighed. "Jerk. All men are jerks."

Lucy frowned. "That's usually my line. After which you tell me that all men are jerks except for Dave, and the one who's going to fall madly in love with me at some future moment in time. A moment, by the way, which I'm still waiting for."

"So you think," Jana muttered around another swig of Coke.

"What?"

Jana hiccuped twice, then burped. "Do you think guys have any idea that we belch better than they do?"

"Do you think I don't know when you're trying to change the subject?"

Jana just smiled. "So, don't you want to know why the happy tears?"

"What? Oh, right! What didn't Grady tell me because he was too busy being a closed-minded jerk?"

"Nothing. I mean, I barely mentioned it in passing. He probably forgot. It was hardly even newsworthy at that point, since we'd only started trying, and I only mentioned it then because I wanted to take his mind off of—" She broke off, looked panicked for a split second, then downed the rest of her drink. "Work," she managed. "Take his mind off work. He really is busy."

"You're babbling," Lucy said, more confused than ever. "You never babble. Come to think of it, you never cry, either." She grabbed the empty can away from Jana. "What's in this, anyway?"

Jana just grabbed another one and popped the top. "My last night of caffeine, that's what." She swigged, hiccuped, then looked at Lucy with a big scared-as-hell grin plastered on her face. "What I've been trying to tell you is, Dave and I decided it was the right time to start thinking about, you know, moving to stage two, and—"

"'Stage two'? What was stage one?"

"Marriage," she said, as if Lucy was completely dim. "And well, you know neither of us had an exactly traditional upbringing, so it made sense for us to wait. To be sure we could handle it. Except when it comes to the two of us, we're apparently incapable of waiting. I should have learned that when I slept with him on the first date, then married him eight months later. And really, who ever really knows if they're ready, right?" She polished off the rest of can number two in one long swig.

Lucy took the empty can when she was done, staring at her like she'd lost her mind. Mostly because she was fairly certain she had. "Did you try and play hockey again with Dave?" She reached out and groped around Jana's scalp. "Because you're acting like you got hit with a puck."

"Actually, that's a pretty good description," Jana said. "My short-term memory is shot and I'm constantly forgetting where I put things, probably because I throw them down wherever I happen to be standing when I have to suddenly run to the bathroom."

"You're sick?"

"It's okay; I'm getting used to it. Well, I'm not, but then, I don't seem to have any real say in the matter. They tell you saltines, but that's crap. Sour balls are the real key to survival."

"'They'? Who are 'they'?" Lucy finally grabbed Jana's waving hands and gripped them tightly so her friend had to look her in the face. "Survive what? For God's sake, just tell me already!"

"I was all prepared to make charts, the whole routine, you know? But we won't have to."

"I'm so glad for you. What kind of 'charts'?" She'd known Jana almost her entire life and she'd never once seen her like this. Giddy, bordering on hysterical.

"We won't need the charts!" Now Jana was squeezing Lucy's hands so tightly the blood flow had stopped and the tips had started to tingle. "God, Luce, it's all so damn scary. And I swore I was going to wait a while, until I was sure, you know, that it was going to take, before saying anything to anyone. Or at least until I got used to the whole idea. But I can't wait."

"Great. Please don't hold back on my account."

Her smile shifted then; it became sort of smug, like she had this awesome private secret. Her eyes, on the other hand, were filled with a kind of awe and more than a little fear. "Terror" still seemed the appropriate adjective. "Apparently Dave is as good at scoring off the ice as he is on the ice, because we only stopped using protection last month and I'm already—"

"Pregnant!" Lucy gasped as it finally hit her. "Oh, my God! Oh! Jana!" Then she smacked her friend on the arm—lightly, given her condition, but still. "Why didn't you tell me?"

Jana laughed, sounding almost drunk. "What do you think I've been doing? You just needed to listen."

"And Grady knows? And he's not here to celebrate with us? God, all men *are* jerks."

"No, you're the first. Outside of me and Dave, that is. I only told Grady we were trying. It was while you were gone. I was going to tell you, too, but it all sort of progressed past that part really fast. God, now that I think about it, I guess I was already pregnant when I told him we were trying!" Her laugh was a bit dazed, and Lucy noticed her hand hovering protectively over her stomach.

"How long have you known?" Lucy felt even more awful now. Here she'd been all preoccupied about playing dress-up for a stupid school dance and her best friend was embarking on one of the most exciting and terrifying journeys of her life.

"Not long. A week."

"A *week*? You've known for an entire week and you didn't tell me?" Lucy couldn't imagine keeping something that huge from Jana, but then, this was huger than huge. Life-altering huge.

"You know I wanted to call you first thing, but Dave and I were sort of in a state of shock. I couldn't even really process it. I mean, I was a few days late, which I figured was like Nature's joke on me, just to psych me out or something. We'd really just gotten comfortable with the idea of not using anything, you know? It's easy to say you want to start, but scary as shit when you actually don't put that diaphragm in. Then, *bang!*, no period and, well, we both knew there was no way I was pregnant the first time out. But we went out and bought the tests."

"Plural?"

Jana smiled a bit sheepishly. "You see one blue line and you don't believe it. But when you're surrounded by blue lines and pink X's, well, it's sort of hard to deny reality then."

"How did Dave react?"

"We were both sort of stunned speechless. In fact, we're still kind of in a daze. Like it's not real yet. Except I've spent the past five days puking my guts up and it's not because I ate the moo shu at Pagoda House again." Again with the somewhat loopy-terrified grin. "So I guess it's real."

Lucy leaned forward and pulled Jana into a tight hug. "I'm so thrilled for both of you," she whispered fiercely. "You're going to be a great mom."

Jana shuddered. "Please, dear God, don't mention the M-word. Not yet."

Lucy laughed. "You might want to start applying it, since you're gonna come out the other side of this as one whether you want to or not."

Jana shook her head. "I can't even contemplate telling mine, much less think about all the ways I can screw up being one myself."

"All first-time parents think that."

Jana nodded. "Some with more reason than others."

"I bet Dave isn't worried."

"About being a dad?" Jana paused for a second. "Once he gets the stupid I-knocked-her-up grin off his face, he might be. But, nah, you're probably right. With his gargantuan family, he's got nothing to worry about. He's already diapered half of Quebec, just with his nieces and nephews alone."

"When are you going to tell his family?" She knew Jana was in no hurry to tell her own mother, who would just as likely freak out at the prospect of being forced to admit she was a grandmother than anything else.

"Not until I'm through my first trimester. Unless he can't wait that long. We'll see them at Christmas like we always do." She groaned. "I'm not even letting myself think about that. I'll be suffocated."

Privately Lucy thought that would probably be the best thing that could happen to Jana. But she knew better than to say it. "Well, I think it's amazing and fantastic and I can't wait to play Auntie Lucy."

"Yeah, don't be so smug, Auntie," Jana informed her. "Just because you don't have to lug this thing around in your stomach all winter and give birth to it at the end, don't dare think I don't have every intention of completely using you afterward. Dave and I will need personal time to deal with the whole being-parents thing, so you and Grady will be our default babysitters. Dirty diaper changes and all." She pointed at Lucy. "Fair warning." Then she snagged the cookie bag. "Now, can we please dive into that pizza? I'm eating for two here."

Still digesting the whole idea of babysitting, Lucy didn't move fast enough and Jana commandeered the pizza box, as well. "Should we, you know, call Grady?" Lucy asked. "Maybe if he knew your news, he'd get over being mad at me long enough to come celebrate with us."

Jana flipped open the box and took out a heavily meat-laden slice.

Lucy craned her head to look over the lid. "What happened to our veggie special? You hate 'greasy meat products' on your pizza."

"Apparently, pregnancy hormones bring out the carnivore in me. I'm just going to puke it all up, anyway," she said, happily sinking her teeth into the cheesy slice.

"Gee, thanks for that lovely visual." But Lucy's stomach growled as the smell of bacon and sausage assaulted her senses. She snagged a slice of her own. "If I gain more weight during this pregnancy than you do, I'm going to make you pay. I don't know how, but I will."

"Yeah, body weight being such a big issue for you."

Lucy snorted. "Says the woman who has never been called 'scarecrow.' "

Jana patted her belly. "Which means you get to smirk when they call me 'balloon belly.' "

"Except your balloon will naturally deflate," she reminded her dryly. "Scarecrow is forever." Just because Lucy was tall and skinny didn't mean she'd thought of herself as having a good body. Ever. When you spend your adolescent years being called "beanpole," "stick," "praying mantis," and the like, you didn't look in the mirror and see Heidi Klum staring back at you. You saw knobby legs, scrawny arms, lumpy hair, and a seriously flat chest . . . no ass or hips, either. In her world, everything was baggy and shapeless, because she was shapeless.

And yet, somehow, Vivian had managed to find clothing—and padded lingerie—that created at least the illusion of a shapely figure. Vivian dePalma, the Houdini of dressers. Lucy had begun to see why she'd been so popular with the Hollywood stars. But she was still getting used to having clothing that felt so . . . binding. Even if it was the binding that created the curves in the first place. Slight as they were.

Beauty, it turned out, was a merciless mistress.

# Chapter 14

It wasn't until Jana had left several hours later that Lucy realized they never had called Grady. She stared at the phone in the kitchen as she shoved the half-empty pizza box into the fridge and tossed the empty soda cans in the recycling bin. It wasn't her place to tell him. And Jana hadn't said what she planned to do about telling the rest of the world, other than she didn't want her editors to know until absolutely necessary. It was hard enough being a female reporter in the bastion of male-dominated sports. But surely she'd tell Grady.

Lucy snagged the crumpled bag of Milanos before retreating to her bedroom. If he called her, what would she say? They'd never kept anything from each other. It would feel weird, like lying by omission.

She snorted and shook a cookie loose before tossing the bag on her nightstand and heading off to turn on the shower. "Like he's going to call me, anyway." Her heart squeezed a little at that.

She was alternately pissed or hurt at his recent cold shoulder. But at the moment, she just felt guilty. This was Jana's time, and they had to be there for her, a united front.

She stepped into the shower and squirted on her specially purchased shampoo for highlighted hair, swearing when she raked her scalp with her acrylic tips before remembering, again, that she had talons now.

So, the only question was, would she just confront Grady on her own, tell him to act surprised when Jana spilled the beans, then demand he patch things up with her for their friend's sake? Or did she hang back and hope he wasn't being such an ass that he wouldn't figure out for himself that their friendship came first?

She still hadn't figured out what to do as she slathered on her tan-maintenance moisturizer and creamed the makeup off her face. *God, this is exhausting,* she thought, missing her old Dove-and-water routine. Then she caught sight of herself in the mirror.

"You did the right thing," she told her reflection. "You've finally figured out how to shed the ugly duck and don your inner swan." Even she couldn't spew that crap without laughing.

But as she yanked on her shapeless, comforting ratty old nightgown—so what if it was like a pacifier and she was pushing thirty—she admitted that, while she wasn't entirely comfortable with the new Lucy, she wasn't ready or willing to revert to the old one.

She unwrapped the towel from her head and was just detangling the snarls, which highlighting made worse, by the way, when there was a knock on her apartment door. She checked the clock, frowned, then scuffed to her front door and eyeballed the peephole.

An instant later she was flipping the locks and opening the door. "Grady? What are you doing here?"

"Any pizza left?" He didn't even bother trying a sheepish smile, much less a single word of apology.

She knew this was the opportunity she'd so badly wanted, but now that he was here, unrepentant and looking tired and grumpy, she couldn't seem to stop herself from bracing her arm on the door, blocking his entrance. "I let Jana take the leftovers home for Dave," she lied. "The Pagoda House is still open this time of night."

"Very funny."

"Not really." And she knew from the way he shifted his feet that he understood they weren't talking about death-by-moo-shu.

"So, does that mean I can't come in?"

"It depends. I'm really not in the mood for another lecture on the evils of self-improvement."

"Good. I'm not in the mood to talk about the reunion. So we're even."

The comment stung, though she knew she probably deserved it. Even if he hadn't been present for her endless analytical dissection since her return, no doubt Jana had filled him in.

"So what are you here to talk about?"

"Did you really send the rest of the pizza home with Jana?"

Lucy wanted to be mad at him. He'd abandoned her in her time of need. But then, she hadn't been there for Jana when she should have been. Maybe Grady was also in the throes of some life-altering event and here she was making it all about her. "No. I was just trying not to be a pushover after being all but shunned for the past two weeks."

"Not everything I do or don't do is about you."

Well. Hadn't she just thought that? She should have been relieved. It wasn't her. It was him. Except she was still pissed. "So your playing Invisible Man since you dumped me on my doorstep is all about you?"

His lips quirked a little, while his soulful eyes still managed to look a little sulky and oddly intense all at the same time—a Grady Matthews trademark.

"No," he said flatly. "That was totally you."

She started to close the door. He stopped it. For a guy with shaggy hair, who looked like the only muscle he flexed was the one between his ears, he had surprisingly fast reflexes. She knew it was from all the racquetball. So, okay, maybe it wasn't just the puppy-dog eyes that attracted women.

"But this isn't about either of us," he told her.

*Jana.* Had she called him after leaving earlier? "Okay." She stepped back and let him in. "Help yourself to the pizza and I'll be out in a minute. If I don't finish detangling my hair, it will be murder with the flatiron tomorrow."

Grady shot her an unfathomable look, but wisely remained silent. He just shook his head and sauntered to the kitchen.

"What?" she asked, knowing better, but when the hell had that ever stopped her? "What's with the look?"

"You're just so . . . girly now."

She clasped her hand to her chest in mock horror. "Oh, my God, no. Not that. Please tell me it's not true." She flipped her wet hair at him and walked to her bedroom door. "And I thought tonight wasn't about me."

She closed the door behind her before she could hear his answer.

# Chapter 15

"It's always been about you," Grady muttered as he yanked the pizza box out of the fridge. He wasn't remotely hungry when he'd showed up at her doorstep, but suddenly he was feeling ravenous.

He didn't need a shrink to dissect that one.

He'd promised himself he was going to stay away from her until the damn reunion was over, or until he got his head screwed back on straight. Whichever came first. Even Jana was losing patience with his lame, morose attitude. Of course, Jana wasn't exactly acting normal lately, either. Which was why he was here now. Or so he'd told himself.

"Okay," Lucy announced as she flounced into the kitchen. "So what's this all about?"

*She never used to flounce,* he thought, biting savagely into a cold piece of pizza. "Jana," he said after swallowing. He rummaged in her fridge for a Coke, both to wash down the cold lump of pizza and give him an excuse not to look at her.

"What about her?"

"She's not acting like herself. She's all distracted and moody and, I don't know, just not herself. Did you notice it tonight? I wondered if she'd said anything or given any indication there was a problem. Are she and Dave okay? Is it a work thing?"

"Why didn't you show up earlier tonight and ask her yourself?"

He paused at the sharp tone, but decided not to go there. So she was pissed at him for all but vacating her life the past two weeks. She'd have to get over it. She was better off without him, at least for the time being, even if she didn't know it. "I got caught up at work late." Which was only a partial lie. He was always caught up in work. Lately more than usual. Specifically the past two weeks. And that was only partly due to the funding approval. He hiked himself up on her counter. "So, did you notice?"

Lucy didn't answer right away, which made him immediately suspicious. She was the world's worst liar and she knew it. But that didn't stop her from trying if and when she thought it necessary. "Notice what?" she asked, with next to zero innocence.

"Jana. She's been acting weird." He polished off his pizza while watching her try and decide how much, if anything, to tell him. He would find out all of it anyway, now that he knew there was something to find, but it could be amusing to watch her go through the motions.

In the end, she just sighed and said, "Yes, I noticed. I'm just not sure I should be the one to tell you."

Surprised by her candor and the seriousness of her expression, he lowered the Coke can he'd been about to drink from. "What do you mean? Why not?"

"She has . . . news. And she should probably be the one to share it."

"I take it she's shared it with you." At Lucy's nod, he continued. "So why wouldn't she want me to know, too?" Then it clicked into place. "Oh, wait a minute. This is about the baby thing, right?"

Lucy's eyes narrowed. " 'The baby thing'?"

"Yeah. While you were in Barbie Rehab, she let it spill that she and Dave were trying to start a family. I just didn't think it would distract her as much as it apparently has." He gave her a leering grin over the edge of the can as he polished it off. "I guess boffing your brains out night and day could do that to a person."

"You should know," Lucy commented as she tore the crust off the last remaining slice and popped it in her mouth.

"Excuse me?" He tossed the empty can into the plastic bin. "What was that supposed to mean?"

"Nothing. Except you're the Hugh Hefner of one-night stands." Her words were muffled as she chewed. "Okay, okay," she swallowed hard, lifting her hands, "maybe two-night stands, three max. I mean, you are single, so it's your choice." She shrugged, condemning him in tone, if not in words.

"Yes, I date. And no, I haven't been interested in looking for anything permanent with anyone I've met so far. But I'm hardly with a different woman every night. Or even every week."

"All I'm saying is you can be cavalier when it comes to sex, so I wouldn't go casting stones."

"I wasn't 'casting stones,' " he said, his voice rising, "I was only making a joke about Jana and Dave and . . . wait a minute." He leveled a stare at her. "You're purposely misdirecting this conversation, aren't you? What do you know about Jana, or Jana and Dave, that I don't?"

Lucy grabbed the empty pizza box. "Why don't you go bang on their door in the middle of the night and ask them?"

Grady grabbed her wrist as she turned to throw the box out, tugging her back around. "This *is* about the baby thing, right?"

Lucy turned and looked up at him, her unnaturally straight hair swinging in a perfect curtain as it skimmed over her shoulders. Devoid of makeup, she still looked mostly like the Lucy he knew and loved, but the fake tan, the blonde hair, the new attitude, still threw him. Badly.

Just not badly enough to make him not want to tug her closer and—

"Yes, it's about the baby thing, okay?"

He frowned. "Why the hostility?"

She pulled her arm free and finished disposing of the pizza box. "I'm not hostile. I'm tired. It's late and I want to go to bed."

So did he, but he didn't need to be going there at the moment. Talk about purposely misdirecting a conversation. "So, what is it? She wants to try and he doesn't? Are they having fertility problems, what? I mean, they just started trying, so how do they even know if they're going to have problems?"

"I swear, you're worse than us."

"What? How?"

"Gossip Guy. You can't stand not being in the loop."

So he did the Offended Guy look. Because she was exactly right and it was his only defense. "I'm just a concerned friend, that's all. That's what friends do, they look out for one another." And as soon as the words were out of his mouth, he realized the trap he'd walked into.

Her newly tweezed Barbie brows came together in perfect harmony with her arms folding across her chest. How did women do that, anyway?

He took the offensive before she could launch her first volley. "I know you're going to blast me for being in absentia these past couple of weeks, but I've been swamped at work."

"You're always swamped at work. Super-secret spies never tire of obtaining new gadgets to better snoop out the scoop on the bad guys."

"It's a new and dangerous world out there," he said, actually serious.

"So it is. And I'm sure we're glad to have our surveillance needs securely in the hands of your twisted genius. But that has nothing to do with you being a friend to both me and Jana at the same time."

"What needs have I abandoned exactly?" He waved a hand in front of her. "Look at you. You don't need me."

She snorted. "Is that what you think? Really? Come on, I expected better of you. The packaging might be different, but I'm the same Lucy Harper I've always been. And if you think it's been easy adapting to the changes—"

"Wait, wait, wait a minute. Are you saying you don't like the new you? That you wished you'd never gone?" A smug smile began to curve his lips. "Are you saying 'You were right, Grady, and I was wrong,' that superficial changes are shallow and lame?"

She smacked him in the chest.

"Ow," he said, rubbing the spot over his heart. There was symbolism for you.

"Sissy."

"You have bionic arms. Be careful where you wield them."

" 'Shallow and lame,' am I?"

His smug smile turned instantly sheepish. "So that's not what you were saying, then? My mistake."

"Don't get all Pound Puppy on me. You know I have no defense for that."

He stuck out his bottom lip and whimpered.

She swatted at him again, which he easily deflected as she tried hard not to smile. "You're such a loser geek."

"So were you," he said without meaning to.

She sobered instantly. " 'Were'?" Her shoulders slumped. "Is that what this is about? You think I've abandoned you or something? Do you know how ridiculous that is?"

"You've become one of them and you're calling me ridiculous?"

"'Them'?"

"You know, one of the shiny pretty people."

Her eyes lit up. "You think I'm pretty?"

"Oh, for God's sake." He slid off the counter. "You're right, I shouldn't have come over."

"Grady!"

She trailed after him as he walked—okay, stalked—to the door.

"Come on," she cajoled, "don't be a jerk about this. You're the brainiac; why is this so hard for you to comprehend? For God's sake, it's just lipstick and hair!"

He turned abruptly at the door, bracing her shoulders with his hands to keep her from running into him. "What was wrong with staying the way you were?" he blurted out. "Were you really so unhappy that you thought you had to do all this?"

She looked both sad and weary. "I liked who I was on the inside. Was it really so bad for me to want to spruce up the outside a little?"

"You didn't just change the outside. You're . . . different."

"Maybe when you look better, you feel more confident in yourself." She gave a stubborn little shrug, trying to shake him loose.

He didn't take his hands away. "You've always been your own person. It's one of the things I admire about you most. You know who you are and you've always been fine with that. Screw the rest of the world."

"You just described you. Not me. And, well, the world wasn't noticing Lucy Harper. It's hard for someone to get to know who I am on the inside when I can't get their attention in the first place. So I decided to change that."

His heart constricted a little. "And are you getting the attention you wanted?"

"Yeah." She said it a bit defiantly.

And just like that, he got his head back on straight.

"I do want you to be happy," he told her. Then he leaned in and pressed a kiss to her forehead. He swore that wasn't him shaking. "I'll try to have a better attitude."

She closed her eyes and let out a relieved sigh. "Just be my friend." When she looked at him again, her eyes were shining. "That's all I've ever wanted."

"Yeah," he said, his voice suddenly rough. "Me, too."

# Chapter 16

Lucy was supposed to be getting ready for the reunion. God knows, she'd had plenty of notice to plan ahead. And yet, there she was, staring in the mirror, wondering why in the hell she'd ever dreamed she could pull this off.

The dress, the black and slinky number from Lorna's Closet, hung on the back of the door. The come-fuck-me heels leaned seductively against each other on the floor beneath. (Jana had corrected Vivian's terminology, saying, "Nobody calls them CDM pumps." Lucy wasn't sure she was grateful for that.) She was grateful that Grady had seemed to pull his head out of his ass after their little talk two weeks ago. He hadn't come so far as to laud her self-improvement campaign, but he had at least shown up on Pizza Night. They'd reached a détente of sorts. Mostly because of Jana.

Jana had sprung her news on Grady that next day. And every day since then, their world had turned from talk of the reunion and Lucy's conquest thereof, to topics that were loads more fun. Like what breast pump worked best and which monitor could pick up the whimper of a meerkat from five hundred yards away. In a dense jungle.

Okay, so perhaps Grady had taken to the technological aspects of his impending godfatherhood a bit too keenly. But if Grady's nursery suggestions were, in fact, implemented, nothing would ever happen to Little Baby Pelletier that wasn't monitored, scanned, coded, and recorded for posterity.

To be honest, it had been a bit of a relief to have something else to focus on. The ever-exhausting Back-to-School night had come and gone. To her surprise, she'd been hit on by not one, but two of the dads. Only one of them had been single. And though he'd seemed very nice, she'd had to turn him down—dating a student's parent was strictly forbidden.

She smiled. But that didn't mean she couldn't privately gloat over being asked in the first place. Jana thought she should have gone out with him anyway. Called it a "conference lunch" or something. Grady had—well, come to think of it, he hadn't really passed judgment one way or the other. A tactic she just now realized he'd come to use more and more often. Well, she wasn't going to go there tonight. Right now she had more pressing concerns.

Like should she even attempt lip liner when her hands were shaking?

She glanced at the phone, debating for the hundredth time whether she should call Vivian. She wanted to. Vivian had called several times to check up on her over the past month, though the last time she'd been forced to leave a message when Lucy had been kept late at school for a staff meeting.

So she knew Vivian wouldn't mind the plea for a last-minute pep talk. She couldn't call Jana or Grady. They both meant well, and they were her support unit, come thick or thin. But their support in this was a kind of hollow offering. They wanted the best for her, but they really didn't get it. Not the way Vivian seemed to.

Grady invariably changed the subject to the latest developments in nanotechnology or sports. Any sports. Basically any topic Lucy would have no opinion on. Jana didn't exactly leap to her defense, either. In fact, she usually willingly followed Grady's lead.

But she hated to bother Vivian. Especially on a Saturday night. It might have seemed like her godmother was always on the job, at least during Lucy's stay at Glass Slipper, but Vivian had alluded—often—to a very active social life. Which Lucy took to mean "sex life." Whatever the case, she doubted Vivian was at home much in the evenings.

"So, you're on your own," she told her reflection. "Final-exam time is now." Visions of Jason Prescott popped into her head. And she just as quickly shut them out. This wasn't about wooing Jason. Like that was going to happen, anyway. She planned to represent herself better this time around, but she had no grand illusions about how the evening would end. "Just show them Lucy Harper kicks ass, and you'll have aced your exam."

Still, she admitted privately that she wouldn't mind if he at least looked at her like he wanted to throw her over his shoulder and find the nearest bed.

Or wall. Or hallway carpet.

"Oh, for God's sake." Tonight was about proving something to herself. *So why have you turned down the few offers you've gotten for dates in the past couple of weeks, hmm?* Sometimes she hated her little voice.

But she went through the mental exercise anyway. She'd turned down all offers because, after all, she hadn't aced her final yet, right? She'd just felt like she had to see the reunion through, and then she'd be ready to really unleash herself on the world.

God, that was so lame even she wasn't buying it.

Sure, one offer had been from a married man and yet another from a grimy construction worker, and while there had been something of a cheap-thrill factor in eliciting a business card from the former and a catcall from the latter, she'd never considered actually accepting either offer. Just like she couldn't accept dates with her students' dads. But that didn't explain why she'd turned down the guy she'd bumped into—literally—in the Comedy section of Blockbuster. She was still a klutz on occasion—all right, on more than one occasion—especially when she wasn't concentrating on being the New & Improved Lucy Harper. And yet the guy—Todd something or other—had smiled at her and fumbled his way through a few cute ice breakers before asking her if she'd like to get a drink sometime.

Looking back, she should have said yes. I mean, wasn't that at least partly why she'd done all this? To attract attention? He'd been cute enough, and seemed sort of funny in an endearing kind of way. They even had the same taste in movies. Well, his pick had included Adam Sandler, and hers, Harrison Ford. But they were both comedies. "Harmless" had been the adjective that had come to mind at the time. So she told herself she'd learned a valuable lesson. Cute or not, "harmless" didn't turn her on.

"And because men are just throwing themselves at your feet, you can afford to be so damn picky," she told her reflection. She had to stop doing that. She had to put herself out there. So what if he didn't make her pulse race right off, it was still a date. Maybe, even with all the improvements, that was all that was out there for her.

"Well," she told herself, "I guess you'll find out once and for all tonight." She started with the bra and panties, liking how the silk felt against her skin, but paused before putting on what came next. Namely, the matching garter and stockings. She'd tried them on before. Exactly once. But she'd felt so incredibly naughty that she'd giggled the entire time she'd spent wriggling back out of them. She hadn't dared buy herself more of them, despite Vivian's heartfelt sermons on how when a woman wore garters she projected sexual tension. She didn't need to project sexual tension in the classroom, and frankly, she didn't need to in Blockbuster or Safeway, either.

Tonight was different.

Lucy fingered the satin straps and finally unhooked it from its personal little padded hanger. Vivian shopped at places that actually hung up their lingerie on hangers. She tried to imagine opening her closet and shifting through rows of padded hangers as she selected today's underwear. Couldn't do it. Hers were all in a jumble in her dresser drawer. Oh, they might start out perfectly folded and sorted, but, inevitably, one morning of sleeping through her alarm clock and her dresser looked like the white sale at Bloomingdale's. After the sale.

Still, she'd kept this set on its little hanger. And she did have to admit that just looking at it and imagining herself in it raised her pulse rate a few notches.

Lucy gingerly unclipped the strips of slinky satin nothingness. "Here goes nothing." She fastened the hooks in the front, then spun it around so they were in the back, then bent down to slip on the stockings. They were Parisian, pure silk, another Vivian find, with a very thin seam up the back. After three tries, the seam still wriggled up the back of her calves, looking like a map of Rock Creek Parkway.

The stockings were starting to get stretched out and she was losing patience when the phone rang. Sighing in frustration, she strode into her bedroom, garters slapping against her thighs, and yanked up the phone. "Hello," she said, knowing she sounded harried. She *was* harried! She'd had all day, and somehow there was only an hour left and she still had to finish dressing and do her makeup and get out before traffic became a nightmare.

"Darling!"

Lucy slumped in relief. "Vivian. Hi."

"You're sounding vexed, darling. What is the problem? This is your night and you should be shining. I know you will be triumphant."

"At the moment, I can't even triumph over a pair of stocking seams. I'm about two seconds away from another glass of wine and a package of Safeway panty hose."

" 'Panty hose'?" Vivian made the two words sound like some dreadful disease.

"It's the seams. They look like I let one of my students loose with a marker up the backs of my legs."

"Well, then, I suppose it's a good thing I'm here with backup."

Lucy's head swiveled toward her door. " 'Here'? As in—?"

"As in, go open your front door. We're coming up."

" 'We'?" she squeaked, but the line went dead.

Lucy scrambled off the bed, tripped over the CFM pumps, ended up staggering into the bathroom, looking wildly around for something, anything, to cover herself with. Her bathrobe. Where in the hell had she left her bathrobe? Then she remembered she'd had it on earlier in the living room while attempting to paint her own toenails. (Money saved toward the Brazilian.) Major mistake for several reasons. Her toenails looked like they were done by the same eight-year-old who had helped with her stockings. And her coffee table had come dangerously close to a serious polish spill. Fortunately, Jennifer Lopez's breasts had borne the brunt of the disaster. Lucy knew that subscription to *Us* magazine would come in handy someday.

But her bathrobe had sacrificed itself in the name of frugality. That, and L'Oreal Jet-Set Red.

So she grabbed the next best thing. The towel she'd slung over the curtain rod after her shower. It was still damp, and immediately soaked her flimsy lingerie, but it was better than answering the door in peek-a-boo silk.

A brisk knock, followed by a "Yoo-hoo, darling!" sounded at the door. She tossed a frantic gaze at her not-so-tidy apartment, wishing Vivian had given her more notice. Like a week. She could have hired a cleaning service by then. Or moved.

She stopped in front of the door, managed to catch her breath, push her hair out of her face, and attempt at least some semblance of the new sophistication she'd supposedly learned at Vivian's master hand. With one hand firmly clutching the towel knotted between her breasts, she opened the door. "Hi! What are you doing here?"

Vivian's expertly outlined and painted lips spread into an immediate knowing smile. "Darling, you didn't think I'd leave you to the wolves without a last-minute pep talk, now, did you?"

Lucy couldn't even pretend to fake it. She all but wilted against the doorframe, she was so grateful. "I was going to call you, but I wanted to handle this on my own. Shouldn't I be able to do this myself? Isn't that the real test?"

Vivian patted her on the shoulder, then futzed with her hair a little, before smoothly barging her way inside Lucy's apartment. "Darling, life is a series of tests. I've learned never to turn down a helping hand. It's hard enough being a woman in demand. We need all the assistance we can get."

Lucy went to close the door behind Vivian, when someone cleared their throat. She looked into the hall to find not one, but three people standing clustered in front of her door, carrying an assortment of what looked like luggage. "Hi," they all chimed together.

Lucy looked from them to Vivian and back to them. "Hi?" she managed.

The tallest one, a guy who looked like the love child of David Bowie and Sting, spoke first. "'Ello, luv. I've brought along my magic pots. We'll 'ave you ready for the ball in no time." He bustled past her frozen form. "I'll just set up by the windows in the parlor," he said after a quick scan of her apartment. "Best natural lighting there."

"'Magic pots?'" Was she so far gone she required supernatural help? And she hated to break it to him, but the "parlor" he'd referred to was the central room of her entire home.

"I've got your headgear," the next one said. She was elfishly small, with spiky, white-blonde hair and tortoiseshell glasses that, on her pixie face, somehow looked trendy rather than nerdlike.

"'Headgear'?" Lucy repeated numbly as the woman moved past her, pulling a wheeled suitcase. Images of padded helmets floated through Lucy's mind. "I'm really doing much better with the heels," she commented, earning a confused look from both Sting and the elf.

"She's talking about brushes, hot rollers, that sort of thing," the final member of the makeover trio said as he skirted around her, careful not to let the lumpy garment bag he was carrying over his shoulder so much as graze the doorframe. He was wearing leather pants so tight Lucy could see the DNA of his children, and an extremely short haircut that was as black as Spiky Elf's hair was blonde.

"And who are you?" she asked.

"Why, your fairy godmother, of course," he said, his blue eyes twinkling quite devilishly as he swished his hips and tight little tushie.

So, she thought, the stereotype lived. But he was pretty cute.

"What's in the bag?" She bumped the door closed behind her,

still with a death grip on the towel wrapped around her. She looked at Vivian. "I was going to wear the dress we picked out at the consignment store, remember?"

"Of course I do, darling. And every woman needs a drop-dead little black dress, but you'll find many, many uses for that on future dates. When I saw this little frock, I knew it was for this night. For you." Vivian nodded to Swishy Elf, who hung the heavy black garment bag on her bedroom door, then unzipped it with a flourish.

"Voilà!" he said with an extravagant hand gesture that Vanna White would have killed for. "Sex on a hanger!"

Lucy gulped. "It's—it's . . ." Well, she didn't know what it was. There was hardly enough fabric to even qualify it as a dress. She'd thought the plunging neckline and above-the-knee slinkiness of the little black dress was pushing boundaries. This dress never knew boundaries existed.

She looked from the ice-blue, sequiny wisp of nothingness to Vivian. She didn't want to sound ungrateful, nor did she want to offend Vivian. But she couldn't pull that off. Even if she wanted to. Which, of course, she didn't. That dress did not shout Lucy Harper. Old version or new.

That dress shouted Sharon Stone.

"Wait until you see it on," Vivian assured her. "It's positively perfect with your coloring. You'll be drop-dead gorgeous in this, darling. Drop-dead."

"It's Donatella," Swishy Elf added. "That woman knows better than any man how to drape fabric on a woman's body." He looked her up and down. "The more leg, the better. And honey, have you got some leg on you."

Lucy blushed and clamped her arms down more tightly on the towel. "Vivian, really, it's gorgeous. But I—"

"You haven't seen the rest," Swishy announced.

She looked at him. "So that's just the top, then?" Really, it looked like nothing more than a slightly long tank top, held up by two thin silver chains, with another, thinner chain that held it together between the breasts.

Swishy just laughed at her little joke. She wished she'd been joking.

"Look at these," he said, pulling a shoe tote from a Velcro hook inside the garment bag. "On his best day, Manolo could only dream of designing shoes like this."

They were strappy sandals with a clear Lucite heel that was every bit of four inches, tipped in silver at the bottom, with something glittery floating inside the lucite. The sole was trimmed in silver also, with a slender strip of silver leather that cupped the back of her heel, and incredibly slender, sequiny straps that tied around the ankle, matching the narrow sequin-crusted strip that crossed the top of her foot. The color was a perfect match for the dress. In fact, the sequins looked exactly the same.

Swishy must have read her thoughts. "Donatella's new young assistant, Fabricio, designed these personally. Mark my words, he'll be the next Jimmy Choo, and then some."

Lucy realized she was still ogling the sandals—they were really amazing—and jerked her attention back to Vivian. "I can't let you do this."

"Why darling, it's already been done."

"It's too much. And I can't repay you—"

Vivian gave her as maternal a smile as she was capable of, which still came off like a tigress defending her young.

Lucy couldn't deny that for a moment, a very tiny moment, a hot thrill of excitement shot through her. All she had to do was work up the nerve to put it on. "It's really something. I just don't think I can pull that off." She shifted the knot in the front of her towel. "There's nothing holding that dress up, and I sure as hell can't."

Swishy reached into an inner pocket in the bag and pulled out two foam pads and a roll of what turned out to be double-sided tape. "Don't worry, honey, with this we can give you cleavage so you look like Julia Roberts in *Erin Brockovich.*"

Lucy stared at the foam pads, trying not to let her mouth drop open. "I, uh . . ." She glanced at Vivian. "I don't know. It seems a little deceptive. Sort of like false advertising."

Everyone in the room laughed. "Men love the illusion, lovey," Sting said, then wiggled his eyebrows and winked. "Trust me."

She felt her cheeks heat again. "You all are being so nice, and you've gone to so much trouble. I'm amazed you came out to help me like this." She turned to Vivian. "I feel like I'm already so indebted to you. This almost feels like cheating or something."

Vivian came over to her and put her arm around her shoulders, gently nudging her toward her bedroom door. "You don't owe me anything but to go in there tonight and knock them dead." She turned Lucy at the door, bracing her shoulders so she looked her in the eyes. "I know we're known as the godmothers of Glass Slipper, but you've really made me feel like I am one. Watching you transform into such a lovely butterfly has been a very rewarding experience for me." She squeezed Lucy's shoulders. "You've already emerged from your chrysalis. You've arrived, darling. Just let me wave my magic wand and make this one special night perfect for you."

Lucy felt tears gather in the corners of her eyes. "I never thought I'd feel like a princess going to the ball," she said, her voice tight with unshed tears. "But you're sure doing your best to make me feel exactly like that."

Vivian beamed. "That's what I want to hear. Now," she instructed, as if all had been settled, "one last thing before I turn the team loose." She held out her hand and Swishy gave her a slender velvet box. With a smile that was part sly and part avid excitement, she opened the box.

Lucy gasped as the gorgeous icy blue stones of the slender pendant and earring set winked up at her. "Oh, my God."

"I know. Understated, and yet the perfect icing to this little cake." She went on before Lucy could protest. Surely she would have protested such extravagance. "Fred has long been a close friend, so don't worry. He lets me dip into his personal vault all the time."

" 'Fred,' " she repeated. "As in—?"

"Leighton." Vivian smiled. "Old connections are the best ones."

"How much—?" She was stuttering.

Vivian merely patted her on the arm. "You don't want to know dear."

"Wow." She gulped. "That much?"

"Just wear them and enjoy. They'll come alive on you. Now," she pushed Lucy into the bathroom, where Spiky Elf had set up a small salon's worth of utensils. "Off you go, gorgeous."

# Chapter 17

The limo pulled up in front of the Hay-Adams Hotel on Lafayette Square, one of Washington's famous landmarks. With stunning views of the White House and the Washington Monument, the hotel was steeped in history. Aside from its political foundations, it had hosted many famous patrons, from Charles Lindbergh to Ethel Barrymore. Which is precisely why her fellow alumni had chosen it, to be sure. With them, it was all about appearances and bragging rights.

Lucy had felt beyond ostentatious climbing into the stretch limo that had been Vivian's final surprise of the evening. But as they pulled up alongside the structure, with its gorgeously restored Italian Renaissance motif, she felt a tiny bit glad she'd accepted.

"Every princess needs a carriage," Vivian had announced. "I prefer mine sleek and black, with a full bar and a handsome driver." Lucy smiled, remembering Vivian winking at the driver, who was young enough to be Vivian's son. He'd given his employer a cheeky smile in return, at which Vivian had fanned herself and privately confided in Lucy that she "loved a man in uniform. And out of it."

Lucy tried not to let that image into her head, but then again, she wouldn't be surprised if Vivian ended the evening seeing the sights in a private limo tour of her own.

Lucy had had to restrain herself from turning the lights on around the vanity mirror in the rear of the limo to marvel at herself. Or, the self that Vivian's trio of elves had transformed her into. Okay, so she'd had to refrain *after* the first half-dozen times. But honestly. No one was going to recognize her. Her own mother wouldn't know it was her.

Of course, her mother was still reeling a bit from her daughter going blonde. Lucy had been careful not to overwhelm her mom or her dad with her new, updated look. Immersed as they were in the world of academia, they didn't take dramatic change well. For them, reading the business section of the *Post* before doing the crossword—in pen; black, never blue—would be a major upset to their morning routine.

She had told them she was going to a spa for a makeover, but that was pretty much the extent of it. Like most parents, they wanted her to be happy, but fitting in with regular society—aka anything off campus—simply didn't register on their list of concerns. They'd never really understood their only daughter's discomfort and feelings of awkwardness.

"Well, dear, it's quite . . . lively, isn't it?" her mother had said, in reference to her new hair color and style, when she'd met them for dinner a few days after emerging from Glass Slipper.

"They've certainly relaxed the dress code in the public school system," her father had grumbled, hiding behind his menu so he didn't have to see her short skirt.

She'd patiently explained that she didn't wear miniskirts to school, but that, as a young woman, certainly she should be allowed to express herself, fashion-wise, in her private life however she wanted. He'd *harrumphed*, but hadn't said anything. Still, Lucy was pretty sure he spent the entire meal worrying that someone from the university was going to come in and—God forbid—see Lloyd Harper's daughter looking like anything other than the very cliché of a repressed librarian.

Their less-than-relaxing evening had ended—thankfully, with both their professorial reputations still intact—with her mother hugging her and whispering in her ear, "Just tell me you didn't . . . pierce anything."

Lucy still hadn't completely gotten over that one.

The driver got out and she snapped out of her reverie. Game time.

God, she wasn't ready for this. She glanced down and took a quick inventory. Her taped-up breasts appeared evenly spaced and elevated. She still couldn't believe that was her cleavage. Well, hers with a healthy bit of foam padding, anyway. The tiny silver chain that hooked the two narrow front panels of her dress together actually sat away from her skin. *Where had this stuff been when she was in high school?* Awesome.

She smoothed her damp palms down her bare legs. The one consolation prize of the evening was that she didn't have to wear the garter or the stockings. Vivian had been disappointed, and maybe there was a teeny bit of Lucy who felt the same, but ultimately she had enough to worry about tonight. But no matter how smoothly the garter lay against her skin, the slinky little sequin tank dress was too clingy for it not to be noticeable. So she was barelegged. Wearing a thong, no bra, and a dress that weighed about two ounces. Soaking wet.

And diamonds. She couldn't forget the diamonds. She hurriedly tugged the mirror down one last time. Only she didn't check her makeup, or the super-straight, fringy bob her hair had been styled into. She just ogled the discreet but incredibly sparkly diamond-and-aquamarine pendant and dangling earrings she had on.

The driver opened her door.

*Please, God,* she thought, *don't let me humiliate myself.*

Pulling her beaded silk pashmina around her shoulders, thankful the late September weather had been relatively balmy, she smiled at the driver and took his hand as he helped her out of the limo.

"Have a wonderful evening, Ms. Harper," he told her. "I'll be here whenever you depart." He pressed a small pager into her hand. "Just use this and I'll pull around."

"Thank you," she said, her smile beginning to tremble a bit as the immediacy of her situation began to sink in. For a wild second, she was tempted to slide right back into the anonymous privacy of the leather-appointed interior and beg him to circle the block a few more times while she extensively sampled the contents of the fully stocked bar. She wished now she'd taken up Vivian's suggestion of enjoying a glass—or three—of champagne on the ride into D.C. She'd wanted a clear head. At the moment, she couldn't imagine why.

Well, worst case was she'd drink herself into a stupor on the way home. Best way to forget whatever kind of nightmare this evening turned out to be.

Clutching her shawl and the minuscule beaded bag that went with the dress, she took a deep breath, then immediately stopped in midsuck when she realized heaving breaths made for heaving bosoms. This had never once been a consideration for her. She carefully exhaled, so as not to dislodge any tape.

"This is going to be a long night."

Fortunately, no one else was being dropped off at the moment. Studying the sidewalk and carpet for any signs of a crack or wrinkle that would send her sprawling face first onto the lobby floor—not the grand entrance she'd dreamed of—she picked out her path and carefully made her way through the gold-trimmed glass doors.

Focusing on keeping her balance and her boobs inside her dress, she turned and looked around the grandly paneled, beautifully appointed lobby. She could hear a bit of a hubbub coming from somewhere on the other side of the room, so she immediately ducked to the right and hid between a cluster of furniture and a big pillar. The dance, being held in the John Hay Room, had already begun—better to make an entrance, Vivian had assured her—so her former classmates were likely crawling all over the place.

Lucy gripped her handbag, feeling the cell phone inside. She'd already called Jana from the limo. But there had been no answer. Jana had called her earlier in the day to wish her luck and demand a full play-by-play tomorrow over lunch.

Jana had almost sounded sorry she and Dave hadn't RSVP'd just so they could watch her take Jason Prescott and the rest of the gang down. Lucy would have loved the moral support of having her best friend close by, but she'd known from the beginning she was in this on her own. And frankly, if Jana had come with her, they'd have either spent the entire night in the bathroom, or, with the last-minute attack of chickenitis she was presently having, she'd likely have let her best friend talk her out of the whole thing. But that didn't mean she couldn't use a lifeline right about now.

She toyed with the idea of calling Grady, but decided against it. It bothered her that she couldn't share this moment with him. Not that he'd fully comprehend the princess-at-the-ball aspect of the evening, but in the past he would have made some kind of observational comment that would have put the ridiculousness of the event into the kind of detached perspective she badly needed. Now she wasn't sure what kind of comment—

thinly veiled or not—she'd get. So she didn't risk it. And that saddened her.

She smiled and shook her head when a bellhop motioned to her, asking if she needed help. She shifted so she could see the room—and not be ambushed off guard—but remained far enough in the corner so no one would notice her, then pulled her cell phone from her bag. That's when she noticed that something else had been tucked in with the new lipstick, her ticket for the dance, and the few bills she'd folded in earlier. She kind of liked the idea that with a limo, not only didn't she need her car keys, she didn't need her ID, either. It lent a sort of anonymous freedom to the evening. Add the dress and the hair, and she felt like a woman of mystery. She wanted to embrace that vibe, make it work for her. But first she needed a pep talk.

She punched in Jana's cell phone number and pulled out the little folded packets, thinking Vivian might have put in hand wipes or something. "Come on, please pick up," she murmured, letting the packets unfold. Her gasp drew the attention of the bellhop. His lips twitched as she quickly folded the condom packets and turned her back to him. "Thanks, Vivian," she muttered, even as she stifled her own urge to snicker.

Jana's voice mail kicked in just then and Lucy was forced to leave a brief SOS. Of course, once she was inside the ballroom, with the music blaring, she'd be lucky to hear herself think, much less her cell phone ringing. She'd just have to check it. Often. It would give her something to do besides stare down in awe and wonder at her newly formed cleavage.

With that thought, butterflies in her stomach, and a knowing smile from the bellhop, Lucy edged her way through the lobby until she spied a table set up outside the ballroom. All the name badges were lined up on the table, waiting for the guests to claim them. Lucy had visions of pinning her badge on with pride, then striding into the ballroom, head held high.

She did not have visions of mincing her way through the lobby, worried about tripping on the rug, which would send her, boobs flailing, into the ballroom. And yet that was exactly what she was doing. Disgusted with her lack of conviction, she boldly removed her pashmina, then had to fight not to ball it up and clutch it between her overexposed, double-taped breasts.

*Some femme fatale you're turning out to be.* She draped her shawl over her arm, took a steadying breath, and proceeded past the registration desk. "Inner rhythm," she whispered, over and over.

A small group was moving up to the table ahead of her. Lucy instinctively ducked back behind a potted plant and plastered her back against the side wall. She swallowed a little yelp as her bare back hit the cold marble. She peeked around the foliage and realized she didn't recognize any of the people at the table. They all grabbed their badges, chatting and laughing as they moved en masse toward the double doors leading into the ballroom. The woman manning the table, whom Lucy didn't recognize either, walked over to open the ballroom doors and ended up stepping inside for a moment. Seizing the now-or-never moment, Lucy took fast little scuffy steps toward the table and quickly scanned the alphabetically ordered badges.

To her horror, each badge was plastered with a name and senior-yearbook photo. While she appreciated the reasoning behind the idea—God knew, she hadn't recognized a single person yet—the idea of pinning that horrible picture to her newly plumped up and blush-enhanced breast . . . well, no. Sure, the looks on people's faces when they glanced from her badge to her Lucy Harper 2.0 face would be momentarily gratifying, but there was a sort of National Zoo exhibit feel to the whole idea that was suddenly repugnant to her. She wanted to wow people, but she wanted to do it in her own way. On her own terms.

So she quickly stashed the badge in her tiny purse, and when the woman manning the table stepped out of the ballroom, Lucy flashed her a fast grin, shoved her ticket at her, then ducked inside before the woman could stop her.

Once inside she automatically sidled to the left and back against the wall. Once a wallflower, always a wallflower. But there was security there by the wall, out of the spotlight, a moment to catch her breath, to rally her will, and to make sure her boobs were still pointing in the same direction.

"Okay, showtime." She closed her eyes briefly and pulled up images of her dance lessons with Arturo. The disc jockey working the reunion dance was playing Tears for Fears, which wasn't helping her much. Then, as if it was a sign from God—or her godmother, which would have surprised her less—the song abruptly changed to an early nineties hip-hop anthem. Not her first choice, or even her hundred and first, but she could follow the downbeat.

Words she'd never thought to utter slipped past her lips. *"Thank you, Vanilla Ice."* Keeping her eyes closed, focusing on the beat, letting it sink in, connecting to the pulse of it. She let her hips sway a little, singing, "Ice, ice, baby" under her breath until she finally worked up the nerve to lift her chin, stand straighter, even thrust her chest out a little. She owned this song. She owned this room. She could do this!

Then she opened her eyes and saw the throngs of her former classmates filling the dance floor.

Sure. She could do this. Right after she had a drink. A very stiff drink.

Her ticket came with two free-drink coupons. She wondered if they'd let her use them both at once for a double. However, inner rhythm or no inner rhythm, she was pretty sure her heels came with only so many stumble-free steps in them. Alcohol would probably reduce that number dramatically.

She stared at the writhing masses, thinking that right there in front of her was pretty much everyone who had made fun of her all through her years in the public school system. The girls who had made fun of her klutzy lack of coordination in grade-school gym class. The guys who called her up in middle school only to ask her if she could do their homework, or get the phone number of the current babe-of-the-week. Like she would know.

The same group who had laughed at her the night of the prom.

Her stomach lurched, and she was glad she hadn't had any champagne. Or dinner. She pulled her phone out and punched the DISPLAY button, but no call from Jana. "Shit."

Well, she told herself, it would mean more if she did this on her own, right? She'd show her former classmates and her current best friends what she was made of. And herself, while she was at it.

God, she wanted to throw up.

Then she thought of it from a different perspective. Because the thing about that prom-night fiasco was, she could hardly go down in anyone's estimation. Reading the loop, it was clear how much everyone was trying to prove they'd maintained their level of cool into adulthood. This was pressure she didn't share. In fact, anything she did here tonight was likely to be a major step up. She already looked better. So basically, all she had to do was not make a spectacle and she'd come out ahead.

The music segued from Vanilla Ice to MC Hammer. Filled with renewed determination, she straightened away from the wall.

"You're damn right you can't touch this," she muttered, and marshaling every bit of nerve she had, she tossed her hair back, pointed her Austin Powers fembot boobs forward, and plunged into the throng.

She immediately slipped a tiny step, almost upending an entire tray of canapés. Two waiters swung smoothly away before she could take them out. She mercifully got her balance back before she went down herself, but just barely. Cheeks flaming, she inched her way to the edge of the room. *A wallflower once more.*

The very thought gave her the courage to begin carefully edging her way around the room. It wasn't exactly plunging headlong into the crowd, but it was a step up from hiding by the door.

She took her time and made a complete circuit, and though she'd gotten a few glances, even a few downright leering ogles, everyone was so caught up in excited conversations with their long-lost classmates, no one *really* noticed her. There were no gasps. No pointed fingers. No whispered "Oh, my Gods" as she trolled the alley created between the large round tables set up around the perimeter of the dance floor, and the wall, which ran parallel to the busier, more heavily peopled dance floor table lane. She'd work her way up to navigating that one. And it was possible no one noticed her because she was mostly walking behind their backs. Nor was she making direct eye contact. At least not on purpose.

Still, she hadn't tripped or fallen out of her dress once. And for the moment, she rather liked being one of the anonymous. No badge, no way anyone could know who she really was. Sort of like Clark Kent in a dress. She used her "disguise" to drift again around the table track, and shamelessly listened in on snippets of conversations. Eventually, she planned to attempt to join in one or two. Right after she worked up the nerve to make eye contact.

After lap three, she admitted she wasn't any closer to doing that than when she'd started. She'd recognized a few people by now, but had not the first clue what to say to any of them. "Hi, I'm Lucy Harper. You remember me, the one whose gym uniform you stuffed in the locker-room toilet in sixth grade?" Or,

"Hi, it's me, Lucy Harper. You know, the one who did your science homework for two years, but whom you pretended was invisible if I so much as made eye contact with you in the halls?"

Somehow, they just didn't seem like the ice breakers she was looking for.

So she began looking in earnest for her ultimate quarry.

Because, while it would be gratifying to have a Carrie-like moment—sans all the blood, of course . . . well, maybe there could be a little blood—where she'd have the complete and utter attention of everyone in the room as she told them where they could stuff their insufferable egos, catty criticisms, and condescending, bullying, mean-spirited bullshit, the truth was, there was only one person she really wanted to blow away tonight.

The rumor buzzing about the room was that he was still godlike and had shown up wearing Armani. How hard could it be to find a six-foot-five god in a two-thousand-dollar tux?

Towering, tux-clad gods, however, seemed to be in unfortunate abundance. Mostly spousal gods, as far as she could tell. Apparently the Debbie Markhams of the world still had all the luck.

Of course, in some cases, a tuxedo, no matter the designer, hadn't been a wise fashion option. She'd accidentally bumped into a now beer-bellied Buddy Aversom, cinched into a severely strained cummerbund, with a too-tight bow tie that looked like it was trying to pinch his head off at the neck. A visual, she was sad to say, she actually spent a few moments savoring. Fortunately, even up close, he hadn't recognized her. She liked to think it was because the Glass Slipper transformation had been so complete that all her former classmates were presently whispering behind their hands, wondering who the hot, Amazon goddess in the sequin dress and fabulous designer heels was.

It was a nice fantasy. And it gave her the necessary strength to continue trolling. Nametag still tucked inside her purse, she scoped out the thickening crowd and let her imagination spin out on how their little reunion would play out. Of course, without her name tag, he'd never recognize her. So, should she simply introduce herself right off? No, no. Better to tell him after they'd finished their first dance. He would be all but drooling over her by then, right? Or her boobs, anyway. Whatever.

She was deep into her little fantasy now, picturing the immensely satisfying look of complete shock on his face when he realized the hot chick with the tan tits was dorky old Lucy Harper. That moment, of course, would be followed by a stuttered yet very sincere apology for how badly he'd treated her that long-ago night . . . maybe there would be some begging involved at that point, she wasn't entirely sure. And she hadn't forgotten the condoms in her purse. While she'd never been a sex-on-the-first-date kind of girl—okay, so no one had exactly begged her to have sex on the first date—every rule had an exception.

All she knew was that if she wanted to ace this final test, she was going to have to make him sweat. One way . . . or the other.

Her fantasy scenario then took a decidedly R-rated turn. She was quite vividly imagining him begging her for just the chance to be the one who took her home tonight, when someone politely tapped her on the shoulder.

"Hi, there."

Startled from her reverie by both the warm touch grazing her bare skin, and the deep timbre of the voice, she spun around, wobbled badly, and had to grab onto the owner of said deep voice to keep from going down. "Sorry," she said, flustered, trying to quickly regain her balance. She dug her fake, French-tipped nails into the sleeves of a very expensive-looking tux. Just as impressive were the big, taut biceps beneath the finely woven fabric. *Wow.* Her heart rate kicked up a few notches, which made letting him go that much harder. After a few more gravity-negotiating moments, she finally managed to release her death grip and stand on her own two spikes.

The initial rush of attraction was compounded further when she found herself having to look up—up! even in four-inch heels!—to see who she'd wobbled into. Until her gaze collided with the intense blue eyes of the one looking back down at her. Then her heart stopped completely.

She didn't need a yearbook photo to recognize those eyes. She'd seen them often enough in her dreams.

Jason Prescott was officially in the building.

And he'd found her first. *Shit.*

All of her carefully planned conversation starters evaporated into the ether. Or the subtle scent of his aftershave. Whatever. Along with her highly detailed fantasy scenario. Which she'd been totally insane to believe for one second would ever happen to her. Leaving her able to do little more than stand there, gaping at him. In all her carefully calculated planning, never once had it occurred to her that he would track her down. Honestly, Glass Slipper reincarnation or not, her karma just wasn't that good.

She knew for sure she was hallucinating now when he sketched a slight bow, offered her his arm, and in a voice that had only gotten deeper and more incredibly male, said, "Care to dance?"

She looked behind her, half expecting to see Debbie Markham and the rest of the varsity cheerleading squad tittering behind their real French manicures while they waited for the punch line of what was surely a ghastly joke about to play itself out. Except there was no one behind her. She was standing in a corner. But another furtive glance proved there was no one standing behind him, either. At least, no one who was paying any attention to them. Yet. That would surely change if she took his arm and stepped out onto the dance floor.

Desire warred with common sense. And she didn't have much of a handle on either at the moment. Her whole entry strategy had been to get his attention, then set him on his heels. Only she hadn't counted on him knocking her back on hers first. She'd expected to feel nothing more than cold and calculating vengeance as she went about taking him down. It was all about making him want her. She'd sort of overlooked the fact that she might want him. She wasn't counting on the clammy palms, the racing heart. Okay, so she might have expected a little of that, but that would have just been due to nerves from facing down her enemy.

Not because she wanted to strip her enemy naked and beg him to take her up against the nearest wall.

Christ. She was *so* not equipped to handle this.

Then another thought occurred to her. *Duh!* No badge. He didn't know who she was! She still had the edge. She just wished like hell it felt that way. In the end, all she managed to do in the face of his questioning, attentive, and incredibly sexy gaze, was nod in the affirmative. With what had to be a stupidly glazed look on her face. But they were making their way to the dance floor, weren't they? She was still in this. She'd just have to reformulate her plan of attack while they danced.

More tentatively than she'd hoped for, she laid her hand on his offered arm. He grinned, the same blinding white, perfect smile that beamed out at her from the yearbook photo pinned to his jacket lapel, and covered her hand with his own. She almost swooned right then and there. *Get a grip.* She couldn't lose it just from a brush of his fingers on hers. Not if she had any hopes of completing her plan. Although, at the moment, there was a part of her that felt pretty damn complete.

The DJ was playing a song that was just slow enough so that he held her hand and put his other hand on her waist . . . but not sappy enough that he pulled her close. Where she might have pressed her cheek to that broad chest, inhaled the scent of his cologne, and lost herself in the fantasy completely. Only the fantasy was real. Living, breathing, just-like-in-the-movies real.

She had to stop this. Right now. If Jana were here, she'd be rolling her eyes in disgust at this very shallow display of, well, absolute shallowness. All of Lucy's endless talk about how this was all about her personal emancipation and not nailing Jason Prescott . . . would be pretty hard to defend at the moment.

*Good thing Jana didn't come after all, then, isn't it?* her little voice whispered. Her wicked, wicked little voice. *No one is going to know what goes on here tonight but you. You . . . and Jason Prescott!*

She bravely tried to shut her little voice out. *Focus on the plan!* Right now she should be shifting back a polite space, just enough to allow him the obvious ogling opportunity. She'd wait for him to leer down at her perfectly plumped-up breasts, then dip her chin just enough so that he realized she'd caught him looking. While his cheeks turned an endearing shade of red, she'd gaze ever so coolly into his big, blue eyes and make some perfectly slice-worthy remark about "my, how times had changed if he couldn't do any better than be reduced to begging dorky old Lucy Harper for a dance."

Except in the real world, her cheeks were frozen in a perma-grin as she stared at some vague point beyond his shoulder. What was worse, she couldn't seem to unstick it long enough to make even the most banal kind of mindless dance-floor conversation. The music was too loud for talking, anyway. At least that was the reason she gave herself for not trying harder.

After. After the dance was over and they floated over to the bar for a drink, then she'd spring her cleverly worded set-down on him.

Hopefully by then she'd have thought one up.

And be past the pathetic "Oh, my God, Jason Prescott is

touching me!" phase, having ascended to something resembling actual maturity.

Her thoughts veered wildly as the music played on . . . and on. From *Please, dear God, don't let me step on his toes,* to *How can I get him to stay with me when the song is over?,* to *Is the air getting a whole lot warmer in here or is it just my pounding heart making me hot?*

The song ended before she was ready, but thankfully segued into another slow song. He just kept on dancing. She didn't stop him. Halfway through, she finally dared a glance at his face, and flashed what was probably a totally gawky smile at him when she discovered he was looking at her. Her cheeks heated and she looked away again. Perma-grin firmly in place.

By the time the second song came to an end, she knew she had to do something to break this spell she seemed to be under, or she'd never be able to live with herself after this night was over. But then the third song started. And it was, in all improbability, Seal's "Kiss from a Rose."

The song that was her song, that she'd been so sure on prom night was going to be Their Song. Finally really was. Not even Jana could say that wasn't a huger-than-huge honkin' sign.

She looked into his eyes again. Only this time she didn't look away. And neither did he. For the duration of the song, she swore her feet never touched the ground. Nor did her heart stop pounding. And she couldn't seem to care.

By the end she felt like she was glowing. Then belatedly realized the glistening sensation was actually from perspiration. Hers. And suddenly all she could think was *Please, God, let two-sided tape be waterproof!*

Why hadn't she asked Vivian the important questions?

No matter what song came on next, she knew she had to call a halt to this magical moment before she embarrassed herself. Or exposed herself. It had been too perfect up to that point to chance ruining it. And her fantasy bubble didn't have to burst just because they'd stopped dancing, did it? Of course not. She just needed some air.

Wait! Maybe she could get him to take her for a romantic walk on the roof terrace! The invitation had clearly said they'd have full and exclusive access, complete with magnificent views of Washington under the stars.

Jana's imaginary look of disgust chose that moment to surface in her mind. Yes, okay, she was supposed to be looking for the right moment to cut him to the quick. And she would. Really. But would it throw her plans off so much if she sort of enjoyed his company first? Just for a little while? I mean, wasn't that a kind of revenge, too?

At the moment, what was important was to keep him from disappearing on her. To do that, she was actually going to have to speak.

The DJ announced a short break. Her perfect cue. Another sign. She swished her hair a little, mostly to get a slight breeze along the damp nape of her neck, then offered him what she hoped was a scintillating smile, and . . . said nothing. Even the soles of her feet felt sweaty now. Which, in four-inch spikes, was just begging for disaster.

Paranoia set in, and she quickly waved her hand in front of her face like a fan, then tilted her head in the vague direction of the doors. She tried not to be obvious about her huge sigh of relief when he smiled easily and said, "Would you like to get some air? I understand we have the use of the rooftop terrace."

It was like their minds were one! All she had to do was nod and he understood. Then he put that wide, warm palm on her lower back and she had to use all of her concentration not to slide right out of her heels and her thong panties as they crossed the room. She couldn't even say if anyone was paying attention to them. Her gaze was focused like a tractor beam on the doors, which they were taking an agonizingly long time to reach.

But surely the whispers were starting now that the music was over and everyone was just standing about. Jason Prescott was always the center of attention. Which meant she was now the center of attention. Because she, Lucy Harper, was officially *with* Jason Prescott.

She wobbled a little just then, and he moved up and slid his hand smoothly around her waist, pulling her lightly to his side. "Careful there."

Oh, God! At this rate she was going to dissolve into a puddle of gooey, lust-filled mush before they ever reached the terrace. So freaking pathetic. But, damn, the man smelled good. And he felt even better. It had been forever since she'd been this turned-on.

Okay, okay, so she'd never been this turned-on. Not when she was actually *with* the man in question, anyway. She had to refrain from doing a little happy dance right there, sweat or not.

She was finally getting her *bam!* moment! And it was *exactly* how she thought it would be. Or hoped it would be. She'd take one look at Mr. The Right One, and, *bam!*, that would be all it would take.

And as Jason Prescott, aka Mr. The Right One—and really, hadn't she always known?—moved in front of her to open the door, looking down—down!—long enough to grace her with that perfect smile, she finally admitted her original plan was toast.

# Chapter 18

The autumn night air felt lovely, and as Jason guided her to the quiet, unpopulated end of the terrace, she worked hard to stay calm and collected.

Having given up formulating the ultimate put-down, she could focus on other, more important things. *Don't blow it now. Say something clever. Do that sexy hair flip. Entice him with your perfectly modulated laugh.*

She hadn't exactly mastered that last one. Last two. Okay, so she couldn't do any of them. But she couldn't stop wishing she could. This was her moment. Finally, all the stars were lining up just right for Lucy Harper. And if she was really lucky, she was going to get kissed beneath every single one of them.

Every rule that Vivian had taught her rolled through her mind in a hopeless jumble. All she could think about was the way the palm of his hand had slid to that spot, right at the center of her lower back. So gentle, but so strong. His step was easy, but sure. Lucy swore she felt the tension spiking between them the farther they drifted away from the terrace tables to a quiet spot by the railing. Unable to stand the suspense a moment longer, she turned to tell him—something. Anything. Now that she was finally here, she couldn't wait a second longer to reach the moment she'd waited for her entire life.

She was saved from whatever moment-ruining thing she might have said when, at the exact same moment, Jason pulled her into his arms. Again, their thoughts were as one! Her head tipped back, his bent down. Their eyes met for a split second, then hers drifted shut as his mouth descended to hers, ending in a kiss that could only be described as fairy-tale magical.

His lips were warm and firm. His kiss confident, if not exactly bold. She didn't care. Jason Prescott was kissing her! And he'd initiated everything! She hadn't had to flip her perfectly straightened hair, bat one lengthened and separated eyelash, or laugh at any of his jokes, in a well-modulated tone or not.

Her fingers slid up his chest, sinking into the delicious bunching of muscle at his shoulders. She tilted her head and was just debating on whether she should open her mouth—just a little, nothing too forward or desperate—to let him know she'd be okay with a deeper kiss, when he broke contact and lifted his head.

She blinked her eyes open, but nothing seemed to want to come into focus. Was the world spinning? Or was it just her?

"Wow."

Had she blurted that out? She quickly tried to force her scattered thoughts and emotions into some semblance of normalcy. Ha. Fat chance. She'd just been kissed senseless by Jason Prescott. Surely she was allowed a kind of stunned "wow."

Except she was pretty sure that "wow" had been uttered in a distinctly deeper voice. Which meant . . . She blinked again, and her heart pounded even more furiously. She finally brought

Jason's smiling face into focus, and though it was indulgently smug to even think it, she could swear he looked a little stunned. She smiled at him. Okay, so it might have been a full-out loopy grin. There might have even been a little drool. She couldn't be sure. Nor could she seem to care. Not only had Jason Prescott kissed her, her kiss had rated a slightly stunned "wow"!

She'd done it! Well, she and Vivian and a staff of highly trained professionals. Which was when she had her first breath of reality.

He'd gone for the fantasy of Lucy Harper. Not the real Lucy Harper. What happened if—could she be that lucky!—he asked to see her again. Or, God forbid, offered to take her home?

Suddenly it was like the condoms in her purse were radioactive. She felt a distinct disturbance in the atmosphere by their mere proximity. She had made it through the kiss without incident, but that didn't mean she was ready for anything that might require any kind of discussion regarding birth control. Much less the actual use thereof.

*Okay, Lucy, plan, plan.* But Jason was staring at her with a look that had all the hallmarks of desire—hooded gaze, intent focus. Yes, this was a man contemplating another kiss. And she hadn't had time to correctly analyze the first one. Moments like this didn't come along every day for her. Or even every year. In fact, putting this into the once-in-a-lifetime category probably wasn't overstating things. So she could hardly risk being spontaneous about it, now, could she?

She needed to buy a few moments to collect herself, to get her act together and reformulate her entire strategy. She did the first thing she could think of. She fanned her face a little—yes, it was lame, but it was all she had in her trick box at the moment. Besides, it had worked before! She could only hope he thought it was his kiss that had her overheating. When, in reality, it had been the mercifully brief vision she'd had of him taking off that tux . . . then patiently waiting for her to get out of this dress.

Was there a seductive way to peel off double-sided tape?

"I—I could use something to drink." She recalled seeing a bar set up on the opposite end of the terrace.

"Certainly," he said, his perfect White Knight teeth gleaming. "Wait right here."

Her ploy worked a little too well, however, as she found herself altogether too quickly abandoned at the terrace railing. Maybe she should have attempted at least a moment or two of clever banter. "Right, because the witty bon mots were just waiting to trip off your tongue." "Trip" being the key word, most likely.

But instead of bemoaning her suddenly single status, she would use these critical minutes to figure out how she wanted the evening to go. Then come up with a plan to make that happen. "Sure," she muttered beneath her breath. "Right after I solve the world energy crisis and bring peace to the Middle East." Once a nerd, always a nerd.

They had yet to actually have even the bare minimum of a conversation. Surely he planned to talk to her. In between more kisses, that is. She shivered a little at the thought of his mouth on hers again. She'd never dreamed that—

"Didn't your fairy godmother tell you never to leave home without your cape?"

Lucy jerked her head around at the familiar voice. "Hey! What are you doing here?"

Grady stood before her, wearing a retro 1980s tuxedo-print T-shirt and a loosely constructed black suit jacket, holding the beaded shawl she must have dropped somewhere between the ballroom and the terrace.

"Coming to the rescue of a damsel in distress?" he said, offering her the silk wrap.

He had that same wry twist of the lips of the Grady of old. And for a split second, her entire being seemed to settle down and relax. Except Grady hadn't been her sanctuary lately. And as much as she wanted to hide in the shelter of his confident charm, she resisted. Wasn't tonight all about learning to stand on her own two feet?

She took the shawl from him and smiled briefly. "Thanks." She prayed he disappeared before Jason came back. He hadn't recognized her yet, but he might remember Grady. She didn't want him putting two and two together until she had a better handle on what was happening between the two of them. Seeing her together with Grady, he of the curly mop of hair that hadn't changed much since his senior-year photo, which she noted he hadn't pinned to his lapel, either, might trigger some latent memories. None of them good. She wanted to build a few more current ones before risking dredging up any ancient ones. If she ever did.

Plus, Grady wasn't always known for observing a proper sense of decorum. If he thought action should be taken, he took it. If something needed to be said, he said it. And damn the consequences. So there was no telling what he'd do when he found out who she was with. Especially after her repeated insistences that she was here for herself, not to land Jason Prescott.

Which meant she had to get rid of him. The irony. After wanting him to be there for her these past couple of months, when he finally came through, she couldn't wait for him to disappear. She told herself she'd make it up to him later, explain everything. That is, if she could. She just wanted this one fairy-tale night. Was that too much to ask?

"I, uh, I thought you wouldn't be caught dead at a, how did you phrase it? 'An event that glorifies the age-old coda of class distinction and the importance of being popular through the ages.' "

Grady shrugged, gave her his most endearing, puppy-dog look. What most people missed was the wry, twisty lip smile thing. Always a sign to never fall for the puppy-dog part. Women never seemed to get that about Grady. Of course, she wasn't sure Grady cared all that much. The puppy-dog look had its bonuses, as well, apparently.

"Jana made me."

Lucy's eyes widened. "She did not!"

The twisty smile grew. "Well, no. But she lobbied awfully hard. She was actually planning to come. With Dave. As a surprise to you. And maybe a collective finger to our lovely graduating class."

The three of them had discussed, early on when the invites had first arrived, the pros and cons of attendance. On the pro side was the fact that Jana was both a well-respected journalist now, and she happened to be married to an even more well-known local icon, the Capitals' goalie. This would have given her instant entrée into the inner circle they'd so coveted in their stupid formative years.

They'd even debated on how, once Jana was firmly ensconced, she'd bring in Lucy and Grady, then make some scathingly grand social commentary on how shallow they all still were, to hold job titles and marital status higher than personal truths and real friendship.

Ultimately they'd discarded their plans for global reunion domination. Mostly because Jana didn't need to make a scene that might be overheard, or, God forbid, photographed, and elevate their little-known event into the national eye. She didn't need to be quoted in the gossip column of her very own paper.

Grady hadn't wanted to go at all. Which left Lucy to make the decision on her own. So as much as she appreciated the Musketeerian show of support, she also kind of resented the idea that, in the end, her friends had thought she couldn't handle it on her own.

"She's still having a really hard time with her round-the-clock morning sickness. So she blackmailed me, instead."

Lucy smiled despite her mild annoyance. "Oh? I didn't realize she had 'blackmail' material on you. I see we're going to have to have a little talk."

Something flitted across Grady's face, a brief expression of . . . well, she couldn't really name it. But it hadn't been positive. "She'd probably appreciate the visit," he said.

What went unsaid, but was well heard, was the attendant, "when you can find time to squeeze her in."

Lucy knew her obsession with tonight had caused her to exclude her friends more than she'd have liked to. But if they'd been more supportive, maybe she wouldn't have felt like she had to. They didn't want to know all about her plans. So she hadn't felt inclined to share the details with them. She'd just have to defend them, and frankly, she was a little tired of it.

For a split second she thought that maybe it would be a good idea if Jason were to stroll back to her just then, after all. Show Grady, who would certainly tell Jana, that she could hold her own. That in fact, not only had she not embarrassed herself tonight, she'd landed the very available, much-talked-about former prom king as her dance partner and up-on-the-roof kissing partner. One she wanted to reclaim before any more of her perfect evening was wasted. Speaking of which, where was Jason, anyway?

She surreptitiously glanced beyond Grady's shoulder. "Well, tell Jana I really appreciate her concern from afar. And her sending in the Black Knight to do her dirty work. But I'm holding my own just fine, thank you very much." She'd meant to say that last part with a smiling sense of reassurance. Perhaps it had come out a bit more defensive than that.

Grady's expression had faltered a bit at the Black Knight comment. He looked her up and down for the first time. And in that one look Lucy felt every bit the imposter they both knew she was tonight. Any charitable sense of kinsmanship she'd felt she owed him fled in that second. How dare he come here and try to ruin her night when he knew how much it meant to her? No matter whether he believed in it or not.

"You do look amazing, Cinderella," he said. And she was momentarily caught off guard by the almost sincere-sounding note in his voice, the hint of what had sounded a lot like awe. She'd been prepared for acerbic. For dry. Maybe even sarcastic. His expression had telegraphed as much, after all.

So she didn't answer right away. She fidgeted for a moment. Suddenly feeling like Lucy Harper, circa senior year. The tape was itchy. And these heels were killing her arches. Her calves were knotting up from the unbalanced gravitational pull she was placing on them. Plus her thong might need to be surgically removed at this point. Not one of these things had occurred to her the entire time she was with Jason. She'd been floating on air.

She wanted to float again, dammit.

"Thanks. I, uh, I need to go see what happened to my date," she finally stammered, then tried not to look mortified that she'd given it away, so inelegantly, after all her worrying and to-and-fro-ing.

" 'Date'?"

He'd said it with surprise. And she could hardly blame him. After all, he better than anyone knew she hadn't had one when she'd shown up tonight. But it hit her the wrong way. As if she couldn't land a date. Even looking like a princess. And she blasted him before she could stop herself. "Yes. Date. The kind who asks for a dance. Holds me like I'm priceless piece of china. Kisses like a dream. And is presently fetching me a little libation."

"'Kiss'? You kissed someone?"

How dare he look outraged? He wasn't her keeper. "Yes. I did," she shot back, very satisfied with the look of surprise on his face at her heated response. "Dorky Lucy Harper landed herself a hottie. Hard as that might be for you to believe."

"I didn't mean it that way."

But she wasn't hearing him now. She was finally delivering the set-down she'd come here to deliver. Only never in a million years did she think she'd be delivering it to the one person who was her champion in high school, rather than the hordes who had been her enemies.

"No," she spat. "Of course you didn't. You only ridiculed me the entire way through this whole preparation thing. You've refused to listen to why this is so important to me, much less even try to understand."

His surprised look faded. But she didn't notice that it wasn't remorse that filled his expression now. That it was, in fact, quite shuttered from exposing any expression at all. "Lucy, I'm—"

"I know you don't want to hear this, Grady. But I did it. I came here tonight to find out something about myself, and I did. I held my own. Lucy Harper finally arrived." So what if no one knew that was who she was? Or that she'd yet to actually talk to any of them? That was hardly the point. Besides, she was on a roll. "And to cap it off, I've managed to catch the eye of the one person I wanted to notice me. And let me tell you, he's noticed me."

Grady's face might as well have been carved in stone at that point. "Prescott is your date?"

"He is," Lucy crowed, only the announcement didn't feel quite as victorious as she'd hoped. Probably because Grady wasn't giving her the pleasure of looking appropriately chastened. In fact, he looked downright pissed. Fine, let him be pissed. "And he's been a perfect gentleman. I know you don't like what he did to me all those years ago. Neither do I. But people change. We were kids then." And why in the world was she defending herself?

"So, I take it he's apologized, then?"

The quietly asked question caught her badly off guard. Dammit. "I—uh—" Just then she spied Jason's blond godliness towering over the clusters of people who had been steadily drifting up to the rooftop. "There he is," she gushed, more relieved for the escape than anything else. Feeling a moment of remorse for how badly she'd treated her best friend, she looked back at him. "Listen, I do appreciate that you came all the way down here to protect me," she told him with utmost sincerity.

His hard-as-granite façade didn't crack. Not even a tiny fissure. She felt more sad than mad at this point. It was like they'd been traveling toward this moment ever since she'd decided to come to this dance. And now that it was here, she wished, almost desperately, that nothing had ever changed and everything was still the same between them. She wasn't even exactly sure why it wasn't. They didn't always agree with everything the other one did, but this . . . this had been different. And she was at a loss to fully understand why.

All she knew was that from this moment on, it was likely that nothing would ever be the same between them again. And for that she was truly and sincerely sorry. But she wasn't going back. Not that she could really, even if she wanted to.

She reached out, briefly touched his arm. "Maybe I don't need rescuing anymore," she told him softly. "But that doesn't mean I don't need a friend."

Grady glanced down at her hand on his arm, then back up at her as she let it fall away. He said nothing.

Lucy saw Jason weaving through the small clusters of people. She desperately wanted to end this before he arrived. This was hard enough without adding what would surely be a disastrous finale to the crumbling of a lifelong friendship. "I—I have to go," she told him.

"I think you already have," he said, then turned and walked away.

She watched him depart, his mop top and lanky height making him easy to spot as he wove through the crowd without so much as a pause. Lucy didn't know if it was by accident or design, but for the narrow space involved, Grady had taken the only path clear to him that removed any chance he'd bump into Jason. Either way, for that final gesture, she was grateful.

It was only when he ducked inside and she was left to face the rest of her evening on her own again that she had a mad, almost overwhelming impulse to run after him. She'd beg his forgiveness, then plead with him to stick around in case things went south and she needed him. Which was so utterly selfish an impulse, it stopped her cold.

Had she always been so self-centered and needy where he was concerned? Honestly, she didn't think so. At least, not any more than normal close friends were with one another. After all, everyone needed somebody they could be a complete bitch with. And she was luckier than most; she had two of them. But in all fairness, she'd been there for him, too. And for Jana. Okay, maybe not that much of late. But Jana was all wrapped up in her impending motherhood, about which Lucy was so clueless, she could hardly do anything more than listen as Jana went on and on about the trials and travails of interviewing the newest rookie drafted to the Wizards while trying to keep down her saltines and sour balls. The candy, not the drink.

And Grady . . . well, he was wrapped up in his work. Even more than usual. Sure, Lucy had blamed part of it on his distaste for what she was doing, but even after they'd made their peace treaty of sorts, he'd been absent even when he'd been with them.

At least it had seemed that way to her. She'd even tried to talk to Jana about it, but inevitably any discussion with Jana ended up back on the pregnancy thing within two minutes. So Lucy had been left to decipher Grady's random attentiveness on her own. And she'd come up with exactly nothing.

Okay, that and she'd been a little more preoccupied with her own chrysalis-to-butterfly date with destiny.

As Jason finally navigated the last group, having been waylaid several times by old friends and hangers-on, she made a solemn vow to herself—she'd soon be done with her self-centered fairy-tale story and once again become the devoted best friend to her buddies. She'd be the best friend-of-the-mom that Jana ever had; maybe she'd even read a few books or something so she could better understand what Jana was going through. And she'd force herself back into Grady's good graces, no matter what it took.

Just as soon as she had her one memorable night. Even her best friends would wish her that much. Wouldn't they?

She glanced up to find Jason still yards away, caught up in yet another conversation. She took the moment to smooth her hair and decide just how she should stand at the terrace railing. Poised with a come-hither smile? Or looking out over the Washington night scene, a self-assured woman confident that her man would return to her?

She opted for the latter. Not because she was confident. Or self-assured. But because she seriously needed to pick at a piece of the tape that was pinching the tender skin just below her faux cleavage. Moments passed. Tape was subtly picked at. More moments passed. No Jason.

She practiced flicking her hair over her shoulder, figuring she'd need that later when they were talking. Her stomach tightened up. Talking. What on earth were they going to talk about? She knew from the loop that Jason had been a promising pick by

NBA scouts in college before a knee injury had ended his future. He'd gone on to law school and had recently made partner in a firm with offices in New York and D.C., specializing in the field of sports and entertainment. She was a third-grade teacher in the Virginia public school system. She definitely didn't run with the same crowd of people.

Jana and Grady were her crowd. Their idea of hobnobbing was trying to cook Thanksgiving dinner in her galley-size kitchen. Thank goodness it was Jana's turn this year. Her spirits fell momentarily when she wondered if they'd even have a Thanksgiving together this year. Surely Jana would be feeling better by then. And she'd have gotten Grady over his funk.

They'd been having Thanksgiving together since Grady had relocated back home after college. His uncle had passed on by then. Jana's mom wasn't one for sentimentality and was usually off somewhere with her current paramour, preferably someplace balmy. Lucy's folks always dedicated that day to a soup kitchen run by one of their college alumni foundations. So they'd adopted a round-robin system, taking turns doing the traditional dinner for the three of them and whomever else they wanted to invite. Of course Dave was a staple now, when he wasn't on the road. They'd invited various strays over the years, but for the most part, it had just been the three of them. Her crowd.

She turned her thoughts to what she and Jason would talk about once he finally got back with her drink, which by now was probably warm. She slipped her shawl around her arms. The evening air had a bite to it now, so maybe warm wasn't such a bad thing. Even better would be Jason's arm around her shoulders. Or maybe he'd be a real gentleman and offer her his jacket. It would smell of his aftershave. Which meant it might rub off on her dress, then she could get a whiff of it and remember tonight forever. My God, she was seventeen all over again. Only worse. Because she was really twenty-eight.

Conversation starters, she thought, fighting to stay focused. All she needed was one or two, then she'd let him take over while she listened attentively, laughed at his stories, and inserted a clever comeback here and there so he could be impressed with her sharp mind and witty nature.

Unfortunately, his client list was on the sports side. Not a soap star or Broadway actor in sight. All her years of watching the Tonys and reading *Soap Opera Digest* would be wasted.

Finally abandoning her post, she turned to see where he was and found him still chatting. He looked up just then, and her heart caught. *Just like in the movies,* she thought. He was so in tune with her that he'd felt her gaze land upon him and had looked up, linking his gaze to hers with unerring precision. So yes, he'd known exactly where she was standing, it was right where he'd left her, after all, but still, it was romantic. Further proof her karma was finally kicking in.

She imagined that Jason had probably been right in the middle of his exuberant recounting of winning the state basketball championship with his three-point jumper on the buzzer, but was now unable to speak because his gaze had once again connected with hers. Then all the excited buzz of the crowd around him would die as everyone looked from him to the object of his obvious lust and affection. Of course he'd cross the floor, setting their drinks on the tray of a passing waiter, never once breaking their soul-deep eye-to-eye contact. Heedless of the heads turning in his wake, he would make his way to her side, take her hands, bringing them to his lips as he apologized for leaving her alone for so long. Then, after brushing his warm lips across her bare knuckles, he would bend her back over one arm for a soul-searing kiss that left the men in the room grinning and the women swooning.

Instead, to her absolute horror, he grinned broadly, then gestured for her to come over. To join him. And other people. His crowd. People who knew exactly who he was, and who he'd been, and what he was now. People who had no clue she was Lucy Harper, high school geek-o-rama-cum-third-grade-teacher-and-wannabe-swan.

She swallowed hard, wishing a passing waiter would appear now so she could down a glass or six of whatever happened to be on his tray at the moment.

"Vivian, where are you when I need you?" she whispered beneath her breath. If there was any way she could have dissolved and magically reappeared behind the safety of the tinted windows of the Glass Slipper limo, she would have. As it was, her only means of escape lay beyond the beckoning Jason.

She should have gone with spontaneity.

# Chapter 19

As one, all eyes in his adoring crowd turned to see who he was motioning to. *The moment was finally upon her.*

"Don't trip. Find your rhythm," she whispered beneath her breath. Clutching her shawl, wanting desperately to check her hair, but not even daring so much as a hair flip, she cautiously made her way over to the small group. *Attempt a winning smile? Or play it cool and casual?* As if she wore stuff like this, dripping in fine jewels, every night of the week. She was so nervous she wasn't sure she could pull off anything more than a sickly grin at this point. And what would she say when they looked for her badge and asked for introductions? Jason couldn't know it was her, so that would prove awkward right from the start, pointing out that even he didn't know her name. So how special could she be?

Then she was there. And the time for subterfuge plotting was over.

Jason beamed at her and made room for her in his circle—the inner circle—as he handed her her drink. "Sorry, I got waylaid by this merry band of revelers."

Everyone chuckled like that was the funniest thing they'd ever heard. Boy, she wished she had a portable backup support group. That would come in handy when she was trying to explain multiplication tables to a bunch of hungry, tired eight-year-olds. "Look, they think it's fun, so will you!"

She managed a light smile as she glanced up at Jason while simultaneously avoiding making eye or badge contact with anyone else. If she didn't know who they were, and they didn't know who she was, well, then it was safe to say she could pretend none of this mattered. Right? She stifled the urge to down her champagne in one unladylike swallow.

"They insisted I tell them the story about the championship final point." He grinned his handsome-prince grin at the group. "I haven't thought about that night in years."

Everyone knew that was a lie, including Lucy. He'd made it sound like he'd had so many amazing moments since then that he could scarcely remember something as minor as winning the state championship for their high school for the first time in its fifty-year history. With a three-pointer. On the buzzer. In double overtime.

Sure, he'd gone on to some better-than-modest success in college, but he probably had the front-page story laminated and tacked to the ceiling over his bed for daily motivation.

Jason's bed. Not a safe thinking topic, no matter how much stimulation-numbing alcohol was at hand.

"So, it was down to three seconds," said someone in the crowd, encouraging the story back on track.

Lucy had no idea who the speaker was because she was too busy slowly taking sips of her champagne and casting her winning smile at Jason. Lucy had a feeling she rated winsome more than winning. Not the kind of thing that got his attention. But at the moment she was more interested in getting him back into his story so the rapt attention of the clustered group would turn back to him. And away from her. Before anyone realized no introductions had been made.

She felt a few assessing glances thrown her way, but they were all quickly swept back into the excitement of his moment. And, before she knew how it happened, she was quickly relegated to the starstruck wanna-be-seen-with position. No one cared about her, because she obviously didn't matter.

*Well, look on the bright side,* she told herself. *You didn't make a fool out of yourself. You got your dance. You got your kiss. On the rooftop, under the stars, no less. All in all, maybe not a slam-dunk ace on her final, but a pretty decent showing. Sleeping Beauty has finally awakened . . . so what if she's still a bit groggy?*

Lucy sipped the rest of her drink as the high-school championship game story segued directly into the college hoops sagas. She had to admit he was a very dynamic speaker. She hadn't the vaguest clue about the difference between running the two-three down low and taking the defense to a perimeter feed, or why running the latter had saved them from early elimination, but he made it all sound so exciting, she was almost as entranced as the rest of them. She bet he made an awesome trial attorney. All he had to do was stack the jury with any representation of the opposite sex and he was well on his way to securing victory for his client. Guilty or not.

Well into his element now, the crowd grew, and she eventually got shuffled back into the second row, behind Jason's elbow. Then the third. He was giving the play-by-play of his latest trial victory now, and her champagne glass was empty. No one was paying her any attention, and she decided that was perfectly fine with her.

So it wasn't quite the fairy-tale ending she'd imagined when he'd kissed her. So he wasn't Mr. The Right One, but Mr. The Right One Tonight. Or just Mr. The Right One for a Brief Moment. The true test was that she was able to enjoy what she had gotten, be satisfied with her fiasco-free performance here tonight, and leave with fond memories of the evening intact. Lucy Harper really had grown up. She was bulletproof.

Placing her drink on an empty tray, she headed carefully for the door. No point in giving anyone a last-minute, full-scale Harperesque production.

After navigating her way back down to the ballroom, she zeroed in on the lobby and the freedom that lay just beyond. She paused just outside the ballroom doors to fish out her limo pager, when someone put a hand on her arm and lightly tugged her back. Her heart tripped, and she realized then that she wasn't quite as grown-up and mature as she'd thought. But she turned to find it was Grady. Not Jason. She tried to mask her disappointment, but Grady knew her all too well.

"I thought you'd gone home," she said.

He shrugged. "I figured it was my reunion, too. And I'd paid for the ticket. Might as well have my free drinks out of the deal. Besides, Jana wants me to bring back the best dirt to take her mind off her puke-o-rama sessions."

Lucy smiled. Grady was the best guy friend ever. A sad little pang followed as she remembered that he didn't seem interested in being her best guy friend. Not anymore.

"So, leaving before the ball is over?"

She knew him all too well, too. She'd hurt his feelings earlier. And though she still wasn't entirely sure what she'd done to put herself in the wrong, she hadn't meant to hurt him. "The princess didn't wear comfortable slippers," she said, unsure with him for possibly the first time ever. "Why do women wear these instruments of torture, anyway?"

The ballroom doors opened as a few other alumni came out. They both looked inside to see Jason, still the center of attention, now holding court alongside the dance floor. "What happened with Prince Charming?"

"He has a lot of loyal subjects."

"Not you?"

She lifted a shoulder. "It was a nice evening. While it lasted."

Grady smiled then, his true smile. The one she'd been missing so much. Her heart filled with relief, even as guilt poured in to fill the remaining nooks and crannies. She wanted her best friend back. To that end, she made a solemn vow right then to be a better best friend in return. To both Jana and Grady. Lucy's Big Night was over. And in the end, both of her friends had come through for her, or tried their best. Now it was her turn to focus on being there for them.

"I said earlier," she began, "that I didn't need you to rescue me anymore. Maybe that's so," she said, then quickly hurried on when that warm smile flickered. "But that doesn't mean that I don't still need you. I might need to fall down on my own sometimes, and I know I need to try new things, figure out exactly who I am, on the outside and the inside." She took his sardonic glance at her dress in stride. "I didn't say I'd mastered it just yet. This was Vivian's idea. But I had to give it a shot. How else am I going to get the answers I need?"

"You could just listen to me. You know I'm always right when it comes to what's best for you."

She knocked her knuckles into his arm, then rubbed the spot when he winced. Two-carat prongs made a good weapon, as it turned out. "Sorry. And maybe you are the great arbiter of all things Lucy Harper. Your guidance has always meant a great deal to me. But you're more at peace with yourself than I am. So you don't understand when I want to push at the status quo. You think I should be happy as is, just like you. You want me to play it safe and be the same old Lucy Harper. Only I'm tired of playing it safe. I don't like the status quo."

"So, you like this?" He motioned to her dress, then nodded back toward the door, beyond which Jason was holding court. "This was the real you all along, just dying to get out?"

Lucy stared into the eyes of her best friend . . . and realized there was no way she would ever be able to make him appreciate the benefits a Brazilian wax could bring to a woman's psyche. How was he really going to understand any of this? "I'm not going to lie and say I didn't get a little thrill being accepted into the cool-kids group with nary a blink."

"I can see where the shocked wow-is-that-really-you reactions would be satisfying. I get that."

Something in her expression must have given her away.

He cocked his head, then zeroed in on her badgeless state. "Wait. They don't know, do they?"

She shook her head. "It was enough just to fit in. I didn't want or need the rest."

To her surprise, Grady chuckled.

"What?" she said, really trying not to be defensive.

He shook his head, then pulled her into a surprising hug. "Nothing. You're just . . . so you."

"I'm not sure whether to be flattered or offended," she said, the words muffled against the sleeve of his jacket.

"Flattered." He set her back, and his gaze rested on hers, quite sincere. "I'm sorry if I was holding you back. My mistake."

"Really? You get it?"

"Will you ever let me live it down if I tell you that you make a smashing princess?"

She lit up. "You really think so?"

"Everybody should be the belle of the ball sometime, I guess."

Grady offered her his arm. "Allow me to escort you to your carriage?"

She gave him a sideways glance, wondering about the sudden shift in mood. Maybe it was her just being her overly analytical self, reading too much into every little thing of late. Maybe Grady was actually fine with her experimentation into dabbling in the world of the swans now that it seemed to be over. Whatever the case, he was trying, which was more than she'd hoped for earlier, and she was just grateful enough to go with the flow.

Smiling back at him, she held up her pager thingie. "Wait till you see my carriage, mister." She pushed the little red button. "Play your cards right and I'll get the nice driver to take us for a spin around the town." She slipped her arm through his, but as they turned to head out, the big doors opened behind them and suddenly there was Jason. Larger than life.

He saw her, his easy, natural smile widening, before flickering slightly when he took in the scene. "Are you leaving?" The question was for her. He barely glanced at Grady.

Her heart bumped against the inside of her chest. *He had come for her after all!* She didn't dare glance at Grady. Dammit! She'd just sort of made peace with him again, and the last thing she wanted was to chance ruining their fresh accord by swooning all over Jason Prescott. And yet . . . the ball wasn't over. Prince Charming was right in front of her.

"I was," she said. *Was.* Such a nice, wishy-washy kind of word. Not "I am," all definite, as if he couldn't change her mind. Saying *was* implied that she might have been thinking about it, but now . . . who knows?

He flashed his game-winning smile. "Could I talk to you for a minute before you go?" He finally spared a glance for Grady, all supreme confidence. "You don't mind, do you?"

Lucy tensed in that moment, praying silently that Grady didn't choose that moment to make a point by saying something snide. Oh, he'd be all subtle about it, leaving Jason to wonder if he'd just been insulted or not, but she didn't even want to risk that much. *Please, please, don't mess this up for me.*

"I have a moment," she blurted quickly. She glanced at Grady, whose expression was unreadable. "I'll be right back," she promised him. "If you can wait."

"My time is yours."

Now she was left wondering. He was being entirely too inscrutable.

"Friend of yours?" Jason asked, as he took her gently by the elbow and led her several steps away.

"Yes," she said, more breathless than she should have been. Damn, but his hands were big. And warm.

"Date?"

She laughed. "No. Not in the sense you mean. We've known each other since we were kids."

"Ah," he said.

And for a split second, she wondered if Jason had actually been worried that Grady might be competition for him. *Boy, wouldn't Grady get some serious mileage out of that.* She hid the amused smile that accompanied the thought.

"I guess I was a little surprised to find someone like you here, unattached. Just wanted to make sure I wasn't stepping on any toes."

Her first thought was that if he was so enamored of her, he surely hadn't shown that back inside the party. But then she felt petty for thinking so selfishly. After all, it was his reunion, too. Surely she couldn't hold it against him that he wanted to visit and chat with everyone. Considering he'd known everyone—most everyone, anyway, present company excluded—he had a lot more visiting to do than most.

She glanced up at Jason then, saw the same unshakable smile, and realized that despite the polite chatter, he'd already completely dismissed Grady. Grady might not be competition in her specific case, but it bugged her a little that he'd been so easily dismissed as a challenge. She imagined it was the old us-versus-them, cool-kids-snubbing-the-geek-kids thing that had provoked the feeling. And God knows, Grady was the last guy who needed, much less wanted, defending. But it put a little tarnish on her White Knight's heretofore blindingly shiny armor.

"I suppose the same could be said of you," she replied. Not the snappiest of responses, but she was happy to be stringing intelligible words together. It was far more attractive than just staring at him, entranced and drooling.

He chuckled. "True. I haven't been in town much of late. I've been defending a big case up in New York."

There was a slight pause, and she wasn't sure if he was setting up a let-me-impress-you name drop (she'd overheard he was defending some NBA star on a felony charge) or if he was expecting her to bat her lashes and ask him to please, please, tell her all about his big case.

The moment passed. And she couldn't tell if she'd gained or lost momentum by not responding in the allotted time. "I suppose that makes it hard to date anyone steadily," she said.

"Exactly." If he was miffed that she hadn't shown appropriate exultation over his big-time occupation, he didn't let it show. "But I'm beginning to think that's a good thing."

She raised her perfectly plucked eyebrows.

"Because I would have hated to run into you tonight and not been able to pursue you."

She couldn't help it. It was such a line. And yet it made her knees go woozy. Yes, yes, she should say something like, "Well, just because I'm here alone tonight doesn't mean I don't have men lined up for blocks. Maybe I'm not available for pursuit." If only she had the nerve to say something so provocative. Bait the big cat.

But she was pretty much overwhelmed with just standing and not falling over while keeping up the barest pretense of maintaining her end of the conversation. All the while her inner voice was jumping up and down and squealing, "He wants to *pursue* you!"

"Well, then," she said to him, "yay for Fate."

Somewhere, Gloria Steinem was weeping.

He laughed then, a charming little self-deprecating laugh. "You know, I can't believe we've danced, had drinks, the whole bit, and I still don't know your name."

He'd missed the part about the kiss. He couldn't have forgotten that kiss, could he? Maybe he didn't want to embarrass her.

"You are an alumnus, right?" he asked.

She'd confirmed she'd come alone, so it was the only conclusion he could have drawn. But she experienced a moment of panic. She wanted to cling to the relative safety net of her princess front. At least for now. As long as she wasn't Lucy Harper, she could pretend she was capable of pulling this off.

He was looking at her chest, but she was pretty sure he was just looking for her badge.

"I was absent for senior pictures," she blurted. "So they didn't have a name tag for me up there. Some sort of snafu."

"Ah."

Again with the all-knowing "ah." Except he looked sort of cute when he had that deep-thinker look on his face.

"Well, I'm Jason," he told her, the same self-deprecating smile edging at the corners of his mouth. "Jason Prescott."

"I know," she said, motioning to his badge, lest he get a swelled head, thinking that he was just that popular. Even though, of course, he was. Still, point for the former geek. She stuck her hand out. "I'm Lucy."

"Lucy," he said, shaking her hand, then not letting it go.

Making her pulse do a little samba and shaking her train of thought.

Point for the former prom king.

She knew he was waiting for a last name.

His smile turned sheepish. And it was just as affecting. He must be amazing in front of a jury, she thought, partly dazed to be the exclusive focus of all that charm.

"I must admit, I don't remember you from our senior class. It was a big group, but I'm surprised at myself. Someone like you, well, I should remember."

"Don't worry about it," she told him. "I've changed a lot over the years."

"Yes, well, I'm just glad I've found you now." He squeezed her hand.

She tried not to sigh too obviously.

"I'm sure you're probably a busy woman, and like I said, I've been traveling a lot, but I'd love the chance to take you out to dinner. Get to know each other a little better." He chuckled. "Well, get to know each other, period." He motioned to the ballroom behind them. "This is better suited to catching up on old times." His smile broadened to a grin and she swore she heard a wolf howling at the moon. "Not creating new ones."

Okay. She so did not have the skill set to handle someone like this. Shew! Her circuits were already on overload and he was just holding her hand, asking her for a simple date.

"Agreed," she somehow managed. First thing, as soon as she got home, or tomorrow morning, whatever, she was calling Vivian's private line and setting up some kind of appointment with her. Multiple appointments, if necessary. She needed pointers. Hell, she needed a whole new toolbox of skills. Her credit card was going to melt, but she didn't care.

"I'm taking the train back up to the city tomorrow, but I'll be back home in a week," he was saying.

*Concentrate, Lucy. This is important.* This is your dream moment. Relish it. Her mind was a huge jumble of worries, thoughts, insecurities, excitement, and anticipation. "Uh-huh," she said. *Oh, brilliant. Scintillating. Christ.*

"Could I call you? Or should we just make plans now?"

"Now," she blurted. Because who knew what might happen five minutes from now? He might never call. He might meet someone on the train. But if they *had plans*, wouldn't he at least be compelled to see them through?

She tried to cover her complete social awkwardness with a smile. "I'd like that." There, much better. Almost cultured. "When would be good for you?" *I'm pretty much free until the next millennium.*

"I wish I could say right now—"

*So say it!* She swore she felt the condoms vibrate inside her clutch. Or maybe that was just her.

"—but there are a few people I haven't had the chance to talk to tonight," he finished saying. "I don't know when I'll get the chance again. You know how it is."

*Not really,* she wanted to say. *There is not a single person in that room I'm compelled to talk to.*

He surprised her by pulling out a BlackBerry and flipping it open. Ever the busy, important attorney, he apparently didn't leave home without it. Even to his high school reunion.

He tapped the screen with the stylus. "How is a week from Tuesday?"

She had course-development classes with the other third-grade teachers on Tuesday nights. Rats! "Actually," she said, somewhat tremulously, "Tuesday is difficult for me." She mentally crossed her fingers. "How about a week from Friday?"

A few more taps. "That will work." He grinned up at her.

And she beamed with pride. *See?* she wanted to say. *I'm not a loser with no social calendar, even if I don't need a personal digital assistant to keep track of mine.*

"There's a little Mediterranean place in Adams Morgan I've been wanting to check out. Chirra. Have you heard of it?"

She just nodded. She'd Google it later.

"We could meet there, or I could come pick you up."

Torn, she went with the one less likely to give her a heart attack. "I'll meet you there. Would seven be okay?" She ran the pregame play-by-play over in her mind. She would have a full two hours after she got home from school to have a complete nervous breakdown, try on everything she owned, phone Jana at least a dozen times, and debate the merits of moving the volatile contents tucked away in her evening bag tonight, to whatever purse she took with her that night.

*Like you're going to sleep with him on the first date.*

Her little voice—which sounded a lot more like Vivian as the night went on—just laughed and laughed. *Like you'd be able to say no if he asked!*

"Seven is fine," he said with a satisfied smile. Then he finished off the fairy-tale evening perfectly after all, by lifting her hand, pressing a hot kiss to the back of it, and lifting his head just enough to give her a secret little just-between-us kind of intimate smile. "Until next Friday, then."

"Friday," she gasped.

Then he stepped back through the ballroom doors and was absorbed into the crowd before the doors swung shut.

She, on the other hand, floated through the lobby and out of the building, completely unaware of the blisters on her heels. She beamed giddily at the Glass Slipper driver as he opened the door of her limo and gently ushered her inside its warm, purring interior.

"Sleeping Beauty has left the building," she murmured as they pulled away from the curb. Then the wide smile she'd been harboring finally broke through and she gave in to the overwhelming urge to celebrate. She kicked up her heels, laughed like a loon, and did just as Vivian instructed. She reveled.

And it was good.

# Chapter 20

So, he's not coming, right?" Lucy sighed and slumped down on Jana's couch.

Jana and Dave lived in a nice two-bedroom condo on the top floor of one of Alexandria's nicer buildings. It was comfortably furnished with a mix of prints and solids, sturdy furniture suitable for team get-togethers, along with the requisite sports-journalist-and-athlete must-have: a television set in every single room, with a satellite dish feed of every sporting event on the planet.

"No, he's not," Jana said as she opened two peach Snapples and set them on the small kitchen table. "But you can't blame him. You ditched him. You of all people know what that feels like."

Lucy hung her head. "I know, I know. I owe you both a huge apology. And since Grady won't answer the damn phone to accept his, I'll give them both to you."

"For?"

Lucy looked up to find Jana leveling a steady gaze on her, and realized just how badly she'd screwed things up. Jana was always the understanding one. Good cop to Grady's bad cop. She didn't look much like nice Officer Pelletier today.

"For having my head stuck so far up my butt these past couple of months." She'd wanted to tell Jana all about the reunion the minute she got home. Hell, if Jana hadn't been so sick lately and not getting enough rest, she'd have called her from the limo. In fact, it was when she'd picked up her cell to leave Jana a voice mail, telling her to call as soon as she got up, that she'd remembered Grady. "For the record, I did have the driver turn around. I went all the way back. He was already gone. I called his cell and his house. Last night and all day today. But he's not picking up." She sighed. "I'm really sorry we all seem to have gotten so off track lately. I know I've been preoccupied and you guys are sick of me, but I never meant for it to cause so much grief. If I'd known, I'd have never signed up for the stupid course."

Jana sighed, too, unable to keep up the stern front. "Don't be silly. You were just doing something for yourself, and God knows, you're allowed. Don't beat yourself up too much. It's not like you're the only one who's been preoccupied of late." Jana laid her hand across her still-flat stomach, an instinctive gesture Lucy found endearing and terrifying all at the same time. "I think we all need to pull our collective heads out of our butts. Shoot," she said with a weary grin, "I'd be happy just to pull mine out of the john."

Lucy shuddered in sympathy. "I can't even imagine what that's like for you." She shifted her gaze to Jana's stomach, really thinking about the fact that a life was growing inside there. "I work with kids all day, but they're all potty-trained and talking in complete sentences." She smiled at Jana. "'I don't know nuthin' 'bout birthin' no babies.' "

Jana laughed a bit shakily. "Neither do I. And if anyone is sick of anything, it's of me being sick."

"We're not sick of you, or the baby," Lucy said, wanting to reassure her friend. She really had no idea what Jana was dealing with. It was overwhelming to Lucy, and she was just an innocent bystander. "Worried about you, yes, but this is such a huge thing, Jana. And you've still managed to be a good friend to both me and Grady, and I haven't."

"We all go through Me-Me-Me phases," Jana said.

"The difference is, Grady isn't treating you like a leper because you got pregnant and talk about things like mucous plugs and jaundice. Me, on the other hand, I don't know what to say to him anymore that won't make him suddenly moody or withdrawn." She slumped back in her chair. "And just when it seemed like we'd finally found accord, I go and do something so stupid, even I don't blame him for never talking to me again."

"So your head was in the clouds." Jana raised her hand. Not the one protecting her belly. That one stayed put. A permanent shield, perhaps. Lucy could use one of those right at the moment.

"Listen," Jana said, "I know how it feels. I get so preoccupied by the idea that something is growing inside me right now that I lose track of entire conversations. I can't tell you how badly I've screwed up at work lately. And no one around me understands. I've made a real conscious effort not to bore everyone else to tears with the subject, but—"

"You haven't 'bored' any of us. Terrified us, maybe. I mean, that Miracle of Birth PBS special? That's true friendship right there, watching that on Pizza Night instead of a rerun of *Pretty Woman.*"

Jana smiled, and Lucy couldn't help but notice just how deeply the fatigue was lining her friend's face. She'd tried to ask Jana how she was really doing, but she always deflected the answer or cracked some joke. Potty humor, literally.

"I do understand that this has been a major change," Jana said, "and that it hasn't been as easy handling the new you as maybe you thought." Jana sighed a little, sipped her Snapple. "And I know that we haven't exactly been the support network you've needed. But you have to understand that you being so dissatisfied with yourself, to the point you felt the need to remake yourself . . . well, it's kind of like saying we're not good enough."

Lucy's mouth dropped open. "That's so not true!"

"I know that. Which is why I've been the good guy. But Grady . . ."

"Does he really think that just because I wanted to feel better about myself, that I'm condemning him somehow? Because that's ludicrous. Yes, we were all misfits, but you guys were always more accepting of it than me. You came into your own in college. You got the job you coveted, met a fabulous man, married, bought a nice place, you know, settled. Felt comfortable. Grady has never once questioned who he is. I think he came out of the womb certain of his role in life. Me? I never got over feeling like a misfit. I never got past the idea that I wasn't supposed to turn out like this, all nerdy and forgettable."

Lucy lifted a hand, stalling Jana's response. "No, really. I'm not memorable. I'm likable enough once you get to know me, sure. But it's hard as hell to get a guy to know me when they never see me in the first place. I'm invisible. I'm human beige." She rubbed at the condensation on the label on her bottle. "I don't look at either of you that way. You have to know that. And changing how I look, or learning how to be more confident about myself, my body, whatever, doesn't have a thing to do with what bonded us together. I know it was our misfitness that brought us to one another, but I'd like to think that there has been a whole lot more keeping us together all these years."

"Of course there has been," Jana said gently. "I do know this. I think Grady knows this, too. He's just . . ." Jana let the sentence dangle and Lucy didn't know what to say. It hurt that, through all of this, Jana had seemed to understand Grady's bad attitude, while Lucy was baffled by it.

"I understand why he's mad now," Lucy said. "But he's had such a hard-on about this from the very beginning. He's acting all hurt by this, but I've been a little hurt by his rejection, too." She looked down at the designs she was tracing with the water ring left on the table. "When he first showed up at the reunion, it didn't go too well. But then he was still there later on, and maybe it was because the stupid thing was finally over and we were literally leaving it behind us, that things finally looked brighter." She swore and scrubbed the water off with her fist. "I can't believe I screwed that up."

"That you did," Jana said, blunt as ever. "How could you forget him?"

"I already told you all about that night," she said, frowning a little. Jana's moods were definitely more unpredictable of late. Lucy never knew what to expect. One minute laughing, the next bitchy, the next sobbing, then back to laughing again. She didn't know how Jana coped with that kind of roller coaster, so Lucy wasn't sure how much of her current irritation to take personally. "You haven't been married so long that you don't remember what it was like, crushing on someone like that. And I did it again and again. Only to be invisible, again and again. Guys I'm attracted to *never* give me a second glance. So to have one finally notice, *and* have that one be Jason Prescott? Are you kidding me? I was lucky to be able to string two sentences together."

Jana just sighed, sipped her Snapple, and remained noncommittal.

"Yes, I know that's no excuse, there is no excuse for abandoning

Grady or anyone. But it wasn't intentional. God, he has to know that! And he would if he'd just pick up his damn phone and let me explain and apologize."

Jana raised an eyebrow. "Somehow I don't think telling Grady that Jason Prescott had just asked you out on a date, which made you so giddy with vindication that you completely forgot about your best friend, is going to be the apology that will get you back in his good graces. Call me crazy."

"So what can I do? He's hated Jason forever for what he did to me, and yet *I'm* the one who got dissed and *I'm* over it. I just want him to let it go. Be happy that I'm happy. Am I supposed to turn Jason down to make Grady happy? I've never told him who he could date and not date."

"You soaked Grady's shoulder for months over Jason's asinine treatment of you. And now you have a hot date with the guy."

"I guess I'd hoped he'd see it as I do. Like some kind of poetic justice, retribution, karma coming full circle."

"I doubt that will ever happen," Jana muttered.

"Why? What is it you seem to get about his attitude that I don't?"

Jana didn't say anything, seemed lost in thought for a few moments. And Lucy noted again how tired she looked. Only looking at her now, it seemed like maybe there was more to her weariness than battling morning-noon-and-night sickness. Lucy shifted closer and reached across the table to take Jana's free hand in her own. "I'm so sorry I've put you in the middle of this. You shouldn't have to play referee to the two of us. We're adults and we should start acting like ones."

"No, that's not it. In fact, I've been happy to have the distraction."

Lucy squeezed her hand. "Are you okay? Is there something else going on, with the baby, or Dave, or you, that you haven't told us about? You know, we might not understand, but we really do want to be here for you." She smiled encouragingly. "Isn't that what godparents do?"

Jana smiled a little, glanced her way, then back to some vague point across the room. "I think godparents are supposed to take care of the baby, not the mommy." She let out a shaky breath. "Mommy. God."

Lucy dragged her chair around until she was seated facing Jana without the table between them. "Maybe we take our jobs more seriously than others. We like to start our watch while the baby's still in the works. Which means taking care of its housing and development." When Jana didn't smile, Lucy tugged at her hand, worried now. "What's wrong, sweetie?"

Jana looked at her closest and dearest friend, and her heart tightened up a little. Sure, Luce had been preoccupied of late. Like she'd said, they'd all had their problems. And if she hadn't felt so torn between her loyalty to Grady and her loyalty to Lucy, she'd have been right in there with her best friend, poring over every detail of Lucy's princess-at-the-ball night, examining every nuance of what Jason had said, how he'd looked at her, the whole neurotic girl-talk ball of wax.

But knowing what she did about Grady and his feelings for Lucy made her feel like a traitor if she gave even the appearance of rooting for Jason.

"Is it the baby?" Lucy asked, concern clear in her eyes.

Jana shook her head. "Not the way you mean, no. As far as we know, things are moving along like they should. Our first sonogram is coming up."

Lucy smiled uncertainly. "That's a good thing, right? Are you going to find out the sex?"

Jana shrugged a little, then suddenly burst into tears, surprising them both.

Lucy immediately pulled her into a hug and Jana accepted the moment of solace like a battered ship finally finding port in a storm. She'd been telling the truth when she said she hadn't minded the Lucy-Grady-Reunion drama. Between that, work, and puking her guts up every few hours, she'd had blessed little time to worry about what was really bothering her. But now that the dam had broken, she wasn't sure she was going to be able to pull it back together.

"Oh, honey, what's wrong?" Lucy asked, still holding her, rubbing her back, stroking her hair. "Is it Dave? Is he freaking out or something? Because, you know he'll come around. He seemed really excited about this."

Jana was crying too hard to answer. All she could do was shake her head. She reached across the table, grabbed a few napkins, and finally managed to pull away from Lucy to blow her nose.

Lucy stroked Jana's hair from her forehead. "Can you talk about it? I know I haven't gone through anything like this, so maybe I won't be any help. But it still might make you feel better to get it out, whatever it is."

Lucy was sweet to offer, and Jana knew she didn't have a big support network. Her colleagues were all men, and most of them considered her the enemy at any given moment, depending on who got the most inches in print that week. She was also a little competitive about winning that particular who-has-the-biggest-penis contest on a semiregular basis, just to shut them up. Which certainly didn't endear her to them, either.

Jana grabbed another tissue. She needed her friends. It wasn't like she could rely on her mother. Hell, she hadn't even told her about the baby yet. Wanted to get used to the puking first. No way she could handle that and the obligatory visit from Angie Fraser at the same time. After all the years of distance between the two of them, Jana wasn't sure how her mother would take the news that she was going to be a granny, but she was damn sure it wouldn't go over well. Jana was still not allowed to address her as "Mother" in public, but she would take enormous delight in ensuring her child's first word was "Nana."

She took another fortifying sip of peach-flavored tea, thankful to have Lucy here. "Dave's been great. His whole family is just beside themselves with excitement. The way they're behaving, you'd never know he had seven brothers and sisters who'd already given his parents and assorted aunts and uncles a pile of grandbabies."

Lucy smiled a little. "It's good they're happy, but I guess it's a bit daunting."

"A bit," Jana said dryly. Dave *was* great. In fact, her husband was over the moon and had been incredibly attentive. Being from a huge family had left him with absolutely zero fear about having a child. The Pelletier clan was great, too, but Jana was thankful they didn't live nearby. For an only child of a single parent who had been largely absent her whole life, being sucked into the bosom of the extended Pelletier family was all a little overwhelming at times.

Then there was Lucy and Grady, who were without a doubt the only two people in the world she could always turn to, though she wasn't sure they could help her this time around.

"But that's not really the problem," she said, blotting her cheeks with another napkin. "I mean, it is, but it's not." She sighed. "I'm not making any sense, I know. It's just . . . this is hard to even think, much less say out loud." She looked at her best friend. "But it's making me crazy, keeping it to myself."

Lucy squeezed her hand. "So don't. That's what I'm here for."

Jana held her friend's gaze steadily, and even though she knew Lucy was right, it still didn't make what she had to admit any easier. "We had just started talking about having kids, you know? Dave has been ready since forever. I was the one who wasn't sure. My career is going well, I'm making my mark, but I have to fight so hard just to keep a toehold in that world. I . . ."

She trailed off, shrugged a little. "Selfishly speaking, I wasn't sure if I was ready to give any of that up."

"Do you have to?"

She looked at Lucy. "I don't have to, no. But you know better than anyone that I was left alone a great deal of my life growing up. I don't want to do that to my kid."

"Having a job isn't exactly like what your mother did to you. Physically being gone for eight hours a day is an entirely different thing than complete emotional abandonment."

"I know that. In here," she said, tapping her forehead. "And I think maybe I can juggle it, at least a little. But it still means making a major compromise. And then I worry that maybe I'm exactly like my mother, putting my own needs first, being so selfish."

Lucy snorted.

Surprised, Jana said, "What's so funny about that?"

"You. Selfish. Are you kidding me? You're like the Mother Teresa of our little group. You're what keeps us together: the settler of squabbles, the arbiter of conflicted plans, and overall general nurturer. How you of all people could question your maternal instincts is, well, to laugh."

Jana felt a warm spot loom in her chest as her heart swelled. And, as was the case more often than not lately, her eyes immediately stung with a fresh wave of tears. She sniffled and wiped them away. "Don't mind them. I've turned into a virtual waterworks lately. The other day I went through half a box of Kleenex after reading the fat content on the package of Double Chocolate Milanos I just polished off." She laughed a little even as she sniffled. "Thanks for saying that, though."

"I meant it."

Jana looked down for a moment, tried to collect herself. "It's more than just having to possibly give up my job, or worrying that I'll resent the baby for it. I mean, there's nothing wrong with having kids later in life, but I'm fortunate enough to have Dave and be financially solvent now. It's just . . ." She let the sentence trail off. Because how could she admit that she was pretty sure she'd made the biggest mistake of her life?

Bless Lucy's soft but wise heart. She didn't push, she just stroked Jana's hand, let her come to it in her own way. That was Lucy's gift. Patience. Grady was always the first to find the humor in any situation, the defuser of tension. Jana was the first to leap in and try to make it all better, to soothe over ruffled feathers. Lucy was the thinker, the ponderer of the group—the one who patiently analyzed the situation, came up with a game plan, then announced the rational solution.

Only Jana didn't think there was any rational solution to this problem. Not one she could even consider, anyway.

She tried a weak smile. "So, about that date with Jason."

Lucy pulled the corners of her mouth downward. "Oh, sweetie, that bad?"

Fighting the tears, she nodded. "I—I thought it would take longer, you know? That I'd have time to get used to the idea. And then *wham!*, it happened all at once and I'm . . . I'm—" She gulped a little air, frowned fiercely to keep the tears at bay, sniffed again, then lost the fight. Helpless and more hopeless than she'd ever felt in her life, she looked to Lucy with tears streaming down her cheeks. "I don't think I'm ready for this, Luce. Not now. I shouldn't have agreed to even try." Hands clutched over her stomach, she sobbed. "I thought I could handle it. And I—I can't. I—I don't want—oh, God, Lucy, I can't even say it."

Lucy tugged her from her chair and they stumbled awkwardly to their feet as Lucy pulled her into a tight embrace. "I'm so sorry," she whispered fervently. "So sorry. I so wanted you to be happy."

"Me—too," Jana said between sobs and gulps of air.

Lucy held her away, still gripping her shoulders, but looking into her eyes. "Don't take this the wrong way, but do you think this might be the hormones, too? Every expectant mom is probably plagued with doubts like this. If you can't talk to Dave about it—"

"God, no, it would crush him."

Lucy pushed Jana's hair back. "Then maybe you should consider seeing someone. A trained someone. To talk it out. I mean, you can talk to me all you want, but I don't know enough about this to know what's what. I mean, it's coming no matter what, right?" Then her face went pale. "You're not—"

Jana shook her head vehemently. "No. I couldn't." Guilt filled her. "But I won't lie and say I didn't lose a little sleep thinking about it."

Lucy hugged her again. "I can't believe you've been torturing yourself like this and haven't said anything. I'm so sorry I haven't been more aware."

"It's not you. I've done a pretty good job of hiding it. Even from myself. I kept thinking I'd get past it, that, like you say, it's normal to be besieged by doubt and fear."

"You're not even past your first trimester. Maybe that is what this is. And if you weren't throwing up every other hour, that might help you gain some perspective, as well."

Jana sniffled, scrubbed her cheeks with her palms. "I wish I could believe that. You have no idea." She plopped down in the chair. "You can't know how ridiculous and foolish I feel, having taken such a major step so unprepared." She laughed without humor. "I mean, I'm the one who does all the prep research for every interview; I'm the one who plots out every story idea before I even approach my editor about it. And yet, for the biggest event in my life, I just leapt off the cliff and never even looked down to see if there was water below, or just rocks."

Lucy sat down in her chair. "Didn't you and Dave talk this through?"

"Yes, of course. But he's just so enthusiastic about all of it. To listen to him, it's one great big adventure." She smiled through her misery. "And you know how cute he can be when he's wound up about something."

Lucy smiled, too. "Yeah. Pound puppies could take lessons from Dave."

Jana's smile turned wistful. "I trust Dave with my life. He has my whole heart. And I just, I don't know, sort of went with the flow of the whole thing. I want him to be happy and I guess I felt like if he was this excited, it would be fantastic for both of us. Crap, I don't know what I thought." She huffed out a helpless sigh. "I wasn't thinking, obviously. And then, you know, we started anyway, and I figured it would take some time before anything happened. I'd have time to explore my feelings more, read a few books on the subject, talk it to death with you and Grady, you know, all the things I normally do when I'm tackling a new project." She picked up her bottle, then remembering it was empty, set it back down. "Little late to be doing all that now, huh?"

Lucy sat there, staring at her hands, and didn't say anything for a few moments. Finally she looked up. "Pregnancy strikes a lot of couples when they aren't ready. On the good side, you have one half of this couple who is more than ready, and he has a big old teddy-bear heart that will support you no matter what."

"I can't tell him, Luce."

"Yes, you can. You have to. You can't take this on all by yourself."

Jana visibly shuddered and her hands fluttered across her stomach. She shook her head.

"The baby *is* coming. What do you think Dave would do if he found out you'd been torturing yourself with this alone and didn't tell him?"

"He'd be crushed. And probably a little angry."

"Exactly." Lucy leaned forward and grabbed her hands again.

"You're in this together, for better or worse. So get him to help you deal with this. And get outside support, too, if you need it. You know I'm on call twenty-four-seven, but I think the one person who can help you with this is—"

"The guy that got me knocked up in the first place?" Jana said, wisecracking even as she wiped away the last vestiges of her tears. More would follow, a lot more, she knew that.

Lucy laughed. "Well. Yeah."

"Thanks, Luce," Jana said, as heartfelt a thanks as she'd ever given. As long as they'd been friends, she felt ashamed now that she hadn't been more trusting, more open. She should have known Lucy would be there for her. "I should have said something sooner."

"It's okay. We've all been going through a lot lately."

Jana gave a watery laugh. "You should see the way Dave is behaving lately. It's pathetic how adorable he is, shaking the rattles and squeezing the rubber duckies. Go figure." She leaned back, took a full breath, and pasted on a huge grin. "What say we go storm Grady's place and drag him out for some pizza or something? If I'm not allowed to hide from my problems, then neither is he."

She might not have a clue what she was going to say to Dave, or how she was going to handle things in the months to come, but Lucy was right. Torturing herself by keeping it all in wasn't doing her any favors, either. Far better to torture others and share the pain.

What were best friends for, anyway?

And if she had to grow up and deal with stuff that was this terrifying, then dammit, it was time Grady did, too. Maybe she wasn't doing him any favors by letting him sit and mope and feel sorry for himself. Torturing himself over his feelings for Lucy wasn't getting him anywhere, either. And she'd let him get away with it for far too long.

Lucy said Jana was the maternal one. So maybe it was time, as lead hen, to look after her fellow chicks. She had to practice the maternal arts on someone, right?

Besides, screwing around with someone else's future was a hell of a lot less terrifying than facing her own.

"Are you sure we should do that?" Lucy asked as Jana went and fetched her purse and made sure she had what she'd come to call her "American Express Package"—a baggie of sour balls, a liter bottle of seltzer water, and a small bottle of Listerine. Ice blue, please. She never left home without them.

She looked at Lucy and laughed. "Hell, no. But why should that stop us?"

"Right," Lucy said, sounding less than sure as she led the way out of the condo. She paused, turned back. "It's just—"

"March," Jana commanded, pointing forward.

Lucy scowled at her over her shoulder as she continued down the hall to the elevator. "And you doubt you'll make a good parent."

# Chapter 21

"I'm not surprised in the least, darling," Vivian assured her. "I'd have only been surprised if he hadn't tried to sweep you off your feet."

Lucy sipped her mimosa, dazzled as always by Vivian's natural aplomb. She'd called to give Vivian the requested update on the reunion and to thank her once again for all her personalized attention, and Vivian had promptly demanded Lucy meet her for Sunday brunch in Old Town to hear all the juicy details firsthand. Lucy eagerly accepted the invitation, knowing Vivian was the perfect person to cast a fresh perspective on her current situation.

Just in the past week alone she'd survived the annual October outbreak of lice in the school—always a thrill, and the timing couldn't be worse. Like she didn't have enough to worry about on her date with Jason next week. Just thinking about it made her scalp itch.

Then there was Jana, who was stoically trying to make her believe things were okay between her and Dave and the whole baby issue, when Lucy suspected things hadn't really changed all that much. She still had that lost look about her and her eyes were perennially red. The morning sickness wasn't getting any better, either. Jana had confided to her that she'd finally worked up the nerve to talk to Dave on Wednesday—blurting everything out right in the middle of their first sonogram together. Lucy agreed that her friend could have chosen a better venue, but Dave, stunned and hurt by Jana's confession, hadn't exactly been as supportive of his wife's problem as either Lucy or Jana would have hoped for. So Lucy had been doing a lot of Friendship 911 these past couple of days.

Grady, on the other hand, hadn't been home last Sunday when Lucy and Jana tried to storm his castle, wielding a sure-to-bring-him-down Domino's pepperoni pizza and a steaming pack of cinnamon sticks. Jana had talked to him since, but even with her intervention, Lucy's calls were going unanswered.

With all of this going on, Lucy hadn't been able to indulge herself in a detailed rehashing of her fairy-tale reunion night with Jason, much less obsess over their upcoming date this Friday. So when Vivian had been excited for her—the first and only person to feel that way besides herself—she'd jumped at the chance to spill all.

"You'll have to tell him, of course," Vivian stated, spearing a cherry tomato with deadly accuracy.

"I have to tell him what?"

"Who you really are."

"I didn't lie. I told him my name."

"First name. Clearly he has no idea who you were in high school."

"Clearly," Lucy readily agreed. "And I plan to keep it that way. I mean, it's enough for me to know I managed to get his attention ten years later. Besides, why put myself up for the possible fresh mortification of explaining prom night to him, and have him *still* not recall me. A highly probable scenario."

Vivian sank her teeth into her tomato, making quick work of it. Vivian did everything with a confident intensity. Even the salad wasn't being spared.

"You do have a point," Vivian went on. "Could make things somewhat awkward. Unless of course you wait until after you've bedded the man."

Lucy choked on her snow pea. After taking a throat-clearing sip of water, she said, "Excuse me?"

Either oblivious to her embarrassed blush or simply not caring, Vivian went on as if this were perfectly normal brunch conversation. "Darling, what's the point of becoming a beauty if you're not going to sleep with beauty?" She reached across the table and patted Lucy's hand, then shot her a wicked smile. "The spell has been broken, sweetheart. Sleeping Beauty is alive and well and ready, as they say, to get her groove on."

Lucy's lips quirked. "There's more to it than that."

Vivian waved her empty fork. "Yes, yes. Confidence, self-esteem, of course, of course. But let me tell you something," she said, leaning forward, the recessed lighting glinting off the heavy earrings dangling from her lobes and the multitude of gold bracelets adorning her wrist. "Having a gorgeous man woo you to his bed is a great way to put an exclamation point at the end of your personal mission statement."

Lucy couldn't help it; she laughed. She was no prude. God knows, she'd harbored many a detailed fantasy over the years. But actually acting them out? Entirely different scenario. She might not be a virgin, but clearly her experience up to this point had left her sadly lacking certain . . . skills. Namely the ones that would help her figure out how to go from reunion dance kiss to naked in Jason Prescott's bed. Preferably without revealing what a total dweeb she really was in the process.

Five minutes into their salads, however, and Vivian not only made the idea of turning those fantasies into reality seem possible, she made it seem downright probable. Exciting, even. What a coup!

Lucy's thoughts drifted to how the night in question would play out. . . .

*"Care to have a drink at my place?" Jason murmured next to her ear as he helped her on with her coat. She could only nod in excited agreement as they left the restaurant together, deep in each other's personal space. Lucy all but floated behind him into his apartment, tingling with anticipation for what was surely to come next. She watched with mounting desire as Jason slid off his evening jacket and sauntered over to the wet bar to pour her something dark and potent. He rolled up his sleeves, revealing tanned forearms, corded with muscle, then wrapped those big hands of his around the bottle before turning back to her, with that look in his eye.*

*You know. That look.*

*"You think to seduce me with cognac?" she purred as he crossed the room, the expression on his handsome face making it clear that was exactly his intent. She rewarded him with a clever smile, careful to stay cool and composed on the surface, not giving him the merest hint of the tempest her raging hormones were swiftly becoming.*

*She took the glass of amber liquid as if she parried like this, with men like him, every Friday night. Maybe even on the occasional school night. He laughed at her wry sense of humor, his sexy eyes twinkling with ever-increasing desire as he slid his hand down her bare arm and asked her if she wouldn't like to take their drinks somewhere, you know, more comfortable.*

*His bedroom was pure animal magnetism on four-hundred- , no, make that six-hundred-thread-count sheets. He set his drink on his mahogany dresser and unbuttoned his shirt before sliding his slim leather belt through the loops of his perfectly tailored pants. The lights were low, the music a purring background rhythm perfect for . . . that. He crossed the room to where she still hovered by the doorway, obviously expecting a more direct invitation, the kind of seduction a woman like her demanded as her right. He slipped his tie around her neck and tugged her into the room with a smile meant to melt her resistance . . . and possibly her stockings.*

*"Would you like to get more comfortable?" he asked, and the Lucy she wanted to be smiled with wanton abandon and proceeded to put on a show worthy of any Vegas showgirl, ending with her wearing stockings, her CFM pumps . . . and little else. Swirling the remains of her drink, she crossed the room to where he now sat in his over-stuffed leather chair, and propped her heel on his knee.*

*He slowly ran his hand up her calf, trailed it along her thigh until he reached the smooth, bare skin at the lacy edge. Then his fingers slid a fraction higher and she—*

Who was she kidding? She'd excuse herself and run to the bathroom so she could cling to the toilet bowl while she lost her dinner. That was what the real Lucy Harper would end up doing.

"There is no possible way that I can go to bed with Jason Prescott!" Lucy put down her fork with a small clatter, as several heads turned.

"Of course you can, darling," Vivian calmly replied, then shot a wink at the spectators, causing them to quickly return their attention back to their own salads, as if they hadn't been caught gawking. "Ah, some things never change," Vivian said with a delighted sigh as she turned her attention back to Lucy. "People love anything that smacks of scandal."

Lucy could only shake her head. Vivian dePalma was in pure diva form today.

"Women just like you bed the Jason Prescotts of the world every day," Vivian firmly stated. "And I daresay the Prescotts of the world somewhat expect it as their due." She stabbed a pepper. "Doesn't mean they shouldn't have to work for it, mind you. Keeps them humble." She glanced up and grinned before sinking her whitened and perfectly capped teeth into the hapless vegetable. "And more dedicated to the art of pleasure." She chewed with relish before swallowing. "Men don't understand how much better it is to give than receive. Until we show them why, that is."

Vivian's voice had risen just enough to rouse the interest of the spectators once again. Lucy was sure the added inflection in her tone, along with the wicked smile, were also calculated to draw attention. She loved her for it, while also realizing just how many of the important details her mother had glossed over when they'd had their "little talk" all those years ago.

"Vivian, I'm not sure I can keep up this pretense." There. She'd finally uttered the words.

Now Vivian lowered her fork and leveled her with the most serious gaze Lucy had ever been on the receiving end of, though between the Botox and the exquisitely tattooed eyebrows, it was sometimes hard to tell. " 'Pretense'?"

Lucy searched for the right words. The ones that would convey her growing concerns about this whole princess business, while not offending the woman who'd been mostly responsible for her transformation in the first place—one she'd asked and paid handsomely for. "Part of me, a big part of me," she hurried to assure her, "is very happy with everything I've learned. I do feel better about myself, more confident, and at least some of the times, less dorky. Or at least I know how to come across that way if I have to." She fiddled with the linen napkin in her lap.

"Why, of course you do, darling."

She forced herself to meet Vivian's gaze, relieved to find no judgment there, just honest interest in her concerns. "But there is a part of me that still feels like I'm playing dress-up or something."

"Darling," Vivian said, pausing just long enough to run a glossy, bloodred, exquisitely manicured nail across the netting adorning her black pillbox hat, then slowly outlining the knife-edged lapel of her vintage Chanel suit as it dipped elegantly between her abundant bosoms, before finishing her thought, a knowing smile hovering around her perfectly painted mouth. "Playing dress-up is the best part of being a woman."

"I guess. And I admit, I did feel good in that outfit, those jewels. I don't want to sound ungrateful."

"No worries on that score. Just tell me what's bothering you."

"I like the attention. Being noticed. It's . . . nice. More than nice. But I can't help feeling like I'm putting on some kind of show. That when I hit it off with someone, the person in question will figure out I'm really a fraud. That beneath the highlights and the French tips, I'm just doofy old Lucy with big feet and lumpy hair."

"Darling, no one expects us to wear our best face all the time."

Lucy stifled a little sigh.

"You went to that dance to prove to yourself that you could fit in anywhere and everywhere you so pleased. You chose to remain anonymous."

"I was already anonymous. I was invisible in high school. College, too, for that matter. It wasn't about seeing shocked faces. In fact, most of them probably don't even remember me, so they wouldn't get the transformation anyway. It was just for me. My own experiment, a little rite of passage. Proof, I guess, that I'd achieved my desired goal."

"You achieved a little more than that."

"Jason Prescott." Just saying that filled her with both a delicious sense of anticipation. And abject terror.

"Precisely. In fact, as a measure of success, I'd say that was your master's degree."

Lucy flushed a little.

"So, he noticed you. He asked you out. No need for any additional proof. You've definitely fulfilled your stated goal and then some."

Lucy nodded.

Vivian lifted her hands, palms up. "So if you feel that by continuing to embrace the new, improved version of Lucy, you are setting him up for some kind of false expectations, then why not call it a day?"

"What?"

"No one is holding a gun to your head, you know. You don't have to remain a blonde. And fake nails aren't forever, darling. You can certainly wear whatever you feel most comfortable wearing. Beauty is in the eye of the beholder. And it is certainly true that now you are both the beholder, and the beheld." Vivian rested her chin on her folded, heavily accessorized fingers. "Just ring up Jason and tell him you won't be able to see him. Then move on with your life, date whenever and whoever makes you feel comfortable. The kind of man with whom you don't have to feel you're something you're not." She paused and smiled. "Unless, of course, you behold Jason Prescott as a desirable thing of beauty. It's not simply about what he sees and wants, my dear, and you already know he wants you." Her smile grew. "Tantalizing position to be in, isn't it, darling?"

Lucy thought about that, about being the beholder. The very idea that this could be about what *she* wanted from Jason Prescott—or any man, for that matter—was a rather dazzling proposition. And a little intimidating.

She didn't know whether to laugh or cry.

"Too trashy." Lucy tossed the slinky red dress—the last of her shopping-spree-with-Vivian purchases—on her bed and held up the other hanger in front of her as she stared at her reflection.

"Mirror, mirror on the wall," Jana quipped from behind her.

Lucy stuck her tongue out at Jana's smiling reflection, then tossed the button-down black knit on the growing pile on her bed. She gazed warily inside her closet at the rapidly thinning selection of Big Date dresses.

"Maybe you should have done this, oh, I don't know, sooner than an hour before you're supposed to meet your date?"

Jana was propped up on the Oreo cookie pillows lining the headboard of Lucy's double bed, eating straight out of a pint of Ben & Jerry's.

"Yeah, says the pregnant, married lady eating Chunky Monkey. You don't have to worry if your dress purrs 'Hey, big boy, I'm an easy lay' or screams 'Repressed librarian, run for your life!' "

"True," Jana readily agreed, swallowing yet another heaping spoonful. "I knew if I spent long enough talking to you, you'd finally make me see why having a baby was a good thing." She licked her spoon. "Thank you for that."

Lucy was happy to see that Jana's dry humor had made its return, but she was still worried about her friend. "So, things between you and Dave improving at all?"

"What, can't a girl enjoy her ice cream in peace here?"

"Sorry," Lucy said, wincing with regret as she dragged another two hangers from the rack. She didn't want to push things with Jana, she just hated seeing her so miserable.

"Tonight is all about your neuroses, not mine," Jana said, using her spoon to punctuate her sentence.

"Deal," Lucy said with a sigh, tossing the latest two fashion victims on the pile without even bothering to hold them up first. "You know, maybe Vivian was right. Maybe I should have just called this whole night off and been happy with being asked in the first place."

"Is that what she said? Because I don't recall that in your detailed reiteration of your brunch."

Lucy looked over her shoulder. "Hey, I wasn't going to breathe a word. You begged me to tell you what happened, remember?"

Jana suddenly became interested in freeing a huge chunk of chocolate from her cup. "We all need distraction from time to time," she finally muttered.

Lucy immediately sat on the side of the bed. "That bad? Still?"

Jana smiled ruefully. "It's been over a week. Feels like a year."

Lucy rubbed Jana's knee. "He's that upset? I'm just so surprised he's not being more understanding."

"Oh, he's being understanding. He's convinced that this is a phase and all I need is to drown myself in the Pelletier family sea of mass procreation and all my true maternal instincts will surface."

Lucy recoiled. "What? How?"

Jana pointed her spoon. "Exactly what I said. Along with 'Why?' Okay, maybe it was 'Dear God in heaven, why?' I don't think I said that part out loud."

"His family is coming? Down here? For what, the holidays or something? You don't need that kind of stress. Not the visit itself or playing hostess when you're still—"

Jana waved her silent. "You say it, I'll want to do it."

"Sorry." Lucy nodded. "Just nibble the ice cream. Can I get you anything else?"

"I'm pregnant, not dying. Although there are times . . ."

Lucy's mouth pulled down at the corners. "I hate this for you, you know that. I can't fix it and I hate that, too."

"No more than me, trust me. And just to answer your question, no they aren't coming here. Dave wants to take me home to Canada next month during the Thanksgiving holiday. It's a special occassion. The family is rallying round for the christening of the most recent grandchild."

"Meaning the whole gang is going to be there? And it's all

about annointing babies?" Lucy looked properly horrified, which seemed to satisfy Jana immensely.

"See? Exactly how I felt."

"Isn't it enough you visit his immediate family at Christmas? All sixty-two of them?"

"Sixteen. If you don't count the four dogs and assorted infants. Which I don't, since they can only drool on me, not interrogate me. Sometimes it might as well be sixty-two, though." She stuck her spoon in the carton and sighed. "They're so . . . huggy."

Lucy didn't instinctively shudder like Jana did at that thought. In fact, she thought it might be kind of nice having a big bosomy kind of family. Of course, her mom and dad were huggy, too, though on a more normal scale. And she only had two sets of aunts and uncles. No cousins. No drooling infants or animals, either, come to think of it. So it didn't seem as overwhelming to her as it did to Jana. "Did you agree to go?"

Jana shrugged, dug back in. "Dave thinks that if I open up to his sisters, aunts, mom, and other assorted successfully reproducing family members, that I'll get my 'head in the game.' " She crooked her fingers in mock quotation marks on that last part, dripping ice cream onto Lucy's bedspread.

Lucy dabbed it up and licked her finger before Jana could worry about the mess. "He didn't actually use a sports analogy, did he?"

"Yep."

"So, are you going to be a *team player* and head up there?"

Jana just gave her a look, then they both cracked up a little. "I don't know," she said. "It's my turn to do our Thanksgiving this year."

"Well, don't let that stop you. I mean, use us as an excuse if you want to stay, sure, but you know I want you to do whatever you have to. I'm sure stick-up-his-butt would want the same thing."

Jana snorted a little, but said, "Don't be mean."

Lucy flipped up her hands. "I'm not. Yes, I was a horrible friend to go off and leave him like that. But he can be a man and answer the damn phone. So the nickname holds for now. I'm sure he has one or two for me lately."

When Jana dove back into her ice cream, Lucy just swore under her breath.

"Actually," Jana said, stirring, "it's precisely because of the rift in my little external family that I don't want to go."

Lucy just looked at her. "Even I don't buy that one. Grady and I will be fine. Someday. As soon as he pulls his—"

Jana leveled her spoon at Lucy. "No graphics for the pregnant woman."

"Fine. But we will be fine, you know." She gripped Jana's knee. "Just do what you need to do for you. You and Dave."

Jana looked over the edge of her carton. "Are you really really sure?"

"Yes," Lucy said without hesitation. "And you know Grady will say the same thing when you call him. Because he answers your calls."

"Stop. He'll come around."

Lucy bent her head and peered into Jana's face. "Are you sure?"

She was teasing, but Jana must have heard something else. "Yes," she said quite seriously. "I am. He's just . . . going through some stuff. He'll come around."

Lucy wanted to ask her what "stuff" she was referring to. It hurt to know he wasn't involving her with whatever was going on in his life.

But Jana suddenly stuck her spoon in the now-empty carton

and impulsively grabbed Lucy's hand. "Okay, promise me something."

"Anything."

Jana raised her eyebrows. "Careful throwing that around."

Lucy just smiled. "Only with you. What's the promise?"

"If I end up going to Canada, you and Grady have to do Thanksgiving together."

Lucy's smile faded. "I'm not sure I'm the one who can make that promise. Maybe you should run this by him first."

"If he says yes? It would be the perfect time to get all this out in the open and over with once and for all."

"Without you there to moderate, so no blood is spilled?"

"Lucy, please? For me?" She rubbed her tummy and looked pathetic.

Lucy rolled her eyes. "Please. Do not start pulling that crap on me."

"Hey," Jana said, eyes twinkling with her old mischief, "I gotta use this to some advantage, right? All the ice cream I can eat, *and* giving guilt trips on a whim. I think I'm beginning to get the hang of this motherhood thing already."

"Gee," Lucy said dryly. "So glad I could help."

"So that's a yes?"

"Yeah, yeah. Get Grumpy Butt to agree, and you've got yourself a deal. Of course," she said, her words muffled by Jana's sudden and surprising hug, "if you change your mind and decide to stay home, please do. I won't even make you cook. Just show up."

"Great!" She held Lucy by the shoulders and squeezed a bit too hard. "This is really great!" Her eyes were huge and a bit glassy.

Lucy looked at her friend with wary curiosity. Jana seemed awfully excited about all this. "Whatever it takes to make you happy."

"Knowing you guys will patch things up is the best thing you could do for me right now."

Lucy chalked up Jana's animated reaction to hormonal

surges and climbed off the bed. "So help me figure out what to wear tonight. I've got—" She looked at her watch and panic set in. "Less than forty-five minutes to look fabulous. Ack!"

Jana sat up and rustled through the pile, pulling out a slim black skirt with an almost indecent slit up the back, and a soft blue cashmere sweater with a demure neckline. "Here."

Lucy took them. "I would have never put these together."

Jana smiled smugly. "I may still play for the dork squad, but I've been married long enough to know that that combination purrs 'Come and get me' while screaming 'But be a nice guy about it.' " She cocked her head. "Is that about right?"

Lucy took a deep breath and let it out slowly. "I hope so. Since when do you know all about slit skirts, anyway? You don't even own a dress."

"Every man has his own version of the little-black-dress hots. For Dave, it's my black bike shorts with a cutoff Gretzky jersey."

"Another combo I'd have never put together."

"Well, there you have it. A match made in heaven. As to this little dream outfit, well, I also work with enough men to know what toots their horn."

Lucy shuddered. "I've met some of the men you work with." She cast a dubious look at the sweater and skirt. "Now I'm nervous."

Jana laughed. "Trust me."

"What makes you think Jason will go for this?"

"He went for that handkerchief masquerading as a dress the other night, didn't he?"

Lucy felt her cheeks heat up. "It's possible he was attracted by other things."

"If I recall, he didn't get to know any other things. Unless of course you meant your taped-up cleavage. Speaking of which, what are you going to do about that little notion tonight? Because the last time I taped anything, Dave permanently lost all the hair on his legs from the shins down."

Lucy drew the clothes across the front of her chest. "Ow. Don't worry, your taping expertise, or lack thereof, will not be needed tonight." Lucy plucked a padded bra from her bed. "I have the NASA bra."

"NASA is making bras now?"

"That's Vivian's nickname for it. Put it on and your boobs will defy gravity."

Jana snickered.

"Funny for you. You don't have to wear it."

"Neither do you, you know."

"Precisely why I didn't come to you for fashion advice in the first place. You'd have never suggested that I wear something that pushed me outside my personal comfort zone."

Jana laughed. "Well, if you mean wearing something that pushed your boobs into orbit, then you're right." She leaned forward and reached out a hand. "Toss me that thing."

"Oh no," Lucy said, holding it clear. "Make fun of my lingerie, then expect to steal it for some perverted sex hockey with Dave? I don't think so."

"We don't have 'perverted sex hockey.' "

Lucy just arched a brow in her direction.

"We have perfectly normal sex hockey."

Lucy just leveled her a look. "At least you're having sex."

Jana scowled and dug back into her ice cream. "As it turns out, regular sex can be highly overrated." She waved a loaded spoon when Lucy went to apologize. "No, don't. Ignore me. What's that?" she asked around a mouthful of ice cream, and pointed to a pile of shimmery silk hanging over Lucy's closet doorknob.

Lucy scooped up the garter belt and matching stockings and dangled them from one hand.

Jana wolf-whistled.

"Too much, right?" Lucy looked at the black heels she'd already decided to wear. When she paired them with the lingerie and stockings, not to mention that little slit in the back of the black skirt . . . well, it did seem a bit too much. "Maybe panty hose instead?"

Jana rolled her eyes. "Chicken. What happened to Ms. I Want Out of My Comfort Zone? What could be more uncomfortable than strapping yourself up in a garter belt for a guy who might or might not ever see it?"

"The idea is if you feel sexy, you project sexy," Lucy said. She ran the stockings across the skirt and sweater. "I'm not sure I want to feel that sexy. Besides, panty hose might be part of the 'I'm a good girl' signal I want to send."

"Fine. Except if you do eventually want to take them off. Because we all know taking off panty hose is such a surefire way to look sexy. Especially when it's your first time together. Another good reason to give up wearing dresses."

Lucy gulped. "I can't believe we're even talking about this. It's my first date with the guy, and you and Vivian both have me romping in the hay with him already."

Jana just laughed. "Right. With Jason Prescott. Like you haven't pictured that very thing, like, a thousand times. Ten thousand times."

Lucy couldn't pull off that lie, so she didn't even try. "Fantasizing isn't the same as doing. Maybe if I make it through this date without tripping over my feet, spilling something in my lap—or worse, his lap—and he asks me out again, *then* I'll begin to think about whether I'll let him take things to the next level."

"Oh, for God's sake, you sound like a reality dating-show contestant. 'I feel such a connection. We're on this journey together. I can't wait to take it to the next level,' " she said, mimicking the words in a breathy exaggerated voice. "If you want to jump the guy, jump him."

"Says the woman who no longer worries about safe sex."

"Yeah, well, maybe I should have." She raised a hand. "Kidding, kidding." She sighed, looked at Lucy. "You want Jason Prescott. So take him. But tell me, do you really like the guy? I mean, apart from what he represents to you?"

"Sure."

Jana just cocked her head.

"Okay, so maybe we didn't get much of a chance to talk. I don't know him all that well. But he still has that same charm and sizzle he always did. Only now it's all grown-up and even more potent."

"So you're thinking long-term-relationship possibility here?"

"I'm not thinking anything beyond getting through this date."

"Okay. That's fair."

Lucy wondered if Jana's ambivalence about her dating Jason Prescott had more to do with her feelings about Grady not liking it than whatever she might personally feel about the situation. But Lucy didn't have time to delve into that right now. Convenient excuse, that.

Jana slid off the bed and shoved her feet back into her suede walking boots. "Just be prepared for anything. That's my motto."

"Vivian's, too." She didn't tell Jana she'd already moved *all* the contents of her reunion-night clutch to her regular purse.

"I'm liking this Vivian more all the time," Jana called out, as Lucy went off to get dressed.

"You would," Lucy said. Then pulled out her war paint and began preparing herself for battle.

She just wished she knew exactly what it was she was fighting for.

# Chapter 22

Chirra was a spectacular location for Lucy's dream date. So elegant. One look around at the sumptuous Mediterranean design, the pricey art, the serious menu, and she realized that there must be a lot of money to be made in getting athletes acquitted of assault and DUI charges.

"Wine or champagne?" Jason queried.

She was still absorbing her surroundings, not to mention her company for the evening, and didn't respond right away. *My, how The World According to Lucy Harper has changed, eh?* She studied her artsy menu, which was a single page mounted on an abstract-shaped piece of slate. *Handy as a menu or a weapon,* she thought. It was hand-drawn, complete with a small watercolor pattern bordering the edge. Every aspect of the restaurant, down to the tiniest detail, had been handled with care. So elegant, so perfect, it made Lucy a bit nervous.

"Wine would be fine," she finally said, proud that she'd

managed to utter all of four words without dropping, spilling, or mispronouncing anything. She'd even rhymed. Emboldened by her success, she chanced a glance up and offered a smile, hoping for sophisticated and worldly, but satisfied with nice and nominally intelligent. "Why don't you select?"

He beamed. Another male, happy to be in charge.

Lucy was fine with that. Let him handle the ordering. She was still busy trying to figure out what she hoped to get out of this date. Part of her felt that this evening was nothing more than self-esteem payback after Jason's rude dismissal of her so many years ago. But . . . sitting across from him now, in his gorgeously tailored suit, she was forced to admit she didn't feel so far removed from that starry-eyed high school senior she'd been ten years ago, the one with a hopeless crush on the most popular boy in school. He was beautiful then and he was beautiful now.

Vivian's words about her being the beholder floated through her mind. It wasn't just about what he sees. *So,* she wondered, *is this what it feels like to recognize passion?*

Upon her arrival at the restaurant, Lucy discovered that Jason was waiting just inside the restaurant door, watching for her. She saw him first, tall and handsome and hers, and had paused for a moment to really absorb that fact. But even when he turned and saw her, began making his way toward her with unmistakable interest gleaming in his eyes, she still felt like the dorky wallflower playing dress-up in her glamorous older sister's clothes.

If Lucy just pretended to be the hot, sophisticated chick long enough, maybe she'd actually become the hot, sophisticated chick. If it walked like a duck, and looked like a duck . . .

"Duck?" Jason said, startling her.

*Dear God, had she spoken out loud?* "I beg your pardon?"

"The foie gras? Would that work as an appetizer for you? You're not a vegetarian or anything, are you?"

"No, no," she quickly assured him. An easy question, she

could answer this one without thinking. "I'm a big meat eater. Nothing better than a big piece of meat, I always say." *Oh, God!* This time she had spoken out loud. She quickly buried her flaming face in her menu.

"Me, too," he said, chuckling.

She wanted to crawl under the table, but she forced herself to peek over her menu and attempt a good-natured smile, only to be caught once again by his brilliant smile and golden-boy tan. He really was beautiful.

"You look nice," he said, as she ducked back behind the safety of her menu before she started to drool.

With a rather limited but refined set of choices, Lucy feared that she appeared to be either extremely picky or indecisive. She finally set the menu slab aside. He'd been so tickled to have his judgment deferred to about the wine, he'd be downright ecstatic when she told him he could order the whole damn meal. "Thank you," she said, forcing herself to meet his gaze head-on. *Don't picture him naked. Or say anything about meat. Any kind of meat.*

"You look so different from the dance, I almost didn't recognize you."

She froze in mid-casual-smile. "I do?" She knew the sweater was too casual for this place. She was going to kill Jana. She should have gone with the red silk. Jason Prescott was a lady-in-red kind of man. Dammit, she'd known that. So what if she was a woman-in-wool kind of girl? This wasn't about her being comfortable. This was about—

That stopped her. She still wasn't quite sure what this was about.

Proving to herself that she could make Jason want her as revenge for prom night? Yes, Jason had been a jerk to her that night, but that was ten years ago. Right now he seemed more like a great-looking guy who was treating her to a lovely dinner and apparently interested in getting to know her. Wouldn't it be okay if she felt the same way? After all, they were both single, available adults.

Maybe this wasn't about the past at all, but about what the future might hold now . . . years later. Let bygones be bygones, and all that. Could it really be that simple? And if so, why in the hell was she wearing this stupid garter belt?

Because it wasn't regular Lucy Harper who'd gotten his attention in the first place. It was Vixen Lucy. Cyborg Lucy. Fake Lucy.

"Is that a bad thing?" she blurted out. "Looking different?"

"No, no, not at all," he assured her with that smooth, easy charm of his. "I love cashmere." His gaze drifted down to her sweater. "Very tactile."

She was trying to decide if that was some kind of come-on, when his gaze moved back to her face and he said, "I know a guy on Seventh Avenue who does wonders with cashmere. I had him make a winter coat for me last year. Dynamite. Very versatile. Goes with everything."

*My God, he actually meant* he *loved cashmere. Personally. Jason Prescott. Metrosexual?* " 'Seventh'? Is that northeast or west?"

He frowned for a moment, then laughed. "Not in D.C. New York City. Sorry, I should have clarified. If you want, I'll give you his card. You should really check him out next time you go up." He flashed her another dazzling smile of encouragement. "He could do amazing things with you."

She basked in the glow just for a moment because, after all, she was human. And female. No matter how much of her was fake, the original wiring was still all hers. She wondered how to break it to Jason that she didn't just "go up" to NYC on any kind of regular basis. Like ever. She settled for, "I don't get up to the city all that often." Since her seventh-grade field trip, to be exact.

"Oh." He seemed a bit startled by the idea. "Well, there's a place in Georgetown. He's appointment only. But I'd be glad to put in a word." He chuckled self-deprecatingly, all handsome abashed perfection. "Of course, I shouldn't assume. For all I know, you could give me a better recommendation. Do you use a tailor? I guess women call them 'tailors,' right? 'Seamstress' seems a bit dated."

Lucy managed a grin that could only be considered weak in comparison to his beaming smile. She didn't even use a Macy's personal shopper. She spent a few more seconds trying to decide how long she could maintain any kind of real pretense, then gave it up. If this wasn't about revenge, but about truly getting to know the adult version of a guy she'd had a major crush on in high school, then the only thing to do was to be true to herself and see where that took her.

"Actually, I'm a department-store girl myself," she said. No point in dragging out the inevitable. At least she'd get a good meal out of it. She hoped foie gras tasted better than it sounded. "Seamstresses and tailors are a bit outside my budget, I'm afraid."

Jason's bright smile dimmed slightly. "I'm sorry. I've presumed too much. And here I've been going on and on like some stuck-up snob. It's just that dress, and the jewelry, the night of the reunion . . ."

"Borrowed." She waited to see if he was still the same old Jason Prescott from high school. The one that would ask if she wouldn't mind giving him the number of the hot chick who really owned all that stuff.

Instead he lifted one broad shoulder and ducked his chin quite endearingly. "I jumped to conclusions I shouldn't have. I'm sorry."

And the fantasy momentarily gasped back to life, struggling to stay alive.

The waiter stopped by their table then, and after reciting an exhaustive list of specials that weren't on the menu, in a tone that made it clear they couldn't even begin to understand the enormity of their chef's ability, Jason made quick, decisive selections, then smiled easily as the waiter hurried off to do his bidding. It was good to be the Boy King.

When he returned his attention to her, he did it with such focus, she felt like the only woman in the room. On the planet. In the universe.

Okay, so maybe she still needed to get a grip on things. Which was it going to be? Fantasy? Or reality? Could they really be one and the same?

"So, since you're not an international supermodel after all, what is it you do, Lucy?"

He was teasing, but she *so* wished she could say something more interesting right now than "third-grade teacher." *I empower the youth of tomorrow,* however, was too pompous, even for Lucy 2.0.

Reality it was. "I'm a schoolteacher," she said, then offered a wistful smile. "Third grade." No need to be ashamed of what she did or how much it didn't pay. And she wasn't. It just sounded so . . . repressed. And goody-goody. She didn't want to be a goody-goody. Not with Jason.

"Wow, really? Well, I wish I'd had an elementary-school teacher who looked like you. I might have actually paid attention in class."

She flushed at the compliment, feeling decidedly less goody than she had a moment ago. "I'm sure you were an ace student. The teachers probably adored you." She caught herself. Too gushy?

His face warmed a bit, or maybe it was the lighting. But it worked for him, either way. "I guess I did okay."

Their wine arrived and after Jason went through the taste-testing routine, which he carried off with the same casual aplomb he did with everything, he handed her a glass. She took a sip, resisting the urge to down the entire contents in one gulp. She'd revealed the truth about herself, and the date hadn't come to a screeching halt. In fact, if she was any judge, he still seemed interested.

"More than okay," she said, confidence momentarily bolstered.

He grinned at that. "You know, I've been thinking about you these past two weeks. You wreaked havoc on my focus while I was writing my closing arguments. I was tempted to call you, just to get you, that dance, the kiss, out of my head. At least for the moment."

*Okay, the wine must have been laced with a hallucinogen. Was Jason Prescott really saying these things to her?*

"Or at least put it in some kind of perspective."

She almost choked on her sip of wine. Perspective. Now there was something she'd apparently long since lost a grip on where he was concerned.

"But you didn't tell me your last name." He reached over then, traced one of those long fingers along her wrist and over the back of her hand. And suddenly she was very, very glad she'd kept the condoms. "I felt sort of like the prince after the ball, with only your first name as my glass slipper."

She put the wine down. *No more wine.* It sloshed a little in the glass as she fought to clear her throat.

For just a split second, years of wallflower paranoia swam to the surface and she wondered if this was all another setup designed to humiliate her. That at some point everyone from his old crowd was going to magically appear and they'd all point their fingers at her and have a good laugh. But no, even she wasn't *that* paranoid.

"It's Harper." She bit the corner of her bottom lip, heedless of the carefully applied lip liner she was probably chewing off.

Jason's perfect smile and gorgeous face squinched up a little as he tried to recollect the girl she'd been.

Lucy thought he even looked sexy when he squinched.

"Did we have any classes together?" he asked.

*Fifteen in four years.* "A few." *Not to mention the student council and the yearbook staff.* She waved her hand lightly. "I wasn't one of the popular gang back then." *Or ever.* "And, like I said at the reunion, I've changed a little." *Completely. Except on the inside.*

Jason's expression smoothed as he smiled again. "It was a big school, so I guess none of us knew everyone."

"Some of us fewer than others," she mumbled.

"What?"

"Nothing." She was saved by the foie gras. Which, as it turned out, was not going to make her top-ten list of things to order on first dates. Or any dates, ever again.

Lucy forced herself to swallow another bite of pasty duck liver without choking. "So," she said, gagging just a little as the gelatinous glob went down. She recovered by dabbing her mouth with her napkin. Once the duck had slid home, she worked up a smile.

"Very nicely done," Jason was saying as he savored the taste. "I'll have to recommend this place to my partners."

"You're a partner in your firm, then? That's wonderful at such a young age."

Jason beamed. "Thank you. I admit, I'm proud of the achievement. But I worked my tail off. Still do." He chuckled. "Well, enough about me. You probably got bored to tears at the reunion with all the talk of my background."

She could have told him she knew every detail about his background without having listened in to even one reunion-night group-replay discussion. But she was still dealing with the aftermath of her total forgettableness being so blithely confirmed. Not that she'd been surprised. Mentioning she'd spent all four years in high school pining after him like a lovesick puppy was probably frowned on in the first-date handbook.

"What got you into teaching?"

"Both of my parents are teachers. My father is an English professor at Georgetown and my mom also teaches English, but at American." Which made her whole family sound about as exciting as watching mud dry.

Jason's eyes still lit with what she could only assume was feigned interest. "Quite a heritage. Did you feel pressured to follow in their footsteps?"

"No, not at all. There was simply nothing else I was particularly good at."

He paused for a moment, not sure she was joking.

She tried to make a sound as if she were amused by her own self-deprecation, but it came out sounding a bit like a snort. "We can't all be jocks, right?" When he looked confused, she quickly changed the subject. "Do lawyers run in your family?"

He stared at her a second longer, but the team-captain smile quickly resurfaced as he shook his head. "I have two uncles that coach college ball, one at Washington State, one for Indiana. My dad was a collegiate all-star in baseball who made it to the minors before his pitching arm gave out. He runs a personal-training business for executives." Again with the self-deprecating smile. "We're more brawn than brains in the Prescott family tree, I'm afraid."

Lucy smiled. "Well, lucky you, you got both." Okay, that might have sounded a bit more snarky than she'd intended. He was treating her nicely and being perfectly decent. So where was all this attitude coming from? So what if he didn't remember her? Given how things had gone in high school—or hadn't—that was a good thing. Right? Fresh start and all that.

"I wasn't the first Prescott through college, but I was the first through law school."

"I bet your family is very proud of you."

He nodded, chuckled. "Yeah. They only occasionally harass me about not making it into the pros now."

"Did they really give you a hard time? You were sidelined due to an injury, right? Because you were being scouted before then. At—at least, that's what I overheard. At the reunion." *Right. Good save, Luce. Because we wouldn't want him to think you're a stalker or anything.*

"Well, I won't say they weren't disappointed. Devastated, actually. More than I was, I think." He was still smiling, only his eyes weren't quite as twinkly. "Usually it's the parents that force a kid to have a backup career when sports are involved. In my case, I was the one convincing them that sports law wasn't a bad second choice."

He was making light, but Lucy saw beyond the surface. Could it be that Jason Prescott had difficulties, too? Just like mere mortals? Well, of course it shouldn't come as a surprise that he'd faced his share of challenges. Who hadn't? She ducked her chin. Because if she'd been asked that question five minutes ago, she'd have easily pointed to her dinner partner. Now who was the shallow one?

Imagining him with normal problems, however, did little to settle her still-swarming butterflies. He looked pretty darn problem-free at the moment. And there was nothing normal about the rest of him, either. The phrase "god among men" came to mind.

"My dad dreamed of sitting courtside and watching me play in the NBA. It was hard for him to get over that dream."

"I'd think he'd understand more than anyone, seeing as an injury sidelined his career in the pros, too."

"You'd think. But it made it worse. He'd always pushed me, hard, in sports. And I knew he was sort of living his dream through me. He'd been hit hard enough with the reality that I wasn't going to make it in baseball. I got my uncle's height early and my heart was on the hardwood courts, not the baseball diamond. That was hard for him to swallow."

Lucy sat there, trying to imagine her parents putting that kind of pressure on her. Sure, she knew they'd have been thrilled if she'd aimed a bit higher and sought to teach at the same academic level they did. But they'd never made her feel less than good enough for teaching in public school. And though they loved to brag to their friends that she'd followed in their footsteps, Lucy didn't think they'd have given her any real difficulty if she'd chosen a completely different field.

The slight pause in their conversation expanded to the awkward stage and Lucy searched for the right thing to say to get them back on a more lighthearted track. "Well, I imagine as partner in your firm you can still get them courtside seats, right?" *Sensitive to his needs, yet still witty.*

Only he didn't get quite the kick out of her comment as she'd hoped. He smiled in response, perfunctory this time, then looked relieved when their dinner showed up.

Well, she'd made it to the entrée before sticking her foot in her mouth. At least her stomach was still empty. She'd pushed around and rearranged her foie gras and parsley snippet until it hopefully looked like she'd eaten more than she had. She was never so grateful than when the waiter cleared that away. Until he put her next dish in front of her. She swallowed hard. It was that or gag. "Are those? . . ."

"Escargot. I hear they make this cream sauce here that is to die for. I really think you'll love it."

He seemed so enthusiastic.

And—oh, goody—the side dish was steamed asparagus. Her second-to-last favorite vegetable, falling right between brussels sprouts and cooked spinach. Maybe if she was really lucky, they'd have sushi for dessert. She'd accepted an invitation to dinner and somehow landed on *Fear Factor: First Date.*

She must not have hidden her reaction as well as she'd hoped, because Jason paused before attacking his first defenseless snail—so what if it was already dead, it just made the whole thing seem that much more tragic—and glanced over at her. "First time eating escargot?" Mercifully, he didn't wait for the embarrassing—and quite obvious answer—reaching instead for the accompanying Tool of Torture. "Here, you just push the fork in the opening and—"

"I can't even pick crabmeat out of the shell," she suddenly blurted. "I'm not going to be able to do this."

He looked momentarily stunned at her outburst.

*Join the club,* she thought morosely. It was like she was purposely sabotaging the whole evening. But honestly, there was no way she was digging that creature out of its shell, much less dunking it in some white sauce and chewing it up.

"I—I thought you weren't a vegetarian. I'm sorry."

She had to tear her gaze away from her plate. Just in case one of the shells moved. Or something. With her date karma, it could happen. She tried for a winsome smile. Hopefully her skin looked less green than it felt. "I'm not one of those 'I can't eat it if it had a face' types. Really. I just kind of need the face to be gone before I eat it." Her gaze was pulled back to her plate. "Otherwise I feel like I should name it and give it a home."

She glanced back up at Jason, who thankfully wasn't staring at her like she'd just sprouted two heads. But the engaging class-president-by-a-landslide smile was not in place, either. He mostly looked nonplussed.

"I'm really sorry. I should have paid closer attention when you were ordering." *Instead of staring at your stunning flawless-*

*ness and wondering what the chances were you'd ever use the condoms in my purse.*

"No, no," he said, snapping out of his momentary lapse in perfection. "Not a problem. It's just, when we met, you struck me as, I don't know, exotic somehow. You know, no name tag, killer dress, amazing jewelry hanging all over you. First-name-only basis. You were mysterious."

"Really?" She couldn't help it. She grinned. The fate of the snails momentarily forgotten as she basked in the glow of his surprising confession. She might have even preened. Just a tiny little hair flip, but it couldn't be helped. No one had ever used the words "mysterious" or "exotic" in the same paragraph as "Lucy Harper" before. An autobiography's worth of words about Lucy Harper would come and go and never come close to using either of them.

His smile broadened once again and he relaxed, the date once again on even footing. "I was trying to impress you with my worldliness."

Jason Prescott. Worried about impressing Lucy Harper. Her life had officially come full circle. Her world now tilted in a whole new way.

He chuckled. "Of course, I didn't know you were a schoolteacher then."

And *whump.* Back on its regular axis.

"Well, I'm sure there are plenty of schoolteachers who eat escargot." She pushed her plate back. "I guess I'm just not one of them. I'll be glad to take care of my meal," she told him. It wasn't fair to make him pay for something she couldn't—or wouldn't—eat.

"No, no. I invited you, and it was my anxiousness that created the problem." He glanced around for their waiter, and as was usually the case for the Golden People, he magically appeared, as if his only role in life was to serve Jason.

Lucy usually waited far too long in the hopes of subtly catching her server's attention with a lifted hand or a nod. After a while, when she realized even a taxi whistle wouldn't get their attention, she'd nicely ask a busboy to track her errant waiter down. And even then they never rushed out. Maybe that had changed slightly in her post–Glass Slipper experience, but with school in session, and okay, no dates on her social calendar, she hadn't had much of a chance to test it out.

Jason quickly had her plate cleared away. "Would it bother you if I—" He motioned to his own pile of unlucky snails.

"No, no," she assured him. *Go right ahead and dig their poor little bodies out of their little shells. I'll just be over here pretending I'm anywhere else on the planet.* She felt guilty enough about wasting her food, she could hardly ask him to waste his, as well.

From memory, Jason asked the server to bring another dish from the menu. "Chicken marsala okay with you?" he asked her. "Is it free-range chicken?" he asked the waiter.

Which made her feel like the Difficult Date From Hell. She didn't care where the chicken lived before they chopped its head off. She just didn't want to be the one doing the chopping. Or the plucking. It really wasn't all that complicated.

The waiter hurried off to find out the chicken's complete personal history before she could tell him not to worry about it. Which left Jason sitting there politely letting his snails grow cold. Or warm. Whichever they weren't originally. She really didn't want to know.

"I'm really sorry," she said again. "I truly wasn't trying to be difficult." She tried an engaging smile, game to the end. "Normally a burger or a plate of spaghetti and I'm happy as a clam." She stopped short at the unintentional irony, then had to swallow an Inappropriate Snicker.

Jason didn't seem to share that difficulty. In fact, he didn't seem to notice the amusing analogy at all. So much for being witty and engaging.

"Not a problem," he said easily.

"Please," she said, feeling more out of place by the moment, "go ahead and eat. There's no reason your dinner should be less than perfect." *Like me.*

She'd wanted to normalize the evening? Well, she'd done that in spades. She supposed she should be careful what she wished for.

One more evening pretending to be Cinderella wouldn't have killed her. And it might have gotten her laid. *Sorry, Vivian.*

# Chapter 23

"No good-night kiss. That's not good." *Unless your name is Grady Matthews.* Jana sipped her water and stared out at the people jogging by. Dave had been hovering all morning—hell, all week—smothering her. He felt like he'd let her down somehow, and of course he hadn't. This was her problem, not his. Which made her feel guilty for hurting him and more like a freak about this whole thing than she already did. So when Lucy had called and begged her to come meet her somewhere, anywhere, to talk about the Big Date, she'd been more than happy to oblige.

It was a gorgeous October morning, so they sat on a bench on The Mall downtown, in the shadow of the Capitol, watching the weekend warriors play Frisbee, soccer, and volleyball. It felt good to have the sun on her face, even if the air was a bit brisk. Unfortunately, the guilt she'd hoped to leave at home had trailed her here.

"Yeah, I figured my Cinderella story was over."

Jana shifted the sour ball to the side of her mouth. "Are you saying it's not?" She swatted Lucy's arm. "Why didn't you just come out and say so?"

"Ow," she said, rubbing the spot. "You have to let me savor some of this. Don't lie and say you're unhappy with the way the date turned out."

"I don't want to see you hurt." That much was true.

"I was disappointed, not hurt."

Jana smiled. "That part I was okay with."

"Gee, thanks."

Turning serious, Jana shifted around on the bench to face Lucy more directly. "It's just that, to be perfectly honest, I feel like you could do better. I mean, look at you."

Lucy looked down. "What? I'm Regular Old Lucy today."

Jana shook her head. "You might be wearing the old Lucy's jeans and sweatshirt, but, well . . . you're different now, Luce."

Lucy looked a little hurt and Jana rushed to explain. "I don't mean that in a bad way. It's more than the hair and all that. You've got this kind of, I don't know, inner confidence now."

Lucy snorted loudly. "I can assure you that is a total act."

"No," Jana said quite seriously, "it's not. The old Lucy would never have strutted her stuff to the reunion."

"I didn't 'strut.' I almost took out half the waitstaff when I tried that. Mostly I circled the outside of the room, praying I wouldn't fall off my heels and my boobs would continue to defy gravity and double-sided tape until the stroke of twelve."

"But in the end, you pulled it off. Just like you pulled off dinner last night. I'm really proud of you."

"Yeah, I can tell."

She rubbed Lucy's shoulder. "I'm serious. You weren't happy with things the way they were, so you formulated a plan and went after it. I admire that. If I had the first clue how to get over my own problems, I would."

Lucy's expression immediately changed to one of concern. "Dave's still being weird?"

Jana really didn't want to talk about Dave or anything having to do with her impending motherhood. The mere thought made her want to throw up. Of course, everything made her want to throw up. She looked away, sipped her water. "He feels like he let me down. He's smothering me with attention. It's one of the reasons I jumped on your offer to get outside today."

"Aw, Jana. I'm so sorry. Maybe if I talk to him or something. Make him realize it's not him."

Jana made a noise in her throat. It was that or sob. "No, it's just me. The only happily married woman on the planet not thrilled at the idea of having a child."

"You know that's not true."

Jana sighed. "Yeah. I know. Listen, I'm here to talk about your miserable life, not mine." She gave Lucy a sidelong smile.

"Maybe we should be talking about you." Lucy feigned an air of wounded pride. "Unless, of course, you feel I've changed so much you can't trust me."

She was clearly teasing, but Jana knew she'd hurt Lucy more with her comments than her friend was letting on. "Listen, ignore everything I said earlier. You're still you. Blonder, but still a dork at heart, okay? I love you, that hasn't changed. It's me, not you. It's just that nothing is staying the same. Not you. Not Grady. Most definitely not me. And I guess I'm not handling it well."

"If it makes you feel any better, I haven't sorted this all out for myself, either. I mean, you are right, I do feel more confident most of the time. But I also still feel like I'm playing dress-up. Last night I wanted to just be me. See if Jason responded to the woman behind the NASA bra. And that's when the date went downhill." Lucy shrugged. "I like feeling more confident, but I'm not sure I want to do all this"—she gestured to her hair, herself—"girly maintenance stuff to have it."

"Do you think that maybe the reason the date didn't feel right was because Jason doesn't fit with you?"

"Are we back on the prom thing? Because I hope we're not held accountable for life for all the stupid things we said and did as teenagers."

"Fine, fine. He's a prince among men now." She lifted her hand. "A hot, rich prince. I'm still not feeling any real connection between you two. You said the date was awkward."

"It was, but that was because of the snails. And the foie gras."

"And the fact that he shops for cashmere in New York City and has a tailor," Jana added.

Lucy's expression turned stubborn. "I told you about his family, how they were disappointed he got into law, and how hard that's been for him to handle."

"Yeah, poor Jason has to settle for being a big-time lawyer instead of a jock. Lucy, this is a guy who orders weird stuff without consulting his date, then talks about himself all night."

"I asked him to order. I was nervous. Besides, he only ordered exotic food because he was trying to impress me." She paused, wiggled her eyebrows. "He thought I was exotic and mysterious."

Jana choked on a laugh. "Sorry," she said, then lifted her hands when Lucy pretended to swing her water bottle. "Don't clock the pregnant lady for inappropriate laughter. Yet another good reason to be with child."

"See? I am helping. Was Dave happy you agreed to go to Canada for Thanksgiving?"

Jana sighed. Apparently, she wasn't going to avoid this particular topic after all. "I think he was more relieved than anything. He doesn't know what to do with me, and I know he's hoping the women in his family will just fix me and make me happy. Of course, I'd probably be less cranky if I could just stop puking all the damn time. I'm either heaving, crying, or sleeping. And I can't tell you how much fun that makes my workdays, trying to hide all that from my lovely coworkers."

"You haven't told them yet, huh?"

"No. They must think I'm having the world's worst PMS or something. And I'm fine with that. Once I get past this first trimester, I'm praying my stomach settles. I'm still not sure when I'll tell them."

"You could always say nothing and let the bump speak for itself," Lucy said, motioning to Jana's stomach.

Jana just shrugged. Telling her coworkers and her boss was the least of her concerns at the moment.

Lucy squeezed her arm. "I wish I could make this easier on you. I still think you should consider talking to a counselor or something."

"Hey, 'research' is my middle name."

Lucy brightened. "You picked up some books?"

"Did you know there is a ton of info on postpartum depression now, but almost zero for during-partum depression?"

Lucy frowned and Jana was suddenly really tired of this subject. So she did what any self-respecting best friend would do, she changed the subject back to Lucy. "So the Date From Hell is over, no kiss, thinking you'll never see him again . . . what was that secret smile all about?"

Lucy refused to be distracted. "You can't keep ignoring this and hope it will go away, you know."

Jana gave her a weak imitation of her dry smile. "Watch me."

"Yes, and in about seven months you're going to be in for a shock."

Jana groaned. "Don't remind me."

*"Jana."*

Lucy looked so sad for her, Jana knew she had to end this discussion now. She really wasn't up for it. "If you really want to help me, you'll take my mind off of this by talking about anything else. Even Jason Prescott. So what was the big news?"

Lucy paused for another moment, then apparently sensed Jana's desperation and did as she'd asked. "He called this morning."

Jana couldn't help the surprised look. "Wow. Less than twenty-four hours later? Hmm."

"I know. Less than twelve hours, actually." Lucy looked like she barely refrained from clapping her hands together. "He even had to go to the trouble of looking up my number, since I didn't give it to him."

Jana didn't want to mention that Jason had probably put a secretary or assistant on that task. "So, where is he taking you this time?"

"He was asked to speak at some lawyer thing downtown at the Willard and wanted to know if I'd be interested in being his date. It's this Friday."

Jana frowned. "'This Friday'? Sort of last-minute."

"It's a week away. And don't go raining on my parade. I know he's out of town all week and probably couldn't get anybody else and I'm just available, but I don't care." She leaned forward a little. "It's dressy. And I imagine I'll get to meet some of his coworkers, so he must be pretty confident of me."

Jana wished she felt the same confidence.

Lucy huffed out a sigh. "What? Go ahead, crush my happiness."

Jana's dry smile felt far more natural this time. "It's my job to keep you grounded in cold, harsh reality."

"And your version of that would be?"

"That he's probably known for bringing a different woman to every function he's invited to. I don't know that I'd get all excited about meeting the coworkers, is all I'm saying. Sorry," she added sincerely.

"No, no, you're right. And I thought about that, too. But then I figured, why be such a pessimist? I didn't think we'd have another chance, and now we do." She glared at Jana. "Yes, I want another chance."

Jana lifted her hands. "Fine, okay. So, tell me one thing, did he happen to sort of mention what he'd like you to wear?"

Lucy looked immediately guarded. "Why do you ask?"

"Aha! He did, didn't he?"

"So what if he did, what difference does that make?"

"Just that you said he was all 'You're so mysterious,' until you told him you're a grade-school teacher who can't eat snails, and then things got all awkward. I'm just trying to keep your perspective here."

"He knows I clean up nicely."

"He knows you can borrow hot clothes on demand. He wants you to look more like Exotic Reunion Lucy than Demure Dinner Lucy, am I right?"

"Maybe," Lucy said, obviously trying not to sound defensive and failing.

"And wasn't it you who said you felt like you were hiding behind the blonde highlights and fake nails?"

"You know, I'm beginning to think best friends are a highly overrated commodity. First Grady deserts me, now you."

Jana debated for all of two seconds before blurting out, "I talked to Grady yesterday."

Lucy's eyes widened. "Why didn't you tell me? Is he still pretending he doesn't know me? What am I saying, of course he is."

"It was last night, a few hours after I got home from your place."

Lucy's eyes narrowed. "Who called who?"

"Whom. And with not one, but two English professor parents." Jana *tsked.*

"You're stalling. You called him, didn't you? Did you tell him I was out with Jason?"

"He knows."

Lucy slapped her thighs. "Oh, great. First I leave Grady standing in front of the Hay-Adams because I'm too busy revisiting my giddy schoolgirl past, and now he knows Jason asked me out for a date? Fabulous." She swore under her breath. "I guess I'll be eating turkey alone this year."

"I, uh, I haven't told him about that yet."

Lucy just looked more forlorn at the news. "I'm thinking it's not going to matter. What are we going to do, J? I mean, I love Grady; I miss him like crazy. I can't stand that this has broken us up."

"I think we're all going through some stuff right now." Jana laid her hand on Lucy's knee. "It's not just about you." She wished she could say more. She hated seeing either of her friends suffer.

"Okay, so you're dealing with"—Lucy waved her hand in the general direction of Jana's stomach—"and I'm dealing with my new split-personality issues. I know Grady is very disappointed about my seeing Jason, but honestly, it's not such a big thing that he has to treat me like a pariah. It's not like I'm going to bring Jason to Pizza Night. He's still talking to you."

Jana wished she'd kept her mouth shut. It was hard enough talking to him and not forcing the Lucy Issue, as it was. She didn't need to do this with Lucy, too. "Just let him be a jerk for a little while. Let him blow off steam, bury himself in his work, and then when he surfaces and realizes how much he misses you, he'll come around. You know he will."

"I wish I felt as certain of that as you." Lucy shook her head. "I just wish he could be more like you about this. I mean, it's obvious you've no love lost for Jason, either, although I really think you should reserve judgment until we see where this thing goes. But you've managed to put aside your personal animosity and focus on what I'm getting out of this."

When Jana pointedly looked away, Lucy dragged at her arm until she met her gaze again. "What?" Jana said. "I'm trying to be open-minded, but you're right. I think Jason was a prick in high school. A good-looking, charming-as-the-devil prick, but a prick is a prick."

"Why don't you say that a little louder?"

Jana opened her mouth to shout it to the world, only Lucy jerked her arm and shushed her. "Okay," Lucy said, glancing around. "I get it."

"And just what are you getting out of it, anyway?" Jana asked.

"There's chemistry there. When he danced with me, kissed me—"

"You were so caught up in the idea of being kissed by Jason Prescott I bet you don't even remember how it felt." When Lucy didn't immediately reply, Jana pointed a finger. "Aha! I'm right. The chemistry is just you being desired by a desirable. When you get down to it, you don't really like the guy much."

"He didn't treat me badly on the date. I just think . . ." She trailed off and picked at the label on her bottle of water.

"What?" Jana asked more gently.

Lucy sighed a little, looked up. "Yes, he seems a bit bigger than life, but he has that kind of life. He was also more human than I expected, and nothing but polite with me. If the fault on the crappy date lies anywhere, it's with me."

*"You?"*

Lucy smiled a little. "See, that's why I have you as my best friend. Thanks for the instant defensive reaction. I feel better now."

"You're welcome. Now, explain how the Date From Hell was your fault."

"Because he was exactly what I knew him to be. But I wasn't what he expected me to be. The dance night was a sham on my part. I mean, that was me in that dress, with those jewels and that hair. But we didn't really get any chance to talk there, to know anything more about each other than that there was chemistry between us. That was enough for me. Enough to want to go out with him when he asked. I just thought when he started to get to know the real me, the chemistry sort of died a little on his side of things." She smiled. "Then he called me. So maybe I was just too flustered to read things right."

"So you're going to the Willard this Friday."

"Sue me. I'm human. He's interested. I'm still curious."

"Except the person he asked out was Vixen Lucy."

"You're making me feel even more schizo about this whole thing than I already do."

"Well, you were the one who said you wanted to start keeping it real. How long do you think you can keep up the Glass Slipper Barbie front?"

She abandoned her attempts to peel the label off the bottle and looked squarely at Jana. "Vivian thinks if I just walk the walk and talk the talk, eventually it will become more natural for me."

"So, okay, let's go with that theory. You start to like the whole spike heels, siren dress, perfectly-plucked-everything deal. You get used to the whole girly-girl routine, embrace your outer Barbie. Fine. But that doesn't change who you are on the inside. You're still a third-grade teacher from Alexandria with a goofy sense of humor, no personal shopper, and two dorky best friends."

"A more confident third-grade teacher from Alexandria with a goofy sense of humor and two dorky best friends. Or one, anyway."

"Can you be confident enough to go mingle in Jason's world and still feel like you can be yourself?"

"Honestly? I don't know," Lucy answered. "I guess I feel like I've come this far and I want the chance to find out." She grinned. "Look at it this way, even if Jason never calls me again, I'll have dipped my toes into a whole new dating pool."

"Just be careful they don't get bitten off," Jana muttered.

"Your confidence in me is so inspiring," Lucy said dryly.

"It's not you I lack confidence in. I just don't want to see you—"

"Get hurt. I know. And I appreciate that you guys worry about me, even though I think it's misplaced. But I think I've got my eyes pretty wide open at this point. It's still just as much about figuring my own self out as it is in getting a man."

Jana just gave her a look.

"Okay, so if I happen to get laid and he happens to make six figures a year and drives a Carrera, I'm not exactly going to complain."

Jana sipped her water and didn't say anything, and for a few minutes they both turned their attention back to the action on The Mall. "You know I do get that you're just trying to figure things out for yourself. I don't want you to limit yourself, or not reach for new things."

Lucy shot her a sideways smile. "Now you sound like a mom." Her smile grew when Jana scowled. "Maybe *you* should embrace that reality. Reach for it instead of being so terrified of it."

"I thought we were talking about you."

"Oh yeah, you're all for me taking risks," she teased, but gently.

Jana smiled a little. "A girl has to try."

"Yes," Lucy said, quite seriously, "a girl does."

Jana ducked her head, wishing she could duck the whole issue. "So," she said, taking a deep breath, then looking at Lucy, "what if I reach for it, embrace this whole motherhood thing . . . only to find I can't hack it? That I resent the hell out of my own child for having the nerve to be born and wrecking all my carefully laid plans?"

Lucy pulled Jana into a hug. "You won't be in this alone, you know."

"Parts of it I will," Jana said testily.

Lucy loosened her hold on her and smiled. "Yeah, but they make really good drugs for that part." Then she took Jana's water bottle and set both bottles aside before taking Jana's hands in hers. "We'll be with you every step of the way. Before and after."

They were both sniffling and Jana could only nod. "Thanks," she managed, wishing she could better articulate what Lucy's support really meant to her. Instead, she pulled her into another hug. They held on to each other tightly for several long moments, sniffling occasionally, before finally letting go.

They picked up their water bottles and each took a sip, their thoughts their own for a few moments.

"So," Jana started, after clearing her throat, "if I promised to work harder at finding a solution to my problems over my pregnancy, would you give up seeing Jason? You know, to get back in Grady's good graces? For my sake?"

Lucy swung a surprised gaze to Jana, then rolled her eyes when she realized Jana was kidding. "I'll deal with Grady," she promised her. "One way or the other."

Jana wished she could trust in that, but Lucy had no idea what she was really dealing with. And Jana simply couldn't be the one to tell her. That would have to come from Grady. If it ever came at all.

# Chapter 24

All he wanted was a hot shower and the sweet oblivion of sleep. It had been a long week. Who was he kidding? It had been a long month. And only part of that was the project he was currently heading up. As daunting as it was exciting, most of his waking moments and a goodly number of his sleeping ones were spent dreaming about carbon nanotubes and microfluidics.

He stepped out of the elevator and was fishing out his key when he turned the corner and stopped short. The person who consumed the rest of his waking and sleepless moments was presently slumped on the floor next to his door, apparently asleep.

He glanced at his wristwatch, but he already knew it was past two in the morning. What the hell was she doing here? *Stupid question, jerkoff.* Apparently he'd ignored her long enough, and now it was time to pay the piper.

He'd wanted to call her. She wasn't the only one who wanted

to get them back to some semblance of normalcy. He just had no idea how to go about it. He'd gone to the reunion dance with the intention of . . . hell, he wasn't quite sure what his intentions had been that night. Confronting her? Being there for her in case Jason was still the same asshole? Both? Neither?

All he knew was that when he'd laid eyes on her wearing that sequined getup guaranteed to give even a dead man a hard-on, he'd been both disappointed and disconcertingly turned on. Hey, he was a red-blooded male and very much alive, thanks. But hard-on or not, the disappointment was worse. That hadn't been the real Lucy there that night.

Now, however, as he examined the woman curled up sleeping next to his door, he wondered if he'd been wrong.

She was wearing Regular Lucy clothes. But that was pretty much where Regular Lucy began and ended. He stood there for a long moment, blatantly using the edge she'd unknowingly given him to look at her. Really look at her. He'd watched her across the room at the reunion, circling the floor . . . dancing with fucking Prescott. But that had been like watching a stranger. Looking down at her now made him feel that oh-so-familiar pang inside his chest. The way her hair fell across her face in a scatter of long, messy strands, casting shadows beneath the lashes brushing her cheek. The way her mouth turned down in one corner and up in the other while she slept, like even in sleep she was the one in on the best joke.

How many concerts had they gone to over the years where she'd slept on the way home, and he'd parked in her driveway and watched her for as long as he could stand it? He'd always wondered what she was dreaming about, if it was as amusing as her slumbering expression insinuated. He remembered thinking how he wanted to be part of her dreams. She'd long since become a staple in his.

He shook that memory loose and stared at her hands, lying

limp in her lap, hands he'd held many times in friendship, a connection he'd cherished, even if it always left him wanting more. The endlessly long tangle of legs. Dorky, spastic legs that she'd never seemed to get total control over, in youth or adulthood. "Grace" wasn't her middle name, or any of her names, for that matter. She'd come striding into that ballroom like a Valkyrie, but then he'd watched her stick to the sidelines, taking careful steps, weaving the path of least resistance . . . the one least apt to gain notice. Proving she was still, underneath it all, the awkward, somewhat insecure Lucy he knew and loved.

And he was left wondering if he was the one who'd become the stranger. She'd only wanted to feel better about herself, to fit in. And he'd just wanted—desperately—for her to be happy fitting in with him.

Jana had been right. Again. They were both searching for fulfillment, but only Lucy had gone out and done something about it. While he'd been a completely selfish ass because he was too afraid to make the same leap of faith and reach for what he wanted.

Now she was dating fucking Jason Prescott. And he was avoiding her calls like they were both fifteen years old and having some stupid, immature argument.

It had been three weeks—God, four—since the reunion, and though he really had been buried in work, he could have returned at least one of the increasingly graphic and pointed messages Lucy had been routinely leaving on his machine. He knew he'd hurt her by abandoning her like he had. But dammit, she'd hurt him, too. The only difference was, she'd hurt him unknowingly. Yet he had sighed in admitted selfish relief that Jana had apparently elected to keep silent and leave the decision on how to handle things between them with him.

Of course, that hadn't kept him from hearing inside his head the advice he knew she'd give him. *Be a man, grow a pair, and go after her, jerkface!* Well, she might have been nicer about it. But then again, maybe not. He'd apologized to her for the added drama that she definitely didn't need. But even knowing that, knowing it wasn't fair to Jana right now to pile this on her, too . . . he'd found himself listening to Lucy's messages, hand hovering over the phone, knowing the right thing to do was to suck it up and call, only to hit the DELETE button. Again.

Looking down at Lucy now, he didn't know where he thought it was all going to end. Or what he wanted from her. And so he'd let work consume him, conveniently avoiding coming to any kind of actual decision. Like maybe it would just take care of itself. In the back of his mind he supposed he knew Thanksgiving was coming and they'd all be together. He'd figure something out by then. Probably.

"Why'd you have to go and upset the routine, Luce?" he murmured. *Because she wanted a life filled with more than having two best friends and a good job, asswipe.* Which forced the hard question: Didn't he want more, too?

*Not if it meant losing Lucy.*

And there was the crux of the whole thing. Be happy with what he had? Or push for more and possibly lose it all?

Maybe it was already too late for that. Maybe fucking Prescott had already snagged her heart. And God-knows-what else.

He nudged Lucy's leg with his toe. Perhaps with more force than absolutely necessary. "Oh, my God," he said flatly, in what Lucy called his James Spader voice, "there's a homeless person in my hall. Vagrancy being a crime and all, I guess I better call the cops."

Lucy came awake the way she always did, almost instantly alert. Considering the hour, and the fact that it took him at least two cups of coffee to be coherent at any time of the day or night, the feat was, as usual, impressive.

"Hey," she said, looking up at him, blinking against the hall lighting. "About time."

"Did we have an appointment I was unaware of?"

She ignored his sarcasm. He didn't bother asking her what she was doing, sleeping by his door. They both already knew the answer to that question.

"Should you be out this late on a school night?"

"What time is it?" she said, pushing her hair from her face, then covering her mouth with her fist as she yawned wide.

"Late. Or really early, depending on your view."

She looked up at him, those sooty lashes looking even darker than usual. Could be the crappy lighting in the hall. Or the dark circles under her eyes. "You probably don't want to hear what I think of my view at the moment."

"Something tells me I'm going to hear it anyway."

"You would be right. Which is one mark in that column, one lonely mark. Up against the whole pile of marks you've accumulated these past few months in the 'I couldn't be more wrong if I tried' column." She yawned again. "And Friday night is only technically a school night."

"Is it Friday already?"

She narrowed her gaze. "It was. I believe it is now very early on a Saturday morning. And while I can believe you've lost track of the day of the week, that's not going to save your pathetic, chickenshit ass. Unless you were really going to attempt to pull off the lie that you've been so caught up at work that you've misplaced an entire month."

"Gee, and to think I've missed you all this time."

She'd opened her mouth to make some retort, only his words stopped her. He saw a flash of . . . what? Yearning? Sorrow? Hope? Or was that all just wishful thinking on his part?

He reached out a hand, bracing himself for the contact.

She refused the help, scrambling to a stand herself.

Admittedly the snub stung, even though he knew he deserved it.

She squinted at her watch. "I can never tell which of Mickey's hands are which. But I'm guessing it's not ten past midnight." She looked at him. "Which means you've either been putting in the heavy-duty hours Jana says you are, or I'm really lucky you came out of that elevator alone."

He didn't owe her an explanation, but he was too busy wondering if it would have bothered her to wake up to find some random woman pawing all over him while he fumbled to get his key in the lock to keep his mouth shut. "The former. But unlike me, you knew what day it was, so you willingly ran the risk by camping out here in the first place." He turned away from her before he blurted out anything else. Like, there really was no risk because he never brought women home. Other women, anyway. If he wanted sex, the woman in question usually had a bed. Or a couch. Whatever. And if he didn't want sex . . . well, then he worked. When he wanted companionship, he hung out with Lucy. And wished they were having sex, too. Couldn't she see how perfect they'd be together?

He really needed to not be thinking about sex at all right now.

"I'm guessing you want to come in."

She leaned against the doorframe, far too close to him for his peace of mind. Basically, anywhere in his range of vision fit that description. "Your genius never ceases to amaze."

He didn't want to be amused, and yet his lips twitched anyway. He'd missed her sharp-ass mouth. Dammit. He flipped on the lamp by the door and tossed his keys on the end table. His place was a mess of overworked bachelor neglect, but she'd seen it in worse shape. Another plus in her favor. No early-dating game-playing behavior would ever be necessary. On either part. "There's beer and Coke in the fridge. Coffee in the filter. But if you make coffee, you better put in a new filter when you're done."

"Yeah, I know. There will be no place good enough to hide if you awaken to anything but the sound of your beloved Krups percolating. Maybe I should have snuck in here a month ago and stolen your coffeemaker. Then you'd have come after me and we could have settled this whole stupid thing."

He felt a sudden surge of completely uncalled-for anger. He wanted to turn and shout at her that he *had* come after her, dammit! But she'd been dancing in the arms of another man. The very man who'd first shattered her tender teenage heart. Whereas Grady had done nothing but cosset and protect it. And where the fuck had that gotten him? He managed to rein it in but turned his back on her as he slid off his coat and tossed it over the living-room chair. Just in case his murderous expression might tip her off.

He had a sudden attack of the yawns, probably a self-protection reaction as much as pure fatigue. Go to bed, tomorrow is another day. And this problem standing in his living room would be but a memory. He had to get up in about five hours and head right back to work. He didn't want to do this now. Or ever. Really.

He rubbed his stomach, which had been grumbling on the way home, but which he'd refused to heed. He'd learned the hard way that eating this late, when he was this tired, would make what little sleep he could get almost impossible. But he was suddenly as ravenous as he was tired. He didn't want to examine that one too closely.

Hollow-eyed, he looked toward the kitchen, wondering if he should just fire up the coffeepot and shove some cold pizza in the toaster oven. It wouldn't be the first time he'd pulled an all-nighter. But this time there was a lot more on the line than the usual. Discovering a new way to improve national security seemed simple in comparison to what he was about to face.

If only he'd invented the time machine he'd dreamed about as a kid. He could transport himself to anywhere else but right here. Right now.

Fortunately, she spoke first, relieving him of finding some way to start what was bound to be a really difficult conversation. Especially given the fact that he still had no idea how he was going to resolve the issues between them without coming out and telling her he was only acting like an ass because he was insanely jealous and hopelessly in love with her.

And he'd held off blurting out that particular fact for over a decade now. Surely he could last one more night.

"You know, for a genius rocket-scientist type who can make cameras small enough to thread through a needle—"

"Fiber optics. And I didn't invent them. Just new ways to use them."

She gave him the stink eye. "For an arrogant genius with nothing better to do than play with fibers, you've been acting monumentally stupid lately."

"That's it," he said lightly, wagging a finger, "no coffee for you." But he was having some. A few gallons at least, just to start. He walked to the kitchen, glad she was already sitting on the couch. Then he didn't have to come within hitting distance. Sure, she had lousy aim, but why chance it?

"I don't want coffee, Grady. I want—"

*You.* He paused by the door, his heart wanting that answer so badly, he'd been stopped in his tracks by the need to hear it. "If you're going to keep me from the much-needed nirvana that is my bed, then I do want coffee," he said, cutting off whatever she'd been about to say. Safer that way. Once he was sufficiently caffeinated, he'd risk the more dangerous conversational territories.

"I didn't plan on talking to you this late," she told him. "I thought you'd be home earlier."

He didn't ask her how long she'd waited out there for him. His guilt column was quite full already, thanks.

"I just couldn't stand this any longer," she said. "If for no other reason than it's stressing Jana out and she doesn't need that right now."

He punched the button on the coffeemaker. Hard. "So, you're here because you're worried about Jana?" First he didn't want her here confronting him about his bad behavior, then he got angry when it wasn't all about him. Christ, but he wanted to go to bed.

"I'm here because I'm worried about all three of us. I don't understand why things can't go back to the way they were."

She had no idea how badly he'd prayed for the same miracle. More sober than he'd like to be, he briefly considered skipping the coffee and going for the beer, but decided against that course of action. As tired and screwed up in the head as he was, no telling what he might say if he was chemically impaired.

The first fumes of perking coffee fueled his stamina instead, and he turned to find her lounging in his kitchen doorway. She'd shed her winter jacket. So he was now treated to the view of her small and apparently non-Wonderbra-enhanced breasts pressing lightly against one of her dad's worn-out Georgetown sweatshirts. His body responded anyway. Because apparently he was so pathetic and starved for her that she could wear burlap and he'd still get hard. He turned back to the coffee. And tried really hard to think about anything that didn't have to do with Lucy or his bed. Together or apart.

"Things aren't the same, Luce," he told her, digging the half-and-half out of the fridge, hoping the blast of cold air would provide some much-needed relief. "You know that better than anyone." He shut the door. Okay, it might have qualified as an almost-slam. He didn't look at her, so he didn't know if she'd noticed or not.

"Goddammit, Grady, what the hell is so wrong with me fixing myself up a little?"

*Because you fixed yourself up for the wrong man, when I would have gladly taken you the way you were!* he wanted to shout. Instead, he made big business out of selecting just the right coffee mug and digging a spoon out of the dishwasher. "Nothing."

She snorted. "Yeah, you always go out of your way to avoid me for weeks—weeks, Grady!—over nothing." Then, just like that, her anger seemed to evaporate and she slumped back against the wall just inside the door. "I know I left you that night and I'm a thousand times sorry for that. It was a horrible mistake to make. But, my God, don't you think you've punished me enough?"

*No*, he thought selfishly, *because it doesn't come close to how much I've punished myself all these years.* Unfair? Sure. Did he care at the moment? Not really.

"You abandoned me, too, only in a much worse way. And you won't even talk to me about it, or let me try and fix it. That hurts. A lot."

*Join the club*, he thought. It wasn't fair for her to get to be the martyr when *he* felt like the one who'd been abandoned. Somehow he didn't think she'd see it that way, though.

"No comment? Are we that broken?" She pounded her fist against the wall, startling him into looking at her.

When he saw the raw pain on her face, it was all he could do not to throw his spoon down and pull her into his arms, hold her close, apologize for everything. Then beg her to never leave him again.

*Be a man. Grow a pair.* "I'm sorry. It's not you—"

Her eyes flashed. "If you even think about trotting out the 'It's not you, it's me' crap, then you deserve to lose both my friendship and Jana's."

Impatient, almost desperate now for his fix, he pulled the coffeepot out and shoved his mug beneath the filter. "I haven't lost anything with Jana," he said defensively.

"Don't bet on it."

He glanced up. "What is that supposed to mean?"

"It means she hates this as much as I do. You don't think that your treating me like a leper puts her in an awkward position? And if you're such a good friend to her, you'd know that's the very last thing she needs right now."

"So you camped out in my hall to force a peace treaty for Jana's sake."

"For all our sakes. Have you been happy with the way things are between us lately? Or is it just me and Jana who are miserable?"

"Of course I'm not happy about all this."

She threw up her hands. "Well, then, why in the hell haven't you tried to do anything about it?"

"I did try!" he shouted, no longer able to keep his anger in check. "I came to the damn reunion to show you I was still in your corner. We all know how that turned out."

She had the decency to look abashed. "Okay, I deserved that." She glanced up then, through those short stubby lashes of hers, and his anger bled out. Like it always did. "I tried to apologize," she said quietly. "You wouldn't take my calls. It's been almost a month, Grady."

A month during which she'd been out with Jason Prescott four times. That he knew about, anyway. A month that he'd spent working himself to the brink of exhaustion so that when he did finally crawl in bed at night, he didn't have to lie there and imagine what they might be doing with each other. To each other.

His fingers curled into his palms and he'd never wanted so badly to hit something. Hard. Jason's pretty face would have been handy.

Slowly he flexed his hand and turned back to his coffee mug, which was full almost to spilling over. He carefully swapped out the pot for the mug. "Sure you don't want any?" he asked, working hard to keep his voice smooth and even.

"No. I don't want any coffee." She came to stand behind him and it took all his willpower to not leave the room. Or turn and grab her. "I just want you to talk to me. Tell me what's really wrong." She rested her hands on his shoulders and his hands tightened so hard on the mug he was surprised he didn't shatter it. "You know, we all go through big changes in our lives. Jana is pregnant, for God's sake, which terrifies me even more than it does her, which is saying something, believe me. And you've handled that okay."

*Because Jana getting pregnant didn't take you away from me.*

Maybe he should just say it, he thought morosely. Just put it out there. It wasn't like he had much to lose at this point. Their friendship was toast, as things stood, so maybe he should finally suck it up and go for broke.

"It's this thing with Jason, isn't it?" she said quietly.

And any hope he had of telling her how he felt vanished. Because she had "this thing with Jason." And though he was a grown man, secure in himself, confident about his place in the world . . . part of him was still that dorky teenager who knew he could never compete with the likes of golden-boy Jason Prescott. Ten years ago he hadn't had to. Jason had screwed up his chance for the best thing going, all by himself. Leaving Grady to be the shoulder, be the one who put the pieces of her broken heart back together . . . even if it put an enormous strain on his own.

Now? Now it was too late. He'd wasted ten whole entire fucking years when he'd had the upper hand. Or whatever edge he'd ever had, anyway. Blown all to hell. Because of complacency. And his chickenshit heart.

"It's not about Prescott," he heard himself say. Because, when you got down to it, it wasn't. It was about him not taking chances when he should have. And then unfairly taking it out on her when she'd moved on with her life.

"Sure it is," she said, not buying that lie for a second. "You've never liked him, even before the stupid prom."

*So, okay, maybe it is a little about Prescott.*

"I know it's confusing after the big whoop I made about him in high school, to be going out with him now, but people change."

"Not usually," he muttered. Once an asshole, always an asshole. He wondered if the same was true about chickenshit hearts.

"Well, you and Jana will just have to learn differently."

So, Jana was still on his side. That made him feel marginally better. "I don't really want to hear the nitty-gritty about your dates, thanks." *Because they might be even worse than the ones I've already constructed on my own.* "And I definitely don't want to look at him across the table at Thanksgiving."

"Actually, that's something else I wanted to talk to you about. And partly why I'm here. I didn't want to wait until the holiday to clear things up, because I'm not even sure that we're having a holiday or what we're doing. Or if we're doing anything."

He turned around, which had the added benefit of dislodging her hands from his shoulders, but the disadvantage of putting her that much closer to the one part of his body he didn't need her close to. He tried not to think about it. Gripping the counter behind him to keep from grabbing her, he said, "What in the hell are you talking about? It's Jana's turn, right? I mean, I know she's not feeling great, but—"

At the look on Lucy's face, and her accompanying, "Shit," he frowned.

"What don't I know?" he asked.

She raked a hand through her hair. He took partial pleasure

in the fact that, even with all the blonde streaks and the flatironing, at two in the morning, her locks still reverted to lumpy Lucy hair. He curled his fingers into a tighter grip on the counter, to keep from ruffling her bangs. He was a hopeless case, really.

She huffed and swore again. "I can't believe she didn't tell you." She looked at him, all accusatory. "I thought you said you were talking to her."

He lifted his hands. Tactical error. "I have! I can't help it if she's keeping something from me that I couldn't possibly know she was keeping from me." He needed to do something with his hands. Immediately. So he raked his fingers through his own hair, which only proceeded to tangle it up more. He needed to get a haircut. He always needed to get a haircut, but it was even worse than usual. "I'm too tired to be having this conversation."

"Jana is going to Canada for Thanksgiving. Dave thinks his family can help her come to terms with being pregnant."

"I'm an only child and a man, to boot, and even I know that's a plan doomed to fail."

"Yeah, well, she sort of hurt Dave pretty badly when she confided her fears about motherhood to him."

"She did tell me about that."

"So she's doing this more for him than because she really thinks it'll work. He just needs to feel like he's doing something to help her, that's all."

"Which means . . . one of us is supposed to do Turkey Day?" Grady realized immediately why Jana hadn't told him.

A second later, the light dawned on her face. "She's playing peacemaker, isn't she?"

*Peacemaker, matchmaker, who knew what was going on in Jana's head.*

Lucy shook her head. "You know, if she realized just what a nurturing person she really is, she wouldn't be so freaked out about the baby."

"I don't think it's just about her ability to be a parent," Grady said.

Lucy looked at him. "Yeah, me either. She's worried about all of it. About her life, her career, whether she's up to the dedication it requires. I think she's worried she's going to be like her mother."

Grady snorted. "No way. She's stable, married to a great guy, with a steady job. Three things her mother has never done individually, much less concurrently."

"Or her father. Who didn't even stick around to see her born," Lucy went on, undeterred. "I'm not saying it makes any sense, okay? Just that she has little confidence in herself when it comes to this big step. She hasn't even told her mother yet. And the only other people she can talk to besides Dave and his happy brood of reproducers, is us."

"Who have the collective experience of navel lint when it comes to babies."

"Exactly." Surprisingly, Lucy smiled at him. There was a shadow to it, mostly in her eyes, which effectively crumbled any resistance or anger he might have left to hide behind.

"What?" he asked, because there was a message that went with that sad smile.

"Nothing. Everything. I miss this. You know. Talking. Figuring shit out. Communing as one. No one thinks the way we do about stuff."

*Not even fucking Jason Prescott?* he thought, but managed by some miracle not to voice out loud.

"Jana didn't tell you because she was afraid if she did, you'd work through Thanksgiving and we'd never get back together."

And Jana was right. He probably would have.

"It would mean a lot to her if we could put aside this . . . whatever it is we're having, and spend the holiday together,"

Lucy went on. "We don't even have to cook a turkey. We can get Chinese carryout and watch football all day and never even talk to each other. She'll never know the difference. But she will know if we don't see each other. She just will."

"Yeah."

Lucy rolled her eyes. "It's like pulling freaking teeth, I swear. You're so stubborn and you make me crazy on a regular basis and I have no idea why I'm killing myself to force a reconciliation between us. Except I refuse to consider the alternative." She reached behind him and grabbed his coffee, downing half the mug before he could take it out of her hand.

"Hey!" he protested. "Get your own mug."

"You weren't drinking it."

Only because he'd completely forgotten about it.

"So, can we at least agree to give Turkey Day a shot? My place is fine with me if it is with you. Or we can meet anywhere you want. Who knows, it's three weeks away. Maybe by then we can have an actual productive conversation about it."

*Only if fucking Prescott gets hit by a truck.*

"Maybe if it's at some kind of normal daylight hour, that would help."

"Like you have such a thing as 'normal' hours. But fine, name a time and a place and I'll be there."

Grady hoped Jason appreciated her loyalty and fierce tenacity. Grady did. Always had. He just wished it wasn't focused on him right now.

He downed the rest of the mug, then mercifully turned away from her to rinse it out and sit it on the drain rack. "Can I get some sleep first?"

He felt as much as heard her sigh. "Sure. But don't make me camp out on your doorstep again."

"I won't."

He didn't turn around, but instead went about dumping out the rest of the coffee and setting up the filter for the morning. Which was now only a scant few hours away.

She let out a long, disappointed-sounding breath, and moved to the door. "Well, that's a start."

He wasn't sure about that. And as she let herself out of the apartment moments later and closed the door behind her, he could only think that it felt a lot more like an end to him.

# Chapter 25

"So, have you talked to him since?"

Lucy juggled the phone to one ear as she held up first one dress, then another, frowning at both. "Once or twice, but only for him to tell me he's too busy to get together."

She heard Jana sigh on the other end of the line. "Yeah. He's working—"

"On a really top-secret project, I know."

When Jana didn't say anything, Lucy wished she hadn't brought it up. "So," Jana said with forced cheer, "where is hot-shot taking you tonight? You've become quite the Capitol Hill socialite these past few weeks."

Lucy smiled, but she didn't feel as giddy about it as she wished she did. "He does move in interesting circles," she said, discarding yet another dress. "I'm going to need a raise if he keeps taking me out to these fancy functions. My wardrobe can't keep up."

"Are they the same people? Can't you recycle?"

"Yes, a lot of the same people. And no one recycles."

"Well, I wish I could help you out, but somehow I don't think anything in my closet screams 'socialite.' 'Sociopath,' maybe."

Lucy grinned at that. But the next dress still went into the discard pile.

"So, how are things going with Jason? I mean, really going?"

"You mean, have we gone to bed together yet?"

"Actually, I was thinking about conversation, bonding, affection, but, yes, that question had crossed my mind."

"Well, you know how it is, there are so many people at these dinner parties and he's trying to make the rounds, be impressive where he needs to be, charm the ones he needs to charm. My job is just—"

"Arm candy. Got it."

That should have stung, but it didn't. Mostly because it was true. She'd become increasingly aware that Jason was using her, but she could hardly run to Jana with her suspicions. Not unless she wanted a big fat "I told you so." And she wasn't ready to hear that yet.

"But when he picks you up, or on the way home, don't you two talk then? And he calls, right?"

*Only to ask me to be his escort again.* "Of course we talk," she said. *About how busy he is, how he wishes he had more free time.* "But he's a busy guy. I guess I should be glad he's wining and dining me."

"Sounds more like he's wining and dining his clients, or prospective clients, I should say, and taking you along for show-and-tell."

"Hey, can you believe Lucy Harper would ever be considered 'show-and-tell' for a hotshot lawyer?" she joked, trying to lighten the tone.

"Is that what this is for you? Just an ego-stroke thing? God knows, we all need that from time to time, but . . ."

"I know." Lucy dropped any pretense she had about trying to paint a better picture. "He's always the perfect gentleman. He kisses me hello and good night, but they're not passionate kisses." Not like that night at the dance. Or maybe that one hadn't been, either, and she'd been so caught up in the moment that she hadn't really noticed. "He always compliments me on how I look, makes me feel good about myself."

"I'm not surprised about the first part, since that's what he needs you for. But there's more to making a woman feel good than flattering her outfit. Do you two talk about you? About your day?"

She wanted to say they would if they just had more time. But she didn't have the energy required to try and pull that off. "I've been telling myself he would if we had more time. I guess I'm realizing we don't have time because he doesn't make time. And I can't call him because he's always in a meeting, or out of town. But a week hasn't gone by when we haven't gone out."

"Have you ever gone out to something that's not a business function?"

Lucy sat on the edge of her bed, her latest selection puddling in her lap. "He says he wishes we had time alone, too. But, no. No, we haven't. He really is busy. And yes, I know that's a lame excuse, but it happens to be true."

"You won't buy it from Grady, so why buy it from Jason?"

She started to say "Because I don't want Grady to fall in love with me," but stopped herself. Until that moment, what she thought she wanted was for Jason to realize the prize he really had on his arm. He kept asking her to be his date, so obviously he was impressed with her. Or maybe he was just impressed with her availability. "I don't know," she told Jana morosely.

"Maybe I'm going out with him because other prospects aren't lining up."

"Maybe they aren't because they think you're spoken for."

"So what do I do?"

"Just say no?" Jana quipped.

"Ha-ha."

"Maybe you should," Jana said, serious now. "Tell him you're busy. See if that nudges him to give you more of himself than an arm to another business function."

"If I say no, he'll just go to the next number in his Yellow Pages–size black book. I think I say yes because I like it that he calls me first. I feel like I have an edge; I just have to exploit it."

"And do you? Do you feel like you two honestly know more about each other than you did that first night at dinner? Has he made even the smallest effort to get to know you better?"

"Well, he's not putting the moves on me, either, so it's not like he's using me for sex." Much to her dismay. "He does seem to respect me."

"I don't want to hurt you, but I think you're being blind as a bat. He is using you as an escort service. And don't take this the wrong way, but if he wants sex, chances are he's hooking up with someone else for that. Sex with you would lead to expectations. You're his No-Strings Business Party Date and they are his No-Strings Sex Hookups. It would be exactly his style."

Lucy sat there, knowing Jana was absolutely right. "He's supposed to pick me up in an hour."

"So answer the door in your bathrobe. Tell him you're sick and can't go."

"I should do that," she said with absolutely no enthusiasm. It would mean never seeing him again, and though she should probably embrace that idea with everything she had, the truth was, she wasn't ready to give that up.

"Are you really enjoying rubbing elbows with the upper crust?"

"At first it was a little exciting, sure. But I think that's wearing off a bit. No one expects me to make conversation, which was a relief initially, but now it's sort of condescending and irritating."

"Lucy Harper, bimbo. Another title you never thought you'd have."

Jana had said it kindly, and they both laughed. "God, I don't know what to do, J."

"You still want him in bed, don't you?"

"Wouldn't you? I mean, he's gorgeous and he's dating me, and hell, I haven't had sex in, like, forever. Of course I want him in bed. At least once."

"Yeah, because he's proven himself to be such a giver. I'm betting he's a lousy lay."

Lucy sighed. "I'd defend him, but I'm too afraid you might be right about that, too."

"Well, I do understand the neediness. Dave hasn't made love to me since I confessed my deepest darkest. It's like he doesn't know what to do with my fragile emotions and he's afraid he'll hurt me somehow. And I'm needing the intimacy, you know?"

Lucy had no idea and couldn't imagine what Jana was going through. But she was miserable for her, that much she knew. "I'm so sorry."

"He'll come around in time. He's too much a guy to go without forever."

Lucy laughed with her.

"So if you really mean it about getting laid, why not answer the door in your sexiest slinky-little-nothing, with a bottle of champagne in one hand and a fist full of condoms in the other, and just seduce the guy. You know by now the kind of things he likes. He all but tells you how to dress, right?"

"It's not like that," she said, except it was just like that. Jana had pointed that out after their second date, and though Lucy liked to think it was flattering that he noticed what she wore and he always told her in such a way as to make her feel good, in the end, it was what it was. Jason being a control freak. "Maybe he's a control freak in bed, too," she said, then was disappointed when there was no accompanying shiver of anticipation to go along with that mental image.

"Maybe." Jana didn't sound too enthused at the idea, either.

"And maybe I don't think I can seduce him. I mean, why risk ending this relationship on the humiliating note of yet another rejection by Jason Prescott."

"So, what are you going to do?"

"I don't know."

Her doorbell sounded just then and she leapt off the bed. "Oh, my God, that can't be him already. It's early. He's never early. I was supposed to meet him downstairs and I'm not even dressed."

"Maybe that's destiny calling, then. Hang up with me and just go answer the door like you are. And let whatever happens, happen."

"Jana, I'm in ratty sweats, with my hair in hot rollers and a green clay mask on my face." She looked down. "And cotton swabs between my toes."

"Oh, my God, you're Patty Duke," Jana teased.

"Shut up," she said, even as she laughed. "No more TV Land for you. It's just what I've gotta do. It doesn't mean I like it."

"You don't 'gotta do' anything. You're gorgeous just like you are."

Lucy groaned as the doorbell sounded again. "Yeah. A real knockout. Listen, I gotta go do . . . something. With my face. With my . . . everything."

Jana was laughing on the other end of the line. "I'm telling you, just grab him by the tie and drag him to bed. He won't care what color your skin is as long as most of it's naked. You'll get what you want, then you can kick his ass out when you're done. Use him for a change, sweetie. Fair is fair."

"You are so not funny." Lucy clicked off on Jana's continued laughter.

The ringing doorbell was replaced by sharp knocking.

"Coming!" she called out, then did one of those panic dances where you take two steps to the bathroom, then turn around and grab everything off the bed, hop up and down while trying to figure out where to stash all your crap. Just in case, you know, the bed did come into play. In some alternate universe. Then she caught sight of her face in the closet mirror, promptly dropped the clothes and raced to the bathroom. "Just a minute!" she yelled as she turned on the knobs full force and began scrubbing the green goo off her skin. She was supposed to steam it off with towels, and as the stuff started to crack and grab at her skin as she all but clawed it off, she began to see why. "Ouch! Shit! Dammit!"

More knocking, more bell ringing.

"For God's sake, hold your horses!" Giving up on the goo, happy that most of it was gone, she yanked at the rollers as she hurried to the door, knowing it was too late to do anything about her clothes. She was tossing rollers and pins onto the chair by the front door when a voice called out:

"Lucy, darling? Are you home? I have something for you!"

She slumped against the door. Vivian. She peeked through the peephole and sure enough, her fairy godmother stood on the other side in all her teased-red-flames of hair and painted-face glory.

She unbolted and unchained and unlocked the door and opened it, not sure if she was happy to see her or dreading whatever—or whomever—the hell she might have brought with her. She sighed in relief to discover Vivian was alone.

Unless you counted the bulging garment bag she'd slung over one bangle-braceleted arm. "Hi there, darling," she said, giving Lucy an air kiss on one cheek as she breezed into her apartment on a wafting cloud of Black Cashmere.

"Hi, yourself," Lucy said, closing the door behind her. She caught her reflection in the tiny hat-stand mirror by the door and blanched. Her face was a vista of blotchy red patches from ripping off the mask and her hair was still half in rollers, the other half having already drooped into a rat's nest of tangled loop-de-loops. Great. She looked like Princess Leia after a three-day coke binge. Pasting on a smile, she turned to face Vivian. "What brings you to this neck of the woods?"

If she noticed Lucy's less-than-desirable appearance, she was too politic to say anything about it. Or, more likely, simply chose not to. Vivian was rarely politic about anything. "A little birdie told me you were attending the Governor's Ball at the Kennedy Center tonight. So I thought you might need something smashing to wear. I'd have come sooner, but I only managed to wangle the delivery of this sumptuous confection this afternoon." She looked around for someplace to hang up the bag.

Lucy crossed the room. "Here," she said, pointing to her bedroom door. She took the bag, surprised by the weight of it, and hung it on the outside of her door. "Wow."

"Bugle beads," Vivian said by way of explanation. "One of Bob's favorite designs."

"Bob?"

"Why, Mackie, darling, of course. You're going to knock all their socks off tonight." She stepped closer and peered at Lucy's face. "Oh, dear. I thought it was unfortunate lighting."

"Mask incident."

Vivian brushed her hands together. "No matter, foundation will cover a multitude of sins." She grinned. "And I should know."

Lucy smiled weakly in response. "You didn't have to do this, Vivian. You know how much I appreciate it, but—"

Vivian took one of her hands between both of her own, her expression turning surprisingly serious. "I know that, child." She let go with one hand and covered her heart. "But it gives me enormous pleasure to see you become the swan you want to be." She winked. "And I happen to like playing fairy godmother, and I have the wherewithal to do it. So deal with it!"

Lucy felt like a total fraud, and something of that must have shown in her face because Vivian frowned. "What's wrong, darling?" She tugged Lucy over to the couch. "Come, come, sit. Tell your fairy godmother everything."

Lucy and Vivian had spoken a handful of times as she'd continued dating Jason. Vivian had seemed so excited and happy at the prospect of Lucy's grand "coming out," as she'd called it, to the Washington social scene, that Lucy hadn't had the heart to tell her she wasn't enjoying it all as much as she'd hoped she would.

"Has that gorgeous Prescott boy done wrong by you? Because I happen to know several of the elder partners in his firm and—"

Alarmed, Lucy raised her hand. "No! I mean, no, no. It's not Jason. Per se." That last part slipped out.

Vivian's expression turned shrewd. She missed little. Which was why Lucy had begged off her repeated requests to meet for lunch over the past month. She knew Vivian would figure out her quandary in a heartbeat.

"Then what is it?"

Lucy searched for the right words. How to explain to Vivian that the world they'd handed her on a string, was, well, unraveling. "I know you told me that the longer I kept up appearances, the more natural it would feel to me. And there is a lot about the new me that I love. There is no doubt I'm more confident about myself, and for that I can never repay you."

"Oh, dear, I never meant for you to feel obligation." Vivian looked so upset that Lucy took her hands now and squeezed them.

"It's not that. I—I just didn't want to disappoint you, that's all."

"You know, darling, you can't operate your life by the fear of how others perceive you. Obviously you don't want to disappoint, but you can't do it at the expense of your own happiness and well-being. Nobody gains then. Tell me what's wrong. Just come out with it. I promise not to be offended. Your happiness is what I most wish for you."

"I don't fit in," Lucy blurted. There, she'd said it. "I mean, I look like I do, and everyone accepts me just fine, but *I* don't feel like I fit in with them. I have nothing in common with Jason's friends or coworkers. For that matter, I have nothing in common with Jason."

"Come now, dear, people from all walks of life can find common ground."

"Maybe that's just it. I'm not particularly drawn to that lifestyle or those people enough to want to find out what that is. And I don't think Jason does, either. He hasn't learned anything about me in the time we've been dating. You can't even call it 'dating.' It's always a business function. I'm pretty sure I'm just being used. You know, arm candy." She felt ridiculous saying that.

"And I'm sure you make smashing arm candy. But why continue to date him?" Vivian's eyes widened. "I hope not out of some misguided idea that I expected you to—"

Lucy waved her silent. "No, no, not at all. I mean, you seemed so excited about me seeing him and all, and I didn't want you to think I wasn't trying."

"Oh, dear," Vivian said, sighing. "I'm so sorry, darling."

"It's not your fault, really. I wanted to know for myself, too. And I guess part of me was hoping that if he kept asking me out and I kept being the perfect escort, things would change. But Jason only wants the part of me that shows up on his arm and doesn't speak much." She leaned back on the couch. "And to be honest with you, I'm not sure he has anything I want, either."

Vivian gave her that woman-to-woman look.

"Well, of course I wanted *that*. Who wouldn't?"

"So use him as he uses you. Quid pro quo. Happens all the time in acceptable society."

"That's what my friend Jana was just telling me."

"Wise woman, Jana."

"Believe me, if I thought I could pull it off, maybe I would try. But I'm not cut out for that lifestyle, either. I don't just want to be wanted sexually, or want someone sexually, I want—"

"To be loved," Vivian said solemnly. She rubbed Lucy's knee, the rings on her fingers clinking together lightly. "Don't we all." Then that wicked smile returned. "But no need to dismiss the one while waiting for the other."

Lucy had to smile at that. She really was incorrigible, this godmother she'd somehow adopted. "I just don't think I'm cut out for it."

"Well, that's fair, too." Vivian sighed a little, then patted her knee as the determined look came over her face again. "So what do you plan to do?"

"I'm not sure," Lucy said. "Jana and I were talking about that when you rang. I thought it was Jason coming early and I was sort of scrambling around."

"Maybe you should have just let him see you in all your preparatory glory. I firmly believe men would have a great deal more respect for us if they had even a glimpse into the horrors we submit ourselves to for their viewing pleasure."

"Amen to that. Except, knowing Jason, he'd have turned around and walked away. I'm sure he could find any one of a dozen suitable last-minute dates before he reached his car."

"Don't be so hard on yourself. That little black book might be filled with names and numbers, but they are hollow entries."

"What do you mean?"

"If he's only investing his energy in advancing his own cause, then all the names and numbers in the world won't make him a more enriched human being. How many people in that supposed book of his do you think really know the man and not just the figure? And how many of those names and numbers do you think know anything more about him than he knows about you?"

Lucy thought about that.

"So what if you can't dial up a dozen men at the drop of a pin—though I could make that happen for you, too."

Lucy waved her hand. "Thanks, but no."

Vivian just smiled. "Just keep that in mind. But as I was saying, just because you don't tote around a similar pile of entries doesn't mean you don't have him beat where it really counts. Friends. People who know and love you and would do anything for you. I seem to recall one rather nice one waiting for you outside Glass Slipper."

"Grady?"

Vivian smiled. "He seemed quite taken with you."

Again, all Lucy could do was say "Grady?"

Vivian lifted a shoulder. "Maybe I'm wrong." But she said it in a way that left little doubt of what she believed.

"He's my oldest friend. We talked about that way back, remember? Although lately things have been a little rocky."

" 'Lately' . . . since you've been dating Mr. Prescott?"

Lucy frowned. Vivian couldn't really think . . . her and Grady? "It's a long story, but suffice it to say, he has no love lost for Jason."

"Hmm. Well, I suppose that's really neither here nor there." She smiled brightly, but Lucy wondered if she was really letting the matter drop or saving it for later. "All I'm saying is you don't need a pile of friends, but you do need them. I'm not sure the Jason Prescotts of the world understand that. Until, of course, the tides of fortune turn against them and they find out the hard way."

Lucy studied Vivian for a long moment. "You sound like you speak from experience."

"I do, dear. Unfortunately, I do. Back in my Hollywood days I was much like Jason. A 'player,' I think they call them now. And I ended up hurting a man who loved and trusted me, because I thought everyone was like me." She smoothed her face with a smile. "I readily admit there is still more Jason in me than I'm proud of. But then, I am comfortable in that world. However, I know the value of friends now, and I am most loyal to those who have been loyal to me." She took Lucy's hand. "I hope you know I'll be there for you, and accept my apologies for perhaps pushing you down the path that I mistakenly took myself, so many years ago. One thing I have learned is you have to be true to yourself above all else."

"Which means breaking up with Jason," Lucy said.

Vivian just shrugged. "If that's what you think is best for you." She stood. "I'll leave the dress here anyway. It might be fun just to play dress-up." She checked her watch. "And as much as I hate to dash off, I'm expected at a dinner shortly. Aurora will nag me all evening if I'm late."

Lucy followed Vivian to the door, then when she turned to say good-bye, she impulsively hugged her. Careful not to muss Vivian's hair or her makeup, of course.

At first Vivian was startled by the display, but she quickly returned the hug, perhaps even more tightly. She bussed Lucy's cheek, then used her thumb to remove the lipstick print. "You are a strong one, Lucy Harper," she told her, her eyes glistening with affection. "You'll always be a swan to me."

Now Lucy's eyes began to swim, and when they both sniffed, Vivian laughed. "God, aren't we a pair."

A knock on the door startled them both.

"Jason!" they both whispered, eyes wide, as they stared at the door, then each other.

"I'm not ready!" Lucy whispered heatedly. "For any of this." She clutched Vivian's arm. "I know you have to go. But can you, I don't know, work your godmother magic and somehow get him to wait outside for . . . a few days?" She was being ridiculous, of course, but panic did that to her.

Vivian turned her head and peeked out the eyehole, then looked to Lucy in surprise as she stepped back and opened the door.

"Vivian!" Lucy hissed. She leapt back, prepared to dash to her bedroom and simply lock herself in forever, or until Jason left, whichever came first.

But then the door swung wide.

"Grady?"

# Chapter 26

"Ah, hi! What brings you by?"

Vivian looked back at a clearly startled Lucy, then to the young man who'd rattled her composure. Tall, lanky, nice cheekbones. He was even nicer close-up. Of course, she personally preferred her men a little more groomed, but she supposed his thick mop of glossy dark curls would appeal to some.

She gave him a smile, then nudged Lucy. "Aren't you going to introduce me to your gentleman caller?"

"What? Oh, right. Vivian, this is Grady Matthews."

Vivian smiled and extended her hand. "We were just talking about you."

Lucy rushed on with the introductions. "Grady, this is Vivian dePalma." Lucy shifted her gaze to Grady.

Vivian didn't miss the warning note. Interesting.

"She's one of the owners of Glass Slipper."

Grady held Lucy's gaze for a challenging moment, then took

Vivian's extended hand in his own much larger one. Quite large, Vivian noted with approval. Some old wives' tales weren't tales, after all.

"Pleasure to meet you," he said, his voice a lovely mellow bass to go along with his height. "Lucy has had nothing but nice things to say about you."

*Pleasant and polite, too.* And if she wasn't mistaken—and she rarely was—the intensity with which Grady held the regard of her Lucy spoke of feelings far stronger than an old friendship. So she hadn't misread the situation that day. She held on to his hand a scant moment longer than necessary, quite aware of Lucy fidgeting beside her. Of course, her beau was set to arrive any moment and it was obvious she didn't want the two men's paths to cross.

If Lucy wasn't so busy worrying about tuning in to her own signals, maybe she'd have already picked up on his.

She reluctantly released Grady's hand, but her smile grew as she began to put a plan together. Lucy clearly adored this fine young man. And friendships were often the basis for some of the strongest love matches. Lucy wanted someone who both loved her and wanted her. All she had to do was have something—or someone—open her eyes to what was right in front of her face. Well, that shouldn't be too hard for a fairy godmother to pull off.

"The pleasure is all mine, I assure you." She smiled at Lucy. She was going to get lucky, all right. In ways she'd never imagined. "Well," she said with a note of finality, "I wish I could stay and chat with you both, but I must be off."

Lucy appeared uncertain how to juggle yet another visitor and the impending arrival of her date. Vivian's heart tugged a little at the beseeching look she darted her way. She was going to help her. She only hoped Lucy appreciated her interference when the dust settled.

"Grady," she said, then offered him her best smile, "you don't mind if I call you Grady, do you?" She kept her hand on the sleeve of his coat.

He managed to pull his gaze away from Lucy long enough to look down at her. She admired his barely restrained patience. *My, my.* How could Lucy not see what she had here? The intensity was all but scorching. Yum.

"No, not at all," Grady assured her.

"I so hate to be a bother, but would you mind terribly fetching me that garment bag?"

"But—"

She talked over Lucy's startled reaction. "It's right inside, hanging on the bedroom door. You can't miss it."

"Ah, sure. No problem." Grady ducked past Lucy and headed inside.

Lucy bent closer to Vivian and in a hushed whisper said, "What are you doing? I thought I was supposed to wear that dress on my date tonight?"

"I thought you were going to cancel?"

"I don't know what I'm going to do!"

Vivian took hold of Lucy's forearms and tugged her close. "Honey, if you're smart, you'll dial up Jason's cell phone and beg off. Your . . . friend here looks to me as if he has something important he needs to discuss with you."

"Grady? Why would you think that? Besides, if Grady needed to talk to me, he has had ample time over the past few weeks. Whatever he has to talk about now can wait."

Vivian looked past her to where Grady was wrestling the garment bag into submission over his arm. Her time was short. "You were going to put Jason off anyway. And if you and Grady have been having problems, then you should see to those instead. After all, isn't he more important to you than Jason?" She looked up and smiled. "Ah, there you go." She stepped past Lucy and took the garment bag from Grady's arm. "Aurora would have had my head if I'd forgotten this." She glanced back to Lucy. "You know what, let me take care of that other little matter for you." She glanced at the wall clock. "In fact, I imagine I can handle it on my way out."

Lucy glanced at the clock, then at Vivian, and pointedly not at Grady. "Vivian," she said, clearly worried.

"Now, now, darling," Vivian said, beaming up at the two of them. Such a handsome couple they'd make. "What good is it having a fairy godmother if she can't handle the small details, hmm?" Before Lucy could say anything, Vivian glanced at Grady. "It was a pleasure to meet you. And, if you don't mind a bit of advice from someone who's been around the block a few times, a woman can't make up her mind about what she really wants unless she's aware of all her options."

Lucy looked nonplussed, but Grady's gaze sharpened instantly. Vivian smiled in satisfaction. "'Night, you two." She ducked into the hall and hurried to the elevator. If she was going to intercept Mr. Prescott before he got on the lift coming up, she had to hurry.

Lucy watched Vivian disappear in a cloud of garment bag and Black Cashmere, slipping into a conveniently available elevator before Lucy could call her back. Sighing in defeat, she closed the door. "I'm sorry," she said to Grady, "I have no idea what she was talking about."

Grady's jaw twitched a little. Was he angry at her again? Now what? "Actually, I think she understands more than the both of us put together."

He lifted his hand toward her and she ducked back, having no idea what his intentions were, but if his expression was any indication, it wasn't good. He scowled when she ducked, and reached farther, touching her cheek. "You had something stuck to your cheek. It looks like dried lettuce."

She paused, raised her hand to her face, and cringed at the crusty little bumps she could feel around the edges. "A facial mask that didn't come off right," she said defensively, though she didn't know exactly why. "What are you doing here? I'm getting ready—"

"I know. For a date with Prescott." At her arched brow, his scowl deepened. "Jana told me."

Lucy sighed. "I know I've been begging you to talk to me more, but now really isn't a good time."

"Actually, I can't think of a better one." He turned around, walked into the living area and made himself at home on her couch.

"Grady! Didn't you hear me?"

"The whole floor heard you."

"Well, given the fact that you can't even utter the man's name without grinding your teeth into stubs, you'll understand if I'd prefer you not actually be here when he shows up at my door."

"I don't think he's going to show up at your door. Not if your fairy godmother has anything to say about it."

Lucy's eyes narrowed. "Okay, what's really going on here?" Because Vivian had taken one look at Grady and changed her thinking on everything. And Grady had looked a bit taken aback by her mysterious bit of advice. Now, however, he seemed totally on the same page. "I'm really getting tired of everyone else knowing what's going on besides me."

Her doorbell rang.

"Oh, for God's sake!" She stomped over to the door and flung it open, thinking Vivian had come back for whatever reason and fully prepared to keep her locked in the apartment until she explained her cryptic remarks. Only it wasn't Vivian. It was Jason.

Jason's broad smile dimmed instantly as he took in her disheveled appearance. "Hi. I thought you were going to meet me downstairs." His gaze traveled to her hair, still half in and half out of rollers, then down her body, still in sweats. "So . . . I assume you're running a little behind schedule? You did remember we had a date this evening?" He said it in a way as to make it clear that he couldn't possibly believe she'd have forgotten something so important. As if her social calendar was a wasteland except for those nights that he so graciously chose to fill it. But then, by always being available for these last-minute functions, hadn't she sent him that exact signal?

Still, she was flustered and embarrassed and in no mood to be patronized. "Yes, of course. A—a number of things sort of came up and delayed me. Ah, actually, I was going to call you."

Now Jason frowned. "About?"

"Well . . ." Why, oh, why, hadn't Vivian stalled him? Given how quickly he'd arrived after her departure, Lucy could only guess that Jason had been on his way up in one elevator as Vivian had descended in the other.

"Can I come in? I'd rather not have this conversation in the hall."

Again with the tone. She was tempted to say she'd rather not be treated like an empty-headed bimbo, either, but Jason peered past her just then. "Who is that?"

*Shit.* "A—a friend of mine. He just dropped by."

Any hope her ego might have had that Grady's presence would incite a flare of jealousy on Jason's part died a swift death. He barely glanced at him. "Didn't you tell him you were going out tonight?"

As if there could be no competition when the great Jason Prescott came calling, commanding her attendance at yet another staggeringly boring legal soiree. It was really only in that moment that she realized just how true that was. Sure they were dazzling affairs filled with dazzling people. All of whom ignored her after the perfunctory introductions, whereby she spent the remainder of the evening sipping drinks and eating food she didn't order, all the while doing her best to appear the ever-fascinated date while Jason charmed everyone with his center-of-attention stories.

Much like he'd been in high school, she realized. Jana was right, tigers didn't change their stripes. Just their audience. And their arm candy. God, where was Debbie Markham when she needed her?

"I told you," she said evenly, "he's a friend. And this isn't about my having company."

Jason stepped past her into the tiny vestibule inside her front door.

Grady smiled and waved from his perch on the couch. Still frowning, Jason waved back, then looked immediately back to Lucy. "Can you get rid of him? Would you like me to?"

Lucy had noted the twinkle of devilish delight in Grady's eyes. She sent him a warning glance, then turned back to Jason. "Listen, I—I'm sorry to cancel on you like this—"

Jason's eyes widened. "Excuse me? Lucy, my firm had to buy tickets to this event tonight. It's a political fund-raiser, and very important to me."

Not, Lucy knew, because Jason harbored any strong sense of patriotism or political views, but because it was likely the guest roster contained several names that might "fund-raise" his firm's bottom line. She knew the drill by now. Just as she knew the firm wouldn't miss the money for her one measly ticket. "I understand that." Lucy also understood his only real concern at the moment was showing up sans trophy, not that he was going to miss spending any time with her. "I wish I could have given you earlier notice so you could find another date."

This is where he should have realized his social gaffe and assured her that it wasn't all about him, but now that her blinders had been torn the rest of the way off, she already knew he wasn't going to.

Jason's cheeks flushed with agitation. "Like anyone else is going to be available at this late date," he snapped.

Lucy's face flushed, too, but in mortification. Anyone else, that is . . . except her. "I'm sorry," she said instinctively, then immediately wondered why in the hell she was apologizing. Except she *was* sorry. Sorry she'd ever entertained the idea that Jason Prescott was her dream date, much less her dream mate. That if she just hung in there long enough, he'd see what a gem he had in her. When, at the moment, all she could wonder was why she'd ever thought she had a gem in him.

She'd been sticking it out because it was too embarrassing to admit that Jana and Grady had been right all along. And too personally mortifying to admit that she'd been so far gone about this whole makeover thing as to think that being considered arm candy was actually flattering.

"I'll be glad to reimburse your firm for the price of the ticket."

"It was fifteen hundred a plate."

Lucy gulped.

"Somehow I don't think that's going to fit into a schoolteacher's budget."

She looked at Jason's sneer and realized just how deeply embedded those blinders had been. She'd never seen this side of him during their time together. In fact, not since high school. But then, she'd made sure she was the perfect date, so why would he have to? Jason Prescott thwarted was not a nice thing to behold.

"No, you're right," Lucy said, temper heating up. The fact that she felt so intensely foolish for letting herself be used like this only fanned the flames. And while that was her own stupid fault, at the moment it felt perfectly acceptable to target Jason. "I imagine you wouldn't miss it, though. Not that I believe for a moment that your firm won't absorb the cost. All you have to do is schmooze an additional client tonight and you'll more than make up for the investment."

Jason looked at her like she'd sprouted two heads. "Excuse me?"

"No need. I know it's hard to comprehend that I can actually think and speak for myself. In full sentences, too."

"What the hell are you talking about?"

"I'm tired of being nothing more than an arm piece in carefully selected evening wear."

"I've taken you to some of the most sought-after functions in Washington!"

"Sought after by an entertainment lawyer trying to fatten his client list, maybe, but what was in those evenings for me?"

Jason didn't have an immediate retort for that. In fact, he seemed stunned speechless that anyone would expect or need to have anything other than his sterling presence to have a wonderful time. But the lawyer in him snapped out of it. "I don't know, I suppose I thought that someone like you would like seeing how the other half lives."

"Someone . . . like . . . me?" Lucy's slow boil went full tilt. She carefully folded her arms. "Exactly what is that supposed to mean?"

Jason huffed, even while saying, "Don't get all huffy, you know what I meant. You'd never mingle in those circles if it wasn't for me."

"And what makes you think those 'circles' are so fascinating? I've never been more bored in my life."

Now his cheeks flushed. "Then why in the hell did you keep accepting my invitations?"

"Because, silly me, I thought maybe you and I were, at some point, going to develop a relationship."

He looked momentarily stunned. "But . . . we are."

Lucy laughed. "No, Jason, we're not. You tell me what to wear and where to go, and I'm expected to show up, smile pretty, then shut up and let you be the center of attention."

He gaped. "I was just doing my job. And it wasn't like you knew anyone there or—"

"Had anything of interest to offer to such an obviously elite group of sterling individuals?"

"Now you're putting words in my mouth. I'm just saying that they run in different circles and it was doubtful you'd have anything in common. I thought I was being a gentleman and saving you from—"

"What?" she said, no longer keeping her voice down. "Embarrassing myself? Or embarrassing you? Oh, wait a minute, that's right, arm candy isn't supposed to want anything more than to see and be seen." She snapped her fingers. "Gee, I guess I haven't gotten the hang of that quite yet. But then, this whole arm-candy thing is new to me, you see."

"What are you talking about?"

"Let me ask you something . . . in the past month, have you been seeing anyone else?"

Caught off guard, he looked instantly wary. Question answered.

"I—we, uh, we didn't make any claims on exclusivity."

"Riiight. So, have you taken any of these other dates to bed?"

He gaped once again, then snapped his mouth shut. "I—I don't think I have to answer that."

"No, no you don't. There's no court stenographer here."

"Now wait a minute. I've been nothing but a complete gentleman with you. I never once pushed you for—"

"Anything. I know. You're right." Lucy sighed. "And I didn't push for anything, either. Because I think I knew all along it was never going to be there, so I tried to make myself believe I would be satisfied with whatever attention you decided to shower upon my poor little schoolteacher shoulders." She laughed hollowly. "My mistake."

"Again, you're putting words in my mouth. I thought we had something good going here."

Jason was never one to allow himself to be made to look bad, so Lucy supposed it was inevitable that he'd end up spinning this so that he was the good guy.

"Yeah, I was always available when you needed a date and you knew I wouldn't push for more. I'd say that was a better than good thing."

"You got to attend some really big and powerful events."

"I know. Yay, me."

Jason shook his head in that way men did to make it clear to anyone who might be paying attention that it was clear the woman in question was being a typical crazy female who had no idea what she wanted.

"I don't get it," he said, diving more deeply into the role. "I thought I was being a nice guy."

"Yes, helping poor little Lucy experience the high life she could never hope to discover on her own. God, you are so condescending and you don't even realize it."

Now his gaze narrowed. "Now, now, no need to get ugly."

Lucy burst out laughing. "Oh, if you only knew."

"What's that supposed to mean?" Then he raised his hand. "You know what? Never mind. It's obvious we're through here. And I'm going to be late. I have a car waiting."

He turned to go, then Grady spoke up. "Not until you offer her an apology."

Jason turned slowly, his gaze shifting to Grady, who had risen from the couch and come to stand a few feet behind Lucy. "I beg your pardon? I don't believe this conversation involves you."

"She's a close friend. And when someone insults a friend of mine, I tend to take it personally."

"Insult *her*? I think you have that backward, my friend. Now, if you don't mind—"

It was Lucy's turn to gape when Grady moved swiftly past her and took hold of Jason's arm. Jason—who was a good several inches taller and easily out-muscled him by thirty pounds or more.

"Grady!" Lucy said, panicking and grabbing at his arm.

"I'm not your friend," Grady said, jaw clenched. "And I believe I said you owe the lady an apology."

"Come on," Lucy pleaded. "Jason, just go. *Grady.*" She turned a look on him that clearly signaled "What in the hell is wrong with you?"

But he wasn't looking at her.

Jason shrugged off Grady's hand. All traces of the charmer fled. He was still smiling broadly, but there was nothing endearing about it. In fact, it made the hairs on Lucy's arms stand up. She remembered that exact smile. She'd seen it once before. Ten years ago, to be exact.

"I'm the one being stood up here," Jason explained with exaggerated patience. "For a three-thousand-dollar date. If anyone owes an apology, I believe it's her."

*Her.* She didn't even warrant a name anymore. "I already apologized for not attending tonight," she said between gritted teeth, but she was pretty sure the testosterone twins weren't listening to her.

"You have no idea what you had," Grady told him, his tone calm, but Lucy saw that clamped jaw and knew he was furious. "She's witty, funny as hell, far more charming than you'll ever be. Unlike you, having to tell stories and work so hard at being the life of the party, she lights up a room without even trying. She'll debate you into the ground on such a wide variety of topics you'll find yourself reading more newspapers and watching the late show just to keep up with her. In fact, I've never met a woman as fascinating and interesting as Lucy Harper. All you saw was the perfect hair and hot body."

Now Lucy was seriously gaping at Grady.

"Your loss, Prescott. You were blind ten years ago, and you're still blind now."

" 'Ten years ago'?"

Lucy's expression swiftly turned to one of horror.

"Prom night of our senior year, to be exact."

"*Our* senior year?" Jason squinted. "Do I know you?"

Grady's smile could cut diamonds. "Hardly. Thank God. I didn't run with your crowd. I chose instead to cultivate real friendships, not potential future business contacts."

"What the hell is that supposed to mean?"

"Do you still keep in touch with anyone from our class?"

Jason stuttered. "I went away to school, and—I'm not going to defend myself to you! I don't even know who the hell you are."

"I'm the guy who should have done this ten years ago." And with that, Grady pulled back his right hand.

Lucy realized in an instant what Grady's intentions were and threw herself at him before his punch could connect. "Grady!"

Grady swore as he stumbled off balance.

Jason laughed. "Right. See, that's the difference between us. I never needed a girl to fight my battles for me." He looked at Lucy. "My only mistake was not realizing who I was dealing with here from the start." He shook his head and muttered, "Losers then, losers now." Still chuckling, he turned to the door.

And Lucy saw red. "You're right," she said. "You don't know who you're dealing with." And out of nowhere came this insatiable urge to finish what Grady had started. Before she could think it through, she yanked him around and swung as hard as she could.

Her fist connected with his nose and made a sickening, if somewhat satisfying, crunching noise. Jason screamed and so did Lucy.

Cradling her hand—who knew faces could be so hard?—she

bent over and swore a long stream of foul words she didn't even know she knew.

Jason started swearing, too. "You bitch! You broke my nose!"

She looked up to see blood running over his lips and down his chin.

Cupping his face with one hand, he took one step toward her.

Her heart still pounding, Lucy took a step backward. *Shit, shit, shit!*

But Grady stepped in between them and shoved Jason through the open doorway. "Oh yeah, I forgot to mention. She also has freakish arm strength for a girl. Her aim is usually really lousy." He grinned. "I guess she just got lucky."

Jason's eyes narrowed in rage. "I'm suing you both for assault."

"And you'll lose," Grady said. "I'll be the eyewitness from hell and she'll back me up."

"You try it." He pushed off the wall and stumbled toward the elevator. "I'll see you in court."

"Yeah. I'm off to call the media. I'm sure they're going to love hearing how hotshot entertainment attorney Jason Prescott got punched out by his date after being an insulting asshole. What else was the poor, defenseless little schoolteacher to do? Your firm's clients will love reading over that with their morning cappuccino."

"Now hold on." Jason turned. Considered. "Maybe I was a tad hasty." It sounded like he was talking with a bad head cold.

"Right. Because it's all about image with you, Prescott. Never anything important, like substance. Now who is the loser?" And with that, Grady nudged Lucy back into the apartment and closed the door. As an afterthought, he locked it and threw the dead bolt. He turned to Lucy and smiled. "I may be hotheaded, but I'm not completely stupid."

Lucy's hand was throbbing like a mofo (another word she'd

never used before, but was thinking about using again real soon), but she could only stand there and stare at Grady. "My hero," she said, somehow finding the dry smile to match her tone.

Grady grinned and nodded to her hand. "I wasn't the one who decked the guy."

"Only because I stopped you. I was afraid he would have slaughtered you."

"Gee, thanks."

"Come on. Words have always been your weapon of choice. And I must say, you wielded them quite effectively there." She grinned. "What a team, eh?" She tried to shake the numbing pain from her fingers, which only made her yelp.

Grady put his arm around her and herded her immediately toward the kitchen. "God, Luce, what did you do?"

She shot him a sideways grin. "What you've been wanting to do since senior year." She winced when he held her hand under running cold water. "Damn. It's not fair. It shouldn't hurt the puncher, only the punchee."

He quickly made an ice pack and wrapped it in a damp towel. "Here." He took her hand and gently dried it, then wrapped it in ice and terry cloth. "Do you think we should go to the emergency room?"

She tested flexing her fingers, swearing only a little. Okay, more than a little. "Everything works. I don't think I broke anything." She couldn't help it, a giggle slipped out. "Except Jason's nose." Another sputter of laughter. "God, I shouldn't laugh. Really. I'm a bad person." She glanced up at Grady, and they both busted out laughing.

"Did you see the expression on his face?" Grady asked between snorts of laughter. "He was just so shocked that something like that could happen to him."

"As much as this hurts now, and as much as I don't advocate

violence . . . I have to admit it felt good to smack that smarmy smile off his face."

" 'Smarmy'?" Grady snickered.

"Smug, smarmy, condescending, whatever." Her laughter finally faded. "I owe you an apology. And Jana, too. I'm sorry I didn't listen to you guys." She gave him a dry smile. "I bet you're dying to call Jana and tell her."

Grady smiled, too. "Nah." He paused a beat. "I can wait until later."

Lucy mock punched him in the shoulder with her good hand. "I really am sorry. For everything."

"Ah, Lucy." Grady sighed. He pulled her into a loose hug, careful of her wrapped hand. "I'm sorry for being such an ass. It was just hard watching you with him."

"I know," she said, her face muffled against his shirt. It felt surprisingly good being held by Grady. Out of nowhere, Vivian's comments about him popped into her head. She'd been completely mistaken, of course. At the moment, as revved up on adrenaline as they both were, it was only natural to feel good at being held. After everything that had happened, she was just glad they'd finally gotten back on track.

"I should have done something sooner, ended it sooner. I just wanted . . ." She trailed off, shook her head. In some ways, she felt clearer about things than ever before. And in other ways, she was even more confused.

"You were just trying to figure yourself out," he said. Then he tipped her chin up so she looked at him. "I should have been more understanding about that. More supportive. It's just . . ."

His gaze was so steady, so reaching. Lucy felt so warm, and good, and, well, safe. Right here, with the one person who truly cared about her for who she was, inside and out. Vivian was right about that much.

Which got her to thinking entirely inappropriate thoughts.

Like, had Grady's body always fit with hers so perfectly? And why hadn't she ever felt the little *zing* she was very definitely feeling right now, at the way he was looking at her? It was all just the power of suggestion. Grady would be horrified if he knew she was even thinking about what he was like as a kisser. She should be horrified. Only she was too busy looking at his mouth.

"You've always been there for me," she said softly, forcing those renegade thoughts from her mind. Except she couldn't help but realize just how true her words were. "I never meant to turn my back on that. No one knows me better than you, but there was a part of me that I didn't know, that I wanted to find out about. I just wish I'd found a way to do it without making you feel like I was pushing you away." *Why had she ever pushed him away?*

"It was stupid, but I felt threatened. Like by changing yourself so much on the outside, it was changing who you were on the inside."

"I have changed, Grady. I mean, not just the hair, the makeup, and all that. That's surface. But doing that allowed me to discover something else about myself, about what I can do, or be, if I want to. The old Lucy would have never stood up to Jason like that. I have more confidence in myself now. That's something I'll always know about myself, that I never would have if I hadn't done this." As she spoke the words, she realized just how true they were. And slowly, things began to click into place. She knew now what parts she'd keep and what she'd discard, as Vivian had advised her to do.

The most important thing she intended to keep was standing right in front of her, holding her, being her rock, and her best friend. "That never meant I didn't still need you. Your friendship, and Jana's, are everything to me. I just needed to know I could be more than teacher, daughter, and friend. I wanted to expand my comfort zone, so I could reach further, find . . . I don't know. Something. Someone. Someone I might not have been confident enough to even try and connect with before."

Grady stroked her face, tipped her chin toward him. "Maybe you didn't need to look so far."

Her heart started to pound. *Oh, my God!* Could Vivian have been right about . . . everything? Suddenly she was nervous as hell, and she babbled when she was nervous. "I know Jason was a stupid choice; it was just, I was really getting confused about what I was doing this for. You and Jana were at odds with me and I felt I had to prove something, to you guys and to myself. Jason was an obvious target. And when he came on to me at the dance, it just seemed like the best way to prove myself."

"You never had anything to prove. Not to anyone that mattered." Grady slid his fingers into her hair, slowly took out the last remaining drooping hot rollers. He set them on the counter without ever breaking eye contact. "Not to Jana. Not to me."

Lucy felt her heart swell, even as her pulse raced so fast she thought she might faint. She really had been blind. The way Grady was looking at her, with such honest affection and . . . and love. Her eyes welled. "I had to prove it to myself," she choked out, throat tight. "But I never meant to hurt you in the process."

"I know you didn't." He paused then, staring into her eyes for so long she wasn't sure he was going to say anything else, then he took a deep breath and said, "All those things I said about you earlier, to Jason. I meant them all, you know."

She smiled and sniffled. "You always were my best champion."

Grady's eyes grew a little glassy then, but his expression had never been so serious. "Yeah," he said, his throat working. "I've always felt that way, known that about you. You—you're right. No one knows you better than I do."

She felt his hands tense on her shoulders. His whole body

seemed tense. Or maybe that was her. She felt like they were standing on the edge of a very high cliff. The moment seemed to shrink down, condense, until she swore she could feel his every breath because it matched her own. It was all going to come down to who jumped first.

"And no one knows me better than you do," he said, stepping closer to the edge. "In fact, I can honestly say I've never felt connected to anyone the way I feel connected to you." He paused, and she could swear she felt him tremble, just a little. "If I was the type to believe in fate and karma and destiny, I'd have to say I knew from the first moment I saw you, in the cafeteria, staring down Buddy Aversom. But even if I don't believe in all that, all the years we've had together since have proven it true anyway."

She didn't know what to say.

"Jana saw it, too."

Now Lucy frowned. "She did?"

But Grady wasn't listening to her, he was too intent on getting the words out. "I never wanted to risk it. Our friendship meant too much. But I can't seem—" He broke off, his voice seemingly choked.

"What?" she urged him, wanting him to jump off the cliff first. Just in case she was wrong, and he wasn't trying to tell her what she thought he was.

"I can't seem to find a way back, to what we were before. For years I managed to seal that part off, be content with the friendship, knowing I was far, far luckier than most, to have that much. I don't know what the hell I would have done if you fell in love with someone else. But when it looked like, after all this time, it was going to be—"

"Oh, Grady."

He choked on a laugh that was totally devoid of humor. "God, please don't say my name like that. Pity, I don't need. Any more than you ever did."

She grabbed his face then, when he went to look away. Her pack fell off and hit the floor with a clatter of scattered ice cubes. But she didn't even feel the pain as she turned his head back to hers. "I don't pity you. I just—this is a shock, that's all. I didn't know." She found herself stroking his face, his much-beloved face, she thought. "I didn't know how you felt." She swallowed hard and stepped right up to the edge herself. "Or that maybe, maybe I might feel the same way."

His gaze intensified so fiercely she began trembling. His grip on her tightened. And then things paused between them. Like the whole world came to a complete stop. They looked in each other's eyes and connected like they always did. She saw all of him, and he saw all of her, like it had been since the beginning. Except she'd missed that one vital element, that one clue. That he loved her. Really loved her. And always had.

Her heart started to pound again. And her knees went a little wobbly. Grady Matthews. In love with her. And maybe, it could be, that all this time, she'd been searching for what she wanted, what she needed, and it had been right there in front of her all along.

He was right about one thing. There was no turning back time, erasing the knowledge they now shared. It was terrifying, really. The enormity of what had just happened. What would happen next. The world, as they knew it, was never going to be the same.

So . . . what did she want to do about it?

She hadn't trusted him before when she should have. Maybe it was time to trust him now. She wasn't sure who moved first, or if they both moved together. But an instant later the gap between them closed, and his mouth found hers.

# Chapter 27

Grady tried really hard to savor the moment. The moment he'd been waiting for his entire life. But he was sweating, shaking, and his heart was pounding so hard it was a miracle it didn't spontaneously combust right through the wall of his chest.

He was finally kissing Lucy Harper.

Her lips were soft, just like he'd known they'd be. They'd kissed before, friendly pecks. But this was different.

Add rock-hard to the list of things his body was at the moment.

He tangled his hands in her hair, swearing he wouldn't lose control, wouldn't rush her. She'd had no idea. He didn't want to overwhelm her.

Then he realized she was the one clinging to him, returning his kiss. Pushing for more.

*Anything you want.*

She opened her mouth beneath his, and he thought if he died right then, he'd go out a happy, satisfied man.

He couldn't quite stifle the groan in his throat, nor could he seem to keep his hips from crowding hers. She bumped up against the counter, but when he went to pull back, she yanked him closer. And took the kiss even deeper.

*Sweet Christ* was all he could think as they tangled tongues and limbs. She was squirming against him and he wasn't sure how long he could hold out. But it seemed a bit premature to start ripping her clothes off. Shouldn't they be taking this more slowly? For all he knew, this was just a knee-jerk reaction on her part.

She suddenly broke their kiss and he wondered if she'd read his thoughts. He gasped for air, scrambled to regain control so she wouldn't realize how close he'd come to losing it.

"Wait a minute," she said, as if just realizing something.

He'd wait forever. Just so long as they got to pick up where they left off. He thought better of saying that out loud. But just barely.

"You said Jana knew. How long?"

She looked a little hurt, and he supposed with reason. So he treaded carefully. "She figured it out a long time ago, only I didn't know that until recently. I'm pretty sure Vivian figured it out, too. And I only just met her."

"'Vivian'? What? Wait, wait." She pushed him back a half step. But her back was still against the kitchen counter, and he didn't give her any more room than absolutely necessary.

"So, you and Jana talked about this?"

"Not in so many words, no."

"But she knows how you feel? About me."

"I'm pretty sure she does. I didn't want to talk about it."

"Yes, that is your M.O. lately."

His lips twitched. "Apparently I'm losing my ability to hide it from anyone."

"Vivian." Light dawned. " 'A woman can't make up her mind about what she really wants unless she's aware of all her options.' "

He could only nod. "That's why I'm here. I just couldn't stand the idea of you and—"

Now she smiled. "He Who Shall Never Be Mentioned Again?"

"Yeah," Grady said, smiling, too. "That guy."

"So you've really felt like this for? . . ."

"Forever, Luce."

She grew serious, then looked down for a moment before looking back up at him. "Why didn't you tell me?"

He lifted a shoulder. "I couldn't tell if it would be reciprocated. I'm not exactly your type."

Her mouth dropped open, offended.

"Come on, Lucy, I'm not. You don't ever want to date guys like me."

"There are no other guys like you!" she shot back.

"That's because I'm your best friend, but you never once thought about me that way. And I couldn't stop thinking about you that way. Why do you think I went off to MIT?"

"Oh, I don't know, a full-ride scholarship?" she said dryly.

"I had other offers. I chose the one farthest away."

"From me," she said, unable to hide the quick flash of hurt.

He held her shoulders. "It was about protecting myself. I had to figure out how to stop feeling . . . what I felt. I swore I wasn't going to come back, to keep some distance between us. I wanted to remain friends, and . . . and hopefully find someone else."

"What happened?" She shook her head and looked around the room, as if the answers to her questions would be found printed on the walls or something. "I just can't believe this. Really. I feel like I've been blind or something all this time."

He reached out, nudged her to look at him. "If I told you, and you didn't feel the same way, we could never go back."

She covered his hand with her own. "Nothing's changed. Why now?"

"Everything changed. You changed. I—I was afraid you'd found someone else. I couldn't even stand thinking about it. That's why I've been such a prick. It was all me. But it was just too much."

"Grady," she said softly.

"I already knew how wonderful a person you are, and I didn't want the secret to get out, you know? You were mine and I didn't want to share. I never really understood just how strongly I felt that until—well . . ." Now he broke off, suddenly feeling—kiss or no kiss—that he'd revealed too much, put too much out there.

Now she tugged at his sleeve, nudged him to look at her. "It's a lot to take in," she said.

His heart squeezed painfully. "Yeah. I know. And you don't have to say anything, okay? It's hard enough—"

She grinned, quite wickedly. "I know; I could tell."

He actually blushed. He couldn't remember the last time anyone had ever made him blush. "Sorry about that."

"Don't be sorry." She tugged on his arms. "I was saying, 'It's a lot to take in.' But I want to try. That kiss . . ." She trailed off, and her eyes went a bit dreamy.

His heart leapt back up so hard he swore it banged against his throat. "Yeah?"

She sighed. "Oh yeah."

He couldn't have stopped the stupid male-pride grin from spreading across his face for all the nanotechnology breakthroughs in the world. "So . . ."

"So," she said, tugging him back up against her, "I say enough of the talking."

His pulse raced. Jesus, she was going to kill him before this was over. "I thought you weren't getting enough talking."

"There're a few things I'm not getting enough of."

He swallowed against a suddenly very dry, very tight throat. His body, however, wasn't having any problems digesting that comment. "Yeah?"

She tightened her hold on his hips. "Remember what I said about that confidence thing?"

"Uh-huh," he said, not even able to understand words at this point. But he'd have said yes to almost anything if it meant she wasn't going to let him go.

"Well, there are some areas that still need a little, you know, boosting."

"Really." Christ, he was going into full cardiac arrest. *Don't think about her naked. Not yet.* Far too late for that bit of advice. But in all of the detailed scenarios of how this moment might play out, he'd never dared allow himself to imagine anything even close to this. He'd just hoped for an outcome that wasn't devastating. It never occurred to him that she'd not only take the news in stride, but take over altogether.

She lifted up on her toes. "Why don't we try kissing some more. You know, just to figure out if we're as compatible as you think we are." She bit his chin.

*Oh, God.* He'd never get his pants off in time. He rapidly contemplated the pros and cons of taking her right here on the kitchen counter. Not the romantic bower he'd imagined, assuming she'd want all the hearts and flowers. And he wanted a nice soft bed. But at the moment, right here on the kitchen floor was looking pretty damn good. *Control yourself, don't scare her. You've had years to build up this need for her; she's had ten minutes.* Which was true, he thought. But come on, she bit his chin! She might have been clued in late in the game, but she was making up time in an impressive manner.

That Lucy Harper, always an overachiever.

"I should have trusted you before," she said, nibbling along his jaw, decimating what ragged edges of control he had left, peck by peck. "You taste like apples, did you know that?"

"No," he stuttered, "I didn't, uh—sweet Jesus." She bit his earlobe. And she was sort of . . . rubbing things. Her hips were moving.

He felt her smile against his jaw and clamped his hands in a death grip on the counter on either side of her waist. Because the instant he put his hands on her again, all bets were off. "I know you trust me, Lucy. But, I'm, uh, I'm—"

"Me, too," she breathed, kissing his neck. "Isn't it great?"

She sounded almost surprised, and as much as Grady wanted to go with the flow, since that flow looked like it was going to lead straight to nirvana, that little note of wonder stopped him. "Lucy."

"Mmm?" she said, trailing what, as it happened, was a quite talented tongue along his jaw. Okay, so apparently there were a few things he didn't know about her. But he planned to dedicate the rest of his life to ferreting them all out. First, however, he had to risk everything she was handing him to ask one last stupid question. Only an idiot would risk that.

An idiot, or a man in love. And he loved her too much to rush her into anything, just because they were all hot and bothered.

"One thing."

"Only one? I was hoping for—"

He let go of the counter and framed her face before she said anything else in that sex-kitten voice. My God, did she have *any* idea what she was doing to him? He doubted it. "Is this about me? Or about not getting him?"

There was no need to spell out who "him" was.

Her eyes had gone all slumberous and too damn sexy for words. She had to blink twice at him before she was able to pull herself out of the sex-fogged haze that had enveloped them both with shocking speed and ease. "I—" And then that deadly pause. "Isn't this what you want?"

He bumped hips with her. "I think we can safely say that's a big yes." The contact made him twitch. The twitch made him groan. Why the hell had he stopped her? *Fool!* "I don't want this to be about what I want. Not just what I want, anyway."

She thought about that for a moment. It was the longest, most excruciating moment of his life.

"I feel . . ." She shrugged, then the most beautiful smile lit her face. "Safe. Loved. Desired. And I want you to feel the same. Plus, I just plain want you." Her smile turned to a wide grin. "Do you think I could be . . . how I've just been, with anyone else?" Even as she said the words, it was like she was realizing the truth of them at the same time. He saw the confidence filter into her eyes, and she held his gaze without a waver or doubt. "No one has ever made me feel like you do. I feel like I've been living in some alternate universe where I was completely blind. I don't know why I never figured this out."

"Maybe," he started, then stopped, the words clogged in his throat. He was either the kindest man in the universe, or the biggest idiot of all time. "Maybe it's because we're just meant to be close friends. The closest. But not more."

She immediately shook her head. "Oh no, no backing out now."

"I wasn't. I mean, I don't want to. I just want to make sure that—"

"Grady, that kiss, that first kiss, was like . . . like I was Sleeping Beauty, or Sleeping Lucy, anyway," she cracked, with that dry grin that he loved so much, "and you woke me up. God, that would sound corny to anyone else, but it's the best way I can describe it. Is that what your ego needs to hear?"

"No," he said truthfully, then wrapped his arms around her. "But it is what my heart needed to hear."

Her expression melted. And so did his heart.

"I want to take it slow," he told her. "I don't want to risk us screwing this up because we rushed when we should have been patient. But . . . honestly, I'm not sure I can. I've waited so long, I just want to devour you."

She shivered against him, and his eyes widened a little. "That's really a good thing, what you just said."

"So you have to tell me if I push too hard, too fast."

"Okay," she said, backing him up, then out of the kitchen. "I'll be sure to do that."

"Where are we going?"

"To a place where you can push hard and fast and I can tell you when to stop."

"Dear God."

She grinned. "You started this."

"Yeah," he said, a dazed grin spreading across his face. "And right at the moment, I'm wondering why in the hell I waited so long." With that he scooped her up and over his shoulder, making her squeal in surprise. "Since when were you such an aggressive wench?"

"Since about five minutes ago." She squealed again when he swung through the living room. "Normally I just think stuff like that, but I'd never dare say it out loud."

"And I got lucky why?"

"It's different with you. I don't have to worry what you'll think." She smacked him on the ass. "I know exactly how your mind works."

"Oh yeah?" He kicked her bedroom door the rest of the way open. "Well, maybe I don't tell you and Jana everything."

"Ooh, sex secrets?"

He flopped her on the bed into a huge pile of discarded clothing. She was laughing and he realized as he followed her down on the bed, so was he.

He pushed his hands into her hair. "No more secrets."

Her laughter faded, but her eyes were still lit up like twin beacons. "No. No more secrets."

He bent down, kissed her. She wrapped her hands around his neck, held him closer.

"Your hand okay?" he murmured.

"Mmm," she managed. "You're a good kisser, you know that," she told him as he bit his way along her jaw.

"I'm inspired."

She laughed. He took that laugh with a kiss, then rolled to his side, taking her with him as he nudged her mouth open and took the kiss deeper.

Their laughter faded, and suddenly the air was charged with a completely different kind of energy. He let his hands trail down her arms, cupping her hips, drawing her leg over his hip.

She was pulling at his shirt. He took the hint and pulled her sweatshirt over her head. She shook her loopy roller curls loose, then gave him that lopsided grin. "Is this going to get weird? Getting naked with each other?"

"Not weird so far. You?"

She shoved him on his back. "Nope. You'll let me know if that changes for you?" She flipped the snap on his jeans.

"Yeah," he said, groaning. "You'll be the first." She tugged his zipper down, and from that point on, all rational thought went on hiatus.

Minutes later, he had Lucy Harper naked and beneath him.

"Can I tell you something?" he said, his breath already coming in pants.

"I have the NASA bra, if you want cleavage," she told him.

He laughed. "No, no. I love your body. It's just, I think I've revised my opinion on the fake-tan thing."

She grinned. "Oh yeah?"

"I'm all for both as it turns out."

"Who would have guessed we'd find détente over smooth skin and tan lines."

"Or the lack of them."

She laughed and wrapped her legs around his hips.

He moaned and arched his head back. "If this is all really a dream, please don't let me wake up for at least another hour."

"An hour?" she queried. "Lucky me." And then she dug in her heels and he was buried deep and she was moaning, too.

Lucy blinked her eyes open some unspecified period of time later. Groggy and trying to figure out where her nightstand clock had gone to, she tossed aside a pair of hose, one skirt, and two blouses. Then her hand landed on something furry, and it wasn't Grady. She dragged the six-foot-long ostrich out from under the blanket, not even wanting to remember how or why it got there in the first place.

Admittedly, things had gotten rather spirited during that second round.

It was pitch-dark now, that was all she knew. Judging by the steady breathing, Grady was passed out beside her. She reached out until her hand met his bare . . . leg? What?

She lifted her head and looked around. What was her clock doing behind her? Then she realized she was facing the wrong way on her bed. And that it was almost six in the morning. Crap.

Then she remembered it wasn't a school day. Saturday. She slumped back on the bed. *Thank you, God.*

Grady rustled then, probably because her hand had slipped up the back of his thigh. He had an incredibly nice ass, as it turned out. Who knew racquetball was such a great workout?

With a grunt, his hand came out and landed on her arm. Another grunt, and he was rolling to his side and pulling her close. More than willing, she shifted around and let him tuck her next to his body. Still sleeping, he let out a deep sigh and buried his face in the back of her hair.

She lay there, staring into the dark, and tried to comprehend all the incredible ways her life had changed in the past handful of hours. Not only had Grady kissed her . . . they'd gotten naked and had world-class sex. Several times! Again she wondered why in the hell it had taken so long for them to figure this out. It wasn't even remotely weird, either. In fact, it had all seemed almost startlingly normal. Imagine. She knew him so well, and he her, there hadn't been any of the traditional first-time awkward moments couples usually have. In fact, they'd had a downright blast exploring . . . everything. She sighed, and realized she was grinning like a mad Cheshire cat or something.

Their compatibility in life had translated to a kind of compatibility in bed that it would have taken eons to build with another person. He'd teased her and aroused her, oh yes, indeedy . . . but he'd also made it fun. God, she'd never laughed her ass off harder than she had while making love with Grady Matthews. She'd been in bed with him less than one night and already she couldn't imagine being with anyone else.

She hoped it wasn't weird later this morning when they got up, she thought, as she dragged his arm higher on her waist and snuggled deeper into his sleeping embrace. She'd just have to make sure it wasn't. Worst case is, she'd drag him back to bed. The very idea had her sighing in contentment.

She was just drifting off again when the phone rang, making her start and Grady swear when her head connected with his chin. She might have also inadvertently mashed something she shouldn't have. Which is when she realized the great thing about making love with your best friend was that he already knew you were a disaster. And he'd still made love to her. Twice. Well, three times, if you count messing around in the shower.

She'd climaxed, so as far as she was concerned, it counted.

Scrambling to reach the phone before it woke him all the way up, she got tangled in the clothes on the bed. She'd almost reached it when it rang again. Grady jerked the rest of the way awake and sat up, which dumped her halfway across the bed.

"What? Who's there?" he said, struggling to be coherent.

"It's the phone; it's okay," she told him.

The answering machine clicked on after the third ring and a second later Dave's voice filled the room. "Uh, Lucy, hi, it's Dave. Listen, I know it's really early. Sorry. I guess you're probably still out." He lowered his voice and Lucy crawled closer. "Jana would kill me if she knew I was calling. But, well, she's in the hospital and, now, she's okay, so don't worry, and she didn't want me to bother you, but I thought she could use a little support."

"The hospital!" Lucy cried.

Grady came instantly alert and immediately reached across her and found the phone.

"How did you do that?" she said, still trying to adjust to the darkness.

"Excellent night vision. You should know that by now."

She couldn't help it, she grinned quite smugly. "Yeah. Right."

Grady clicked the phone on. "Dave, hi, it's Grady. What hospital is she in?"

" 'Grady'?" Dave sounded understandably confused. "I, sorry, man, I thought I dialed Lucy."

Lucy looked toward Grady and felt him shift to look at her.

"Uh—"

"It's okay," Lucy whispered. "They're gonna know anyway." She hadn't even thought about Jana, in terms of all this. But then, she'd been a little preoccupied.

"I'm at Lucy's. She's right here. Jana's okay?"

Lucy groped Grady's arm until she could find the phone. He let her have it. "Hi, Dave, it's me. Is she okay?"

"Yes. She had a little . . . problem. With the baby."

*Oh no. Oh, God.* Lucy's heart leapt to her throat. "Is—" She couldn't get the question out.

"The baby is fine, but she's—well, she's feeling—she's just not herself."

"Oh, thank God the baby is okay," Lucy said. Grady began stroking her arms and she relaxed back against him. How wonderful was it to have support just there for you, so easy, so automatic? "Can we come see her?"

"Would you?" He sounded . . . overwhelmed, and not a little lost. "I know she'll feel better if she could talk to you. Both of you, if Grady can come, too."

"We'll be there."

He sighed in relief. "Thanks. Thank you. I know she'll feel better when you're here."

Lucy frowned with worry. Dave still sounded pretty shaken up. "You sure she's okay?"

There was a pause, then, "Yeah. Physically, she'll be fine. She's going to have to be careful, maybe rest more than some women, but . . ."

"Dave, it's okay. She's strong, you know? She'll be okay." Of course, Lucy still didn't know exactly what had happened, but she'd never heard Dave sound so shaken.

There was a sound, almost like a half sob. "She thinks it's her fault. Because—because she didn't want it."

"Oh, Dave!" Lucy instinctively pulled Grady's arm more

tightly around her waist without even thinking. "No, no, of course it wasn't. She has to know that."

"The doctor explained it all to her, but she just—" He sounded like he was fighting for control. "Come and be here with her. I know you can talk to her. She'll hear it better from you than from me right now."

"Okay, okay. We're on our way."

"Thanks, guys," he said shakily. "Oh, and—" There was a sniff, then another pause while he got his act together. "We found out the sex. It's a boy."

" 'A boy'!"

Grady nudged the phone away from her. "A boy, huh? Dave, that's wonderful! Congratulations, man. We're on our way."

"Great. You guys, just . . . thanks."

# Chapter 28

The ride to the hospital was short but tense. They hadn't said much, but Grady had kept her hand tucked tightly in his the whole way over.

They stopped by the lobby gift shop long enough to pick up a teddy bear with a blue ribbon around its neck, then ducked into the first available elevator.

"She'll be okay," Grady told her, squeezing her hand.

Lucy knew he was reassuring himself as much as anything, and squeezed back. She had told him what Dave had said, about Jana assuming guilt for the situation. He'd been stunned and sad, then immediately assured her that they'd help her through it. "That's what friends do," he said.

And she realized in that moment that she was the luckiest woman on the planet. Because her best friend and her lover were one in the same person.

He punched the button for the third floor.

"What are we going to do about this?" Lucy lifted their joined hands.

"Dave might have already said something."

"I'm not sure Dave put it together. He's pretty messed up about all this. And it's not unheard of for you to crash at my place or theirs, for that matter."

"We'll just handle it as it happens." He looked at her; his hair was a wild halo of curls. She didn't even want to think about what she looked like. As if he read her mind, which she was convinced now more than ever he could, he reached out and picked off another piece of errant facial mask.

"Oh, God," she said, "I should have looked in the mirror before we left."

"She's not going to care."

Lucy stared at them both in the wavy reflection of the elevator walls. Their clothes were a hurried mess of rumpled wrinkles. As were their bodies, faces, and hair. "She's going to take one look at us and know."

The corner of Grady's mouth curled. "Would that be such a bad thing? I'm pretty sure she's going to be okay with this. In fact, it might be welcome news right now."

The door slid open and they hurried down the ward, holding hands, teddy bear clutched under Lucy's arm. They paused at the nurse's station long enough to get the room number.

When they got there, Dave was just coming out. His face was a little pale, and his hair looked like he'd slept standing on his head. His smile was weary but heartfelt. "Hey, guys!"

"Hey, yourself," Lucy said, hugging him. "Is she awake?"

Grady gave Dave the guy backslap hug. "How're you holding up?"

"Well, I've managed to keep my family from boarding the next flight down, so that's a major feat right there."

Lucy breathed a sigh of silent relief. Dave's family meant well, and they were a great bunch, but definitely not what Jana likely needed to deal with right now.

"The doctor says she should take it easy for a while, so we're going to postpone the trip north until Christmas." Dave favored Lucy with his famous snaggletoothed hockey grin. "Any chance we can con you into cooking turkey?" He nodded to the door. "She thinks she's going to be up for that, but if we make plans—"

"You know, I can hear you scheming out there," a voice called out from inside the room.

Lucy lit up and Dave nodded and opened the door. First she pecked Dave on the cheek. "I'll take care of Turkey Day, no problem."

"Thanks."

Lucy promised herself no matter what she encountered, she was going to do it with a smile. Jana was in the second bed, the first one being mercifully empty. There were flowers already on the windowsill and nightstand. "Hey, we brought you something to keep you company," she called out.

Jana was propped up in bed, looking paler than usual. Her freckles stood out in stark relief against her skin, her corkscrew curls frizzed beyond belief in a wild red halo around her head. "I told Dave not to call you," she said, then lifted her arms out to Lucy. "But I'm glad he did."

Lucy tucked the bear by Jana's side, then bent to hug her. "Right. Like we were going to stay home."

"Grady, too?" Jana smiled as she spied Grady behind Lucy. "Wow, is that what a girl has to do to get you guys to communicate? Land in the hospital?"

Lucy purposely didn't look at Grady, already surprised there wasn't a neon sign over her head proclaiming "We did it! We got naked together!"

"Hey, Sunshine," Grady said, leaning down for his hug. "You doing all right? Not giving the nurses a hard time?" He wiggled his eyebrows. "Chatting up the cute doctors?"

Jana smiled and seemed to perk up a little. "I do what I can," she said.

Lucy perched carefully on the side of her bed and folded Jana's hand in between her own. Jana immediately noticed the red knuckles and turned Lucy's hand around to study it closer. "What the hell did you do to yourself?"

Lucy smiled. "I got in a fight."

"I'm afraid to ask how the other guy looks." She immediately glanced up at Grady. "Well, you look no worse for the wear. Thank God." She looked back to Lucy. "Who'd you sock?"

"Well, this will perk you up," Lucy said.

"Wait a minute. You were on a date last night with—" Her eyes widened and she gasped. "No!"

"It was that or let Grady beat him to a pulp." As soon as the words left her mouth, she realized the gaffe.

"'Grady'? What was he doing on your date?" She looked to Grady.

"Hey," Lucy said desperately, tugging at her hand, trying to shift the topic, "we didn't come here to talk about you know who."

But Jana was still looking at Grady. She had that journalist thing going on with her narrowed eyes and forehead wrinkle. "So, I take it it's over between you and—"

"Yeah, it is," Lucy admitted. "But we're here for you, so—"

Jana looked back at Lucy. "Well, you've already made my day. I'm so glad you came to your senses." She was still sending the occasional glance at Grady. Who was looking far too nonchalant about this whole thing.

Lucy rubbed Jana's hand. "You doing okay?" she asked gently.

Jana sighed a little and laid her free hand over her tummy.

"Yeah. No. I don't know." Her eyes welled up an instant later, and Lucy immediately pulled her into an embrace.

"Oh, honey. I'm so sorry you had such a bad scare. I'm just glad you're okay. That you're both okay." She leaned back, then yanked out a tissue and handed it to Jana.

"Might as well give me the whole box. I'm an emotional disaster lately."

Lucy was undecided on how to approach the news Dave had shared with her on the phone. She decided the direct route was best. "You know this isn't your fault. You know you couldn't have prevented this." She didn't even know what had happened, but it didn't matter. Jana might have been an emotional wreck over her pregnancy, but she'd taken very good care of herself and the baby.

"It's like karma. Really bad karma." She kept rubbing her stomach. "I was so uncertain about all this. About . . . him." She gulped and let out another little sob.

Lucy just ripped more Kleenex out of the box, beginning to see why Dave was so at a loss. "You can't make something like this happen because you've had a rough time emotionally. You know that, Jana. I know you do."

Jana nodded, blew her nose noisily, then crumpled up the next wad of Kleenex Lucy pressed into her hand. "I think what scares me is that I almost lost him, and I never even fully appreciated him or what he will mean to us. I was just so stupidly selfish, you know? It was all about me and my life and my world and what I'll have to sacrifice." She looked at Lucy, her face all splotchy, eyes swollen from tears. "It wasn't until I thought I was going to lose him that I realized how devastated I'd be if I did." She hiccuped a little, and Lucy felt her own eyes watering.

"But he's safe. And so are you."

"It shouldn't have taken this to shake me up, to wake me up."

"It doesn't matter, Jana. This was going to happen if it was going to happen. Look at it this way, for all the fear and terror, you also got a gift out of it. The gift of knowing you love your baby."

Jana was nodding and crying and Lucy started crying. They were hugging each other and rocking.

There was a suspicious sniff behind them and they both paused, sniffling, and looked at Grady, who scowled. "Just toss me the damn box, okay?"

Lucy threw the tissue box to him, only she missed and it glanced off of some piece of medical equipment that was thankfully not hooked up to her best friend at the moment. "Oops."

Grady just smiled at her in this amazingly affectionate way and picked up the box. His easy acceptance of her dorkiness, along with the knowledge of how they'd spent last night, made her forget for just a second that Jana was sitting right there. God-only-knows-what kind of goofy smile was plastered across her face.

"You know," Jana said, wiping her eyes, then blowing her nose again, "I'm glad you guys are here. Because there's something I wanted to talk to you two about, anyway."

Lucy started a bit guiltily as she realized she and Grady were still staring at each other all moony-faced. "What? If it's about Thanksgiving, then don't even start. I'm cooking turkey."

Grady snorted behind her.

"Okay, Grady's actually cooking the turkey. No need to bring up the basting-fire incident again. It might upset the baby."

Grady and Jana both groaned. "She's actually using an unborn child as a defense now," Jana said, shaking her head, but smiling.

"Not my fault. You drove me to it. Anyway, we're cooking and you and Dave are going to come over. We're going to watch football and parades and eat until we explode. And you are going to do nothing but put your feet up and relax."

"You know, I've definitely not been playing this pregnancy thing for all it's worth. But that's going to change." She leaned up and kissed Lucy's cheek. "Thank you for the holiday hostessing. But that's not what I was going to say."

"Okay, what is it?"

She waved Grady closer and reached out her other hand to take his. "We've been friends forever, right?"

"Right," Lucy said, wary now. She knew that intent look. Jana was up to something.

"Well, one thing I learned in the past twenty-four hours was to never take any relationship for granted." She sniffled again and Grady immediately handed her the Kleenex.

They all laughed a little, but Jana just squeezed their hands more tightly. "I've watched the two of you for years." She glanced at Grady. "I know you don't want me to do this, but I think you're making a mistake by not telling Lucy the whole reason behind your retreating of late."

Lucy and Grady looked at each other, and there was no way to cover the guilt coloring their expressions.

"Um," Jana said, looking between the two of them. "Is there something else I don't know about?" A smile began to play around her mouth, and her eyes lit up a little. "Would it perhaps have something to do with why Grady was trying to flatten Jason Prescott?" She looked at Grady. "And nice job, by the way. Wish I was there so I could have helped."

Grady smiled. "No need. Slugger here took him out with one punch, direct hit right to the schnoz. Prescott might not be so pretty anymore."

Lucy snorted. "Who are you kidding? I'm betting he had the best plastic surgeon in the country on the phone before he hit the lobby of my apartment building."

"'Lobby'? *Your* building?" Jana looked at Grady. "And you were there?"

Grady came to sit on the other side of the bed. "Yeah. I was there. I, uh, well, remember you told me about the date?"

Jana nodded.

"I guess something just snapped inside me." His smile was wry. "Might have had something to do with that visual image you planted in my brain."

"What 'visual image'?" Lucy asked.

Jana smiled smugly. "You. And Jason Prescott. Doing the—"

"Please," Grady said. "Once was enough."

"Apparently it was enough," Jana said, her voice taking on a note of wonder. "So . . ." She trailed off encouragingly.

Grady reached across the bed and took Lucy's hand. "So I stayed. And we talked."

Jana looked from one to the other.

Lucy knew her hot cheeks were a dead giveaway.

" 'Talked,' huh?"

"Lots of talking," Lucy said.

"So when Dave called you this morning—"

"I answered the phone," Grady said.

"Hot damn!" Jana hollered, which brought Dave crashing into the room.

"What? Are you okay?" He looked wildly around the room. "I didn't want to intrude, but—"

"They did it!" Jana said, then hooted again.

" 'Did' what?" Dave said, calming down now that he realized her scream was for an apparent good thing.

"It!"

Dave looked at the joined hands, apparently added two and two and an early phone call, and went, "Ohhhh. *It!*" A big gap-toothed grin split his face and he strode over to Grady and clapped him on the back so hard it almost sent him sprawling. "All right!"

Lucy and Jana looked at each other. "What is it about guys and sexual prowess, anyway?" Lucy asked.

"Hey, at least he's not rubbing your belly and getting that smug 'Look what I did' smile on his face."

Lucy went a bit pale. The other three laughed.

"We'll have to work up to that," Grady said.

Jana grinned and patted Lucy's shoulder. "Well, when the time comes, I have a stack of books for you."

Lucy just swallowed hard.

"God, I love you guys," Jana said, pulling them both in for a clumsy group hug. "Thanks for being there for me through all this. Before and what's yet to come."

"Of course," they both mumbled as she squeezed them tightly. After letting them go, she suddenly yawned hugely. "God, I'm whacked."

Lucy and Grady immediately got off the bed. "You should get your rest," Lucy said. "We can come back later."

Jana settled back among her pillows, the teddy bear hooked in one arm, and her other hand on her tummy. Her eyes were already drooping, but her smile was pure Jana sass. "Yeah, sure. You're going to go have hours of fantastic hot sex and I'll be here eating hospital gelatin."

"Probably not 'hours,' " Lucy said.

Grady nudged her, and she nudged him back.

"You know," Jana said, yawning again, "I might live to regret hooking the two of you up."

"She's already taking all the credit," Grady said.

"You bet," Jana said. "Never argue with a pregnant woman."

"Yeah, you've got about six months to exploit that rule."

Dave fussed with his wife's blanket and moved the rolling tray down to the foot of her bed. "She'll just have a new rule when the baby gets here," he said.

"True," Lucy said with a laugh.

Grady slipped his hand in hers as Dave leaned down over his wife and kissed her cheek. She was out before he straightened. He mouthed "Thank you" to the two of them, then settled in the chair beside her bed.

Lucy and Grady took their cue and ducked out of the room.

"So," Grady said, as they wandered back down the hall toward the elevator, "where to?"

"Is this the 'Your place or mine' question?"

"Might be."

"For how long?"

Grady smiled, then surprised her by ducking inside a door marked LINENS. "How long do you have?"

"Grady!" Lucy hissed. "We're in a hospital ward!"

"Yeah, but I learned something back there in Jana's room."

She arched an eyebrow.

Grady scowled. "You know, that plucked-eyebrow thing is like a weapon. Like it's got a personality all its own."

Lucy grinned. "Yeah, I'm learning I have a lot of weapons I didn't know about. First thing Monday, I'm planning on calling the tanning salon and buying a lifetime membership."

Grady laughed, then tugged her tightly into his arms. "Speaking of lifetimes . . ." And he bent his head and kissed her.

When he finally lifted his head, they were both a little breathless.

"Wow," Lucy said.

"That's what I figured out in Jana's room. That it's going to take at least a lifetime to do all of that I want."

Lucy wove her hands around his neck. "A lifetime. Hmm."

Grady's expression turned serious. "I love you, Lucy Harper. You've always been the most beautiful woman in the world to me. Inside and out."

Lucy actually felt her heart swell. "I love you, too, Grady

Matthews." Saying it, meaning it the way she did now, wasn't nearly as scary as she'd thought it would be. In fact, it felt just right. "Vivian was right. It's all about finding the perfect inner balance. You've always been that balance for me, steadying me, being there for me. My sounding board, my friend, my ally, my staunchest supporter." She grinned. "And now all that and benefits, too!"

He laughed, smoothed the hair from her face. "You do know you're all those same things for me, don't you?"

"I do now. Maybe if I'd understood that sooner." She smiled up at him. "Or maybe I needed to learn about myself first. Things happen when they do for a reason. For Jana. For us." She tugged his head closer. "And I'm thinking a lifetime sounds just about right." She kissed him deeply, then sighed as he held her close. "Remind me to send Vivian a thank-you note."

"Sure," Grady said, walking her back up against a shelving unit full of towels. "Just as soon as I can stand taking my hands off of you."

Lucy was the one who flipped the lock on the door. "Vivian would be the first one to approve that sentiment." Then she ripped his shirt off.

"God bless fairy godmothers everywhere," Grady said, groaning in pleasure.

# Epilogue

Later that evening, after a lovely call from Lucy, Vivian sat on the lanai behind Glass Slipper, Inc., and raised her glass in a silent toast. She was quite satisfied with how everything had turned out. Dessora Claudette would be proud of her most successful assistant.

Vivian downed the shot in one fiery gulp, then smiled with intense satisfaction. Another job well done, yes. But this one was the most satisfying she'd been involved in, in a very long time.

In fact, she felt so invigorated by her success that she decided she deserved a little reward. Her smile was a wicked one. So maybe it wasn't going to be that little. She deserved that, too. She rose from her quiet spot and went off in search of that gorgeous limo driver. The ever delicious and quite talented Paul. Ah yes, just the way to celebrate a success. The only way, if they asked her. And they often did.

The night was young. And so, at heart—and with the help

of a very nice plastic surgeon, a number of other body parts—was she.

*And so it came to pass that the knight known as Grady, his heart steadfast and true, swept his lady love Lucy off her feet (and frankly, those four-inch spikes were killing her anyway) and carried her into the sunset of their everlasting love (which looked a lot like his apartment in Alexandria).*

*Jana and her true love, the valiant (and virile) Dave, became the parents of a bouncing baby boy (and future goalie for the Capitals) known as Benjamin Ross, who was followed two years later by his younger sister (Olympic volleyball hopeful Sasha Lynn), and three years beyond that, by the twins, Drew and Adria. (Who, between them, won a Pulitzer, a Peabody, and an Oscar. But couldn't sink a foul shot if their collective lives depended on it.)*

*And last but not ever the least, the godmothers known as Vivian, Aurora, and Mercedes were once again free to look toward the future . . . and did so with great glee. For right around the corner was their next Once Upon a Time. . . .*

# About the Author

National bestseller Donna Kauffman resides with her family just outside D.C. in northern Virginia. She recently attended her own high school reunion (we won't mention which one) relatively unscathed and with only minimal assistance from her local day spa. Okay, so maybe it was more than minimal assistance. But she is proud to say that her yearbook accolade of Best Dancer continues to go unchallenged.

Don't Miss

Donna Kauffman's

other fresh and flirty fairy tales for

the modern girl . . .

THE BIG BAD WOLF TELLS ALL

THE CINDERELLA RULES

DEAR PRINCE CHARMING

And coming in
Summer 2006

NOT-SO-SNOW WHITE

"Donna Kauffman writes
smart and sexy, with sizzle to spare!"
—JANET EVANOVICH
the Big
Bad Wolf
tells all
Donna Kauffman
Author of The Cinderella Rules

# The Big Bad Wolf Tells All

*"Women everywhere will be taking* Big Bad Wolf *to bed with them."* —Janet Evanovich

Tanzy Harrington is the Bay Area's most-read romance columnist and self-proclaimed love-'em-and-leave-'em artist—and she's not quite ready to tie herself down to one man. That is, until Riley Parrish lands on the scene.

When Tanzy agrees to house-sit for her eccentric great-aunt, she finds herself sharing close quarters with Riley. At first he seems a bit too much like the "sheep" Tanzy derides in her column—too polite, the classic boring good provider. But when she catches a glimpse of the "wolf" lurking in his eyes, the ultimate alpha female is about to take a fall.

# Tanzy Tells All

So I watched my best friend get married for the third time this weekend and I got to wondering . . . does the wedding bouquet lose its matchmaking karma if the marriage doesn't last? Not that I want to be matched. Well, not for more than a few really good hours. A day or two, tops. In fact, they can keep the bouquet. Why risk it, you know?

I bring this up because it was at that moment that my life-altering epiphany occurred. It all happened when I attempted to dissolve into the crowd of bouquet-catcher wannabes . . . and made the startling discovery that there was no crowd to dissolve into. In fact, upon further observation, I realized I was the only person at the crowded reception old enough to vote and not yet on social security who met the requirements for the Bridal Bouquet Rodeo.

How did this happen? How, at age twenty-nine, did I, Tanzy Harrington, officially become the Last Bridesmaid in a social circle filled with Till-Death-Do-Us-Parters?

Today's query . . . is honeymoon sex really that fantastic? Or do the participants merely indulge in that fantasy as a way to deal with the dawning realization that this is the only kind of sex they will have . . . ever again?

---

Killer column today, Tanz. I like the new tangent you're off on with this whole wolf/sheep thing."

Tanzy adjusted her phone headset and hit save. "Thanks, Martin. Let's just say I was inspired."

"Apparently. Who knew there were so many Last Bridesmaids out there?"

She snarled silently. "Yeah, I'm thinking of forming a club." It had been three weeks since her first column commenting on her wedding reception epiphany. Apparently she wasn't, in fact, the last bridesmaid on the planet. She'd heard from a whole slew of them in the past ten days. Hordes. Somehow, she didn't feel any less alone. "Listen, I'm getting Saturday's column in early. I've got that Single Santa radio thing this afternoon, then this month's stint on the *Barbara Bradley Show* is taping tomorrow morning. They're doing a Single at Christmas show, too." Hoo boy. She could hardly wait.

"Well, chat up this wolf/sheep thing you mentioned in today's column. I have a hunch it's going to play big with the serial solos out there."

She grinned. "Says the ultimate sheep."

He chuckled, not bothering to refute it. "Hey, at least I'm the herd leader." Martin was managing editor of *MainLine*, the hottest online magazine since *Salon* and home to the controversial, much-talked-about "Tanzy Tells All" column for the past four years. Despite being on the cutting edge of publishing technology, though, Martin was still a guy pushing fifty, with a wife of twenty-five years, two kids in college, and a nice house in Pacific Heights. He might as well have "good provider" stamped on his vanity plate.

"Yeah, you da Big Sheep, Marty."

"Hey, herd member I might be, but that doesn't mean I don't have a little howl left in me, you know. Did I tell you about the new ride?"

Tanzy rolled her eyes. What was it with middle-aged men and their toys? "Yes, Marty. Candy-apple red, leather interior, nice wheel package, and a whole herd of horses under the hood."

"Beats a herd of sheep," he shot back, and she heard the pride of toy ownership in his voice. Or maybe it was just sports car lust.

She did understand a little about that. But you were supposed to drive fast cars when you were young, right? Marty was a sedan guy. Marty had probably been born a sedan guy. Which is what made this whole toy car thing so weird. For him, anyway. Portly, balding, prescription glasses . . . nope, she couldn't picture him flying down the highway, top down, singing "Born to Be Wild." She gave a little shudder at the visual. Well, he'd just sent his last kid off to college this fall, so maybe that explained it. She'd heard empty nests made people do odd things. God only knew what Mrs. Marty thought about her husband's new fixation.

"Any time you want a test drive, you let me know, okay?"

She rolled her eyes. "Will do. I'll talk to you after I'm done taping Friday, let you know how it went." She clicked off and stared at her laptop screen, scanning back over what she'd already written, then began to type.

*So, is that why we L.B.'s aren't willing to settle for sheep like the rest of our social circle? Sheep Sex aside, what's wrong with a man who puts family first, who maintains a steady job, has college funds set up for his kids, and builds that nest egg for his retirement? Member of the workaday herd, never straying.*

*Solid, dependable Sheep Guy.*

*Why can't I love Sheep Guy?*

Donna Kauffman
Author of The Big Bad Wolf Tells All
The Cinderella
RULES
Rule #1:
Always try on more
than one glass slipper.

# The Cinderella Rules

*"Fun banter and sizzling sex."* —Entertainment Weekly
*"A sexy, spicy romp."* —Booklist

There's a little bit of Cinderella in every woman . . . except Darby Landon, or so she thinks before meeting the three fairy godmothers of Glass Slipper, Inc. They guarantee they can bring out the princess in any woman. But they'll have their work cut out for them with Darby, who's more comfortable in jeans and cowboy boots than designer gowns. But when she's called from her Montana ranch to squire her impossible-to-please father's star client around the D.C. social scene, Darby has to turn into the queen chic . . . and fast.

Between torture-chamber sessions of tweezing and teasing, and horrifying lessons on place settings, Darby finds herself drawn into a fairy-tale romance of the very adult variety with Shane Morgan, the devastatingly sexy (and reluctant) heir to one of the city's largest companies. But when another Prince Charming arrives on the scene, Darby's caught between the woman she is and the woman she's supposed to be, between two very different irresistible bad boys. Now Darby has to choose her own happy ending . . . and with the help of three very unusual fairy godmothers, this modern-day Cinderella is determined to stay dancing way past midnight—no pumpkins required.

*A GLASS SLIPPER NOVEL*

His lips were . . . well, as perfect as the rest of him. And he definitely knew his way around a woman's mouth. She tried—okay, for about two seconds—to just absorb the kiss without responding, determined not to react, just to see what he'd do. He was far too used to women swooning and sighing over him, and for some perverse reason, she wanted to be the one who didn't. Except his kiss was as natural as his charm.

And it undeniably went a long way toward taking the edge off the ugly stepsister vibe she'd been carrying around since the moment she saw that glass slipper. Okay, maybe for a while longer than that.

His hand came up, slid beneath her heavy braid, and cupped the back of her head as he moved to take the kiss deeper. Now was the time to casually pull away, show him her studied indifference, maybe a little shrug when he lifted those charismatic brows of his, surprised at her lack of response. But who was she kidding? It had been a long time since she'd been kissed like this. Actually, it had probably been . . . never.

So she let him past her lips, into her mouth, and grudgingly accepted that about the best she could hope for in terms of studied indifference was refraining from moaning wildly and ripping his clothes off. It wasn't much of an edge, but she clung to it.

And then he was lifting his head, taking his mouth from hers. "Cinderella packs quite a punch, glass slippers or no," Shane said. The gravelly edge to his voice sent a hot thrill straight through her.

"No regrets, then," she managed, her own voice a shade rougher than she'd have liked.

He held her gaze so steadily, she forgot where she was, what she was supposed to be doing, even her own name.

"Only one."

She lifted her eyebrows in question, but he was already reaching for her. And this time when he took her mouth, there was nothing light or casual about it. This was no preliminary exploration, no assuaging of curiosity. If she thought she'd felt his hunger before, now she felt as if she were being consumed. Devoured, even.

Her fingers found their way into his hair. Someone moaned, someone growled. Then he was pulling all five feet eleven inches of her across his lap as effortlessly as if she were . . . well, Pepper. It was a rather defining moment for Darby, yet she couldn't stop to examine it. She was much too busy being insatiable.

Donna Kauffman
Author of *The Cinderella Rules*
*America's #1 advice author is about to give away his biggest secret....*
Dear Prince Charming

# Dear Prince Charming

"Dear Prince Charming *is campy, ridiculous fun. Kauffman's zippy prose and direct sensibility are a breeze to read. The perfect afternoon read."*
—Contra Costa Times

Workaholic *Glass Slipper* publicist Valerie Wagner needs a prince and she needs him yesterday. Her hard-won career depends on finding a stand-in for the magazine's wildly popular advice columnist, whose scandalous secret is keeping him out of the limelight for the magazine's launch. But where is she going to find a guy who understands women—and also just happens to be drop-dead gorgeous?

Enter sportswriter Jack Lambert, a handsome charmer with a devilish smile and a chain of ruined relationships behind him. With Valerie's help, Jack's about to pull off the scam of the decade: pretend he knows exactly what women want. But the more time Valerie spends with him . . . the more both of them realize that when it comes to love, they're going to need a royal dose of advice.

*A GLASS SLIPPER NOVEL*

At age thirty, Valerie Wagner had begun to fear that the fashion career she'd dreamed of since opening her first *Vogue* at age nine was actually a grand and cruel delusion, and that perhaps medical intervention might be required in getting her over it.

Maybe her fourth-grade teacher, Ms. Spagney, had been right all along. She'd sent *Vogue*-enhanced Valerie home from school the following day with strict instructions to never scare the other students like that again. Privately, Valerie had thought Ms. Spagney could use some heavy kohl eyeliner and spiky bangs herself. It would have done much to hide the deep grooves that came from too many years of frowning down at young, independent thinkers like herself.

However, she'd been objective enough to realize that maybe makeup and hairstyling weren't her strengths. So she'd stared down at her flat chest and thought . . . hmm. Valerie had been the only girl in her sixth-grade class secretly thrilled not to need a training bra. After all, she'd never walk the runways in Milan if she had boobies.

Unfortunately, she'd forgotten about the height clause. By sixteen, even in wobbly heels, with hair gelled to within an inch of its life, she barely flirted with the five-eight mark. Much shorter than the five ten she knew from her by-then slavish devotion to *W* was the minimum of industry standards.

Cruelly, the now-welcome boobies had never appeared.

Undeterred, she'd resolutely turned to design. If she wasn't made to model fashion, by damn, she'd create it. Which would have worked beautifully except stick figures sporting Magic Marker–colored, triangle-shaped outfits weren't exactly going to win her any scholarships. And yet, she'd hung in there, convinced her calling was still within reach. She'd go for a degree in fashion merchandising and work for an upscale chain as a buyer. She envisioned trips to Paris, London, Milan. So what if she had as much chance of balancing her checkbook as she did of discovering the formula for cold fashion? It wasn't like she was going to be spending her own money, right?

Then had come the Big Breakthrough. In her senior year of high school, the brokerage firm her father worked for had transferred him to Chicago. She'd gotten a summer job with *Madame* magazine—for full-figured gals, not call-girl employers—though as switchboard operator she'd heard every hooker joke and pimp pun on the planet. She hadn't minded.

She'd found her people.

Obviously she'd just misinterpreted the gospel according to *Elle*. It wasn't the people populating those glossy pages that called to her. It was the glossy pages themselves. Fashion magazines, the force that drove the industry, deciding what was hip and what was hopelessly last year . . . that was her true calling, her primary function, her niche.

Ten years later she'd become a serial niche killer. There

wasn't a job she hadn't held. Or gone on to abandon, feeling more unfulfilled and depressed with each failure. Fortunately, she'd stumbled upon her last hope before getting a prescription for Paxil.

When she'd heard that the owners of Glass Slipper, Inc., the company renowned for performing *life makeovers*, were looking for a publicist for their new endeavor, the bimonthly glossy *Glass Slipper* magazine, she knew she'd found the career Holy Grail she'd been searching for. And it was do-or-die time.

*And look for the next Glass Slipper novel . . .*

# NOT-SO-SNOW WHITE

Coming in Summer 2006

*Tennis anyone?*

Meet the tennis world's latest phenomenon: Tess Hamilton. Not only is she a fantastic athlete with enough Grand Slam trophies to rival the careers of the best in tennis history, she's also gorgeous, passionate, and supremely stubborn—a female McEnroe.

At the pinnacle of her career, Tess suddenly sustains a career-threatening injury and is faced with one of the toughest decisions of her young and gifted life. And on her heels is a new rising star, Gabby Fontaine, almost half her age and with enough moxie and brazenness to go toe-to-toe with Tess on any playing surface, not to mention the commotion they both can stir up in the media pit.

Now, newly retired Tess takes on the new kid—as her coach—and finds herself in the constant presence of the young upstart's savvy, unflappable manager and brother, Max. And from the French Open to Wimbledon to the U.S. Open, the tennis world's three brightest stars will find themselves on the verge of match point both on and off the courts. Advantage Miss Hamilton? Max may have a thing or two to say about that.

And look for fairy godmother, Aurora Favreaux, to return with her Glass Slipper wisdom in tow to help Tess see beyond the proverbial mirror on the wall.